A
Woman's
PLACE

A Woman's PLACE

A NOVEL

LYNN AUSTIN

BETHANY HOUSE PUBLISHERS
Minneapolis, Minnesota

Published by Bethany House Publishers
11400 Hampshire Avenue South
Bloomington, Minnesota 55438

Bethany House Publishers is a division of
Baker Publishing Group, Grand Rapids, Michigan.

Printed in the United States of America

ISBN   978-0-7642-2890-2

Library of Congress Cataloging-in-Publication Data

Austin, Lynn N.
    A woman's place / Lynn Austin.
       p.   cm.
    ISBN 0-7642-0295-2 (alk. paper) — ISBN 0-7642-2890-0 (pbk. : alk. paper) — ISBN 0-7642-0265-0 (large-print pbk. : alk. paper)
    1. Women—Fiction. 2. World War, 1939–1945—United States—Fiction. 3. United States—Social conditions—1933–1945—Fiction. 4. Michigan—Fiction. I. Title.
    PS3551.U839W66   2006
    813'.54—dc22   2006019417

To Ken
with gratitude
and love.

Books by Lynn Austin

All She Ever Wanted
All Things New
Eve's Daughters
Hidden Places
Pilgrimage
A Proper Pursuit
Though Waters Roar
Until We Reach Home
While We're Far Apart
Wings of Refuge
A Woman's Place
Wonderland Creek

REFINER'S FIRE
Candle in the Darkness
Fire by Night
A Light to My Path

CHRONICLES OF THE KINGS
Gods & Kings
Song of Redemption
The Strength of His Hand
Faith of My Father
Among the Gods

THE RESTORATION CHRONICLES
Return to Me
Keepers of the Covenant

www.lynnaustin.org

Lynn Austin has sold more than one million copies of her books worldwide. She is an eight-time Christy Award winner and an inaugural inductee into the Christy Award Hall of Fame, as well as a popular speaker at retreats, conventions, women's groups, and book clubs. She lives with her husband in Michigan.

"Many women do noble things, but you surpass them all."
Charm is deceptive, and beauty is fleeting;
but a woman who fears the Lord is to be praised.
Give her the reward she has earned,
and let her works bring her praise at the city gate.
PROVERBS 31:29–31, NIV

PROLOGUE
December 1941

★ *Virginia* ★

Virginia Mitchell watched her husband carve the Sunday pot roast and wondered if he was having an affair. He showed more interest in the way the meat was cooked than he did in her. Harold traveled out of town often with his work, so he had plenty of opportunities to stray. He would leave tomorrow on another trip, in fact. He set down the carving knife and nodded his approval.

"Roast beef looks good, Virginia. Not dry or stringy."

She sighed with relief. "I was afraid it might be ruined. The sermon went a little long."

"The new pastor likes to beat a dead horse." Harold gave her his charming smile, revealing an endearing dimple in his left cheek.

Virginia never should have married a man as handsome and intelligent as Harold Mitchell. She worried constantly that he would find another woman who was more stimulating than she was, someone who made her seem dull and boring in comparison. Virginia always sifted through his pockets when he came home from a trip and searched every compartment of his suitcase for telltale signs that he'd been with another woman. She even sniffed his shirt collars and the lapels of his suits for traces of perfume. Once or twice she thought she'd detected an unfamiliar scent.

Worry consumed her the way her family was consuming this Sunday meal: Harold piled thick slices of meat onto his plate; nine-year-old Allan shoveled forkfuls of mashed potatoes into his mouth; seven-year-old Herbert gulped down Jell-O as if racing against time. If only she knew for certain that Harold really was having an affair.

But then what would she do? Ginny had thought it through count-less times as she'd searched his pockets. She couldn't leave him; how would she support herself and her sons on her own? She would have to find a job, and she wasn't qualified to be anything except a housewife.

She watched Harold pour gravy over his mashed potatoes and thought that maybe it was better if she didn't know for certain. This way she wouldn't be forced to decide whether to live with the knowl-edge in silence, forgive him, or leave him. She found it difficult enough to decide what to fix for dinner, let alone wrestle with ques-tions of infidelity and trust. Ginny didn't kid herself—you could never trust a man once he became a *philanderer*.

She had chosen *philanderer* for her newest vocabulary word. It meant someone who made a habit of cheating on his spouse. For more than a year, Ginny had used a thesaurus and a dictionary to try to improve her vocabulary, hoping to converse more intelligently for Harold's sake and to feel less inferior for her own sake. She had purchased the two books during her one and only year in college, and they'd done nothing but collect dust ever since—except for the odd time she'd used them to press flowers. She had looked up *playboy* in the thesaurus, recalling that Harold had a reputation as one before they'd met. The word *playboy* had led to *philanderer*.

Was he one? Did she really want to know? She watched him stab a forkful of green beans, and her chest ached with love for him. If only he loved her half as much as she loved him.

Harold took charge of the dinner conversation, as usual, asking the boys about their schoolwork and Boy Scout projects. Ginny had nothing new to report about her week. She felt dumb, dull, *vacuous*—another vocabulary word. Her life was uninteresting and boring, day in and day out. If only she could do exciting, challenging things, be a woman of vision and purpose like Eleanor Roosevelt. Then Harold would have no reason to *philander.*

The candle flames blurred as her eyes filled with tears. Did anyone even notice the pains she took to make Sunday dinner special: lighting candles, using her good china and silverware, spreading the table with a white damask tablecloth and napkins? Sunday was the one day when her little family was home together all day, and she liked to make it special. They always attended church, dressed in their Sunday finest, the boys looking like little men in their jackets and ties. Ginny was in no hurry for Allan and Herbert to grow up. She wished they were still babies, or at least chubby toddlers in short pants. Harold chided her constantly for babying them too much.

Virginia watched the mashed potatoes and Jell-O vanish, the pot roast shrink to scraps of leftovers. All too soon, Harold and the boys had gobbled down the apple pie she'd baked, excused themselves from the table, and disappeared into the living room. Harold sighed as he slouched into his armchair with the *Sunday Times.* The boys sprawled on the floor with the family dog and the funny papers. Maybe Ginny should do more than skim the news. Maybe she should take an interest in the events over in Europe the way Harold did. Maybe other women would pose less of a temptation if she could discuss current events with him.

But current events would have to wait until she'd washed and dried the dishes. Virginia surveyed the abandoned table and wanted to cry. All that work: ironing the tablecloth and napkins, peeling the potatoes, cutting up the green beans, making sure the meat was seasoned just right and the gravy wasn't lumpy, rolling out the piecrust, peeling the apples, slicing them to a uniform thickness—an hour and a half of work in a steamy kitchen and the meal was over in twenty-two minutes. It would take her another hour to clean it all up. And it was such *vacuous* work. No wonder Harold was bored with her . . . she was bored with herself. She wished she were bolder, smarter, more confident—like Eleanor Roosevelt.

Virginia was drying the last of the pots and pans when the

telephone rang. "Ginny! Are you listening to the radio?" her next-door neighbor asked breathlessly.

"No, why?"

"You'd better turn it on. We've been attacked."

"Attacked? What do you mean?" But Betty had already hung up. Ginny hurried into the living room, stepping over Harold's outstretched legs and Allan's strewn comic books as she made her way to the radio. The humpbacked Philco came to life with a hollow *ploink*.

"Who was on the phone?" Harold asked as the radio tubes warmed up.

"Betty Parker. She said we should turn on the radio. Something about an attack." Static squealed as Ginny adjusted the knob, finally tuning in to a channel. It took a moment for the announcer's words, reported in somber tones, to sink in.

"Thick smoke is still billowing from the United States' Naval Base at Pearl Harbor, where the U.S. Pacific Fleet is anchored, and from Hickham Field, where more than one hundred U.S. planes have reportedly been destroyed on the ground. There is still no word on how many ships were damaged. So far, at least two hundred servicemen are confirmed dead, but the death toll is expected to rise."

Harold lowered his newspaper and sat forward on the edge of his seat. Allan looked up from *Little Orphan Annie*, his eyes wide. "What happened, Dad?"

"Shh ... listen."

"Witnesses report that the emblem of the rising sun was visible on the wing tips of the attacking airplanes. There are unconfirmed reports that the Japanese used aircraft carriers to ferry the planes within striking distance. Once again, we repeat: This morning at approximately 7:55 A.M. local time, the nation of Japan launched a surprise attack on our American military bases in Hawaii, causing widespread devastation. President Roosevelt is reportedly meeting with high-level Washington officials and is expected to ask Congress to declare war."

War! The word sent a chill of fear through Ginny. What would happen to her children, her home? Would Harold have to go away and fight? At age thirty-five he was eligible for the draft. She gazed around at the room that had seemed so safe and secure a moment ago and felt as if the Japanese had attacked her house. The walls suddenly seemed flimsy and vulnerable, her children frail bundles of flesh and bones, a heartbeat from death.

"Harold! What are we going to do?"

"Now, Virginia, take it easy."

"But we've been attacked! What if the Japanese invade us?"

"You worry too much. It's my job to protect this family."

"But I feel so helpless! I want to do something!"

He gave her an indulgent look. "I could use a cup of coffee. Is there any left?"

Coffee? All she could do was make *coffee?* Virginia realized that he was serious, that he was dismissing her, and she stepped over the dog and the scattered newspaper pages to return to the kitchen. She could hear Harold and the boys talking about the Japanese Empire and the war in Europe as she set the pot of leftover coffee on the burner and lit the stove.

"Here, I'll show you on a map, Herbert," she heard Harold say above the sound of rustling newspaper pages.

The radio announcer continued to describe the devastation, her sons were asking worried questions, and all Ginny could do was stand in the kitchen waiting for the coffee to reheat. She knew that her life couldn't possibly continue the way it always had—everything had suddenly changed. Her country had been attacked, and her nation would be engulfed in another terrible world war. She felt helpless.

"I want to do something," she said aloud.

Virginia recalled her earlier fears that Harold was having an affair, and they suddenly seemed trivial in comparison.

★ *Helen* ★

Miss Helen Kimball lay in bed, listening to the distant toll of church bells, and for the first time in her life she saw no reason to attend Sunday services. As of this morning, she no longer believed in God. When the alarm clock had awakened her for church at the usual time, she had shut it off and remained resolutely in bed, gazing out of her bedroom window at the wintry tree branches. But now the aroma of coffee had begun to drift up to her room, and she found it irresistible. She climbed from beneath the sheets, put on her robe and slippers, and went downstairs to the cavernous kitchen.

Minnie, her parents' housekeeper, stood at the sink, humming as she peeled potatoes for the noon meal. A Sunday hat perched on her wooly gray hair, and she wore her best Sunday dress beneath her apron. Minnie turned when she heard Helen enter, and her dark eyes widened in surprise.

"Why, Miss Helen! I thought you'd off and gone to church already, and here you are in your nightclothes. You feeling sick?"

"No, I'm perfectly fine." She found a mug in the cupboard and poured herself a cup of coffee. Minnie set down her paring knife and dried her hands on her apron.

"Let me fix you some breakfast, then."

"No, you go ahead and finish what you're doing. I can make myself some toast."

Minnie's dark face wore a worried expression as she watched Helen pull a loaf of bread from the bread box and place two slices in the toaster. "Ain't you gonna be late for church, Miss Helen?"

"I'm not going."

"Not going? What else you be doing, then?"

"Well . . . I'm not really sure what I'll do all morning. But I know I'm not going to spend it singing hymns and spouting creeds and yawning through a meaningless sermon. What's the point of going to church if I don't believe any of it?"

"Since when ain't you believing?"

"I don't know," Helen said with a shrug. "But I finally realized it this morning, so I decided it was better to stay home than to be a hypocrite."

"Now, you can't go losing your faith, Miss Helen. Don't you know the Bible says, 'What is a man profited, if he shall gain the whole world, and lose his own soul?'"

"Yes, I do recall reading that verse," Helen said as she checked to see how the toast was progressing. "And it surely does apply to me. The doctors say that I'll inherit Father's estate in a few months—more money than I can possibly spend in my lifetime. Especially since I'll be fifty years old soon, and my life is certainly more than half over."

Her life might continue, but Helen knew that her soul was definitely lost. It had shriveled up inside her and died quite some time ago. As of this morning, she no longer cared.

When Minnie didn't respond, Helen looked up. Minnie's worried expression had transformed into speechless shock. "Don't mind me, Minnie," Helen said as she spread butter on her toast. "You'd better finish peeling those potatoes or you'll be late for church yourself."

"Now, how can I be thinking about church or potatoes when you're talking this way?"

"Better yet, leave the potatoes, and I'll finish them myself. It'll give me something useful to do." She carried her toast and coffee to the kitchen table and sat down.

"You already got plenty to do, taking care of your mama and daddy the way you been doing." Minnie moved the colander of potatoes from the sink to the table so she could face Helen while she continued peeling them. "You don't mean what you're saying, Miss Helen. You just wore out, that's all."

"No, actually, I'm not. Between you and the nurses, I don't have much to do at all. In fact, I'm more bored than tired. Last year at this time I was still teaching second grade, and Sunday was a welcome day of rest before another week of school. Now it's just another endless day like all the others as I try to keep from going crazy or roasting to death in this huge, overheated monstrosity of a house. Do you know that no matter how high I set the furnace or how many blankets I pile on mother's sickbed, she still complains that she's cold? The calendar says December, but it feels like August in here."

"You trying to change the subject on me, Miss Helen?"

"In fact, I may not get dressed at all today. Who's going to see me? It's the nurses' day off, and my parents never have any visitors. All their friends are either dead or too old to make sick calls."

"Why don't you invite some of your own friends over?"

Helen stood and carried her plate to the sink without replying. She didn't have any friends—but that was by choice.

"If you don't mind, Minnie, I think I'll listen to the radio in your sitting room. I need to hide in there until after noon in case Father feels well enough to putter around downstairs today. He'll want to know why I'm playing hooky from church, and I don't feel like explaining why I no longer believe in God."

"Miss Helen! I don't believe a word you say. You know perfectly well there's a God."

"Well, if there is, then my father is the spitting image of Him. They're both rich, both powerful, and they both like to order people around like pawns in a chess game. Neither one of them has ever shown much love, and any decisions they've ever made for me suited their own interests, not mine. Together, they've ruined my life."

Minnie gazed at Helen in disbelief. "Now you got me good and worried, Miss Helen. I been working here more than twenty years, and I ain't never heard you talk this way before."

"Even though Father knows he's dying, his heart hasn't softened in the least. I resigned from my teaching job and rented my home to tenants so I could move in here and take care of him and Mother, and he hasn't shown one ounce of gratitude. He orders me around like I'm one of the servants, and he argues with me over every little thing."

"He ain't feeling well, Miss Helen—"

"So he wants everyone else to feel just as miserable. He's unfailingly grouchy, demanding, and ungrateful. Every single day he reminds me that he's leaving his fortune to me. I got so fed up yesterday that I told him I planned to give away every last cent of it and live a simple life. I just might do it, too."

"Ain't so simple living a simple life," Minnie said. "Being poor is hard work. Being a poor colored person is even harder. I don't recommend you try it, Miss Helen."

"I almost did it once, you know, when I was younger. I nearly gave all of this up for love."

"And I'll bet you're glad that you didn't. Nothing good happens when you think with your heart instead of your head, let me tell you."

"Maybe you're right. . . . But it's too late now. I'll never know." And Helen would have to live with *what might have been* for the rest of her life.

Minnie chopped the potatoes into quarters and spread them in the roasting pan with the meat and carrots and onions. "This here will be done cooking at twelve-thirty," she said as she slid the pan into the oven. "But you and me ain't done having this conversation about believing in God, Miss Helen." She untied her apron and hung it on the kitchen door, then shoved her arms into her coat sleeves. "My granddaughter's gonna be here any minute to take me to church. And you better know I'll be praying for you today."

"Don't waste your prayers on me, Minnie. The doctors say that my parents haven't much time left. Pray for them instead."

"Gonna pray for all of you," she said. She closed the back door behind her.

Helen hid in the servants' den all morning, but her father didn't come downstairs. At noon she finally went upstairs to get dressed, then took Minnie's roast beef out of the oven and carried a tray of food to her father. She walked into his room and out of it again before he had a chance to say a word to her. She picked at her own plate of food for a while, sitting alone in the kitchen, wishing Minnie was there to keep her company. Then Helen cut pieces of meat and potatoes and carrots into tiny pieces and took another tray into her mother's bedroom.

"Do you want me to help you with this?" Helen asked.

Her mother cupped her hand to her ear. "Pardon me?"

"Do you need help eating?"

"No, I can do it. And you don't have to shout."

Helen sat in the chair beside her mother's bed, drumming her fingers on the armrest. The long afternoon stretched endlessly before her. "Would you like me to read to you?" she finally asked.

"What did you say?"

"Never mind." Helen would have to shout to be heard and would end up hoarse. She longed to do something, to take charge, but she was helpless, trapped in a silent, loveless house, waiting for everyone to die.

When she could no longer stand the aching silence, Helen carried the radio from the sitting room into her mother's bedroom and tuned it to a channel that played classical music. Halfway through the first movement of Beethoven's Third Symphony, the music halted abruptly.

"We interrupt this program to bring you a special bulletin." The announcer's grave voice made Helen's heart speed up. *"A spokesman at the White House has just confirmed that shortly before eight o'clock this morning, Hawaiian time, the nation of Japan launched a surprise air attack on U.S. military installations on the island of Oahu. All of the principal American military bases in the Hawaiian Islands were struck, including the United States' Pacific Fleet anchored in Pearl Harbor."*

"What did he say?" Helen's mother asked.

"Nothing." Helen quickly turned off the radio. "There's something wrong with the transmission. Technical difficulties."

Helen's mother had mere months to live. Why burden her last days with news like this, especially after all of the other losses she'd suffered in her lifetime? Helen could hardly comprehend the news herself. If it was true, then America was about to become involved in another war. The carnage and destruction of the Great War would be repeated, like a returning nightmare. The first war had shifted Helen's life from its foundations. A second war just might complete the destruction.

"Maybe you should take a little nap," she told her mother. Helen helped her get settled beneath the mountain of blankets, then carried the radio into the den and turned it on again.

"... Several battleships and destroyers are in flames, and the injured are pouring into emergency facilities. There are reports of sailors trapped in their berths in the sinking ships, still asleep when the first wave of enemy aircraft struck without warning. The unofficial death toll stands at more than nine hundred and is expected to rise."

Helen listened in stunned silence for more than half an hour before finally turning off the radio for good. How could a loving God allow such a disaster to happen? How could He stand by and watch as helpless men died in their bunks? If He wasn't able to stop something this evil from happening, then He wasn't very powerful. And if God could have stopped the carnage but had chosen not to, then Helen didn't see why she was expected to trust Him.

"Where were you when all this was going on?" she asked aloud. But there was no God to hear her question, much less answer it.

★ *Rosa* ★

Rosa Bonelli awoke with a humdinger of a hangover. The sun had climbed above the apartment building across the street, and as the light shoved its way into her room, it sent a bolt of pain straight through her head. She squinted at the alarm clock beside her bed. Ten-thirty in the morning. What day was it? Sunday? Oh, for crying out loud! Rosa had to be at work in an hour, and her head felt like it was about to crack open like an egg.

She crawled out of bed, pulled on a bathrobe over her underclothes, and lurched out to the kitchen, hoping to find some tomato juice. The spindly kitchen table had enough liquor bottles on it to start a small nightclub, but there was nothing in the refrigerator except a sour smell. Rosa cursed and closed the door, leaning against it for support.

She wondered where Mona, her worthless excuse for a mother, was. Then she remembered that Mona was working the breakfast shift for a friend today. Rosa ransacked the cupboards for a bag of coffee and the percolator, careful not to bang the cupboard doors too hard and make her headache worse. The percolator had just started to burble when Mona's latest deadbeat boyfriend, Bob Something-Or-Other, appeared in the kitchen doorway in his boxers and undershirt.

"Hey, what's all the racket out here?" He grinned, showing his misshapen teeth. "You killing roaches or something?"

"Nope, just making coffee." Rosa quickly turned away, tying her bathrobe closed. She didn't like the way Bob always looked her over like he was undressing her with his eyes. She had sized him up as a creep the day he'd moved in, and she'd felt uneasy around him ever since—especially when Mona wasn't home. Rosa had known from day one that he'd never be a father to her. She had waited in vain all of her twenty-two years for one of Mona's many boyfriends to step up and be a father to her. It hadn't happened yet.

"You want a cup of this when it's finished?" she asked.

"Yeah, sure." Bob didn't move from the doorway. "Dang, but you sure are a pretty little thing."

She wanted to smack him with a frying pan, but Mona didn't own one. Rosa knew she needed to get dressed and out of there before big-eyed Bob started getting ideas. She quickly found two mugs in the cluttered sink and rinsed them out.

"I gotta get ready for work while this finishes brewing," she told him. "Excuse me." She tried to slip out of the kitchen, but Bob blocked her path.

"Whoa, whoa. What's your hurry, Rosie?"

"It's *Rosa*, not Rosie. And I gotta be at work in less than an hour."

"Seems like you're always running off somewhere. Can't we sit down and visit a little bit? Make friends?"

"Maybe another day." She had half a mind to tell him that they could be friends when pigs learned to fly, but she didn't want to make him mad with Mona gone. She tried to squeeze past him again, but he grabbed her arm.

"I know you like a good time, Rosie. I seen you running around the clubs every night. You and me could have a lot of fun together now that Mona's at work."

"I said, some other time!"

Bob was a big guy and, judging by the grip he had on her arm, very strong. Rosa's heart began to pound harder than her head—and it took a lot to make Rosa Bonelli afraid. She tried to think what to do, but her hung-over brain wasn't working yet. Bob mistook her hesitation for interest and pulled her close.

"Come here, babe. . . ."

"No! Let go of me, you big jerk!" She lifted her knee as hard as she could, and Bob grunted in pain, doubling over. As soon as she felt Bob's grip loosen, Rosa twisted free and ran to her bedroom, slamming the door and locking it. Thank God it had a lock! She heard Bob lumbering down the hallway, right behind her. He pounded on the door as if trying to smash it down.

"Let me in, you little tease! You can't prance around in your underwear every morning and then tell me you ain't interested! Open the door!"

Rosa yelled back, telling him exactly where he could go as she scrambled into her waitress uniform and shoes. Any minute now either the lock or the door was going to break, and the big goon would be inside. The only other way out was through her bedroom window and down the fire escape. She tugged the window open and looked down. Dirty city snow blanketed New York, and judging by the gust of cold air that slapped her in the face, the temperature was below freezing. She had no way to retrieve her coat and gloves from the front closet.

Bob began to curse as he pounded on the door. "Open up or I'll kick the blasted door in!"

Rosa grabbed a sweater and climbed over the windowsill, making her way down the wobbling fire escape, doing her best to ignore the five-story drop. Particles of rust flaked off on her hands as she gripped the railing. She hoped the rickety old steps would hold her weight.

Suddenly they ended, and she had to drop the last six feet to the ground. Her knees were shaking so hard they gave out, and she collapsed onto the sidewalk in a heap. People stared at her as if she'd just escaped from the loony bin. She could imagine what she looked like with half-buttoned clothes and uncombed hair and no coat. She didn't care. Rosa scrambled to her feet again, worried that Bob might chase after her. She took off at a run, jogging the four blocks to the restaurant where Mona worked.

"If you're looking for a handout, you're out of luck," Mona said when she saw Rosa. "I'm not giving you any more money."

"I'm not here for money," Rosa said through chattering teeth. "I just had a narrow escape from your darling Bob. He tried to grab me and—"

"Were you flirting with him? I know how you like to flirt, Rosa. I told you you'd get yourself in trouble someday."

"I wasn't flirting! I was trying to make a pot of coffee, and he came after me!"

"I don't believe you. Bob isn't like that."

"Hey! Did you notice that I don't even have a coat on? I had to climb down the blasted fire escape to avoid being raped!"

"I don't have time for all your carrying-on, Rosa. I got customers waiting. What do you want from me?"

"What do I want? For starters, I could have used a father for the past twenty-two years. Someone to watch out for me and protect me from creeps like Bob. But I suppose that's too much to ask."

Rosa whirled away before Mona could reply and ran for the door, grabbing a customer's coat off the rack on her way out. It was a long walk to the diner where she worked, and she had plenty of time to get her tears under control before she arrived. She would go back to the apartment for her clothes and things when she was sure that Bob wasn't home, but she made up her mind to move out for good. She couldn't live there anymore.

"Hey, do you know anyone who's looking for a roommate?" she asked her friend Lorraine when she finally arrived at work. Business was slow, too early for the servicemen from the nearby navy base to arrive, so Rosa and Lorraine had time to talk.

"I can squeeze you in my place somewhere," Lorraine said after she'd heard Rosa's story. She handed her a handkerchief to dry her eyes. "My place is small, but we can figure something out. You can't live with a jerk like Bob, that's for sure."

Lorraine loaned Rosa some makeup and a hairbrush. It took a long time for her hands to stop shaking so she could pour coffee. She eyed the door nervously all day, worried that Bob would show up, looking for revenge. She thought her shift would never end.

Halfway through the afternoon, the guy from the pretzel stand on the corner burst into the diner, shouting loud enough for the whole world to hear. "Hey, did you hear the news? They just interrupted the Giants game—the Japanese bombed Pearl Harbor this morning! They tried to sink the whole U.S. fleet!"

"Aw, you're crazy," a customer at the counter said. "Japanese planes can't fly that far. They'd run out of fuel."

"Well, they sure as shootin' did! Turn on a radio and see for yourself."

Rosa brought the check to a group of sailors in a booth, pausing to flirt with them so they'd leave her a big tip. Then she hurried to the pass-though window to listen as the cook turned on the radio in the kitchen. Static hissed like frying hamburgers, then the news announcer's voice finally tuned in:

"*. . . in Pearl Harbor where the United States was attacked early this morning. The battleship* Arizona, *the* West Virginia, *and as many as nineteen other ships in the U.S. Pacific Fleet have been damaged or sunk. The Japanese also destroyed more than one hundred eighty American fighter planes parked on the tarmac. The death toll is close to one thousand and rising. . . ."*

"Holy smokes!" the cook breathed. "We're in this war for sure now. I may as well head on down and enlist."

Rosa leaned against the counter, her strength draining from her legs for the second time that day. But Bob's clumsy attack was nothing compared to this one.

"I don't want to believe it's true," Lorraine said. She and Rosa clung to each other, listening to the grim news.

"*. . . The attack on* Pearl Harbor *has effectively crippled the American fleet, leaving the United States vulnerable to further attacks. President Roosevelt is expected to ask Congress for a declaration of war—*" The cook shut off the radio in disgust.

"I'm a mess," Lorraine said, wiping her tear-streaked mascara on her apron. "Come on, let's take a break." She pulled Rosa into the ladies' room.

Rosa leaned against the tiled wall, staring at her hollow-eyed reflection in the dingy mirror. "You know what, Lorraine? I'm sick and tired of not knowing which way things are gonna go when I wake up every morning. My life is like riding the Scrambler at Coney Island: All I can do is hang on tight while it spins me in circles and shifts direction every other second."

"The Scrambler's great if you got a cute guy to hang on to."

"Yeah, but at the moment, I got no one. I'm sick and tired of all the bumps and turns, tired of working dead-end jobs and fighting off creeps like Bob. I can't count on anyone or anything to be there tomorrow. Sure, some of the sailors I dated swore up and down that they loved me, but they didn't stick around any longer than my mother's worthless boyfriends do. And now this—a sneak attack, another war. Everything's gonna change."

Lorraine blotted her lipstick with a paper towel. "Maybe we should join the WACs or something."

"Nah, they make you keep your room clean and get up real early in the morning." Rosa poked at her hair, tucking some loose strands beneath her hairnet. "I know life isn't a fairy tale with a happy ending, but I'm really not asking for much in life—just a nice guy who loves me."

"Yeah, and maybe a cottage in the woods, like Snow White."

"With my luck, I'm gonna wind up with the seven dwarves instead of the prince."

"Hey, Rosa, your customer needs more coffee," one of the other waitresses told her as she and Lorraine emerged from the bathroom.

"So what else is new?" Rosa sighed and picked up the coffeepot. Even when life threw curve balls, some things never changed. If only the carnival ride would end so she could go home with her handsome prince.

★ Jean ★

Jean Erickson sat in the Majestic Theater, holding her boyfriend's hand, but her thoughts kept straying from the Sunday matinee movie to the essay that she needed to write for tomorrow's history class. She silently composed her arguments as the film *Sergeant York* played across the screen.

She'd told Russ that she couldn't go to the movies after he'd driven out to her family's farm to invite her. "I still have homework to finish, and then I have to study for a chemistry test, and—"

"Why? So you can get an A instead of a B?" Russ asked. "Would the world come to an end if you only got a B?"

"I need straight A's so I can get a college scholarship for next fall. My parents don't have any money to pay for college and—"

"Come on, Jean. It's only a two-hour movie. You've got all night to study." Russ had turned to Jean's twin brother, John, seated across the kitchen table from her. "Help me talk her into it, buddy. You should come, too. We'll stop by Sue's house and make it a four-some."

"Great idea." John had closed his history book with a slap and stood up. "Let's go, sis. We can finish studying later." Jean might have been able to refuse Russ, but her twin could talk her into anything. That's how she'd ended up in the Majestic Theater sharing a box of Jujubes with Russ, worrying about her essay.

All of a sudden the movie screen flickered, then went dark. The soundtrack ground to a halt. The audience groaned. Someone in the balcony booed as the house lights blinked on. The theater manager blew into the microphone several times and asked, "Is this thing on?" He blew again. "Testing ... testing ... Can you hear me?" More people booed.

"Ladies and gentlemen," the manager finally said, "we apologize for interrupting the show, but we've just received an important news bulletin. Early this morning, the Japanese launched an air attack on the U.S. fleet in Pearl Harbor."

Jean caught her breath. The theater grew deathly still.

"Early news reports say that more than three hundred Japanese aircraft were involved, including dive-bombers, fighter planes, and high-level bombers. Eight U.S. battleships have reportedly been damaged or sunk, along with three destroyers. As many as two hundred U.S. aircraft have been damaged or destroyed on the ground. Casualties are estimated at hundreds of lives."

Jean gasped. "Russ, my brother Danny is stationed in Pearl Harbor!"

"I thought he was at Great Lakes."

"No, he finished there. He came home on furlough last month, then they shipped him to Pearl Harbor." She hadn't feared at all for Danny's safety until today. America wasn't involved in the war. She leaned forward to face her brother John at the same moment that he leaned toward her. "Is this for real?" she asked him.

"I don't know. We'd better go home and see."

All over the theater, people were standing and putting on their coats to leave. Jean hoped she was dreaming as she grabbed her jacket and hurried outside to Russ's truck. Her legs felt weak and shaky.

"Maybe this is another hoax," she said as she climbed into the seat, "like that radio broadcast a few years ago, remember?"

"You mean 'War of the Worlds'?" John asked. "That caused an awful lot of panic. I don't think they'd dare pull another stunt like that."

They took John's girlfriend home first, then Russ drove his father's pickup truck at breakneck speed down the country roads to Jean's farm. The three of them bounced on the worn springs like popcorn in a hot pan. Powdery snow blew across the barren fields and onto the dirt road as they sped past.

"We just got a letter and photo from Danny," she said, picturing him with his white sailor hat tipped jauntily on his head. "He went on and on about how beautiful the islands were, how balmy the weather was."

"I don't understand how Japanese airplanes could get close enough to attack Hawaii without being spotted," John said as they drove. "Why wasn't there any warning?" No one knew the answer.

Please, God. Don't let anything happen to Danny, Jean prayed.

She ran inside the farmhouse as soon as they reached home, not even bothering to remove her boots. "Ma!" she shouted, "Did you hear the news? The Japanese attacked—"

"Shh!" Her siblings hushed her from the living room. Jean found everyone gathered around the radio, listening intently. She sank down on the arm of the sofa beside her mother.

". . . More than three hundred Japanese aircraft participated in a coordinated attack against American military installations on the island of Oahu, including Wheeler Field, Hickham Field, and Pearl Harbor. All military personnel and civilian defense workers—excluding women—have been ordered to report for duty immediately. Women and other civilians have been ordered to seek shelter and stay inside until further notice."

The family listened in silence until the announcer began to repeat himself, then all of Jean's sisters and brothers began talking at once.

"Did they say anything about Dan's ship, the *California?*" Jean asked her mother.

"They mentioned the *Shaw* and the *West Virginia,*" her younger brother Howie said.

"They can't get a clear view of the other ships," her father added. "There's too much smoke."

Jean struggled to control her tears. "I hope Danny's all right."

Ma took her hand, squeezing it to comfort her. "God is in control, Jeannie. Don't ever forget that. The leaders and nations of this world aren't running things, God is."

"But Danny—"

"He'll let us know he's safe as soon as he can. There's no sense worrying about something until it happens. I leave my worrying to God."

Jean wished she had even half a measure of her mother's faith. "I don't know how you can sit here so calmly after what just happened, and—"

"I'm going down tomorrow to sign up for the air force," John interrupted.

"You can't do that! We're going to college together next fall, remember?"

"College isn't going to happen, Jeannie. If this news bulletin is true and America really has been attacked, then our lives are about to be turned upside down. I may as well enlist before I get drafted."

"Me too," Howie said. "I'll go with you."

"You'll both have plenty of time to enlist after you've finished high school," Ma said calmly. "You can't enlist until you're eighteen, Howie. And they won't allow either one of you into flight school without a high school diploma."

"You don't have to fight at all, you know," Russell said. He had followed Jean into the house without her realizing it. "We can all get draft exemptions because we're farmers." Everyone stared at him as if he'd spoken in Japanese. "It's true. I already read up on it. We're exempt if we stay home and run the family farm."

"But I want to fight for my country," John said.

"Me too," Howie echoed.

"I'd gladly enlist if I were a guy," Jean said. It wasn't the first time she'd felt the frustration of being born female.

"You could join the Women's Army Corps," John told her.

"And be a glorified secretary? No thanks! They don't let women do anything in the army except wear a uniform and type letters."

"Of course they don't," Russ said. "You don't really think women belong in combat, do you?"

Any other time Jean would have argued with him, but not today. She was much too worried about Danny to launch into a debate on equality for women. "Well, I'm going to do *something* useful for the war effort," she said aloud. "I don't know what, but I'm going to do my part."

"The Japanese don't stand a chance with Jeannie on our side," John said. She punched his arm.

"I'd better head home," Russ said, turning toward the door. "I don't know if my folks have heard the news yet." Jean walked out to the kitchen with him. Her schoolbooks still lay open where she'd left them on the table, but the Japanese had just wreaked havoc on all of her plans.

"See you tomorrow, Jean."

She kissed Russ good-bye and tried to return to her essay, but she couldn't stop thinking about her brother Danny and the devastation at Pearl Harbor. And if her nation did go to war, and if Johnny did enlist, would she ever get to college? Jean wished she knew the answer.

PART ONE

"No matter how long it may take us to overcome this premeditated invasion, the American people in their righteous might will win through to absolute victory. . . . With confidence in our armed forces, with the unbounding determination of our people, we will gain the inevitable triumph—so help us God."

★ ★ ★

PRESIDENT FRANKLIN D. ROOSEVELT

CHAPTER 1
September 1942

"A German submarine laid mines
off Charleston, South Carolina, today."

★ *Virginia* ★

Ginny's morning began with the same old routine: fixing breakfast for Harold and the boys, packing their lunchboxes, retrieving all the things they'd lost or misplaced, reminding them to wear their jackets and to tie their shoelaces. But today she watched herself perform these tasks as if detached from it all, almost as if observing from a distance. And what she noticed was that everybody took her for granted. They never seemed to notice *her*, only her mistakes—and they always noticed those.

"I don't want this egg," Allan said, pushing it away. "I like the yellow part hard, not all runny."

"This coffee is too weak," Harold said as he dumped it down the drain. "I'll grab a cup at the office."

"You put oleo on my toast," Herbie complained. "I wanted jelly." She made him a new slice of toast with jelly, but later, when she tried to wipe jam off his face, he squirmed away.

"Stop smothering them," Harold said. "They aren't babies anymore."

Ginny watched as each one grabbed his things and hurried out the door. The family dog lay sprawled on the kitchen floor, but everyone stepped around him or over him, ignoring him as if he were part of the furniture. Poor Rex. They'd loved him as a puppy, but now nobody even saw him. If he ran away from home, how many days or weeks would go by before anyone even noticed? Was it the same for her? No, her family would certainly notice if there weren't any meals on the table.

"I'm a real person!" she felt like shouting. "Not 'Mom' or 'Dear' but a real-live woman!"

Rex's legs twitched as he lay stretched out on the green-speckled linoleum, as if he dreamt of running through fields, chasing rabbits. Did dogs dream of traveling to other places, doing interesting things, challenging things? Ginny had never dreamed of any other life except this one and now it had become meaningless. Tears filled her eyes. Stupid tears! She bent to pet Rex and he startled awake, tail thumping.

"Well, boy, I guess it's just you and me," she said aloud. His tail thumped again, and he licked her hand.

Virginia cleared the breakfast table, washed the dishes, and tidied the kitchen. She spotted an advertisement as she refolded Harold's morning newspaper and paused to read it. Ads for defense workers were everywhere these days, thanks to the Office of War Information—in magazines, on billboards, on posters in every store window—but she saw this one as if for the first time. It sang out to her: *You are needed!*

She fought the impulse to grab her purse and take a bus over to Stockton Shipyard immediately. They would certainly notice her hard work—notice *her*. But it was Monday, after all, and she had laundry to do. Ginny shoved her daydreams aside and dragged the laundry baskets downstairs to the basement. She pulled the string on the light bulb above the washing machine, and a pale circle of light bloomed around her. The furnace and hot water heater rumbled in a distant dingy corner, performing their tasks, and it occurred to her that she was just like those machines: working behind the scenes to keep the household functioning and comfortable but completely forgotten until something went wrong.

She listened to the chugging washing machine, imagining that it was the sound of factory machinery, and she began to dream of a more purposeful life, building tanks and ships and armaments, becoming part of the Allied war effort as the tantalizing advertisement had promised. Doing her part on the home front had challenged Ginny at first, learning all the rationing rules, juggling coupon books, saving waste cooking fat, adapting her recipes to cope with sugar rationing. But it no longer seemed like enough.

She was still dreaming of a more interesting life as she emptied Harold's shirt pockets and found the ticket stubs. Two of them. Ordinary torn ticket stubs that said *Admit One*—or in this case, two. They could have been for a movie, an amusement ride, a coat check—anything. Except that there were two of them, and Ginny hadn't gone anywhere with Harold this week that used tickets like these. She dropped the shirt and ran up the basement steps as if trying to escape from her discovery, collapsing onto a kitchen chair.

If she hadn't just realized that very morning that no one noticed her, Ginny might have done nothing at all about the tickets. But the evidence that Harold might indeed be having an affair prompted her into action. *You are needed!* the advertisement told her. And so she shut off the washing machine, grabbed her purse, and took a bus to Stockton Shipyard. Anger fueled her as she filled out all the paper work.

"The job is yours, Mrs. Mitchell," the personnel director told her. "You can start tomorrow morning."

On the bus ride home, she thought about all the rules the director had outlined and hoped she could remember them all: her hair must be covered, she couldn't wear nail polish, she should wear sturdy shoes, and so on. When she got home her neighbor, Betty Parker, was taking her wash off the clothesline already, and Ginny still had two loads to finish. She had supper to fix, too. Thank heaven there was pot roast left over from Sunday dinner.

Later, the laundry still felt damp when she took it down mere moments before Harold arrived home. He'd be shocked to learn that she had taken a job without asking him. She should confess to him tonight. And she needed to ask him about the two ticket stubs, as well. But Harold always needed time to unwind after his busy day at work, and he wouldn't want to discuss either of those things in front of the children. She waited until the boys were in bed, then sat down with him in the living room, searching for a way to begin.

"Harold . . . I was looking through the newspaper this morning, and—"

"And it's all bad news, I know." He turned another page in the magazine he was reading without lowering it or looking at her. "Hitler's invading Stalingrad, the Japanese just sank another one of our aircraft carriers. . . . That's the third one so far."

Ginny's heart speeded up. "Yes . . . our factories will need more workers to build new ships, and—"

"It's been nine months since the Japs bombed Pearl Harbor," he said, shaking his head, "and the Axis powers are still dominating the world."

"Yes, and so while I was doing the laundry today, I—"

"Isn't it time for 'Lux Radio Theater'?" he asked, laying down the magazine. "Turn it on for me, will you?"

Somehow the evening flew by. When it was time to go upstairs to bed, Ginny was still searching for a way to tell him. She was a grown woman, thirty-three years old, a wife and mother. . . . Why was this so difficult?

She lay in bed, listening to the sounds Harold made in the bathroom: turning the tap on and off, brushing his teeth, gargling with Listerine, blowing his nose—sounds that she found either endearing or obnoxious, depending on her mood. She would tell him as soon as he finished his nightly routine. She drew a deep breath, preparing herself, rehearsing the words in her head.

Harold . . . I applied for a job at the shipyard today. . . . Harold, I found two ticket stubs in your pocket today. . . . Are you having an affair?

"Virginia?" Harold called from the bathroom. "We're out of soap."

She knew that couldn't be true. She had just purchased three new bars last week. She didn't say the words out loud. Harold hated it when she contradicted him. She got out of bed and padded into the bathroom. He was looking in the wrong place—the medicine cabinet above the sink, for goodness' sake! She reached into the linen closet where she kept the soap and held up a bar without speaking. Harold frowned.

"Why did you put it way over there?"

Honestly! That was where she had stored it since they'd moved into this house eight years ago. Again, she didn't say the words aloud.

"We can keep it in the medicine chest from now on, if you'd like," she said. She unwrapped one bar and handed it to him, then put the other two in the cabinet where he'd been looking. The tile floor felt cold beneath her bare feet, so she hurried back to the bedroom and climbed into bed. She drew a deep breath, grateful for the reprieve—but now she really had to talk to him.

"Harold, I went across town today to—"

"That reminds me. I have to go downtown to the rationing board tomorrow and complain about the ration book they gave me. I should have been issued an unlimited X card since I drive all over the state for the government. Instead they gave me a B card for commuters."

Maybe Virginia should postpone telling him for one more day. Tomorrow. She'd tell him tomorrow. But she was supposed to show up for training at Stockton Shipyard tomorrow.

"Virginia ..." He interrupted her thoughts again. His voice sounded muffled as he called to her from inside their clothes closet. "Virginia, where did you put my blue tie?" Harold, a creature of habit, always laid out his clothes the night before.

"Isn't it on the tie rack with all the others?" she called. He stuck his head out of the doorway.

"If it were on the rack, I wouldn't have asked you where it was."

She threw back the covers and climbed out of bed to help him, worried that she had lapsed in her wifely duties. She found the tie on the closet floor where it had slipped off the rack. Harold grunted his thanks and stood aside as she helped him lay out his clothes. His skin felt warm and a little damp from his bath as she brushed against him. He smelled clean and powdery, the way her children had when they were babies. How she missed those days when she could inhale their soft skin without them squirming away. She reached to caress Harold's arm and wished he'd do something totally uncharacteristic like sweep her into his embrace and kiss her the way the hero always kissed the heroine at the end of a movie. But Harold did no such thing.

Virginia climbed back into bed for the third time. Her feet felt like two blocks of ice, and she buried herself beneath the blankets, pulling them up to her chin. She watched her husband putter around. He was still a fine-looking man at thirty-six, in spite of too many frown lines. His hair was still dark brown and thick, his body trim and muscular. She loved the dark evening shadow that colored his chin and the way it prickled when he held her close. She could never quite get over the fact that handsome, bright, successful Harold Mitchell had chosen her for his wife.

She had been in awe of him from the first day they'd met—and she was still in awe of him, even though she knew all of his faults after eleven years of marriage. Her love for him had grown steadily over the years, undiminished. She felt it now as she gazed at him, a relentless ache deep in her chest. The fear of losing his love choked off her words, making it impossible to ask him about the ticket stubs or tell him about her new job.

He was examining the shirt she'd chosen for him, holding it out in front of him with a look of displeasure. He carried it over to the bed, offering it for her inspection.

"Did you starch this?"

"Yes, of course I starched it."

"It doesn't feel as stiff as it should. Did you use the right amount?"

Her mistake sprang immediately to mind. "I bought a different brand last week. It was ten cents cheaper. I'll switch back to the old brand, if you'd like."

"It isn't worth saving a few cents if this is the result. It isn't stiff

enough. Can't you feel the difference? Feel it." She obliged, pulling
her arm from beneath the covers and nodding her head as she rubbed
the fabric between her fingers. But to be honest, she couldn't feel
any difference at all.

Was she really that stupid? And if men could perceive minute
differences that she was incapable of detecting, how would she ever
survive in a man's world down at the shipyard? Anxiety swelled inside
her like soap bubbles in an overflowing tub. What had ever possessed
her to hop on the bus this morning and ride over there? At the time,
she had liked the feeling of independence, as terrifying as it had been.
For once in her life she was doing something on her own, with no
one to answer to, no one to order her around.

"Can't you feel that? The shirt isn't stiff enough," Harold
insisted. "I don't care for it at all." Ginny hoped he wouldn't ask her
to rewash all of his shirts. She didn't want to point out that he'd
worn improperly starched shirts all last week.

He finally hung it up again and walked over to the bed, pulling
the blankets all the way back as if throwing open a door. His frown
of disapproval worried her. If this shirt annoyed him, what would he
say about her taking a job? Maybe it would be better to delay telling
him until she was certain that she really wanted to work—or that
she was capable of doing the work. She had never held a real job in
her life.

She wondered if what she'd done had been *injudicious*. That was
her new word this week. It meant, *"showing lack of judgment, unwise."*
She whispered the word a few times, enjoying the rustling sound of
it, if not the meaning.

"Buying a cheap brand of starch was *injudicious*," she said. "Do
you want me to throw it out or use it up?" It should have been a
simple decision, but she couldn't seem to make it. It was Harold's
money she was wasting, after all.

"Buy a new bottle of the regular brand," he said with exaggerated
patience, "and save the cheaper brand for emergencies—in case you
run out." He sounded irritated with her. She felt stupid for not
thinking of it.

"Oh ... of course." Then the full weight of today's decision struck her: She'd accepted a job at the shipyard, building boats for the war effort. What on earth would Harold say when he found out? Would he lose his temper? Rant and rave? No, he would probably respond with that quiet, deadly anger of his that reminded Ginny of banked coals—innocent looking, yet filled with heat, capable of deep burns. He would speak slowly, pronouncing each word carefully as if she were too slow-witted to comprehend if he spoke any faster.

What if he ordered her to quit?

I won't do it, she thought with a burst of daring. He could hardly tie her to a chair all day to keep her at home, could he? What if he took away all of her shoes or her clothes so she couldn't leave the house? No, Harold wasn't that imaginative. She chuckled at the thought.

"What's so funny?" he asked.

"Nothing." But he studied her for a long moment before picking up his book and his reading glasses from the nightstand.

Did she look different to him? Had her singular act of bravery—or was it *injudicious*-ness—changed her in some barely perceptible way, like the difference between a properly starched shirt and one that wasn't? But it hadn't been courage that had made Ginny hang her apron on the kitchen doorknob this morning and abandon her laundry in the middle of a washday and take coins from her jar of egg money for bus fare. It had been a matter of survival. No one noticed her anymore. And Harold had two ticket stubs in his pocket.

He began to snore. The book he'd been reading dropped to his chest. Ginny loved him, and she wanted him to love her in return, but she also wanted him to respect her, to need her for more than simply cooking his meals and finding the soap and starching his shirts. She reached over to gently remove the book from Harold's hands. He awoke with a snort.

"Huh? What did you say?"

"Nothing," she replied, smoothing his hair off his forehead. "You fell asleep. Why don't you turn off your light?"

He did, and as Ginny lay in the darkness, excitement mingled with fear as she thought about tomorrow and her first day of work.

CHAPTER 2

★ *Helen* ★

Miss Helen Kimball glanced up at the factory's ugly brick walls as she steered her bicycle into the parking lot. Goodness, how this place had grown. In a mere nine months' time, the modestly sized Stockton Boat Works, which had manufactured motorboats in the drowsy village of Stockton, Michigan, for years and years, had transformed into the gargantuan Stockton Shipyard, producing landing craft for the war effort. The air around the building had a greasy, electric smell to it, and she could almost sense the throbbing of machinery, hissing and clanging inside.

What on earth was she doing here? A woman from her station in life had no business working here. She considered turning around and pedaling home again, but she was too winded at the moment to make the return trip. It had been farther than she'd bargained for. And there were more hills on this side of town than she had recalled. The trip would be impossible by bicycle in the wintertime, especially for a fifty-year-old woman such as herself.

The brakes squealed as she halted her bicycle in front of the factory. She wasted several minutes searching for a place to park, but the factory didn't seem to have a bicycle rack. Helen would have to speak to someone about that. She hopped off and smoothed her skirt, then poked at her graying brown hair to rearrange it. The plant

manager had advised her to wear slacks, but Helen Kimball had never
worn men's clothing in all her born days and didn't own a pair. Wearing the drab, shapeless coveralls they'd promised to give her would
be horrid enough.

What am I doing working at a factory? she asked herself again. Then
she remembered: trying to stop the walls of the huge Victorian mansion on River Street from closing in on her. She couldn't bear to
remain in that house one more day now that her parents had passed
away. She could have applied to teach as a substitute, she knew that.
But it wasn't the same as having her own students, doing things her
own way. After twenty years, Helen Kimball knew a thing or two
about how to teach. She wouldn't go back to Lincoln Elementary
School until she could have her own class and teach them proper
behavior from the very first day. There was just no telling how these
younger teachers ran their classes, and Helen wouldn't put up with
wild behavior or slipshod teaching, even if she were a mere substitute.

The last time she had substituted, she'd begun the day by reading from the Psalms, as she used to do before she'd stopped believing
in God, and some wise-aleck boy in the back of the room had called
out, "Our teacher never reads that."

She had given him a withering stare and asked, "Do I look like
your teacher?" Her icy response hadn't fazed him. In fact, the boy
continued speaking out in that same irritating manner all day, telling
Helen how the "real" teacher did things. No, she had no desire at all
to be a substitute.

She wheeled her bike into the scraggly bushes that served as
landscaping and leaned it against the front of the building for lack
of a better place. If someone stole it she would just have to take
public transportation—another first for her. But maybe it was time
to take another step down the social ladder and see how other people
lived. She had never asked God for wealth and social stature, so what
did it matter now if she threw it all back in His face? Being a Kimball
had been a curse, not a blessing, and Helen was ready, at long last,
to prove to God and everyone else that she could live a simple
working-class life.

The air felt cooler inside the building, out of the glaring sun, and she paused for a moment to get her bearings before making her way to the same office where she'd applied for a job two days ago. She nodded a silent greeting to the lone woman in the waiting area, then sat down and pulled a handkerchief from her purse to delicately wipe the perspiration from her brow.

The other woman looked vaguely familiar—and very nervous. The mother of a former student, no doubt. She was in her early thirties, attractive, but round shouldered and timid looking. She sat huddled over her purse, her white-gloved hands gripping it as if it contained state secrets. Helen had to bite her tongue to keep from telling her to sit up straight. Good posture was so important. Then their eyes met and the woman smiled.

"Excuse me . . . Miss Kimball?" she asked. "I don't know if you remember me or not, but my son Allan had you for his teacher in second grade?"

"Yes, of course—Allan Mitchell, I remember. A bright boy. Well-mannered."

"Why, thank you. His father insists on good manners—and so do I!"

Helen remembered Mrs. Mitchell's husband. Firm yet fair, not much warmth, rarely allowed his wife to say more than a peep. But obviously intelligent, articulate, and well-educated. He had reminded Helen of her own father.

Mrs. Mitchell, on the other hand, had struck Helen as a typically dull wife and mother, the sort of woman who does charity work in her spare time, who always buys purses to match her shoes and goes to the hairdresser regularly to refresh her permanent wave. In fact, Mrs. Mitchell was probably the last person on earth that Helen would ever imagine working in a defense factory. She was surprised that Mr. Mitchell had allowed her to. He didn't strike Helen as the sort of man who would embrace nontraditional roles for women. In that regard, he definitely resembled Helen's father.

"What brings you here, Mrs. Mitchell?" Helen asked.

She hesitated, blinking in doe-eyed wonder as if asking herself the same question. "I ... I've taken a job here." Her voice had a tremor of excitement—or perhaps it was fear. Mrs. Mitchell seemed ready to bolt for home at the slightest provocation. "Now that I'm here," she continued, "I'm wondering if my decision was *injudicious.* Why are you here? Surely not to work?"

Helen nodded. "Yes, to work."

Mrs. Mitchell was too polite to ask why, but Helen saw the unasked question in her eyes. It took Helen a moment to recall the reason herself. Five days ago, as the walls of the house had begun to close in on her, she had seen an advertisement in a magazine from the Office of War Information calling for defense workers. The slogan read, *His Life Depends on You.* She had thought of Jimmy.

One would think that after all these years she would have forgotten Jimmy long ago. Heaven knows all the other things Helen seemed to forget at her age, such as people's names or even what day of the week it was. So why was Jimmy's face still as vivid to her today as on the day he left for France in 1917?

She knew perfectly well why. It was this horrid war. And there would be lots of Jimmies, truth be told, who would fight on foreign battlefields far from home. Come to think of it, if America had to fight another European war, then what on earth had the first one accomplished? Helen hadn't wanted to think about any of those things, but the magazine advertisement had forced her to. The soldier in the drawing had even looked a bit like Jimmy with his dark, curly hair and brown eyes.

His Life Depends on You, the caption insisted. If Helen could have gone to work during the Great War, taking a job that would have saved lives, she certainly would have done it. So why not do it during this war? Heaven knows she was weary of visits from the angel of death. He seemed to be working overtime these days, making sure Helen remained alone in the world. She knew it sounded silly, but she wanted to fight back—to give that angel a piece of her mind.

Helen came out of her reverie as Mrs. Mitchell leaned toward her. "Excuse me again, Miss Kimball. But I just wanted to say how sorry I was when I read in the paper that your father had passed away."

"Thank you."

"It seemed such a tragedy after losing your mother only a few weeks before. I'm so sorry."

"That's very kind of you." Helen hated sounding so prim, but as much as she disliked her tone of voice she couldn't seem to help it. What had been considered proper manners when she was a girl made people call you "prim" or "stuffy" nowadays.

"And I was sorry when I heard that you'd resigned from teaching last year to take care of them," Mrs. Mitchell continued in her breathless, nervous manner, "because I was hoping that my son Herbie would have you for his teacher. That's selfish of me, I know, but Herbert is my youngest, and Harold says I spoil him too much. Anyway, he's more high-spirited than Allan and could have used a firm teacher such as yourself to keep him in line."

"Thank you, Mrs. Mitchell. I hope to return to teaching someday when there is an opening. For now, I've accepted employment here."

"Please, call me Ginny," she said with a smile. "Mrs. Mitchell sounds like my mother-in-law." Virginia Mitchell laughed, and Helen tried to smile in return.

How weary she'd grown over the years, listening to married women complain, even in a joking manner, about their in-laws and their husbands and moaning about how tired they'd grown of picking up dirty socks. They should try living in Helen's shoes for a while, waking up alone day after day, living in an empty house that stayed neat as a pin but was vacant and loveless, always wondering what it would have been like to be married. Sometimes Helen thought she would willingly pick up entire rooms full of stinking socks if only she had someone beside her to love.

To her horror, Helen felt tears burning in her eyes. She simply must stop this foolishness! She despised self-pity in others, and here she was indulging in it herself.

"Of course, Ginny," she replied. "Thank you." But she didn't offer to let Virginia call her Helen in return. It didn't seem right.

Ginny couldn't be more than thirty-two or three, and Helen was fifty—old enough to be her mother.

The door to the personnel director's office opened suddenly, and a young, dark-haired woman emerged with him. "You may take a seat with the others," Mr. Wire said. "We'll be getting started in just a few minutes, ladies."

Helen recalled Mr. Wire's doubtful expression as he'd interviewed her for the job, as if he didn't expect her to last a week. Why did everyone seem to doubt that she could be ordinary and do menial work, simply because she'd been raised with wealth? Helen lifted her chin, resolved to succeed, determined to prove everyone wrong.

CHAPTER 3

⋆ *Rosa* ⋆

The persistent knocking on her bedroom door awakened Rosa Voorhees from a sound sleep long before she was ready. Her head hammered along with the pounding, and at first she couldn't recall where she was. Not in her apartment in Brooklyn, that's for sure! For one thing, it was much too quiet—except for the knocking. She rose to her elbows and looked around the darkened room. Even with the curtains drawn she recognized the blond-wood furnishings of her husband's boyhood bedroom, his high school pennants on the wall, his baseball glove on the dresser top, his books and comics arranged neatly on the shelf beside his desk.

She remembered standing before a Justice of the Peace with Navy Corpsman Dirk Voorhees—who had looked dazzlingly handsome in his U.S. Navy whites—and becoming his wife. She recalled their brief month of married life before his transfer to Virginia. She remembered the long train trip alone from New York to Michigan in the overcrowded rail coach. And she remembered the looks of dismay on his parents' faces when she'd arrived at their home one week ago yesterday. Rosa sank back on the bed again and closed her eyes. The knocking continued.

"Rosa . . ." her mother-in-law called. "Are you awake?"

She licked her lips before replying. The bitter remnants of too much gin had left a sour taste in her mouth. "Yeah . . . I'm awake. . . ."

"The water is now hot for doing the laundry. You can do yours with me. . . . No sense in wasting the water."

Even if Dirk hadn't told her that his parents were immigrants from Holland, Rosa would have figured it out by their funny accents. But Dirk hadn't told her how blasted picky and old-fashioned they were about everything. Rosa's head throbbed. She pushed her dark hair out of her eyes and turned to look at the clock that was ticking loudly on the nightstand. Ten minutes to six in the morning! Was the woman crazy? Rosa had been asleep for less than four hours!

"I'll do my wash later," she mumbled, pulling the covers over her head.

"There won't be hot water later. And we do not do the washing again until next week. . . ."

Rosa groaned. Would it break one of the Ten Commandments to do laundry on a different day—or at a time later than dawn? You never knew with her in-laws. According to them, God had more rules than Rosa had ever dreamed of.

"And I need to wash your bedsheets," Mrs. Voorhees insisted. Rosa almost swore aloud but stopped herself in time.

"Right now?"

"Yes . . . please."

"Oh, all right. Give me a sec."

She lay unmoving for another minute, eyes closed, wishing she could open them and be back in Brooklyn. What was the point of getting out of bed so early when there was nothing to do all day after the laundry? But Mrs. Trientje Voorhees—or "Tena" to her husband, Wolter—ruled her household with a strict routine. And every time Rosa had tried to help out this past week, whether peeling potatoes or sweeping the porch or washing the dishes, her mother-in-law had come along behind her and done it all over again. She had even gone into Rosa's bedroom every morning and remade her bed.

All day long Tena never stopped working, cleaning every last inch of the bungalow, scrubbing the floors until they shone, cooking three huge meals a day, and tending the vegetable garden. If this was daily life as a housewife, Rosa wanted nothing to do with it. Besides, at twenty-three years old she was much too young to be a housewife. She had better things to do, a life to live.

Then she remembered that she was a married woman now. Dirk expected her to learn things from his mother, like how to cook and keep house. His parents had gone easy on her all last week, not asking too much of her, allowing her to sleep late and get settled in, but this morning she had a feeling her real initiation was about to begin.

Rosa climbed out of bed and got dressed; Mrs. Voorhees had already spoken to her about "parading around" in front of Mr. Voorhees in her nightclothes. She stripped the sheets from her bed as if she had a grudge against them, then kicked all the dirty clothes that lay scattered around the room into an untidy pile on the floor. She tied her long, dark hair back with a red scarf and staggered out to the kitchen.

The dawning sunlight made her headache worse. It wasn't even six o'clock, but the day was well underway in the Voorhees' household. Tena had set a huge breakfast on the table for Wolter, who would leave for work shortly. He sat in his place at the kitchen table like a kingpin in coveralls, his toolbox waiting on the floor near the back door. Wolter and Tena Voorhees, now in their sixties, had raised two daughters before Dirk had come along as a late surprise. Rosa knew that Dirk's new Italian wife from Brooklyn had been an even bigger surprise.

She glanced around the spotless kitchen, saw the bread dough rising on the stove, the kitchen table neatly set, the laundry tubs waiting on the back porch, and she stifled a groan. She had wanted this, she reminded herself. After living in tenements all her life, Rosa had often dreamed of a cozy cottage like this one. It was everything that Dirk had described to her, everything he'd promised her it would be. Just goes to show you'd better be careful what you wish for.

She slumped into her chair at the table. "You would like some eggs?" Mrs. Voorhees asked. Rosa gagged at the thought. How could anyone eat food at this hour of the day—let alone *eggs*?

"Just coffee. Black." *Gallons of it.*

Her father-in-law cleared his throat. "There is something I must ask you, Rosa."

She cringed. Mr. Voorhees rarely spoke, communicating with gestures and grunts that Tena seemed to understand perfectly. When he did speak, his stern voice and stiff accent made Rosa feel like she was in the principal's office. He never quite looked at her, as if he thought it was a sin to gaze at his son's beautiful young wife.

"Where were you last night—or should I say early this morning?"

"Down at that place on the next block . . . the Hoot Owl," she said with a shrug. "I wanted a bite to eat, a few laughs . . . you know." She also knew, after going to the Voorhees' stuffy little church last Sunday, that having a drink and a few laughs was frowned upon.

"We are happy to share our home with you since you are the wife of our son. Dirk loves you and he has asked us to make you welcome here. But you should not bring shame on our family."

"I haven't done anything shameful!"

"But you have. It brings shame to our family when you spend your evenings in a bar, drinking alcohol and carrying on with the wrong kind of people."

"Hey! I wouldn't have to 'carry on' in a bar if there was something else to do in this godforsaken town." She saw them both flinch at the mention of God and was sorry for her choice of words. "Listen, I'm not doing anything wrong—just hanging out, dancing a little, having a beer or two. It's no big deal." But Rosa saw by the way that Tena's hands trembled as she placed a saucer and a cup of coffee on the table in front of her that it was a big deal.

"Since you now bear our name, you must try to adapt to our way of life," Mr. Voorhees continued. "This is the life that Dirk will have when he returns home. You must get used to it so you will live here happily with him after the war."

"What makes you think we'll stay in this crummy town when he gets out of the navy?" Dirk had liked New York. He had gone with Rosa to all the clubs, danced to Big Band music, drank his share of beer. He would look for a job someplace fun after the war.

"But he will want to work as a plumber with his father," Tena said in alarm—as if Rosa had spoken blasphemy. "This is his home."

"Yeah, well, it's not my home."

She was sorry as soon as the words were out of her mouth. She didn't have a home, and if she lost this one she didn't know where she would live. She had wanted out, and Dirk had been her ticket—out of the diner, out of New York, out of a life that was going nowhere. Sweet, wholesome Dirk Voorhees had helped Rosa imagine a better place than the streets of Brooklyn, a place with green grass and blue skies and cows.

"Sorry," she said. "I didn't mean it that way. I'm not used to getting up this early. It makes me crabby . . . and I don't feel up to snuff this morning."

She saw them exchange glances, probably wondering if she was pregnant. Rosa knew very well that she wasn't, but to admit that she had a hangover would prove Mr. Voorhees' point.

"Look, I'm sorry, okay? I won't stay out so late next time."

"There cannot be a next time."

"Yeah . . . all right . . . sure." She would just have to sneak out of the house after the old sourpuss was asleep, then sneak home again. "What did you want me to do today?" she asked Dirk's mother. "Besides the laundry?"

"This afternoon there is a Bible study meeting at church, and—"

Rosa groaned aloud. She couldn't help herself. She had gone to church with them last Sunday—morning *and* evening—and didn't think she could stand to go there again. But groaning had been the wrong thing to do.

"Our faith is very important to us," Mr. Voorhees said, "and to Dirk, as well. Why do you belittle it?"

She could have told him that religion certainly hadn't been part of Dirk's life when she'd met him. Wouldn't they be shocked to know what their son had done before he'd eloped with her? But she wasn't going to snitch on him.

"Sorry. I didn't mean to *belittle* your *faith*. Church is fine for you. It's just not for me."

"You must try to understand how we feel—"

"You've made it plain as the nose on your face how you feel. You don't like me. You wish your precious son had never married me."

Mr. Voorhees' face turned as red as a stoplight, but he didn't raise his voice. "Nevertheless, Dirk has asked us to give you a home and make you part of our life. We will do that in the best way we know how. But you have not tried to fit in with us."

"I'll never fit in to your world."

"That is up to you, Rosa. But I think there is one thing that we do agree on: We all love Dirk—at least, I hope it is true for you."

"Are you saying you don't think I love him?"

"Dirk must return home safe and sound," he said, ignoring her question. "We must not say anything in our letters or do anything that would upset him and put his life in danger. He needs to put all his thoughts into fighting this war, and he must imagine that we are all getting along and keeping a happy home for him to return to."

"I do love him! I want to spend my whole life with him!"

"Your actions while he is away don't show me that you care about him. You were out until two o'clock last night, and—"

"What gives you the right to keep tabs on me?"

"You live under my roof. We have opened our home to you until Dirk returns."

Rosa scraped back her chair and stood. "I don't have to take this."

"Rosa, please," Tena begged. "Don't be angry—"

"I can wash my own clothes, you know. I been doing it all my life—maybe not to your prissy standards, but I do okay. Just leave my stuff alone. I'll wash them when I'm good and ready." She grabbed her purse from the chair where she had dumped it the night before and strode to the door.

"Where are you going?" Tena asked.

"Out!"

Rosa slammed the door and stalked down the street to the bus stop. It was what she always did after fighting with her own mother. Rosa would ride the New York subways awhile so her mother would know that she wasn't taking any of her garbage. Maybe Wolter and Tena Voorhees would mind their own business and treat her a little nicer, too, after this.

She boarded the first bus that happened along and slouched down in a seat beside the window. At first she paid no attention to her surroundings as she replayed the fight with her in-laws. She had lived with them for only a week, and she already knew she couldn't stand living there much longer. But what else could she do? She really, truly did love Dirk and didn't want to lose him. What if he took his parents' side?

The bus lurched through the downtown area, stopping every block or so to let people on and off, then it continued toward the river on the other side of town. The erratic motion, along with the exhaust fumes, made Rosa's headache worse. Finally the bus stopped in front of a sprawling factory—Stockton Shipyard.

"End of the line," the driver announced. "Five-minute break, then we turn around." The bus emptied as all of the men and women on board made their way toward the brick building. People streamed out of the factory, too, and boarded the bus. A tired-looking woman no older than Rosa sank down in the seat beside her with a weary sigh. She wore dark-green coveralls that were coated with grease, and she carried a shiny metal lunch pail.

"You work in there?" Rosa asked in amazement.

"Yeah. I started two months ago. It's not bad—I like the grave-yard shift."

"What's that?"

"Eleven at night until seven in the morning." She yawned, then laughed at herself. "I'm on my way home to bed."

It was the perfect solution. Rosa knew a godsend when she saw one. She had always been a night owl. Not only could she avoid her in-laws by working all night and sleeping all day, but she could earn a little money, too.

"They pay good?" she asked.

"Thirty dollars a week to start." Rosa's mouth dropped open in astonishment. "They're still hiring, if you're interested. They got a government contract to build ships and they need a lot more workers if they're gonna produce on time. My foreman told me they're training another group, starting today. You got kids?"

"No, not yet. Me and Dirk have only been married a month and a half."

"If you tell them you're willing to work the graveyard shift, they'll hire you on the spot. A lot of women have families and can't work those hours."

"Thanks for the tip. I think I'll apply." Rosa stood and stepped over the woman's outstretched legs, which were shod in heavy work boots, then made her way down the aisle to the back of the bus. The driver ground the gears and released the brakes with a hiss just as Rosa hopped off.

The workers had been going in and out of the factory's side entrance, but Rosa strode straight up the walk to the main door. She went inside, then halted in front of a Negro janitor who was mopping the foyer.

"Hey, can you tell me how I apply for a job around here?"

"Yes, ma'am. You can talk to Mr. Wire's secretary, ma'am. Right down at the end of that hallway." He pointed to the left.

Rosa found the secretary and got an application form. She sat down to fill it out and quickly decided that she needed to lie about finishing high school. They'd never call all the way to Brooklyn to check up on her, would they? When she came to the part that asked her to list two references, she stopped. Should she put down her father-in-law's name for one of them? Rosa decided against it. He would probably have a fit, saying women shouldn't work in a factory—although it was okay for his wife to slave away at home fourteen hours a day, six days a week, scrubbing his clothes and cooking his meals without pay.

She wrote Dirk's name instead, and the name of the cook in the diner where she'd worked in New York. When asked which shift she preferred, she checked all three boxes: 7 A.M.–3 P.M.; 3 P.M.–11 P.M.;

and 11 P.M.–7 A.M., just to let them know she was willing to work any time.

The secretary showed Rosa into Mr. Wire's office when she finished. He looked up from his desk when she entered and stared at her, google-eyed—but Rosa was used to men staring at her. Mr. Wire looked like he was about to give her a wolf whistle when he caught himself and cleared his throat.

"Please, have a seat." Rosa sat. He peeled his eyes away from her figure and studied her application. "I know your husband," he said when he looked up again. "My son Larry went to school with him. Played on the varsity baseball team together. Great ballplayer, your Dirk. And he sure found himself a pretty little wife."

"Gee, thanks."

"Which branch of the service did Dirk join?"

"He's in the navy." She gave him her prettiest smile, careful not to lay it on too thick.

"My boy joined the marines. I know your father-in-law, too." He cleared his throat again. "So . . . you moved here from New York recently?"

"Yeah. Brooklyn. Me and Dirk met there. We got married a month and a half ago, then he got transferred to Virginia for more training. I sure could use this job, Mr. Wire."

"Well, that shouldn't be a problem. We're starting to train a new team of electricians today, in fact. The job is yours if you want it."

"You bet I do!"

Rosa's head spun as she stood up to shake his hand, but she wasn't sure if it was from her hangover or the speed at which everything was happening. An hour ago she'd been sound asleep; now she was accepting a job. She felt a brief moment of panic, wondering what she might have gotten herself into, then realized that she could always quit again if she didn't like it. She'd had a whole string of jobs after dropping out of high school. What was one more? If things didn't work out she could be out of here as fast as she had come in. Maybe by then she'd have saved up enough money to get out of town.

Mr. Wire stood, too. "You may step out here, Mrs. Voorhees, and have a seat with the other ladies. Your foreman, Earl Seaborn, will be with you momentarily."

"Yeah, great. Thanks a million."

Two other women sat in the waiting area, and Rosa could tell by the conversation she interrupted that they already knew each other. It burned her up that every last person in this stupid town seemed to know everybody else. These ladies probably knew her in-laws, too. In fact, Dirk's mother had probably told the whole town about the sleazy wife their darling Dirk had sent here from New York City, and how she was an "Eye-tal-yun" girl who never stepped through the door of a church before. The stares she had gotten last Sunday had been more than Rosa could stand—not admiring stares like Mr. Wire's, but as if she were on loan from the zoo. She would never belong in a million years. She tried to tell that to Dirk when he first came up with the idea of sending her to live with his parents, but he wouldn't listen.

"Oh no, Rosa," he'd insisted. "You'll charm their socks off just like you charmed me. You're so funny ..." Blah, blah, blah. Rosa could see that moving here while Dirk was in the service had been a big mistake. Yeah, they could save money on rent and all that, but he would have to pick her up in the loony bin by the time the war was over and cut her out of a straightjacket. This factory job might get her out of the house for a while, but judging by the way the two hens sitting alongside her were chewing the fat, it looked like Rosa was doomed to be the outsider again. Then the older lady surprised her.

"Forgive us for being rude," she said, extending her hand. "I'm Helen Kimball."

"And I'm Virginia Mitchell," the thirty-something lady added, extending her white-gloved hand to Rosa, too. "Call me Ginny."

"Rosa Bon—" She started to say Bonelli, her maiden name, then caught herself. "Rosa Voorhees. Pleased to make your acquaintance."

"Oh, are you any relation to Mr. Voorhees, the plumber?" Ginny asked. "I always call him when I need work done."

Rosa resisted the urge to roll her eyes. "Yeah, I married his son, Dirk. A month and a half ago, in fact."

"I taught Dirk Voorhees in the second grade," Helen Kimball added. "It's hard to believe so much time has passed, and that he's grown and married now. Is he in the service?"

"Yeah, we met when he was in corpsman school at the navy hospital in Brooklyn. He walked into the diner in New York where I was working, and *boom*. Two weeks later we got married."

"Dirk was a very bright student. Well-mannered, too," the teacher said.

"Yeah? He just got transferred to another navy hospital in Virginia to finish learning to be a corpsman."

The schoolteacher nodded, and Rosa decided she wasn't so bad after all, even if people back home would call her prim.

"So you're a newlywed!" Ginny gushed. She looked neat and well-pressed, every curl in place—the type of woman who would give Rosa's mother-in-law a run for her money in a contest for Housewife of the Year. Both Helen and Ginny looked out of place here. But then, so did Rosa—not just in this factory but in this godforsaken, backwoods town. Well, Rosa had wanted a change and boy, had she gotten one!

"Are you originally from the Stockton area?" Ginny asked.

"Heck, no! I'm a city girl, street-smart and street tough, too. You have to be in order to get by in my Brooklyn neighborhood, or you don't last too long."

They were interrupted by a young, clean-cut guy who strode into the waiting area. "Sorry to keep you waiting, ladies. I'm Earl Seaborn, foreman of your division. Come right this way, please."

Rosa stood with the others, hardly able to comprehend that she really was starting a new job. What would Dirk's parents say about that? She'd be willing to bet that at this very moment Tena Voorhees was washing Rosa's bedsheets. It was no skin off Rosa's nose. No matter how hard she scrubbed, they'd never be clean enough for her mother-in-law.

Mr. Seaborn opened a door that led into the factory, and there was such an explosion of noise and bright lights that Rosa didn't know whether to cover her ears or her eyes. The steady banging made her head feel like the clapper of the Liberty Bell on the Fourth of July. What a dumb idea to start work in a noisy factory with a hangover! Mr. Seaborn had to shout at times to be heard as he led them on a brief tour, describing all the stages in the construction process. Rosa passed row after row of machinery and tools and workers in coveralls. Some of the giant hulks of metal resembled boats, but a lot of what she saw looked like complicated piles of junk. The factory went on and on forever and stank of hot metal and enamel paint.

After several minutes, Rosa wondered if this was a bad dream. She glanced at the other two women, and they looked like they wanted out of here, too. The schoolteacher was trying to keep a stiff upper lip, her chin high in the air, but she looked like somebody had put her in a tub of hot water and shrunk her a couple of sizes. The housewife, Ginny, was fighting tears. If her shoulders slumped much more she would bend in half. No backbone at all, that one. Sweet little Ginny wouldn't last two seconds in the city—they'd eat her alive. Rosa was willing to bet that neither one of them would last the week out in this place. Then again, she might have bitten off more than she could chew, too.

She decided to give the foreman, Earl Seaborn, the once-over to take her mind off her pounding head and jittery nerves. He looked to be about Dirk's age, in his mid-twenties, and she wondered why he wasn't off fighting. It galled her to see men shirking their duty when her Dirk had to go and fight. Then she noticed that there was something wrong with Mr. Seaborn's left hand. He held it funny, when he wasn't stuffing it into his pocket as if trying to hide it. When she did glimpse his hand, it looked thin and shriveled. As she followed him down the assembly line, she also noticed that he limped, favoring his right leg, dragging his left one. Polio, she guessed. Too bad. He'd be a nice-looking guy otherwise, even if he wasn't a hunk like Dirk.

As Mr. Seaborn continued the tour, some of the men along the way stopped working to give Rosa the once-over. "Hey, baby . . ."

someone called. She thought she recognized one of the guys who'd bought her a drink last night. She heard a wolf whistle.

"Keep your eyes on your work, please," Mr. Seaborn ordered.

"How big is this place?" Rosa asked after walking for what felt like miles. She was so tired by the time they came to the end of the line that she tripped over a toolbox and nearly fell into the test pond where a huge boat was floating. Ginny grabbed her arm to steady her.

"This is the last stage, where we test-run the ships," Mr. Seaborn said. "Then they're ready to launch. They'll go down the river to Lake Michigan, then out to sea."

"How often do you complete one?" the schoolteacher asked.

"Not often enough. We're way behind schedule. But if we can hire enough help and gear up to three full shifts, working around the clock, we hope to launch one every month."

"Yeah, right!" Rosa said. "How can we put a whole boat together in a month? It's like working a gigantic jigsaw puzzle with a million pieces."

"We break it down into small steps," Mr. Seaborn said, "and everyone builds a small part of it. You ladies will be wiring the ship's electrical systems."

He escorted them back to what he called the harness shop, where a young girl who looked as though she was barely out of high school sorted through piles of cables and wires and electrical switches. She strode forward to greet them, towering over Rosa. The girl was as tall as Mr. Seaborn!

"This is Jean Erickson," Mr. Seaborn said. "She's going to train you ladies."

"Yeah, right," Rosa said without thinking. Jean looked peeved. She was pretty in a plain sort of way, very blond with blue eyes and fair skin and a boyish figure. She looked exactly like the kind of blah hometown girl that her in-laws would have picked for Dirk—the complete opposite of the curvy Italian beauty he'd chosen. Tough luck for them.

"Hey, no offense," Rosa said quickly, "but you look too young to be bossing everybody around. How old are you? Sixteen? Seventeen?"

"I'm eighteen. And we'll start today by learning to solder wire." Jean's voice told Rosa that she wasn't taking any guff, in spite of her age. "Eventually they'll assign our four-woman crew to the assembly line, where we'll be expected to wire a certain quota of the ship's electrical systems in an eight-hour shift."

"What happens if we don't finish on time?" Ginny asked in a worried voice. She had finally taken off her white gloves, but she still looked like she wanted to run home.

"Any work we don't finish overlaps into the next shift," Jean replied. "But it causes a lot of trouble if the entire production line has to stop while they wait for the ship to move on to the next stage." She gestured to another crew, working on a later stage of construction.

"It sounds like there will be a lot of pressure on us," Ginny said.

"Even more so because we're women," Jean told them. "There are a lot of men in this place who resent women working here and who would love to see us fail. The only way we can succeed is by becoming a team. We have to work together just like the guys in the army do, cooperating as a unit, helping one another and picking up each other's slack. With a war on, there's no time or place for individuals who want to go it alone. We have an important job to do. Soldiers' lives depend on us. I have five brothers in the armed services, and I'm sure you have loved ones fighting, too. Our boys need these ships so they can invade Europe when the time comes. Our marines need these ships in order to take back all the Pacific islands from the Japanese. Do you think we can pull together and do that?"

"Yeah, sure!" Rosa was surprised by her own enthusiasm. She imagined Dirk and all his navy buddies riding in one of her boats, winning the war because of her hard work, then coming home safe and sound again. She felt tears in her eyes.

What had begun as a terrible day was turning out to be the start of something really good in her life—something that just might make a difference. Rosa couldn't wait to begin.

CHAPTER 4

★ *Jean* ★

Jean Erickson could tell by the dazed look in everyone's eyes that her new crew had absorbed enough information for one day. They reminded her of an electrical socket with too many appliances and extension cords plugged into them. Any more and the fuse would blow for sure.

"Okay, I think that's enough for today," she told them. "We'll quit a few minutes early so I can show you where to find your time cards and how to punch in and out. Don't forget you'll need to wear the coveralls I gave you, starting tomorrow."

The three women trailed behind Jean, clutching their folded coveralls as she strode to the time clock. Jean remembered feeling weary and overwhelmed, too, when she first started working here nearly four months ago.

"Sometimes when I punch out at the end of the day I feel like I'm running the gauntlet," she told her new crew. "Especially since Mr. Seaborn promoted me to crew chief."

"Why's that?" Rosa Voorhees asked.

"Well, most of the men don't like working alongside women. They've worked at Stockton Boat Works—or, I should say, Stockton Shipyard—their entire lives, and we've invaded their territory. The fact that I'm only eighteen and a crew chief makes me an obvious target for harassment."

"That must be very hard for you," Ginny said.

"I try my best to ignore them. I grew up surrounded by brothers who excelled at ribbing me, so I've had plenty of practice. Besides, the shipyard is hiring more and more female workers every day, so the men will soon be outnumbered."

Jean showed them how to punch their time cards, then took them to the women's locker room. "You can change in and out of your work clothes here, and lock up your coats and purses and things. Any questions?" When they shook their heads, she led the way out of the locker room and back through the factory, fighting the flow of workers arriving for the next shift.

"I gotta catch a bus home," Rosa said. "Any of you coming along?" She turned to Helen Kimball first. "You going my way?"

"No, thank you. I rode my bicycle."

"You? On a bike?" Rosa said with a laugh. "*That* I gotta see!"

Helen exhaled. "I would have preferred to walk, but I live on the other side of town."

"So you ride your bike all over the place? Wearing a skirt? Did you use to ride it when you taught school?"

"No, I lived close enough to walk to the school where I taught for the past twenty years."

"What're you gonna do when it snows?"

"I'll have to drive my father's beast of a car—assuming I can get gasoline rations for it."

Rosa started to ask another question, but Jean could see that Helen Kimball was getting fed up with her. "We'll see you tomorrow, Miss Kimball," Jean said, steering Rosa away. "I'll take the bus with you once it snows, Rosa. But for now, I walk every day to save money."

"What're you saving up for? You got a boyfriend you're gonna marry?"

"Marriage is the last thing I want!" Jean replied. "I'm saving for college. As soon as the war ends, my twin brother and I are going to go together."

"You must be real smart, going to college."

"I'll take the bus with you, Rosa," Ginny said, linking arms with her. She glanced at her watch. "Hopefully one will come along shortly. My boys will be home from school soon."

Jean waved good-bye to the other women and set off at a brisk pace. The two-mile walk felt very long after being on her feet all day at work, and she came through the back door of her sister Patty's bungalow, wanting nothing more than to sit down and kick off her shoes.

"Hey, you're home," Patty said as Jean walked into the kitchen. "How was work?" Patty had her baby propped on one hip as she stirred a pot of tapioca pudding on the stove with her free hand. One of her toddlers clung to her leg, whining, while the other one emptied pots and pans from the cupboard onto the kitchen floor. A pile of clean diapers filled one kitchen chair, and heaps of clothing that needed to be ironed filled two more.

"Work was very tiring. I've been on my feet all day." Jean pulled out the only vacant chair and sat down to untie her shoes. "They just hired a crew of greenhorns, and I'm supposed to train them. Yikes, what an odd bunch! There's a middle-aged schoolteacher who's old enough to be our mother, a housewife in her thirties who has never worked a day in her life—"

"Hey, watch it!" Patty interrupted. "Housewives never *stop* working!"

"You know what I mean. She's the type who has to look pretty when her husband comes home from work and who believes that a woman's place is in the home—"

"You're really asking for it!" Patty said, raising her fist in a mock threat.

Jean laughed. "Sorry, but it's true. And last but not least there's a pinup girl who asks a thousand nosy questions per minute. Honestly, Rosa is beautiful enough to be a movie star, but she's very rough around the edges. Kind of slinky and slithery, if you know what I mean. She got wolf whistles from the welders. I'll bet none of these three makes it through the two-week training period. I know how hard those first two weeks are; there's so much to learn. And when these three ladies quit I'll be stuck training a whole new crew."

"How come you're doing the training? You've only been working there for a few months yourself."

"I know. But nearly everyone is new. Most of the original work force either enlisted or got drafted. And the men who've stayed behind aren't real pleased to be working with women. You know what the man who trained me said? 'You're not bad, for a girl.' I asked him, 'Why did you add, *for a girl*?' and he said, 'Because this is *men's* work.' I felt like saying, 'Well, it's women's work now, buddy!' Guys like him infuriate me! Anyway, that's why Mr. Seaborn made me a crew chief. He figured the training period would be easier on women if they didn't have to put up with that kind of an attitude."

"Boy, I'd apply for a job down there in a minute if I had someone to watch the kids. At least you have people to talk to. You should spend all day with a baby and two toddlers and a husband away in the service."

"No thanks. That's exactly why I'm going to college. The domestic life certainly isn't for me." Jean decided to change the subject before Patty got the bright idea to work piggyback shifts with her. Jean loved her three nephews, but she had no desire to baby-sit solo for them after working for eight hours. "Did the mail come? Did I get a letter from Russ?" she asked.

"No, but I got one from Bill." Patty looked as if she'd beaten Jean in a footrace. She was four years older than Jean and turned everything into a contest. "Bill says it's miserable over in England. It rains all the time, there's no heat in any of the buildings, and the Germans are trying to wipe London off the map with all their bombs."

"Any other mail?" Jean asked. "Did we hear from Johnny? Or Danny?"

"No, but there was a letter from Ma to both of us." She handed the baby to Jean and began spooning pudding into dessert dishes.

Jean pretended not to notice that the baby's pants needed to be changed.

"Good old Ma. Where does she find the time?"

"She says that money is tight, as usual, so she's trying to get jobs for the boys after school—delivering newspapers, running errands, working as telegraph boys or delivery boys at the grocery store. She said that Danny—"

"Don't tell me everything, you'll spoil it! I want to read it myself."

Jean put her nephew in his high chair, then took the letter into the living room and sank down on the sofa with it, marveling at her mother's endurance. Ma had written the letter unhurriedly, leaving out no detail, telling about life on their small Indiana farm. She never seemed overwhelmed by her huge brood of children but treated each of them as if he or she were her only child. She had written personal words to both Jean and Patty to encourage them: *Cherish your time with your little ones,* she reminded Patty. *You are a natural-born mother. The housework can always wait. Have fun with them. Give Bill my love when you write to him. I'm praying for his safe return.*

And to Jean she had written, *I'm not at all surprised to hear that they're going to give you a position of responsibility at the shipyard. You are such a smart, capable young woman, and I know you can do anything you put your mind to. Reach for the stars!*

Her words brought tears to Jean's eyes. She tucked the letter back into the envelope when she finished reading it and went into the kitchen to help Patty with supper. Afterward, they washed and dried the dishes together, listening to Frank Sinatra and the Andrews Sisters on the radio while they worked.

"So what are you doing with yourself tonight?" Patty asked. "Writing another letter to Russell?"

"I don't know. I'm very annoyed with him." Jean tossed a cooking pot into the cupboard and closed it with her foot. "I've written three letters to him, and he hasn't answered a single one of them."

"He's probably busy with farm work. It's that time of year, you know."

"He could spare a moment to scribble a line or two, couldn't he? Even a postcard would be nice."

"Be glad he isn't overseas. I wish Bill could have qualified for a farm exemption."

"That's what I don't get. Johnny could have taken an exemption, but he didn't. He and Russ were best friends. They did everything together—until now. And all of the other farm boys from school enlisted, too. In fact, every eligible guy I know was eager to join up as soon as he finished high school—everybody except Russ."

"Boy, you really are annoyed with him!" Patty drained the water from the sink and grabbed the towel from Jean to dry her hands. "I have to put the monsters to bed."

Jean got out her box of stationery and sat down at the kitchen table to write another letter to Russell. She got as far as the date and *Dear Russ* when someone knocked on the front door. She opened it to find Earl Seaborn, her foreman from work, standing on the porch.

"Mr. Seaborn! What brings you here?"

"Hi, Jean. Sorry to bother you after work hours—I hope you don't mind. I . . . uh . . . I got busy today and never had a chance to check back with you about your new crew. Do you have a minute? Am I interrupting something?"

"No, not at all."

"Listen, I'd be glad to treat you to an ice-cream cone or a milk shake or something down at the drugstore while you fill me in—to make up for bothering you at home."

"You don't have to bribe me with a milk shake, Mr. Seaborn."

"I sure wish you would call me Earl when we're not at work."

"Okay . . . Earl." The personal name felt stiff on her tongue. "To tell you the truth, it's hard to say how the women are going to work out after only one day. Everyone seems overwhelmed when they first start—I know I was—and these three are no exception." She stood in the open doorway, leaning against the frame as she talked, leaving Earl outside on the porch. When she noticed how uncomfortable he

looked, she motioned to the porch swing and rocking chair. "I'm
sorry. Do you want to sit down?"

"I'd rather walk to the corner drugstore, if you don't mind, and
get that ice-cream cone." He smiled shyly.

"Oh, all right," she said with a sigh. She closed the front door
and followed him down the porch steps. The evening had turned
cool, and after only a few minutes Jean wished she had put on a
jacket. At first she walked too fast, accustomed to strolling at a brisk
pace and eager to finish this task. Then she remembered the limp
that Mr. Seaborn took pains to disguise, and she slowed her steps.
She returned to her analysis of the new women as they walked.

"The older one, *Miss* Something-Or-Other . . ."

"Kimball. Helen Kimball."

"Right. I'm just afraid she'll find the work too boring. She told
me that she was a schoolteacher for years and years, and she seems
very capable. But I'm worried that this kind of work is going to be
too dull for her. It can't be nearly as stimulating as handling a classroom full of kids."

"I wondered about that, too," Earl said. "Mr. Wire told me that
she's been a teacher here in town since Hector was a pup. She taught
all of Mr. Wire's sons, and they're my age. She's sort of a cliché,
don't you think? The old-maid schoolteacher?"

His words made Jean angry. "Maybe she *chose* teaching as her
profession. Some women prefer a career over marriage and a family,
you know."

"Why would any woman choose a career?" He seemed truly baffled.

"For the same reasons men choose careers."

His smile vanished. "I'm sorry. I didn't mean to be insulting."

"Anyway, back to my new crew . . . The dark-haired one, Rosa,
with the Brooklyn accent, is certainly bright enough. She asks
thousands of questions. But she seems really out of place here in
town."

"I'm worried that she'll slow down production, sashaying around
with her curvy hips and tight sweaters. She's really something, isn't

she? Did you hear the whistles she got?"

Jean laughed out loud. So, clean-cut Mr. Seaborn had noticed Rosa, too. He had blood in his veins after all. "You'll be happy to know that I issued her a very baggy pair of coveralls," she told him. "But seriously, I can't imagine that she'll be content here in Stockton for very long. In the meantime, I think she can do the work. She caught on quickly today."

They reached the drugstore, and Earl held the door open for her. They walked to the rear of the store and sat down on stools, side-by-side, at the soda fountain. Jean ordered a chocolate ice-cream cone, Earl a vanilla milk shake. She had never bothered to look at Earl Seaborn in any way other than as her boss, but when she saw the teenaged waitress behind the counter giving Earl the once-over as she took his order, Jean decided to size him up herself.

He looked like an all-American boy—brown hair, a faint sprinkle of freckles, a boyish grin. She would guess his age to be around twenty-six or twenty-seven. He wasn't what you'd call handsome— he certainly lacked the fair-haired, movie-star looks that her boy-friend, Russell, had. Not to mention Russell's hay-baling muscles. But Earl had a nice smile, a pleasant manner. Jean waited until the whirring blender stopped to continue talking.

"The third woman, Ginny, seemed the most overwhelmed to me. She's very nice and willing to try, but she doesn't have much self-confidence. She's like a fish out of water in the factory. I gave them all a pep talk about working together as a team, telling them how our soldiers are depending on us. I think it helped."

There was a long pause while Earl sipped his milk shake and played with his straw wrapper. Jean wondered what he was thinking. Maybe she had sounded too critical of the new women.

"Was there anything else you wanted to know about them?" she finally asked.

"No. That was great, Jean. Thanks for the update. So . . . um . . . did you grow up here in Stockton?"

"I'm from Indiana. My parents have a farm outside a very small town that you probably never heard of."

"How'd you end up here?"

"I'm living with my older sister Patty and her three kids. Her husband enlisted a month after the baby was born, a month after the attack on Pearl Harbor. Patty has only seen him once since then, when he came home on furlough. She wrote and told me they were hiring women at the shipyard, so I moved here after graduating from high school last June."

"Do you have any other brothers and sisters?"

"Oh boy! Do I ever! There are eighteen of us altogether."

"Eighteen?"

"Yep." Jean loved watching people's reactions when she talked about her family. Earl's wide-eyed, openmouthed response had been a good one. "Some of the older ones like Patty are married, but I have seven younger brothers still at home. My twin brother, Johnny, and I are numbers ten and eleven. Five of my older brothers are in the armed forces, including Johnny."

"Where are they stationed?"

"All over the place. Let's see, my brother Danny survived Pearl Harbor and is on a ship escorting convoys to Australia. Johnny, my twin, is in the air force, training to be a gunner-engineer at Jefferson Barracks in Missouri. Peter was a policeman before the war, so he's now in the military police at an army base in Iceland. Rudy's at an air force base in Fresno, California, and might be sent to Dutch New Guinea soon. And Roy is at the Pensacola Naval Air Station in Florida, learning aviation repair. My mother, God bless her, writes faithfully to all of them. She hung banners in the window with five blue stars, one for each of them. When my brother Howie enlists next June, she'll add a sixth."

"I wanted to enlist, but they wouldn't take me," Earl said quietly. "I figured there were plenty of noncombatant jobs they could've given me if they didn't think I could march and shoot. I could drive a Jeep in the motor pool or do a desk job. But Uncle Sam doesn't want me because I had polio as a kid."

"The government can be pretty stupid sometimes.... Did you grow up around here?"

"No. I'm originally from Cleveland. I tried to enlist in Ohio and again in Indiana, but they turned me down in both places. So then I came to Michigan to see if they'd take me, but no deal."

He fell quiet again, and Jean hoped she hadn't hurt his feelings by talking about all her brothers in the military. She was trying to think of something to say when Earl swiveled his stool around to face her, his expression serious.

"Jean, I have a confession to make. I didn't really come over to talk about the new crew—although I appreciate your insights. I . . . I just wanted to spend some time with you. Away from work."

She drew back a little. "I, uh . . . I'd hate to break any factory rules."

"I'm management," he said with a faint smile. "I make the rules."

"Oh . . . that's right." Jean tried to laugh it off but suddenly felt very awkward. She scrambled for something to say. "Gosh, I'm really flattered, Earl, but I'm really not interested in dating. In the first place, I'm saving my money to go to college, and I don't plan on getting married until after I get my degree. And in the second place, I already have a boyfriend."

"Is he in the service?" She could tell that her refusal had hurt him, but he was trying not to let it show.

"No, Russ has a deferment to help run the family farm back home in Indiana."

Earl opened his mouth as if to say something, then stopped. He shrugged and smiled his slow, shy smile. "Can't you just think of me as a friend? Someone to go to a show with or have an ice-cream cone with once in a while? There aren't very many men my age to pal around with, you know. And since neither of us is from around here, you probably don't have a lot of friends in town, either."

"That's true. But I would hate for people at work to get the wrong idea about us. . . . You know, seeing us together."

"I stopped caring what people thought of me a long time ago."

She heard the sadness in his voice, and his vulnerability made her want to protect him, befriend him. "You're right—it would be great to get out of my sister's noisy household once in a while and see a show. I'd like to be friends. But please understand that I think the world of my boyfriend. I'm not looking for a new one. And besides, you're such a good-looking guy that you're sure to have lots of girls swarming around you before too long." She leaned closer to whisper, "Our waitress thinks you're cute."

"How do you know that?" he asked with a frown.

"A woman can tell these things."

They talked for a while longer as Earl sipped his shake and Jean crunched into her cone. He seemed reluctant to leave, but he finally took out his wallet and laid money for the bill on the counter, along with a generous tip. The waitress was busy cleaning the blender.

"Thanks for the milk shake," he called to her. She turned to him and he gave her a dazzling smile that made her blush clear to her toes.

"See what I mean?" Jean whispered.

"Aw, go on." He dismissed her comment with a wave of his hand, but Jean could tell that he was pleased. They walked back to Patty's house and sat on the front porch.

"You ladies at the shipyard are trailblazers, you know," Earl said. "A few years ago, nobody would have believed women could do so-called 'men's work.'"

"No one would have given us a chance to try it."

"And now here you are: welders and electricians and riveters . . . doing just as fine a job as the men did. You'll go down in history, you know."

"Gee, do you really think so?"

It surprised Jean to discover how comfortable she felt with Earl, considering the age difference between them and the fact that he was her boss. Maybe it was because they were both new in town and lonely, but Jean found herself chatting with him as if they were old friends.

"See you tomorrow," he called when they finally said good-bye.

"Who's the cute fellow?" Patty asked when Jean came inside. "I peeked through the curtains."

"Mr. Seaborn, my boss from work."

"That's a very smart career move, dating the boss."

"We're just friends. I'm dating Russell Benson, remember?"

"Oh, *that's* right," Patty said with phony surprise. "*Russell*—the fellow who never writes to you."

"I'm going to bed." Jean tried to pretend indifference, but Patty's reminder had stung. She carried the letter she had started writing to him up to her bedroom but found that she had nothing to say. She crumpled it into a ball.

It took her a long time to fall asleep, but when she finally did, Jean dreamt of Earl Seaborn, driving a tractor with his crippled arm and leg.

CHAPTER 5

★ *Virginia* ★

For the first time in her married life, Virginia Mitchell didn't have dinner ready when her husband arrived home from work. She had just put the potatoes on to boil, the meatloaf had at least another half hour to bake, the table wasn't set and neither was the Jell-O. She'd barely had time to hide her new coveralls and tie an apron around her waist before Harold walked through the back door.

She greeted him with a kiss. "How was your day, Harold?"

"Same as usual." He kissed her absently in return, loosening his tie as he walked toward the telephone table in the hall, where she usually placed his mail. He swung back to her in surprise. "Where's today's mail?"

Still in the mailbox! Ginny had forgotten to retrieve it after arriving home from work to face a near crisis. The bus ride had taken longer than she had anticipated, and her two boys had arrived home from school twenty minutes earlier. Eight-year-old Herbie had panicked when she wasn't there to greet him. Ten-year-old Allan had the telephone in his hand, about to dial the police, when Ginny hurried through the back door. It had taken fifteen minutes and lots of motherly hugs to calm them both down. At least they had noticed she was gone.

Earlier that morning she had hurried off to catch a bus to the factory mere seconds after Harold left—and forty minutes before the boys had to leave for school. They'd seemed baffled that she was leaving them without an explanation, telling them to "Be good" and "Don't be late for school." She'd been afraid to tell them where she was going, worried they would leak the news to Harold before she had a chance to tell him that she had taken a job.

She'd been rushing around ever since, trying to get the boys' breakfast dishes cleared away—they had left their sticky plates and juice glasses on the kitchen table—and to hurry and get dinner made. No, her first day as a working mother wasn't going well at all, and now on top of everything else she had completely neglected the mail.

"I seem to have forgotten it," she mumbled. "I'll be right back." She wondered if the mailman had missed chatting with her. He usually delivered her mail around two o'clock, and she would spend a moment talking with him about the weather if she was feeling bored or lonely.

She retrieved the letters from the box on the front porch and handed them to Harold, hoping he wouldn't ask her to explain her lapse. But before he could respond, Ginny heard a hissing sound in the kitchen and ran out to find the pot of potatoes boiling over on the stove. She had tried to speed things up by leaving the lid on it, and now she would have another mess to clean up. She grabbed a potholder and pulled the pot off the burner, fighting tears.

"What's that awful smell?" Harold called to her.

"Nothing ... it's ... nothing. I'm taking care of it." She had hoped Harold would arrive home in a good mood so she could tell him all about her exciting new job, but the frown never left his face as he scanned the mail.

"Is dinner ready?" he asked when he finished.

"Not quite. I'll call you."

Harold shrugged off his suit coat and disappeared into the living room to wait. She would tell him after they'd eaten. But afterward she had dishes to wash and dry and the kitchen to clean, and the boys needed help with their homework, and then it was time to put them to bed. Ginny was tempted to put herself to bed along with them, but she still had all of her ironing to do. She set up the ironing board in the kitchen and tried to work quickly, afraid that Harold would ask her why she wasn't in her usual place beside him, listening to the radio.

Ginny was in the middle of ironing one of his shirts when she overheard an advertisement for war workers. *"Attention, all American citizens,"* the announcer said in an urgent tone. *"We need your help. If we're going to win this war, we need every able-bodied woman to pitch in and work in the defense industries so our boys will have the equipment and ammunition they need to win on the battlefield. Please, won't you sign up for a job today? No experience necessary. Wages paid while training."*

She set down the iron. This was the opportunity she had been hoping for. "Did you hear that, Harold?" she asked as she walked into the living room.

"Hear what?"

"The advertisement that just played . . . about the need for workers—"

"Which radio station do you have on?" he interrupted.

"I don't know. But the man was just saying how they need women to—"

"Doesn't *The Aldrich Family* usually air on Tuesday nights? I don't think the radio is tuned to the right station." He got out of his chair and bent beside the radio, fiddling with the dial.

"Harold, I need to tell you something. Today—"

"I wish the boys wouldn't fool around with this dial. It's going to fall off one of these days, and then the radio won't work at all."

Ginny gave up and returned to the kitchen. He never wanted to listen to her. She picked up her thesaurus, searching for a word to describe his lack of interest in her life. Under the listing for *uninterested* she saw the word *aloof*. She liked the sound of it—like one of the grunts he gave when he wasn't really paying attention. She looked up *aloof* in the dictionary and read, *"at a distance but within view, unsympathetic, disinterested."* That described Harold, all right—within view as he sat in his favorite living room chair but a million miles away. She wrote the word *aloof* in the notebook she kept, her tears making watermarks on the page, then blew her nose and resumed her ironing.

When *The Aldrich Family* ended, Harold wandered into the kitchen looking for her. "Are you going to be ironing much longer?" he asked.

"I just have a couple more things. Why?" Maybe he was feeling romantic. She hoped so. She could break the news to him when he was happy and relaxed.

"I have to go out of town tomorrow," he said, "and I need you to pack my suitcase."

"Out of town! I hate it when you have to travel overnight. The evenings seem so long and lonely without you." She also hated the constant worry that he would find another woman on one of his trips. Ginny hadn't thought about the two mysterious ticket stubs all day, but she remembered them now.

"Where are you going this time?" she asked. "For how long?" She tried to make her voice sound interested, not upset.

"The plant in Detroit is having some problems. They need me to get things rolling more smoothly."

"I wish you would have warned me."

"I didn't know about it myself until this afternoon." He sounded defensive.

"Well, I was just wondering when you'd be back because there is something we really need to discuss, and I was hoping that we could—"

"Why on earth are you doing the ironing at this time of night?" he asked suddenly. His frown deepened.

Ginny tried not to panic as she scrambled for words. Harold was in a crabby mood, and she knew that if she confronted him now he would order her to quit. She would need this job at the shipyard more than ever if Harold really was *philandering*.

"I . . . I had a busy day. How many shirts will you need? I think I've ironed five—will that be enough?" She unplugged the iron, anxious to get upstairs to help him pack, desperate to change the subject. Her words ran endlessly like water from an open tap. "Are you driving to Detroit or taking the train? Which suitcase will you need, the big one or the small one? How many suits?"

She followed him upstairs and took care to fold his shirts the way he liked, rolling his socks in pairs, and neatly tucking everything into his large beige suitcase. She wished she could go someplace different, even if it was only to Detroit.

When Harold disappeared into the bathroom, Ginny breathed a sigh of relief. She sank down on the bed and finally took a moment to reflect on her first day in the factory. It had been exciting in a frightening sort of way, giving her that shivery, exhilarated feeling she always got when she listened to ghost stories. The bustle and bigness of it all had thrilled her—she was part of the war effort, just like the soldiers! She could do this job. She wanted so badly to do it, to prove to herself and to Harold and to whoever he might be having an affair with that she could make it on her own.

Soldering wire wasn't as hard as Ginny had thought it would be. She was sure she could get the hang of it before too long. She didn't dare think about what would happen if she made a mistake that caused the boat to sink, or she would freeze up with fear. Her heart had pounded with excitement when she'd seen the ship floating in the test pond. Imagine helping to build a ship like that, helping to win the war. Imagine having three new friends to talk with while she worked and while she ate lunch every day.

She'd had one frightening moment when that dark-haired girl, Rosa, had tripped and almost fallen into the water; Ginny's quick reflexes had saved her. And wouldn't Harold be surprised to learn that Allan's former teacher, Miss Kimball, worked there? Harold had always said that Miss Kimball was a fine teacher. Maybe that's how she should prepare him for the news. Maybe she could use Helen Kimball as an example of how every woman ought to do her duty.

"Penny for your thoughts?" Harold said. He had emerged from the bathroom and caught her staring into space. For a long moment she couldn't reply. Why had he picked this very moment when her thoughts were all jumbled together to suddenly become un-*aloof*? Was there such a word as *un-aloof*?

"Oh . . . um . . . What time do you leave tomorrow?" she asked, stalling for time.

"You already asked me that, and I already told you. What's wrong with you tonight? You seem . . . distracted."

"I had a busy day. You'll never guess what I did—"

"Did you finish packing my suitcase?"

"Yes. Harold, I need to tell you that I—"

"Did you remember clean pajamas?"

He wasn't listening. He was within view, but at a distance—*aloof*. And even if he hadn't been *aloof*, Ginny was afraid to tell him. Maybe his trip to Detroit was a good thing. It would give her a few days to adjust to her new work schedule while he was away. She decided to wait until he returned home to talk to him.

She stood and wrapped her arms around him, hugging him tightly, savoring his clean scent and the familiar comfort of his solid chest. She didn't think she could ever live without him, and it terrified her to think of losing his love. But it was even more frightening to feel as though she was losing herself. She stood on tiptoes to kiss him.

"I'll miss you," she said.

In the morning, Ginny got out of bed an hour earlier than usual so she could do a few household chores and pack lunches for herself and the boys and make breakfast for everyone before work. By 6:30 she was frantically watching the clock, waiting for Harold to leave so she could leave, too. He was acting *aloof* once again.

"Boys!" she called up the stairs. "You need to stop dawdling or your pancakes will get cold." Ginny could save time by wearing her coveralls to work, but how would she explain such an unusual outfit to the boys? They probably didn't pay much attention to what she wore, but she didn't want to take that chance.

"Listen, I have to go," she told them as soon as Harold's car pulled out of the driveway. The boys had finally slouched into their places at the breakfast table, but Herbie sat up with a worried expression on his face when she told him she was leaving.

"Where are you going, Mom?"

"We'll talk about it when I have more time. Here are your lunch-boxes. Don't forget them. Listen, I probably won't be here when you get home from school."

"Again?"

"Just let yourselves in like you did yesterday. I won't be long, okay? Maybe ten or fifteen minutes. Let Rex out when you get home, but I want both of you to stay inside until I get here, okay?"

"Can't I go play with Tommy?" Allan asked.

"You'll have plenty of time to play after I get home. Start your homework while you're waiting. I want to find you sitting here, doing homework."

"What's going on, Mom? Where are you going?" Allan was star-ing at her, his frown a miniature version of his father's.

Ginny grabbed her own lunch. "I'll explain later. Please do what I ask, okay? Bye."

She had no time to worry about them as she sprinted two blocks to catch her bus. Harold was always chiding her for smothering them—well, she certainly wasn't smothering them now. He would get his wish at last.

CHAPTER 6

★ *Helen* ★

The jangling alarm clock startled Helen from a deep sleep. She had been dreaming of the rural, one-room schoolhouse where she'd once taught, and she awoke with surprise to find herself in her bedroom. In the dream, Jimmy Bernard had sat in the front row, looking just as he had the very first time she'd seen him: barefoot and wearing a pair of overalls that were several sizes too large for him. His brown eyes looked as dark and mysterious as secret passageways. She longed to close her eyes and return to the dream, to hear his voice and the sound of his laughter, but it was time to get up for work.

The dream had been so vivid that for a moment Helen forgot she was going to the shipyard instead of the school. Her lapse was understandable; she had worked as a teacher for over twenty years and at the factory for only four days. Today was Friday, the last day of the workweek. She would have the weekend off, but to do what? She couldn't say that she enjoyed working at the shipyard—not yet, anyway—but it was better than staying here alone all day. Too many ghosts inhabited her parents' house. If only she could sell it.

"It's not a good time to put a house as large as your father's on the market," her lawyer had advised. "You won't get a very good price for it as long as the war is on. Why not divide it into apartments or rent out rooms if it's too big for you?"

"I'll think about it," she had told him. But of course partitioning it was out of the question. Father would roll over in his grave if Helen dared to change a single thing in his precious mansion. And the neighbors! Turning it into some sort of rooming house was unthinkable, that's all there was to it. She often wished she could move back into her own little bungalow near the school, but it wouldn't be right to evict the people who were renting it from her. Not with the husband away in the service. And who would ever rent this monstrosity if she did move out? Besides, Minnie had been her mother's housekeeper for more than twenty years and she needed this job. No, there was nothing Helen could do but stay here and suffer in silence.

Silence. That was the worst thing about this place—the silence.

Helen climbed out of bed and went into her adjoining dressing room. The first things she saw were her work coveralls lying neatly folded on the chair. She hadn't made up her mind whether to continue wearing them to work or not. Helen didn't want to wear pants a moment longer than necessary and hated the thought of someone recognizing her in such an outfit while pedaling to the shipyard. But she hated the locker room at work even more. Undressing in front of so many other women would be even more dreadful than being seen in coveralls. In the end she decided to wear them to work again, as she had been doing all week.

When she was dressed, Helen made her way down the wide, curving staircase and into the echoing kitchen to fix herself a cup of tea and some toast. It seemed ridiculous to carry such a meager breakfast into the immense dining room, but she liked to gaze through the French doors to the backyard and the gazebo beyond. If she closed her eyes she could picture one of the many dinner parties her father used to host, with the chandelier glowing and a dozen guests gathered around the gleaming mahogany table. She imagined Albert sitting beside her again, looking handsome in his uniform. The soldiers she saw on the street every day reminded her of him, but of course Albert had fought in the Great War and his uniform had looked much different.

Thanks to Minnie, there wasn't a speck of dust in the dining room, and the silver tea service shone softly on the sideboard. But beyond the French doors, the backyard resembled the jungles of Borneo. Her father had hired a succession of gardeners, but none of them had done as fine a job as Joe Bernard had all those years. The current gardener was much too old to keep up with such a large estate—but what else could Helen do? Every able-bodied man between the ages of eighteen and forty-five had either enlisted or been drafted.

Helen finished her toast, packed a lunch, and wrestled her bicycle out of the toolshed. Her legs ached from pedaling to work all week, but she wouldn't be riding much longer. She would have to drive Father's car to work—assuming it still ran after all these months. She wondered who would keep it tuned up for her. Father's chauffeur had enlisted in the navy. And what if she had a flat tire? All of the spare tires in America had been gathered up in rubber drives for the war effort. She saw buses stuffed with people at the factory every morning and evening, but public transportation was for people like that girl Rosa Voorhees, not for her.

An hour later the clamor of machinery startled Helen anew as she entered the factory, especially after being greeted with the high-pitched laughter and squeals of children for most of her life. She was the first member of her crew to arrive, and after punching the time clock, she took a moment to tidy her crew's tool station, setting all their equipment in order.

"Look how nice and neat our workstation is compared to the men's," Virginia Mitchell said, coming up behind her. She gave Helen's arm a little squeeze.

"I've just been straightening it."

"Jean Erickson is such a good teacher, isn't she?"

"A very bright young woman," Helen agreed.

"She said we might be able to start working on the production line by the middle of next week. Can you imagine? I was afraid it would take me months and months to learn everything because I'm not nearly as smart as you and the other ladies are—"

"Excuse me, Mrs. Mitchell—Ginny—but you shouldn't be so hard on yourself. You're every bit as capable as the rest of us."

"But there's so much to learn, and—"

"There are dozens of picky little tasks to master, true, but none of them are particularly difficult. They can be performed one at a time, and I'm sure you're used to doing several chores at once, am I right?"

"Oh no, I'm just a housewife."

Helen sighed and gave up trying to convince her.

"You know, I still can't believe I work here," Ginny continued. "I was in Harris's Drugstore down on Main Street last January when a long line of trucks came rumbling into town. Mr. Harris, who knows everything there is to know about Stockton, told me that the owners had applied for government money to expand the shipyard and build landing craft for the war effort. And now here we are six months later, walking through the employees' gate in our coveralls every morning, carrying lunchboxes. Who would have ever thought?"

Helen didn't say so, but she certainly wouldn't have imagined it, even in her wildest dreams. No one in her family had ever worked in a factory. On the contrary, her father's bank had probably financed the loan to start the shipyard. In fact, if she dug through her father's papers she would probably discover that she owned shares in Stockton Boat Works, as it used to be called.

Jean arrived and assigned everyone a task. Helen settled down to work, concentrating on learning to do the job well. The other three women on her team were rapidly making friends with each other, and that was understandable. Helen felt like an outsider—which she was.

When the lunch whistle blew, her crew filed into the lunchroom with hundreds of other workers. It was not a very attractive place to eat, with its glaring overhead lights and cheap wooden tables and benches, but is was less noisy than the factory floor. The smell of bologna and tuna fish and egg salad drifted out of lunchboxes, mingling with the aroma of stale coffee. Jean, Ginny, and Rosa found an empty table and sat down to eat together as they had done all week.

Helen was searching for a quiet place to eat alone, apart from the others, when Rosa stopped her.

"Hey, how come you never sit with us? You think you're better than we are?"

"Of course not. I thought you younger ladies would have more in common with each other. I'm trying to give you some privacy."

"But we're a team," Ginny said with a worried look. "I feel bad to think we haven't included you in our conversation. Please, you don't need to feel *aloof*. Won't you join us?"

Helen felt awkward as she sat down at their table. Even their lunches were different from hers, with their thick sandwiches and homemade cookies. Helen had a Thermos of canned soup and some crackers.

"We were talking about all the adjustments we've had to make since we started working here," Jean explained.

"I hate getting up so early in the morning," Rosa said. "I wanted the cemetery shift—"

"You mean the graveyard shift?" Jean asked, smiling.

"Yeah, that's it!" Rosa laughed along with the others. "I knew it had something to do with dead people. Anyways, I'm a night owl, so I was hoping they'd let me work here all night so's I could sleep all day."

"You could ask for a transfer once you finish training," Jean said. "They don't let greenhorns work the graveyard shift right away."

"But we would miss you, Rosa," Ginny added. "It's only been a week, but I think we all work so well together, don't you?" The others nodded, their mouths full of food. Helen noticed how hard Ginny always worked to make everyone feel important—everyone but herself.

"Yeah, but I'm not getting along too good with my in-laws," Rosa said. "I wanted to work nights so's I wouldn't ever see them. Me and Mr. Voorhees are always locking horns. He just about had kittens when I first told him I took a job here. He thinks women belong at home. Period."

"So does my husband," Ginny said.

"Did he have kittens, too, when you took this job?"

Helen looked up from her soup, waiting for Ginny's response. She had been wondering all week how Virginia Mitchell had ever talked her husband into allowing her to work. Ginny didn't meet anyone's gaze as she folded the sheet of waxed paper that had held her sandwich into smaller and smaller squares.

"He doesn't know I'm working here," she finally said.

"How on earth have you kept it a secret?" Helen asked.

"I ... I didn't mean to. He has been working out of town all week. . . . I plan on telling him as soon as he gets home."

"When's he coming home?" Rosa asked.

"Tonight."

That will be the end of her working career, Helen thought. Harold Mitchell definitely wore the pants in that family, and if he didn't want Ginny to work, she wouldn't.

"What if he makes you quit?" Rosa asked.

"I'm hoping he won't. I really like working here. I feel like I have a real purpose in life for the first time since the boys were babies. They don't really need me anymore—in fact, they hardly even notice me—and I feel so useless at home."

"Is that why you took this job?" Rosa asked. "To get your husband's attention and make him notice you?"

"No, I . . . I don't think so. I wanted to do something that really mattered for once, besides cooking meals and washing clothes. I went from living under my father's roof to living under my husband's in a single day and never had a chance to make my own decisions. I felt like I . . . like I was losing myself! Anyway, don't mind me," Ginny added with a wave of her hand. "It's the same way for all women, isn't it? What else is there for us to do besides be wives and mothers?"

Helen was about to enter the conversation and set Ginny straight, but Rosa spoke first.

"Just stand up to your husband," she said. "That's what I did with my father-in-law. I told him I'd move back to Brooklyn if he didn't quit trying to boss me around, and he don't want that because he knows it would upset Dirk. He finally stopped giving me a hard time about it, but he shoots me dirty looks all the time, and he doesn't talk to me much—which is fine by me. The next fight is going to be about church. I went with them for two Sundays and I'm not going back. Ever."

Helen understood. She hadn't been to church in nearly a year and didn't miss it in the least. She hadn't thought about God at all since then, and she was quite certain that He hadn't given her a second thought, either.

"Your in-laws go to that little white church over on Front Street, don't they?" Jean asked. "I thought I saw you there last week."

"Yeah. You go to that church, too?" Rosa unwrapped an enormous piece of apple pie that made Helen's mouth water.

"I just started attending," Jean replied. "I only moved to town a few months ago."

"And you actually like that place?" Rosa asked.

"I do. The people seem very friendly—and the minister is a good preacher. I've got five brothers in the service who I need to pray for."

A lot of good prayer will do, Helen thought.

"I don't fit in too good in that church," Rosa said with her mouth full of pie. "Everybody is so stiff and straight-laced—especially my in-laws. Dirk's father shoots daggers at me with his eyes every time I move or make a peep. His mother thought my dress was too short to wear to church, and she kept motioning for me to pull it down every time I crossed my legs. She even made me wear one of her hats to church. Me—in a hat! Hah! It had flowers on it and one of those fishnet things. I'm telling you, it was torture."

Helen couldn't imagine Rosa sitting primly in church. Nor would a hat help her look any less seductive—even with flowers and a veil. She would attract male attention in a gunnysack.

"Listen, why don't you sit with my sister Patty and me next week?" Jean asked. "I'll introduce you to some people our age."

"Gee, I don't know. Religious people are always condemning girls like me, telling us we're going to hell and stuff like that. I only went because my in-laws practically forced me to, but I don't really belong there. I see the church ladies smiling and hugging and being holy, and I know I'll never fit in. I'm nothing like them. Those people started learning to be good from the day they signed up for Sunday school, and they have parents and grandparents who went to church for ages and ages, too. I never met my father, much less my grandparents, but I'm pretty sure they never set foot in no church. Dirk knows the truth about me, but his parents sure don't."

"But it sounds like going to church is important to your husband's family," Ginny said. "Why not give it another chance, Rosa? Sit with Jean next time. It'll help keep peace in your household if you do go."

"And it's only for an hour," Jean added. "There's nothing worse than living in a home that's a war zone."

"Yes, there is," Helen said softly. She didn't think anyone would hear her, but they all turned to stare at her.

"What could possibly be worse?" Ginny asked.

The question embarrassed Helen, but she had to answer. It would be rude not to. "Going home to an empty house," she said quietly.

"Oh, Helen," Ginny said, wrapping her arm around her shoulder. The motherly gesture came so natural to Ginny, but it startled Helen. Her family had always avoided such open displays of affection, and so had she. She couldn't recall the last time someone had embraced her. Had it been Albert, all those years ago? She lifted her chin to keep away the tears.

"Don't mind me. I shouldn't have spoken."

"Of course you should have!" Ginny insisted, giving her shoulder a squeeze. "You don't need to be afraid to tell us how you feel. That's what friends are for."

"Why didn't you get married if you don't like being all alone?" Rosa asked.

Helen ignored her. Didn't anyone ever teach that girl to think before she spoke? No wonder her home was a war zone.

"It's not polite to ask such personal questions, Rosa," Ginny said as the silence lengthened.

"I really admire you, Helen, for having a career all those years," Jean said. "Not too many women do. I guess I'm a bit unconventional, too, because I want to go to college when the war ends. Sometimes I wonder if there's something wrong with me, why I'm so different from other girls my age. They all want to get married or become secretaries, but marriage is the last thing in the world I want. Not yet, anyway. Maybe it's because I grew up surrounded by brothers, but I know I'm just as smart as they are, just as capable of going to college or flight school or anywhere else that they go. But I have a hard time convincing the rest of the world. My school guidance counselor kept trying to steer me into teaching or nursing as a career, and it made my blood boil—no offense, Helen."

"No offense taken. But I hope you're prepared to fight a lot of battles along the way. The world will leave you alone as long as you stick to one of the traditional women's careers, but not if you try to venture out of those boundaries. One of my classmates in college decided to study medicine, and she traveled a very hard road. If women try to compete in a man's world, they have to continually prove themselves. It isn't enough to be as good as the men are, you have to be better. Society still believes that a woman's place is in the home."

"I think it's wonderful that Jean is so determined," Ginny said. "I went to college for a year, but then I met my husband and he wanted to get married, so I never finished."

"What did you want to study?" Jean asked.

"Oh, I don't know ... nothing, really. My father said I should go because I could meet a man who had a professional career. That's the only reason any of the girls in my high school class went to college—to find a husband. It didn't matter what majors we chose because we all knew we would never finish anyway."

"That's absurd," Helen said. Her words came out with such vehemence that everyone stared at her again. "I'm sorry, but I think education is very important for women."

"I'm with you," Jean said. "But we're in the minority in this world."

"What about your boyfriend?" Rosa asked Jean. "You told me you had a guy waiting for you back home. Don't you want to marry him and have kids?"

"Of course I do." Jean stuffed a rather dry-looking piece of cake back into her lunchbox and snapped it shut. "But Russell and I are both pretty young. He isn't ready to get married and neither am I. We'll figure things out after I finish college."

"Well, I lived on my own long enough to know I hated it," Rosa said. "Now I just want this stupid war to be over so's me and Dirk can be together again."

"Dirk and I," Helen corrected.

Rosa stared at her as if she had used profanity. "Dirk and *you*...?"

"No, no. I'm sorry; I was correcting your grammar. I've been a teacher for so many years that I do it automatically. The correct way to say it is 'Dirk and I,' not 'me and Dirk.'"

"You got a lot of nerve."

"Yes, I suppose I do. I'm sorry." Helen never should have joined the other women. She always seemed to be the odd one out. Staying away had made her seem uppity, but now her conversation had reinforced that attitude—at least in Rosa's mind.

"Listen, I'm sorry if I give the impression that I think I'm better than everyone. I don't feel that way at all. In fact, I feel like an outsider for entirely different reasons."

"Oh yeah? Why's that?" Rosa asked. She had her arms folded across her chest, an expression of belligerence on her pretty face.

"Well . . . because you're all so much younger, for one thing. And your interests differ from mine."

"Because we're married or have boyfriends?"

"That's part of it, Rosa. I became a teacher because I wanted to provide disadvantaged young people with a good education. I attended private boarding schools when I was growing up and graduated from Vassar, an exclusive girls' college in New York State. Most of the rural schools in this part of Michigan were one-room buildings, and all eight grades shared the same room and the same teacher.

The teachers weren't much older than their students and had only two years of training at the Normal School before teaching an entire class. Stockton is a fairly large town, so our schools at least have separate grades now—but many of the rural ones are still one-room schoolhouses. I wanted to provide the disadvantaged students and the colored children in this county with a better education."

"So why'd you quit teaching?" Rosa asked. "Why're you working here?"

Ginny laid her hand on Rosa's arm. "You really shouldn't ask such personal questions, Rosa," she said gently.

"I don't mind answering that one," Helen said. "My parents both became ill a little over a year ago, and I had to resign from teaching to care for them. They've both passed away, but now I have to wait until there is an opening at school to reapply."

"Don't you find it kinda boring here? You being an educated person and all?"

"I suppose it's boring at times, Rosa. I would hate to do this for the rest of my life. But any job can become routine if you let yourself get into a rut."

"Housework can certainly be boring," Ginny said with a sigh. "It's nice to do something different for a change." The attention shifted to Ginny, and Helen felt greatly relieved. "I loved it when the boys were babies," Ginny continued. "And I'd love to have more children, but Harold says two are enough."

"Why is it all up to him?" Rosa asked. "Don't you have any say in the matter?"

"Well . . . no. I mean, he's the one who has to provide for them."

"Are you too poor to have more? How much money does your husband make?"

Helen silently shook her head at the girl's lack of tact. Even Ginny seemed taken aback for a moment. "It's not a question of money. . . ." she began. But then the whistle blew. Lunch hour was over.

As the afternoon dragged on, Helen noticed that Ginny was watching the clock, growing increasingly nervous as the shift drew to a close and the time came to face her husband.

"See you all on Monday," Jean said after the whistle blew.

"I hope so," Ginny murmured. "I have to tell Harold about this job when he comes home tonight, and I'm so afraid he'll make me quit."

"Please don't quit," Jean said. "The men heckle us as it is, saying that women don't have what it takes to work here, and blaming us for slowing down the line. As if it's always our fault. Besides, I'd hate to lose you, Ginny. You're a good worker."

"Thank you . . . but—"

Helen could no longer remain silent. "Virginia—if I may say something. I know it's none of my business, but . . ." In fact, Helen had always prided herself on minding her own business and not becoming involved in the lives of the other teachers at school. She didn't know what had come over her now that caused her to speak up. Maybe it was because Harold Mitchell reminded her so much of her own father. Maybe, deep down, she was still angry with him after all these years. Or maybe it was because she hated to see such a warm, caring woman as Virginia have all the love bullied out of her. Whatever the reason, she had to speak up.

"Yes, please," Ginny begged. "I could use some advice. Harold always admired you as a teacher."

Helen drew a deep breath. "Sometimes you have to decide for yourself what's best for you to do. Only you can determine that. Others may mean well, but they usually have their own interests at heart. I wonder . . . if Mr. Mitchell asked you to quit, would it be because it's best for him or for you?"

"I don't want to be selfish. I have the children to think about. . . ."

"Your boys are bright, responsible children. Give them some credit. I'm certain they can handle your working. Besides, I can't believe that you, of all people, would be a neglectful, selfish mother."

"Thank you." Ginny's words came out in a near whisper.

"You're a grown woman, capable of making your own decisions. It isn't up to Mr. Mitchell to decide whether or not you should work;

it's up to you." With that, Helen left. She had spoken her mind, gotten it off her chest. Even so, she didn't expect to see Ginny on Monday morning.

By the time Helen reached home, the big house on River Street looked inviting for once, quiet and serene after the clamor and activity of the shipyard. And she was glad to see that it wasn't empty; her mother's housekeeper, Minnie, was still there, putting away the last of her cleaning supplies in the pantry closet.

"You look wore out, Miss Helen. I got your supper cooking in the oven."

"Why don't you stay and eat with me? I'll drive you home afterward in Father's car."

"Thank you, Miss Helen, but I can't stay. I have my granddaughter Thelma living with me now, and I need to get on home and fix us some dinner."

"Maybe another time," Helen said, disappointed. "It seems like I never take the time to tell you how much I appreciate everything you do—"

"Oh, please don't make this any harder than it already is," Minnie interrupted. "The reason I waited around today is because there's something I need to tell you."

"You're not quitting!" Helen sank down on a kitchen chair.

"I'm sorry, Miss Helen, but the truth is, you don't need me no more. I know you don't. And there's all kinds of good jobs out there where I can make a little more money. They don't even care that I'm nearly sixty-five years old."

"How much are they paying you? I'll give you a raise." Minnie shook her head.

"I can't be taking more money from you for doing nothing around here. This place don't need cleaning every day. My granddaughter can come and clean once a month if you want her to, but that's all this place needs."

"Yes, I suppose you're right. And I do know how to clean up after myself. I did all of my own cooking and cleaning for years when

I had my own house. It's just that ... I'm so sorry to see you go."

Helen gave Minnie a week's pay, along with a hefty bonus, and said good-bye. As she stood in the kitchen doorway watching her walk away, Helen felt a terrible loss.

CHAPTER 7

★ *Rosa* ★

Rosa arrived home from work at 3:45 to find her mother-in-law already busy cooking supper. Talk about an eager beaver! Mr. Voorhees wouldn't even come home from work for another hour and a half!

"Did you have a good day, dear?" Mrs. Voorhees asked as Rosa put her lunchbox in the sink.

"It was okay."

The kitchen smelled wonderful—even better than the diner did where Rosa used to work. She would gain a hundred pounds in no time if Mrs. Voorhees kept feeding her this way. Rosa had never eaten three square meals a day in her life, much less had someone cook them for her. And such delicious meals.

"Did you have enough to eat for lunch?" Tena asked. "Am I packing enough food for you?"

"Yeah, plenty . . . but I can do it myself, you know."

"I always fix a lunch for Wolter, so it's no bother to pack one for you, too."

"Okay, then. Thanks."

The house was so clean it sparkled. Rosa was almost afraid to walk across the floor or sit down anywhere. But when she went into

Dirk's room and saw the mess she had created in the once-spotless room, she felt a stab of guilt.

"Rosa, you're a slob," she mumbled as she changed out of her coveralls. She had ordered Tena to stay out of her room, and now look at it. The bed hadn't been made all week. Clothes everywhere. And the pile of cosmetics on the desk looked like a drugstore had exploded. Rosa was gazing around in dismay, wondering where to begin, when Tena knocked on the door.

"May I ask you something, Rosa?" she said, poking her head inside.

"Hey, I know it's a mess. I'll get to it when I can, okay? I had a long day."

"It isn't about the room."

"What, then?" She wasn't sure she wanted to hear it.

Tena hesitated before speaking, her work-reddened hands fluttering like pigeons. "I know that my husband can be stubborn sometimes. He has opinions about things like women working. But I would like to have peace in this household. To hear you two arguing at the dinner table each night . . . it hurts me. Please, can't you try to get along a little better?"

"Tell him to stop picking on me all the time." Rosa kicked a pair of shoes out of sight beneath the bed.

"My husband has always said what he thinks. You must learn, like I have, to listen and not say anything. Once he speaks, he is done. Dirk is the same. He's so much like his father that I think if you can get used to Wolter, it will help you when Dirk comes home."

"Hey, I'm not the type to just sit back and take that kind of baloney, okay? I can dish it out, too, you know." She corralled her scattered makeup containers into a small mound in the middle of the desk.

"But what is the use? You won't change Wolter's mind. The Bible says, 'A soft answer turneth away wrath.' Please, Rosa. Try it once and see."

Rosa remembered how Dirk had always spoken his mind with the other sailors, but he had never tried to order her around. Of course, they'd only been married a short time, and she hadn't done anything to make him mad the way she had angered his father. She and Dirk had been crazy in love, still on their honeymoon, when they'd had to go their separate ways.

"Yeah, okay. I'll try," she told Mrs. Voorhees.

"Thank you." Tena smiled, but her eyes still looked sad and worried.

Being on her feet all day had exhausted Rosa, and she longed to lie down and take a nap before dinner. She decided to straighten her room instead. She was still sorting through piles of clothing when she heard Mr. Voorhees come home. A few minutes later, Tena called her to dinner.

"So. You have worked for a week," Mr. Voorhees said after he'd prayed over their food. "Are you ready to give up this idea of a job and stay home?"

Rosa's temper flared, but she glanced at her mother-in-law and saw the pleading look in her eyes. Rosa forced herself not to shout at him, but it was the hardest thing she'd ever done.

"I been working all my life, Mr. Voorhees, ever since I was fourteen. I was working when me and Dirk . . . Dirk and I . . . met, and he didn't say nothing about it." She glanced at Tena again and saw a tiny smile of approval. Rosa suddenly had an idea. "Hey, listen, how about if I give you some money from my pay every week for my room and board? How much you want?"

Mr. Voorhees looked startled—and annoyed—by her offer. "It is the man's job to support his family."

"Okay, then, I'll give you money out of Dirk's pay. I know prices are high these days, and I been eating like a pig. The food is so good, you know. And Dirk would want us to help out."

"Have you told him that you are working?" Mr. Voorhees asked.

"Yeah, I wrote him a letter telling him all about it. It's too soon to hear back, though. I told him that working gives me something to do all day. She don't really need my help around here," Rosa said, gesturing to Mrs. Voorhees. "I told Dirk we could save up and maybe buy us a house or something when he comes home."

Wolter grunted. "If he tells you to quit, I expect you'll obey him." It was a statement, not a question. Rosa was about to explode when she felt Tena's hand on hers. She decided to take Tena's advice again and hold her tongue.

The truth was, she didn't know what she would do if Dirk asked her to quit. She remembered how worried poor Ginny had been about breaking the news to her husband tonight and wondered how she was making out. If he was anything like Mr. Voorhees, meek little Ginny would never have the guts to stand up to him. Maybe Rosa should have offered to go over and back her up. She wasn't afraid to stand up to nobody.

"Please pass the potatoes," Mr. Voorhees said.

He had changed the subject! Rosa tried not to gape at him in surprise as she handed him the serving bowl. Tena was right. Once he got something off his chest, he dropped it.

After dinner, Rosa helped Tena clear the table, then took a clean towel from the drawer to dry the dishes. "Just leave them on the counter, dear," Tena said when Rosa started to put the dishes away in the corner cupboard. "I'll take care of them."

"You afraid I might chip them or something? You know, it burns me up that you don't trust me with any job." She was about to name all the complicated stuff she was learning to do at the factory when Tena looked up at her in surprise.

"Oh, no, no, no, Rosa. Of course I trust you. But there is not much room in this tiny house, and the dishes must go into that cupboard just so if they are going to fit. I've had more practice, that's all."

Later, they sat in the living room, listening to the news on the radio. Every evening seemed exactly the same to Rosa, with the three of them sitting around like mannequins in a department store window. Wolter hid behind his newspaper, while Tena got out her basket of yarn and knitting needles. The rhythmic clacking of the needles set Rosa's nerves on edge. Tonight was Friday, the end of a long workweek, and she was bored out of her mind.

"Isn't there anything to do around here?" she asked with a sigh.

"I could teach you to knit," Tena offered.

"Heck no!"

Tena's hands froze; Wolter lowered his newspaper. They stared at Rosa as if she had said the real word.

"Sorry," she mumbled. "All this bad news about the war has me worked up. It seems like the wrong side is winning, don't it? Now the blasted Japanese took over *another* island in the Pacific. I'm dreading the day when it's Dirk's turn to go."

"But Dirk won't be fighting," Tena said. "He will work with a ship's doctor when he finishes his training."

"I know, but just getting across the ocean is going to be dangerous, with German submarines going after all our ships and trying to sink them."

"'Sufficient unto the day is the evil thereof,'" Mr. Voorhees said.

"What's *that* supposed to mean?"

"It means that today's worries are enough. Don't borrow from tomorrow's."

"But I can't help worrying! The whole world is at war, and someday soon Dirk is going to be shipped out into the middle of it, too."

Mr. Voorhees shook his head. "'Take therefore no thought for the morrow,' Jesus said, 'for the morrow shall take thought for the things of itself.'"

"Jesus talked in riddles," Rosa mumbled.

Mr. Voorhees leaned toward her. "Pardon?"

"Look, I'm scared for Dirk, okay? I love him and I don't want anything to happen to him."

"Dirk is in God's hands," he said quietly. "We can only pray."

"Well, I don't know much about prayer, but I'm pretty sure it won't help me stop worrying."

She rose from her chair, too restless to stay seated, and tuned the radio to a station that played music. But before the usual Friday-night shows came on, the Office of War Information gave an announcement, telling people how important it was for women to go to work in defense factories. *"If you're an American citizen,"* the announcer pleaded, *"we need you."*

Rosa glanced at Mr. Voorhees to see his reaction. She was tempted to say, "See? That's why I'm working." But he had his face hidden behind the newspaper once again. Besides, she had promised Tena that she wouldn't argue with him anymore.

Rosa sighed and slumped back into her chair. It was the weekend, for crying out loud. She should be out having fun, not sitting here with two of the world's most boring people. If only she had someone to talk to, laugh with. Didn't her in-laws know how to have a little fun? She stood up.

"I'm going to go write Dirk a letter," she said, stretching. "Then I'm going to bed." She did write the letter, telling him all about her first week at work and how much she wanted to keep her job.

Please don't tell me to quit, she begged Dirk. *I need to do something to keep from going crazy—and the navy needs me to build lots more boats for the war.*

But when she finished the letter, she combed her hair and put on lipstick and her nicest party dress. Then she turned off her bedroom light and paced restlessly around the room, waiting for Dirk's parents to go to bed. She couldn't believe she'd lived here two whole weeks already. Things sure were different from her life back home—if you could even call it a home. Rosa could count six different apartments she and her mother had lived in when she was growing up.

The girls at work today had all been talking about going to college, and Rosa had felt like a Dumb Dora. What would they think of her if they knew she hadn't even finished high school? And the nerve of that schoolteacher correcting her grammar! Rosa had felt like socking her. What did that old bat expect when Rosa had been forced to change schools every time her mother had changed jobs and apartments? Her mother had called herself a cocktail waitress, but the kinds of dumps that Mona Bonelli had worked in were nothing but dives. They made the Hoot Owl down the block look like the ballroom at the Waldorf-Astoria!

What would it have been like to grow up in a home like Dirk's—a place that was clean and orderly, with good, warm food on the table and apple pie in her lunchbox every day? It might have been nice to have a mother like Tena—even if Rosa couldn't seem to do anything to suit her. But she never would have wanted a father like Wolter bossing her around.

"Dirk is so much like his father," Mrs. Voorhees had said. Could that be true? Would Dirk expect her to settle down and be a homebody like his mother who cleaned all day and cooked huge meals and never talked back? Rosa hoped not. She could never be like Mrs. Voorhees in a million years.

At last Rosa heard her in-laws going to bed. She waited ten more minutes, then slid her bedroom window open and climbed out. She wouldn't stay at the Hoot Owl very long—just long enough to have a few drinks, a few laughs, maybe a dance or two. Long enough to help her stop missing Dirk so much that she wanted to cry.

CHAPTER 8

★ *Jean* ★

By the time Jean finished all her paper work at the end of her shift, the line of people waiting to punch out at the time clock was composed entirely of men. She kept her head lowered as she joined them, bracing for the usual comments from the other crew chiefs. She didn't have long to wait.

"Hey, Jean. I saw those sorry-looking co-workers of yours trying to solder their fingers together today."

"Shut up, Doug."

"Think you can teach that pinup girl to solder?" someone asked.

"Hey, that doll can solder my wires anytime she wants," Doug replied. Whistles and hoots filled the air.

"By the time Jean's girls get through working on our ships," another man added, "the Nazi submarines won't have to sink them—they'll sink all by themselves!"

Jean ignored the rowdy laughter that followed. Then the man in front of her whirled around to face her. "All I can say is, your girls better not be getting a man's pay, because it takes twice as many of you to keep up with us."

"Yeah, this place is falling way behind schedule," someone behind her said.

"But did you notice how nice and neat the girls' tools always look?" Doug pranced in place, imitating a woman brandishing a feather duster. More laughter followed.

"I'll be glad when the war ends and the girls all go back to the kitchen where they belong."

The last comment made Jean's blood boil. It took every ounce of restraint she had not to lash back. She finally punched her time card and hurried toward the exit. Earl Seaborn held the door open for her, then followed her outside.

"You're wise to ignore them, Jean. They'll soon tire of this game."

"My brothers used to tease me all the time, too, but I knew they respected me underneath it all. This heckling seems different."

"Those guys feel threatened, that's all."

"Oh yeah? You could have fooled me." Jean had been walking briskly, fueled by anger, but her steps slowed when she saw the same group of men congregating at the bus stop. She made up her mind to walk home, in spite of the cool weather, rather than put up with their jibes all the way home. In fact, she needed to cross the street right now to avoid walking past them. Jean looked both ways, surveying the busy street, waiting for the traffic to clear.

"The men who were employed here before the war," Earl continued, "never had to work with women—much less compete with them." Jean turned at the sound of his voice, surprised to find him still waiting with her. "You and the other women are plowing new ground, showing the world what you're made of," he finished.

"I wish the war would hurry up and end so I could say good-bye to this job and all those jerks and get on with my studies. But every time I read the newspaper or listen to the news on the radio, it seems like the war is going to last forever. Have you heard the latest?"

"I know, it's all bad news. The Japanese have overrun most of Southeast Asia, and now they've set their sights on Australia. The Germans are pounding the Russians at Stalingrad, while more of them are trampling across North Africa with General Rommel the same way they rolled across Europe. Meanwhile, their U-boats control the North Atlantic and are laying mines in Chesapeake Bay. No, the war doesn't seem to be going well at all for our side. . . . But about the other crew chiefs, Jean. Don't let them get to you. Some guys don't feel like real men unless they have a woman to push around." His comment suddenly reminded Jean of Ginny's dilemma.

"Listen, Earl, I should probably warn you—one of my crew members may have to quit. Her husband sounds a lot like those guys," she said, gesturing to the crowd at the bus stop, "and he may not let her come back to work on Monday."

"Oh no. That'll set back production an entire week if you have to train a replacement."

"I know. But there's not much anybody can do about it, unless you want to go talk some sense into Mr. Mitchell. See you Monday."

"Jean, wait." He rested his hand on her arm to stop her. "I was wondering . . . How about a movie tonight?"

His face wore such a hopeful expression that she had to turn away to keep from giving in. Going to the movies with Earl sounded much more appealing than spending an evening with her sister and three rowdy nephews. But Jean had finally received a letter from Russell, telling her how lonely he was and how much he missed her. He'd sworn that he had never even looked at another girl—and Jean had felt guilty ever since for agreeing to be friends with Earl. She scrambled for a way to let him down gently.

"I don't think so, Earl. I'm pretty tired."

"How about tomorrow night, then? Or maybe a Sunday matinee?"

"I don't think so. . . . But thanks anyway." His gentle persistence loaded on more guilt, like adding another passenger to an overcrowded bus. She saw a break in the traffic and sprinted across the street, waving good-bye to him over her shoulder. "See you Monday."

As Jean had feared, she arrived home to chaos once again. Her nephews had overturned all of the kitchen chairs to build a fort, and they howled like banshees as they fought imaginary enemies. The baby stood in his playpen, howling along with them. Judging by the smell, he needed a diaper change.

"Want to do something after supper?" Patty asked above the din.

"We can take the kids to the drugstore for ice cream, or maybe there's a children's movie playing."

Jean stifled a groan as she stepped over the mess, making her way across the kitchen. She longed for peace and quiet—and solitude. If she had wanted to spend Friday night at home with a bunch of kids she would have married Russell and had her own. Jean wanted out of here. She made up her mind to go to the show alone.

"Sorry, Patty, but someone already asked me to the movies." It wasn't really a lie. Someone had asked her. She didn't need to add that she had refused him. "Maybe we can do something tomorrow night."

She helped Patty straighten the kitchen and set the table, then washed and dried the supper dishes to try to ease her guilt. It didn't help. As she said good-bye to Patty and closed the front door on the noisy household, guilt weighed Jean down like a pocket full of rocks.

The lights on the movie marquee a few blocks away cheered her a bit. They were showing an *Andy Hardy* movie starring Mickey Rooney. She joined the line at the ticket booth and was daydreaming about Russell when Earl Seaborn walked up behind her.

"I see you changed your mind, Jean. Did you get a sudden burst of energy?" He looked so hurt that for a moment she didn't know what to say. She decided on the truth.

"I *am* tired, Earl, and I *was* going to stay home, but I live with my sister, and she has three boys under the age of four, and I—"

"You don't owe me an explanation."

"Yes, I do. I needed to get out of there, so I decided to come here for a little peace and quiet. But the real reason I turned you down this afternoon was because I got a letter from my boyfriend this week, and I realized that I wouldn't like it if he went to the movies with someone else."

"I told you, I just want to be friends."

"Well, I don't think that's a very good idea."

"I see." He looked away. Jean might have felt better if he had gotten angry and told her off, but his quiet forbearance made her feel like a heel. The tension between them grew until it felt like a cable about to snap. She paid for her ticket, then waited while he purchased his.

"Listen, Earl, this town is full of girls who are free to date. Why don't you ask—"

"I *have* asked. Nobody wants to be seen with a guy who isn't in uniform. I'm a disgrace."

"It's not your fault."

He shrugged and walked away. Jean went inside and waited in line at the candy counter. Earl stood in line for popcorn. There weren't many empty seats left in the crowded theater, and she had trouble finding one. Earl wandered down the aisle a few minutes later searching for an empty one, too. The guilt-rocks in her pockets began to weigh her down like boulders, and she wanted to be rid of them. She waved to get his attention.

"There's a seat right here, Earl." She pointed to the empty one beside hers.

"Are you sure? Because if you want me to go away, I will."

"No, I'm really, really sorry. Sit, already. The show is starting."

Earl sat. When the cartoon ended and the newsreel began, he held out his box of popcorn to her. "Want some?"

"No, thanks."

He didn't speak again during the entire show. When it ended, they both stood up to leave at the same time. "Want to go somewhere for a bite to eat?" he asked.

"No, thanks. I ate a huge dinner . . . and I should get home."

"Would you like me to walk you? It'll be pretty dark outside if they decide to have a blackout drill. And I'm going your way."

"Okay." She didn't have the heart to refuse him again.

They filed out of the theater with the rest of the crowd, walking side-by-side. Neither of them spoke. By the time they turned onto Jean's street, the silence between them had become tense once again. Earl was a nice guy, and Jean knew she owed it to him to make things right.

"I am really sorry about what happened tonight, Earl. But things get much too complicated when men and women try to be friends, don't you agree?"

He shook his head. "No, because if everyone feels the way you do, I'll be alone until the war ends. All of my buddies are in the service, and the only friends I have left are women."

"I see what you mean. Then I guess it must be lonely for my boyfriend, too. He's the only guy in my graduating class who didn't enlist." They climbed the steps to Jean's front porch and stopped by the door.

"Would it bother you if your boyfriend took a girl to the movies?" Earl asked. "If you knew they were just friends?"

"Truthfully? Yeah, it would. That's what I was thinking about when I turned you down this afternoon. . . . Anyway, thanks for walking me home. See you Monday."

"Out with the boss again, hey?" Patty said as she came inside. It irked Jean that her sister had been spying on her—but at least she would never know that Jean had lied to her.

"Earl and I are just friends."

"Sure you are." She gave Jean a knowing look.

"I'm in love with Russell Benson," Jean said stubbornly—even though she wasn't entirely sure that it was true. She and Russell had never spoken about love.

"What movie did you see? How was it?"

Earl had just told Jean how lonely he was, and she realized that Patty was lonely, too, tied down with three kids and her husband away. Jean decided to sit down with her for a few minutes and tell her all about the movie, mostly to ease her own guilt.

"It's a good thing you didn't go tonight, Patty. The newsreel they showed before the film was of London after a Nazi bombing. I don't know how I'm going to get those images out of my mind. And since Bill is stationed near there . . ."

"Yeah, you're right. Good thing I didn't see it. If anything ever happened to Bill, I don't know how I'd ever raise three boys without him. It's hard enough to cope until the war ends."

It was late when they finally went upstairs to bed. Jean wrote a letter to her twin brother and was in the middle of writing one to Russell when someone knocked on the front door. She was so afraid it would be a telegram for Patty that she leaped off the bed and ran downstairs to answer the door before her sister could.

Earl Seaborn stood on the front porch, his arms all wrapped around Rosa Voorhees from work.

"Hey there, Jeannie Beanie!" Rosa said, smiling crookedly.

Jean's first thought was that Earl was trying to make her jealous. Then she saw the worried look on Earl's face and realized that Rosa was very drunk.

"Sorry to bother you," Earl said, "but I didn't know where else to bring her. I couldn't take her to my place, and I don't know where she lives."

"Hey, looks like ol' Jean's got something to put in her brassiere after all," Rosa slurred. "Hard to tell in those work-thingies.... What do you call them again? Coverovers ... coverups ... coveralls!"

Too late, Jean realized that she'd forgotten to put on a robe over her nightgown. She folded her arms across her chest, embarrassed to be standing this way in front of Earl. He gazed at the floor, politely averting his eyes.

"She's very drunk," he said. "I stopped by the Hoot Owl over on Cass Street after I left here and found her making a fool of herself. I didn't know what to do. I offered to take her home, but she keeps saying that she lives in Brooklyn. Do you have any idea where she lives?"

"No, only that it's with her husband's parents. They won't be thrilled to see her in this condition. They're pretty religious. You'd better come in." She held the door open while Earl hauled Rosa inside. "Put her there on the sofa. I'll be right back." Jean ran upstairs to get dressed. When she came down again, she saw that Rosa had slumped against the couch cushions and was snoring. Earl paced the floor.

"I'm really sorry for bothering you, Jean, but I didn't know what else to do."

"That's okay. It was nice of you to watch out for her."

"I couldn't just leave her there. The place was full of guys—not the best kind, either, if you know what I mean. I recognized three or four of the welders from work. They're all married and they know that Rosa is, too, but everyone was too drunk to care. It's payday."

"How'd you get her to leave?"

He smiled shyly. "I had to flirt with her and pretend like I was taking her to my place for a drink. Listen, should we pump her full of coffee? Does that really work?"

"I don't know. I don't have much experience with drunks." Jean decided to try her hand at talking to Rosa. She shook her awake. "Come on, Rosa. Time to get up. You need to go home, okay?"

"I have to sneak in or my in-laws will have kittens," she slurred.

"Where do you live?"

"Brooklyn, New York." She smiled and closed her eyes again.

They let her sleep and went out to the kitchen to put a pot of coffee on to percolate. Patty came downstairs when she smelled it brewing, and they had to explain everything to her. The three of them sat at the kitchen table talking until the baby started crying upstairs.

"I'd better go up and put him back to sleep," Patty said. "It was nice meeting you, Earl."

"Sorry for all the trouble," he said. "I never would have bothered you if I had known the baby would wake up."

"Don't worry about it," Patty said on her way out.

When the coffee was finally ready, Jean poured it into the largest mug she could find, adding milk to cool it off. "Hey, did Rosa have a purse with her?" Jean asked as she carried the coffee into the living room. "Maybe there's something inside it with her address on it."

"Yeah, she did. I hung it on her arm." Earl sat down beside Rosa and gingerly removed the purse from around her shoulder. He handed it to Jean. "You do it. My mother taught me to steer clear of ladies' purses."

Jean set down the coffee and took the purse from him. "I feel like a peeping tom," she said as she sifted through it. "Bingo! Here's a letter from Dirk with his parents' address on it. And their house is only a few blocks from here. I'll help you walk her home."

Earl nudged Rosa awake. "Come on, Rosa. Time to wake up. We made you some coffee. Drink up." He held the mug to her lips as she sipped. "Better keep our fingers crossed that she doesn't 'whoops' it up all over your sister's sofa."

At last Rosa was conscious enough to function. Earl pulled her to her feet, and Jean helped him support her, each taking an arm. They hooked Rosa's purse over her shoulder again and ventured outside.

The sky had grown cloudy, making the streets dark and spooky. The row of homes on Rosa's street was so dark that Jean could barely read the house numbers.

"Is this your in-laws' house?" she asked Rosa.

"Yeah, that's it, all right. Home of the most boring people in town." They led her up the front walk, but she halted in front of the door. "Wait, wait, wait! I can't go in that way. They'll hear me. I gotta go in the window."

"The window?"

"Yeah. Dirk's folks don't know I'm out," she said with a giggle. "Can't wake them up or they'll have kittens."

Kittens seemed much too small and harmless to describe what Rosa was putting everyone through. Jean and Earl dragged her around to the side of the bungalow and found the open window.

"Is this the right one?" Jean whispered. Rosa nodded.

Earl slid it open a few more inches and they boosted Rosa up so she could climb through it head first. They had to push her the last few feet. As soon as Rosa thumped to the floor, Jean tossed in the high heels that had slipped from Rosa's feet, and Earl slid the window shut again. He and Jean hurried away.

"Let's hope she doesn't escape again!" he puffed.

"Let's hope we don't get arrested!"

By the time they walked up the steps to Jean's front porch they were both laughing. "What a night," Jean said.

"I'm really sorry for bothering you."

"Forget it. It was sweet of you to help Rosa out. She might have gotten herself in an even bigger mess with those goons from work, and I'd hate to lose a good worker. At this rate we'll never get any ships built. See you Monday, Earl."

She hurried inside and closed the door before he could say anything else.

CHAPTER 9

★ *Virginia* ★

Ginny surged forward with the crowd as they spilled out of the bus on Monday morning, excited to be back. The doors to the huge brick shipyard stood wide open, and they seemed to welcome her with open arms. She was needed here. Her hard work would never go unnoticed.

"Ginny! You're back!" Jean said in surprise. "I'm so glad—and very relieved." She looked as though she wanted to hug her. Ginny couldn't help smiling.

"I'm glad, too."

"Hey! You escaped!" Rosa said as she hurried over. "Tell us what happened." Ginny thought Rosa looked a little bleary-eyed, but she seemed interested in Ginny's life, too. Even Helen stood listening from a polite distance. How wonderful to be around people who weren't *aloof*, for a change.

"How did you talk your old man into it?" Rosa asked.

"I ... um ... I didn't tell him yet."

Jean's smile vanished. "Didn't he come home?"

"Oh yes. He came home on Friday night. I made fried chicken for him—his favorite—so he'd be sure to be in a good mood when I broke the news—but he just wasn't listening to me. Every time I tried to tell him, it seemed like his mind was a million miles away, and before I knew it, he was packing his suitcase to leave again."

"How long do you think you can keep it a secret?" Rosa asked.

Ginny shrugged. "I don't know. I'm not trying to keep it a secret. I got up early on Saturday morning and did all the laundry. Then I went shopping for groceries and cleaned the house and did everything else that I usually do during the week."

"Didn't he ask why?"

"I thought for sure that he would, and I was working my way up to telling him. I told him that I was going to be very busy this week, that there were plenty of things a woman needed to do with a war on, and that I wanted to do my part. But he didn't ask for details. As long as his shirts are ironed and his dinner is on the table—" Ginny's throat tightened as she tried to hold back her tears. It was a moment before she could finish. "Harold doesn't seem to care about me anymore. That was why I decided to take a job in the first place. Because if he is planning to leave me for another woman, I'm going to need this job."

"He has another woman?" Rosa asked, wide-eyed.

"I don't know—at least, not for certain. But he travels so much, and he's so handsome, and he doesn't seem to know I exist anymore, and I'm so afraid that he . . ."

She could no longer control her tears. Rosa and Jean huddled around her, consoling her with hugs and murmurs of sympathy. Ginny might have cried for hours, but she stopped when she overheard some of the men mocking her.

"You ladies are gonna rust our ships with all your boo-hooing."

"Yeah, or else cause a short circuit and electrocute yourselves." The other men roared with laughter.

"Get lost!" Rosa shouted back at them. "Mind your own business!"

"Thanks. I'm okay now," Ginny said, pulling herself together. "We'd better get to work."

"I'm very glad you're still with us," Jean said, giving Ginny another pat on the back. "Anyway, today we're going to start wiring consoles."

Ginny pulled a handkerchief from the pocket of her coveralls and blew her nose, determined to concentrate on her job. What Jean was calling a console looked like the dashboard of a car, covered with gauges and dials. Maybe it was the dashboard of the ship. Then Jean turned it over, and Ginny saw dozens of wires dangling from it. How in the world would she ever keep them all straight?

"It isn't as hard as it looks," Jean said, as if reading her mind. "There are a lot of gauges on this thing, but they all get wired one at a time. You'll do fine."

Ginny settled down to work beside Rosa, who seemed very subdued today. Her dark hair hung from a limp ponytail, and she hadn't done her face all up with her usual rouge and bright lipstick.

"Are you feeling okay?" Ginny asked her.

"I'm beat. I had a rough weekend. Hey, you look as tired as I am."

"I did a mountain of housework over the weekend and it's finally catching up with me," Ginny admitted. "And I haven't been sleeping very well. I keep having nightmares about making a mistake and causing a ship to sink to the bottom of the ocean. On days like today this job seems overwhelming."

"I know what you mean. I always I tell myself, 'One step at a time, Rosa.' That's what Lorraine, back home, used to say. Sometimes the diner would get so full that I thought I was going have a nervous breakdown, with everybody yelling for more coffee and things. Lorraine taught me to just take one table at a time, and don't let 'em razz you."

"That's good advice," Ginny said, smiling slightly. "I suppose it's just like any other task I might face—turning a cupboard full of groceries into a meal, for instance. Or tackling a mound of laundry that has to be sorted and washed and folded and ironed. I've handled fund-raising events for the Stockton Women's Club and organized elaborate charity dinners for hundreds of people. And I'm the best bridge player in the club."

"That's the spirit! You can do this, too!"

Jean came over to survey their work a little while later, and it lifted Ginny's spirits when Jean praised her accomplishments. She complimented Rosa's work, too.

"Hey, Jean," Rosa said, pulling her aside, "I'm really sorry about getting so drunk on Friday night."

"Please, don't mention it."

"I was—"

"I mean it, Rosa," Jean said in a harsh whisper. "Don't talk about it—especially here."

"Is Mr. Seaborn mad at me?"

"He was more worried than mad. But he will be mad if we waste time talking when we should be working."

"Sorry."

By the end of the day, Ginny had already gotten the hang of this new task. She felt so happy and proud of herself that she wanted to send up fireworks. If only she didn't have to go home to the nagging worry of how to tell Harold.

As she stood at the stove that evening, frying liver and onions for dinner, it occurred to her that tomorrow was the one-week anniversary of her new job. Seven days had passed, and Harold still didn't have a clue that she was now an apprentice electrician. If he could completely ignore her for one week, then why not two? Or three? He had no idea what her days had been like before she'd started working at Stockton Shipyard, so why should anything change?

She watched Harold and the boys devour their dinner and calmly asked each of them what his day had been like, what he was learning in school, how Harold had fared at work. When they'd eaten the last bite of her pineapple upside-down cake and excused themselves from the table, she realized that not one of them had bothered to ask about her day. She didn't have to keep her life a secret from them— nobody cared! The thought should have upset her, but she felt oddly satisfied. Besides, Harold obviously kept secrets from her, such as the origin of the two ticket stubs, so why couldn't she have secrets, too? At least hers was for a good cause.

She was baking cookies for their lunchboxes after dinner, trying a recipe she found in the newspaper that used less sugar, when her friend Sandra telephoned.

"Virginia! I've been trying to reach you all day. We missed you at Women's Club last week. I should have phoned to remind you. Anyway, I wondered if you needed a ride to Women's Club tomorrow. It's at Gloria's house."

In an instant, Virginia's old life came rushing back to her with full force. It differed so greatly from her new life at Stockton Shipyard that she nearly told Sandra she had the wrong number, the wrong person. It took Ginny a moment to gather her wits and formulate a reply. "I'm sorry, Sandra, but I won't be able to go tomorrow."

"Oh? Why not?"

Ginny didn't know what to say. The gossip would surely fly if she didn't explain her absence. In the past she had been afraid to miss a meeting, because any woman who did was certain to be the subject of gossip. Ginny could almost hear them whispering, *"I wonder if she and Harold are having problems?"* ... *"Ginny always seemed a little high-strung, if you know what I mean. . . ."*

She had hated all that backstabbing and had tried hard not to get involved in it, but now she worried about what they would say about her behind her back. Should she lie to Sandra and say she was sick? No, they'd send some snoop over with a casserole or a pot of chicken soup to find out if she was pregnant.

For the first time, Ginny realized how much she disliked her so-called friends in her social set. She had joined the Women's Club because Harold had wanted her to, but she hadn't missed their meetings in the least. The committees did some good work, raising funds for Stockton Hospital, sponsoring luncheons for war bonds, holding blood drives, and so on. But the women also wasted a great deal of time, turning the organization into an exclusive social club and gossip mill. Wasn't there more to Ginny Mitchell than that? For the second time that day she was reminded that it was exactly what she had set out to learn.

"I'm taking a break from club activities for a while, Sandra. I have too much work to do."

"A break? How long do you—"

"You know what, Sandra? I'm right in the middle of something," Ginny said as the timer she'd set for the cookies began to ring. "I really can't talk. But thanks for calling."

She hung up, smiling to herself as she took the finished batch out of the oven and slid in a new batch. Then she pulled the ironing board out of the pantry closet and began pressing the boys' school clothes while she waited. She could manage to do only a little each night, and the basket of ironing never emptied the way it used to when she could tackle it all on the same day.

Twenty minutes later, Ginny's neighbor, Betty Parker, arrived at her back door. "Yoo-hoo! Anybody home?"

Ginny stifled a groan. The club women must have batted the gossip from house to house like a tennis ball in a championship match, since she'd hung up on Sandra. They'd obviously decided to send over Ginny's closest neighbor to find out the score.

"Come on in, Betty." The invitation was unnecessary. Her neighbor was already through the door, nearly tripping over the pile of shoes that needed to be polished.

Ginny tried not to grimace as Betty took in every detail of the kitchen as if recording it on film for later viewing. The Mitchell home was clearly a mess, from the floor that needed waxing to the dirty dishes towering in the sink: cereal bowls from breakfast and plates from dinner, pots and pans and lunchboxes, mixing bowls and measuring cups. Ginny had decided to wait and wash them all after the cookies finished baking. A basket heaped with ironing sat on the floor by Ginny's feet. Harold's laundered shirts hung on hangers from a doorknob. Betty Parker observed it all with a gleaming, critical eye.

Keeping up with the Joneses was a competition that Betty took seriously—and one in which she excelled. She was the first woman on the block to get her laundry on the line on Monday morning, the first to buy the latest kitchen gadget, the first to sport the latest fashion accessory or hairstyle. In the past, Betty had never failed to make Ginny feel inferior, but now a slow smile spread across Ginny's face. Betty Parker didn't know how to wire an oil-pressure gauge to a ship's console. Betty Parker wasn't building landing craft for the war effort.

"So what's really the matter, Ginny?" Betty's face wore a look of phony compassion, as if to say, *Confide in me . . . you can trust me.*

"Nothing," Ginny said calmly. "What makes you think something's the matter?"

"Well . . . where should I start?" Betty glanced around again with a sniff of superiority. "I noticed that you've changed your laundry day to *Saturday*—"

"So? Is that a crime?" Ginny asked as she resumed ironing.

"And Tommy says you're never home when your boys get home from school."

"How would *he* know that I'm never home?"

"Your Allan told him. Tommy says that Allan says that you said he can't go out to play until you get home."

"I'm always home by three-thirty or quarter to four."

"Home from *where*, Virginia?"

Ginny Mitchell had never been rude in her life. Always unfailingly polite, she'd allowed bossy women like Betty Parker to bully her because she was too timid to tell them off. Ginny would be polite now, too. But she would show a little backbone for once. Like her friends Rosa and Helen and Jean.

"I really don't think my whereabouts are any of your business, Betty." She spoke so quietly that it took Betty a moment to grasp what she had said.

"Excuse me?"

"If I decide to skip a Bridge game or stop attending Women's Club, or start doing my laundry on Saturday, it's really nobody's business but mine, is it?"

"Well . . . but . . . we're concerned about you," she sputtered. "If something is wrong, we'd like to help."

Sure you would. You're just plain nosy. Ginny didn't say the words out loud. Instead, she smiled sweetly and said, "That's kind of you, Betty, but nothing is wrong. I don't need any help—unless you'd like to wash my supper dishes for me while I finish ironing these shirts."

Betty edged toward the door. "This isn't like, you, Virginia. I hope you know that my door is always open if you need to talk."

"Thanks. Good-bye, Betty." The back door closed again as Betty scurried home to file her report on the Mitchell household.

Ginny felt so good she laughed out loud. Why had she allowed that crowd to bully her all these years? She had tried hard to please them in order to feel like she belonged, but they'd always made her feel worse, not better. The nasty gossip and petty backbiting undermined the little bit of good the club did for charity. Enough! Virginia Mitchell wouldn't let women like Betty Parker bully her anymore. Ginny had more important work to do. While the club members sat around playing Bridge tomorrow, she would be building ships to help win the war.

She reached for her thesaurus and looked up the word *bully*. It led her to the word *intimidate*, which the dictionary defined as *"to make timid, or inspire with fear."* Perfect! It would be her new word for the week. She would not let Sandra or Betty or any of the other members of the Stockton Women's Club *intimidate* her anymore. She would no longer allow them to "make her feel timid" or "inspire her with fear." She pulled her notebook from the kitchen drawer and wrote *intimidate* on the line below *aloof*. She was returning the book to the drawer when Allan came out to the kitchen, sniffing like a rabbit in a clover patch.

"Are the cookies done yet?" Ginny marveled at how her son could eat an enormous dinner and a big slice of upside-down cake and feel hungry thirty minutes later. She knew that one of his favorite radio programs came on tonight—*Captain Midnight* or *Superman* or maybe it was *Sky King*. Yet the aroma of baking cookies had lured him away.

"They need to cool," she told him.

"*Then* can I have some?"

"Yes, but I have a job for you to do first."

"A *job?*" He stared at her in disbelief, as if she had pulled a gun out of her apron pocket and pointed it at him.

"Yes. It's high time you learn how to shine your own shoes."

"What?" He started backing away, just as Betty Parker had. "I guess I don't want any cookies."

"Allan Michael Mitchell, get back in here." She spoke firmly, not angrily. He gaped at her as if she had fired the gun. "You'll find the shoe polish and brush in a box under the sink. Spread a piece of newspaper on the table first, and I'll show you how to get started."

"Mo-om!"

"If America is going to win this war, then everyone has to do his part. This is your part—starting tonight. You can practice on your shoes, then your father's need to be polished, too."

He wore the same astonished expression on his face that she'd seen on Betty Parker's. Ginny had to turn away to hide her amusement. The oven timer went off again and she bent to remove the next batch of cookies from the oven, proud of herself for not being *intimidated*.

"Do I *have* to?" Allan asked.

"Would you rather help out by washing the dishes?" She gestured to the cluttered sink, and his eyes grew even wider as he stared at the mound. His mouth hung open, but he couldn't seem to reply. "I didn't think so," she said. "There's the newspaper. Get going."

It took her son a moment to realize that she meant business, then a few more minutes to perform the usual childish hemming and hawing. When Allan finally got around to spreading newspaper on the table, one of the headlines jumped out at Ginny: "Millions of Women Must Be Shifted to War Work." She quickly snatched up the page.

"Not this paper," she said. "Use a different one." She tore out the article and put it in the drawer with her word notebook, thinking she might need it to convince Harold—although he read the newspaper from start to finish every night. He surely must have seen the article.

Allan was still huffing and groaning and slamming cans of shoe polish around when Herbie walked into the kitchen.

"Are the cookies ready yet?" he asked. Before Ginny could reply, Herbie noticed his brother smearing brown polish on a pair of shoes. "Hey! How come Allan gets to shine shoes and I don't?"

Ginny smiled. "I'm sure Allan would welcome your help." In an instant, Allan's attitude did a complete about-face, nudged along by sibling rivalry.

"Get lost, Herbie. This is my job, not yours."

Once again, Ginny could barely stifle her laughter. "Okay, your job will be to feed Rex his dinner," she told Herbie. "Scrape those table scraps into his dish and add a little dog food to it. He needs fresh water, too. And then you can strip all the labels from those tin cans and flatten them."

"Do I have to?"

"Yes. As I explained to Allan, we all have to do our part now that America is at war."

"But feeding Rex is *your* job, Mom."

Her job. In a moment of revelation, Ginny realized that she had always performed every household task herself in a misguided effort to feel needed. She had never demanded that her sons do any chores, as if afraid to allow them to grow up, afraid to discover that her home could run without her. But as the newspaper article had pointed out, Ginny was now needed for a much more important task.

"Feeding Rex *was* my job—but now I could use some help. I know that change is hard to get used to sometimes, and nobody likes it. But if every person in America does his part to help fight the war, then it will end that much sooner."

"Tommy Parker says that the reason the bubble gum won't make bubbles anymore is because of the war," Allan said.

"That's probably true. There are going to be shortages of a lot of things. The ships that used to bring goods from other countries are needed to carry troops overseas now. And remember how your scout troop had that rubber drive a few months ago? It was because the Japanese have taken over all the places where rubber grows."

"Dad said I can't get a new bike because we need the metal to make tanks and things."

"Right. But if we all pitch in, Allan, and do our part, we can win the war, and the factories can make bicycles again."

Ginny scraped cookies off the sheet with a spatula. What would she do once the war ended? As much as she longed for the war to be over and for the fighting and the dying and the destruction to end, she couldn't imagine returning to the life she had always lived. For the first time since the boys were old enough to go to school, she had an important job to accomplish, a purpose in life. Anyone could cook and clean house, and it terrified her to think that she was just an anonymous "anyone."

She squirted soap into the sink and filled it with water, watching the bubbles rise in a fluffy white mountain. She still wasn't certain who Ginny Mitchell really was, but she was determined to find out before the war ended, no matter what.

CHAPTER 10
November 1942

"A joint U.S.–British fighting force under the direction
of Gen. Dwight D. Eisenhower has begun landing at Casablanca,
Oran, and Algiers in North Africa."

★ *Rosa* ★

Rosa squirmed in her seat, waiting for the ordeal to end. Every night after supper—and before she and Mrs. Voorhees could clear the table and wash the dishes—Rosa had to endure what Wolter Voorhees called "family devotions." First he would read a boring passage from the Bible that used words like *Thee* and *Thou* a lot. Then they would all fold their hands while Mr. Voorhees prayed. He would ramble on and on about the war and about Dirk being in God's hands, until Rosa could barely hold back her tears from worrying about him.

She tried not to slouch in her chair and roll her eyes as Mr. Voorhees pulled his worn Bible from the kitchen drawer and cleared his throat. "Tonight our reading is from Proverbs, chapter thirty-one, the virtuous wife," he began.

Rosa braced herself. When she'd first arrived two months ago, the nightly readings had seemed to come in sequence, one chapter following another. But lately she'd noticed that Mr. Voorhees had been skipping around, reading verses that were probably meant just for her. She'd had to endure several references to wives obeying their husbands, then a long warning about lying and drunkenness and "debauchery"—whatever *that* was. Now it looked like Mr. Voorhees was going to harp about wives again. Well, maybe he could force her to sit here, but he couldn't force her to pay attention.

"'Who can find a virtuous woman?'" he read in his stiff accent. "'For her price is far above rubies. The heart of her husband doth safely trust in her, so that he shall have no need of spoil....'"

There was more, but Rosa stopped listening. Her father-in-law had a lot of nerve! Dirk's heart *was* safe with her. Dirk *did* trust her. She loved him and he loved her. And what was that stupid word *doth* supposed to mean? There was no such word. She let her mind wander, trying to decide what she would wear later tonight when she sneaked down to the Hoot Owl. The red dress had been Dirk's favorite. He always told her how beautiful she looked in it.

"'Favor is deceitful, and beauty is vain:'" Mr. Voorhees said, catching her attention again, "'but a woman that feareth the Lord, she shall be praised.'"

His words made her spitting mad. Was he calling her "vain" just because she was beautiful? Well, Dirk certainly praised her beauty, even if his father didn't! According to what Mr. Voorhees had just read, Dirk would rather have some mousy, cowering woman who sat around "fearing God," like those old cows down at the church, instead of a woman who was beautiful and enjoyed life. What a bunch of baloney!

Being good like the people in the Bible was no fun at all. Yet Rosa didn't kid herself about what she was really like deep down inside. She felt like a phony whenever she went to church because she liked to have a good time. She was nothing like those people.

She gave an enormous sigh when Mr. Voorhees finished praying. She hadn't meant to, it had just slipped out. "Sorry," she said when he frowned at her.

When the dishes were washed and the kitchen cleaned, Rosa followed her mother-in-law into the living room, bracing herself for another long, boring evening with the newspaper and the knitting needles and the radio. Even the programs they listened to were boring. What she wouldn't give for some decent music and a cold beer!

At last, Tena put her knitting away, and Wolter turned off the radio. As soon as the last light went out, Rosa climbed out of her bedroom window and walked down to the Hoot Owl. She could hear the music of Glenn Miller's band blaring from the bar's jukebox half a block away, and it put a skip in her step. How she loved to dance! She hung up her coat and was barely seated at the bar when one of the regulars offered to buy her a drink.

"No, thanks," she told him—as she did every time. He never got the hint. The man reminded her of her mother's last boyfriend, Bob, the one who had tried to get fresh with her. At least this guy gave up and went back to his barstool.

As time passed and Rosa sat at the bar, listening to the music and sipping her drink, she began feeling lonelier and lonelier. She was starting to regret sending the first guy away when Doug, one of the welders from work, finished the game of pool he'd been playing in the back room and sat down on the barstool beside her. She could tell by the way he looked at her that he liked what he saw—unlike Mr. Voorhees, who kept throwing Bible verses at her all the time, trying to get her to change.

"Wanna dance?" he asked.

"Yeah, sure." She let him take her into his arms, imagining that she was back in her favorite dance hall in Brooklyn. If she drank enough, if her vision blurred enough, she could almost pretend that she was back in Dirk's arms again. But as she swayed dreamily to the song "I'll Never Smile Again," Rosa noticed that Doug was holding her a little too closely. When he bent to kiss her neck, she pushed him away.

"Hey, knock it off!"

"Don't be a tease, Rosa. You know you're as lonely as I am."

"I'm a married woman."

"So? You let me pay for your drink, didn't you?"

Rosa squirmed out of his embrace as her temper flared. "I'll give you back your stupid money, if that's how you feel. I can buy my own drinks."

"Rosa, wait," he said, catching her by her wrist. "Don't get sore. Friday night only comes once a week. We were having fun, weren't we?" They had been, and she didn't want to go back to her lonely barstool.

"Oh, all right. But behave yourself."

She drank some more and danced some more, imagining that she was holding Dirk in her arms. She began to feel tipsy. "I need to sit down," she said when the music stopped. Doug led her to a shadowy booth in the corner and ordered another round of drinks. Rosa watched as he pulled out his wallet to pay the waitress and saw a snapshot fall out along with his money. Rosa yanked the photo across the table to look at it. A woman sat on a beach blanket with three small children, smiling and waving at the camera.

"You're *married?*" Her words came out louder than she had planned.

"So what?" he said with a shrug. "So are you."

"It isn't the same——"

She stopped. It was exactly the same. What if, at this very moment, Dirk was sitting in a bar with another woman, buying drinks for her, dancing with her? And what if Doug's wife was sitting home at this very moment like poor Ginny Mitchell, crying her eyes out because her no-good bum of a husband was messing around with another woman? Rosa recalled the words that Wolter Voorhees had read from the Bible, *"her husband safely trusts in her,"* and all the booze she had drunk sloshed sickeningly in her stomach. She shoved the photo across the table to Doug and climbed out of the booth.

"I'm going home."

"Rosa, wait. Don't be sore at me."

"Go home to your wife, Doug."

She glanced at the clock above the bar and saw that it was only eleven-thirty—several hours earlier than she usually went home—but she put on her coat and headed home, her high heels tapping loudly in the quiet streets. She glanced over her shoulder every now and then, worried that Doug or someone else might follow her. But this wasn't Brooklyn, she reminded herself. There was no need to feel threatened in boring Stockton. She made it home and hurried across the grass to her bedroom window on the south side of the house.

The window was closed.

Rosa stared at it dumbly for a long moment. She was certain she had left it open. Had it slid shut on its own? She stood on tiptoes and gripped the sash, trying to push it open. It wouldn't budge. Rosa braced her hands against the sill and jumped up to look inside. The latch was locked! The curtains were drawn, too, and she knew for certain that she'd left the curtains open.

Rosa leaned against the house. Booze swirled around in her stomach like a load of rags in a washing machine. Dirk's parents knew! They had caught her sneaking out and had locked her window!

There was nothing she could do except go around to the back door. She would probably find Mr. Voorhees sitting at the kitchen table like he was judge of the world, waiting to condemn her to hell. But when Rosa tried the back door it was locked, too. Her knees went weak. The Voorheeses hardly ever locked their doors. When she'd first moved to Michigan and saw how safe Stockton was compared to New York, she could hardly believe it. But Mr. Voorhees had deliberately locked her out tonight.

She walked around to the front door, certain that it would be locked, too—and it was. The house was dark and very quiet, her in-laws fast asleep. Rosa sank down on the front step in a daze. She didn't know what to do. November in Michigan was much colder than November in Brooklyn, and she didn't want to freeze to death on the doorstep. But she didn't want to knock on the door and be forced to face her father-in-law, either. What if he refused to let her in?

Maybe she should go to Jean's house. It couldn't be far because Jean and Mr. Seaborn had walked her home that one night. But Rosa had been too drunk to remember which house it was. She snorted in frustration and gripped the railing to pull herself to her feet. The front yard whirled like a carnival ride, but Rosa decided to walk back to the Hoot Owl to see if maybe Mr. Seaborn had come there again, like he had that other night.

She quietly slipped inside the bar and looked all around for him, peering into all the booths and even into the dingy pool hall in the rear. Mr. Seaborn wasn't there. She would have to come up with another plan.

"Do you know where Jean Erickson lives?" she asked the bartender.

"Nope, sorry. Never heard of her."

"How about Earl Seaborn who works at the shipyard?" The bartender shook his head.

Just her luck. Any other time, you could ask a question like that and find out the person's entire life history, along with where he lived. But then Rosa remembered that Jean and Mr. Seaborn were both new in town, just like she was. Jean lived with her sister, but Rosa didn't know her sister's name.

She suddenly thought of Ginny Mitchell. She was from Stockton. And Ginny had a heart as big as Lake Michigan. She would take Rosa in for the night. Rosa was about to ask the bartender if he knew the Mitchells when she remembered that Ginny's husband still didn't know that she worked at the shipyard. How would Ginny explain Rosa to him? The last thing she wanted was to get Ginny into trouble.

That left Helen Kimball as the only other person Rosa knew in town. According to Ginny, Helen's family was very wealthy and had founded Stockton Bank. Surely the bartender would know them.

"Hey, you know where the Kimball family lives?" she asked. "The rich ones who own the bank?"

"Sure, everybody knows the Kimball mansion. Fanciest house in Stockton. It's across town, right next to Kimball Park, overlooking the river."

"Why are you looking for them?" one of the regulars at the bar asked Rosa. "You been invited to a dinner party there?" He was laughing at her, making fun.

"Helen Kimball is a friend of mine," Rosa said proudly.

"Sure, and Eleanor Roosevelt is a friend of mine." Rosa walked out to the sound of drunken laughter.

She didn't know her way around town very well, but she decided to head toward the shipyard, which was also on the Stockton River, then follow River Road to the park. It turned out to be a long hike, especially in high heels. Why didn't this stupid town have taxis like normal cities did? She would have blisters tomorrow for sure.

The truth of her situation slowly began to sink in as Rosa hiked through the darkened streets. Dirk's parents had locked her out of their house! They hated her. The tears she had been holding back ever since she saw her locked window finally began to fall. Her life was so mixed up. Dirk's parents had tossed her out and she deserved it. It would serve her right if Dirk was out with another woman right now, dancing with her and buying her drinks.

Rosa felt a wave of homesickness and didn't know why. She didn't feel at home with Mr. and Mrs. Voorhees, so it couldn't be that. She didn't miss New York, either—she had nothing there anymore. How could she be homesick when she had no home? Yet the longing she felt—for something—made her heart feel so hollow and empty it just might blow away on the wind. All she wanted was to be loved, to belong to someone the way all those families at church did. The way she had belonged to Dirk for the few short weeks they had spent together.

Rosa walked on and on, weeping as she went. At last she came to an area of very large homes—and one in particular that was set back from the road and surrounded by a wrought-iron fence. Rosa had never seen a real-life castle before, but this was what she imagined one would look like. Two cement pillars supported the front gate, and she saw the name KIMBALL carved onto one of them. A light glowed in one of the upstairs windows, barely visible behind the curtains. Good. At least Rosa wouldn't have to wake Helen up.

She tried the latch on the front gate and found it locked. The pain of being locked out by Dirk's parents made her tears start falling all over again. Rosa stumbled around to the side street, searching for a driveway. Helen had told them just the other day that it was getting too cold to ride her bike and she'd have to apply for gasoline rations in order to drive her car.

Sure enough, Helen had left the gate open leading to the garage. Rosa slipped through it. The yard surrounding Helen's castle went on and on forever like Central Park. Rosa followed a sidewalk around to the front door, and when she saw her reflection in the glass it startled her. She looked so bedraggled! She dug through her purse, searching in the dark for a comb and some lipstick, but no luck. She didn't have a handkerchief, either. She hadn't done laundry in two weeks. Mrs. Voorhees had offered to do it for her, but Rosa had refused. She had no idea why.

Don't start crying again, she told herself. She wiped her eyes on her coat sleeve and rang the bell.

CHAPTER 11

⋆ *Helen* ⋆

Helen fell asleep reading in bed and dreamed that the doorbell rang. She jolted awake. The clock beside her bed told her it was just after midnight. She knew she must have been dreaming because no one would come to her door this late at night. She set her book on the nightstand and was about to turn off the light when the doorbell really did ring. A shiver of alarm raced through her. Nothing good could come from a visitor at this late hour. It rang again, long and insistent, as if someone had leaned on the button.

Helen climbed out of bed, her legs limp with fear, and put on her robe. "Coming," she called as she hurried down the sweeping staircase, then realized that whoever it was couldn't possibly hear her through the massive oak door. She switched on the foyer light, then the porch lights and peered through the side window.

Rosa Voorhees stood on her doorstep.

"Oh, for goodness' sake," she mumbled irritably. She wrestled with the locks, and at last the huge door swung open. "What on earth are you doing here?"

Rosa stood blinking at her, blinded by the harsh light. She teetered on a pair of ridiculously high heels, swaying as if the front porch was the deck of a ship. Makeup ran down her tear-streaked face, her hair was disheveled, her overcoat buttoned crookedly. Helen wondered if she had been in some sort of an accident. Then Rosa hiccuped and Helen realized that she had been drinking.

"Dirk's father is mad at me," Rosa said. "I got no place to go."

"Perhaps you should have thought of that before you made him angry. Did you try apologizing?"

"It won't help. I mean ... the truth is ... he locked me out!" Rosa began to sob. "I went out for a few drinks ... and he shut the bedroom window ... and he locked me out!"

Helen wanted to ask why on earth Rosa had come running to her. Instead she asked, "How did you know where I live?"

"Everybody in Stockton knows everybody else. Please, you're always saying how lonely you are ..." Rosa was shivering, and if Helen stood here in her robe much longer she would start shivering, too.

"All right. Come in." It wasn't a very warm invitation, but Helen didn't feel very gracious or hospitable at this hour. Or under these circumstances.

Rosa stepped into the foyer and looked around in awe. "Wow! I seen hotels that weren't as big as this place!" She turned and Helen caught a whiff of alcohol on her breath. "I'll pay you for a room if you let me stay."

"Don't be absurd. I'm not taking your money." But she certainly wasn't going to allow Rosa to stay, either. She would help her sober up, convince her to apologize to Mr. Voorhees, and drive her home. "Let's go in the kitchen," she said, leading the way. "I'll make coffee."

The Office of Price Administration rationed coffee now. Helen had stood in a long line to buy some, but it would be worth each precious drop to be rid of her uninvited guest. She filled the percolator with water, scooped coffee into the strainer, and struck a match to light the gas range.

"This is an awful big kitchen for just one person," Rosa said. "You could fit three of Mrs. Voorhees' kitchens inside this one." She stood in the middle of it, gazing around like a child on her first day of kindergarten.

"Have a seat." Helen gestured to one of the kitchen chairs, and

Rosa dropped onto it. "Speaking of Mrs. Voorhees, don't you think it would make life easier, Rosa, if you learned to get along with Dirk's parents?"

"Hey, I can't change who I am."

"Well, you're not likely to change them, either. Nor do I think you can count on changing your husband. His parents made him the man he is. They're part of him. So is this town, whether you like it or not. Do you take cream and sugar?" Rosa shook her head. Helen set a cup and saucer in front of her, then sat down across the table from her to wait for the coffee to brew. A few minutes passed in silence as the aroma of coffee grew stronger and stronger, and the percolator began to burble.

"When Dirk comes back we're gonna move away to someplace fun," Rosa said.

"Stockton is his home. What if he wants to live here?"

She didn't answer Helen's question. There was another long pause before Rosa suddenly blurted, "Know why I came here tonight?"

"I have no idea."

"Because me and you are a lot alike."

Helen was too appalled by Rosa's statement to correct her grammar. They were absolutely nothing alike! Rosa was immature and uneducated and a drunk, and Helen had never been drunk in her life. The girl lived the wild, unrepentant life of a prodigal, and Helen didn't blame Dirk's father in the least for tossing her out. Helen was about to say something scathing when she realized that she would be acting as rude and impolite as Rosa usually did. Which would prove Rosa's point.

"What makes you say that we're alike?" Helen asked.

"I'm used to being alone, like you. Me and you don't need nobody. At least, I never used to ... until ..." She began to sniffle. "Until I met Dirk, and now I need him and I don't know what to do! Oh, you wouldn't understand." She leaned her elbows on the table and covered her face.

"You think I've never been in love?" Helen said after a moment.

Rosa looked up. "Have you?"

"Yes, as a matter of fact."

"What happened to him?"

When would this girl ever learn to stop asking nosy questions? Helen did not want to discuss her life or her past loves.

"Did he die?" Rosa asked when Helen didn't reply.

"We went our separate ways."

It suddenly occurred to Helen that she did have more in common with Rosa than she'd realized. But how could she explain it without giving away part of herself? The last thing she wanted was Rosa's pity. And she certainly didn't want to become involved in Rosa's life.

"I think the coffee is ready," Helen said. "I'll fill your cup and we'll take it in there." She led Rosa to the small den just off the kitchen where Helen usually sat in the evenings to listen to the radio. It had been the servants' sitting room back when this house had servants. Rosa set down her cup and curled up on the sofa with her legs tucked beneath her. She looked like a lost waif with her windblown hair and dark, melting eyes. Rosa was forcing Helen to become involved in her life whether she wanted to be or not.

"I understand what you're going through with Dirk's parents," Helen said, "except that I was on the other side of it. My father didn't approve of the man I loved and didn't want me to see him."

"Dirk's parents hate me."

"Hate might be too strong of a word. But if I could give you any advice, Rosa, it would be that you don't put Dirk in the position that I was forced into: choosing between his love for you and his love for his parents."

"He already married *me*. He made his choice—for *me*."

"True, but there will be a hundred other little choices in the future—like where to live and how often you'll visit his parents, and how involved you'll let them be with your children, and so forth. If you can't get along with them, then Dirk will be forced to choose between keeping you happy or honoring his parents. He'll have to fight with you every time he wants to visit with them. And if he visits them alone they will have nothing good to say about you. I was trapped in the middle that way, between the man I loved and my duty to my parents. I know exactly how Dirk is going to feel. Don't make him choose, Rosa. If you can make peace with Mr. and Mrs. Voorhees now, before Dirk comes home, it will be the greatest gift you can give your husband. He loves all three of you, and he won't want to take sides."

"They dote on Dirk because he's their baby."

"All the more reason to try to get along. I suspect that his parents already understand the position Dirk is in. You're very fortunate that they've taken you into their home. That was a gracious gesture on their part. My father flatly refused to accept Jimmy. He vowed to disown me if I had anything to do with him. If my father had shown any willingness at all to change his mind, Jimmy would have bent over backward to please him. But my father didn't even try to get to know him. He couldn't get past the externals."

"What was wrong with Jimmy?"

"Nothing." Helen sighed. "Our story is a worn-out cliché, the classic *Romeo and Juliet* plot. Jimmy was our gardener's son. His only mistake was being poor and uneducated."

"Like me."

"But there is a difference, Rosa. Dirk's parents accepted you into their home in spite of your background. It's your behavior they are rejecting, not you. They didn't care that you came from Brooklyn or that you were Italian or uneducated. They didn't hold your parents' background against you. I think they object to your going out to bars and getting drunk, am I right?"

"They're real religious."

"Is faith important to Dirk, too?"

"I don't know. We didn't get to know each other very good before we got married."

Dirk Voorhees was going to pay dearly for his rash decision. Helen could understand why he had yielded to temptation, though. Even in her disheveled condition Rosa was undeniably beautiful. But now Dirk would have to live with his choice for the rest of his life.

Helen knew from bitter experience what that was like, too.

"Do you understand what I'm telling you about not placing Dirk in the middle?" Helen asked.

"I guess so. I just get so mad when Mr. Voorhees tries to boss me around."

"None of us enjoys being told what to do, but that's life. Soldiers have to follow orders if they want to win the war, and we have to follow Jean's orders if we want to build ships, don't we? I've heard that it's the same way in a marriage. If couples want to live harmoniously, someone has to take charge and someone has to let him."

Rosa hadn't touched her coffee. Helen was about to urge her to drink up, eager to get her sober so she could send her home. But to Helen's dismay, Rosa suddenly covered her face and began to weep.

"I miss Dirk so much!" Her hands and her tears muffled her words. "If only I could go see him one last time before he ships out! I'm so afraid he's going to die, and I don't know what I would ever do without him! I love him so much!" She began crying as if she never would stop.

Helen couldn't think what to do. It just wasn't in her nature to hug the girl or murmur consoling words. She searched the pockets of her robe for a handkerchief but didn't find one. "I'll get you a handkerchief," she told Rosa.

Helen fled to the kitchen, even though she knew she wouldn't find one there. She went to the window and stood looking out into the darkness toward the gazebo, wondering what to do. Why on earth hadn't Rosa gone to Virginia Mitchell's house instead of to hers? Ginny would have known exactly how to console her—and would have done it well, even if she'd been awakened from a sound sleep.

It wasn't that Helen had no experience with tears. Grief had infused this house for as long as she'd lived here. The sound of her mother mourning for her children had become as familiar as the soulful cries of the doves in the pine trees outside. But nothing that Helen had ever said or done had been able to comfort her mother.

After several very long minutes, the crying seemed to stop. Helen waited, listening in the silence, then pulled a clean kitchen towel from the drawer and steeled herself to go back into the room.

Rosa had cried herself to sleep. It seemed cruel to awaken her, and besides, she might start crying again. Helen covered her with the afghan that Minnie had crocheted and went upstairs to bed.

Even with the lights out and the house peaceful once more, Helen couldn't sleep. Rosa's words played over and over in her mind: *"I love him so much. . . . If only I could see him one last time."*

If only. As Helen lay alone in the dark, the old, hopeless story of Jimmy Bernard slipped down from the shelf where she had carefully stored it and came to life once again in her mind. . . .

The first time she saw him he looked as he had in her dream: barefoot and dressed in an oversized pair of overalls. Helen had spotted him from her bedroom window, romping around the backyard and had asked her nursemaid, "Who's that boy down there?"

"He's nobody. And you're supposed to stay in bed. You're still recovering from a fever."

Helen didn't feel sick, but the nurse hustled her back into bed as if her life depended on it. And maybe it did. After all, Helen's sister Beatrice had died of a fever a year earlier. But as soon as the nurse left the room, Helen got out of bed to watch the boy again. He scrambled up a tree as if he'd been born in the wild, then hung upside down from one of the branches.

A week later, the doctor listened to Helen's heart with his stethoscope and finally pronounced her well. But before allowing her to get up, he sat on the edge of her bed to talk to her.

"I'm afraid I have sad news, Helen." The lines in his face drooped with sorrow. His voice sounded weighted with grief. "Your sister Ophelia has gone to heaven to live with the angels."

"Like Beatrice?" she asked. He nodded, looking away. "Will they be together? Can they play up in heaven?"

"I'm a physician, Helen, not a minister. I'm sorry."

Months passed before Helen was allowed outside, even though she could leave her room, finally. She watched the boy from the dining room window as he frolicked outside, wishing she could run and jump and climb trees the way he did. "His name is Jimmy," Cook told her. "He's the new gardener's boy."

As she grew older, Helen continued to watch Jimmy from afar, marveling at his strength and vigor, a startling contrast to her siblings' fragile health. Then one glorious day in the first summer of a brand-new century, she and her older brother Henry went outside to join him. Their mother had been confined to bed, expecting another baby. Helen and Henry were too old for the nursemaid, who was busy taking care of their frail brother William and sister Blanche. As the strongest of the four remaining Kimball children, she and Henry were the only ones who didn't seem to be chronically ill with coughs and congestion and diarrhea.

Helen reveled in her freedom, roaming the estate's grounds with Jimmy and Henry, playing hide-and-seek among the bushes and pretending that the gazebo was the deck of a pirate ship. They knocked wooden croquet balls around the yard, whacked birdies back and forth over the badminton net, and pitched countless games of horseshoes. For Helen, the gentle whirrs of Mr. Bernard's push mower and the steady snip of his hedge clippers eclipsed the sound of mourning during those warm, endless summer days.

Jimmy was wild and alive and bursting with energy. When Helen read *Tom Sawyer* and *Huckleberry Finn*, she recognized the same exhilarating love of adventure in Jimmy. She gladly abandoned her dolls and her books to play with him all summer—and for the summer after that—running through the cool, green grass and chasing fireflies among the hedges. Following Jimmy's fearless example, Helen grew bold enough to scale the rear fence and scramble down the ravine to the river.

In the fall, Jimmy raked leaves with his father while Helen studied indoors with her tutors. In January, he shoveled snow so mourners could attend the wake for four-year-old Blanche, who had died of pneumonia. By spring, Helen could barely concentrate on her schoolwork, aching to join Jimmy outside as the earth budded with new life and tulips and daffodils flowered by the gazebo. At last summer arrived. As soon as Helen's father excused her tutors for the summer break, Helen left the gloomy confines of her house and escaped to the yard with Jimmy and Henry.

"Let's pretend we're in the circus," Jimmy said one hot August day. He leaped onto the railing of the gazebo, imitating a tightrope walker as he performed a daring balancing act from post to post.

"Watch me!" Henry yelled as he climbed onto the railing to mimic him. But Jimmy had walked barefoot, and Henry wore slippery-soled shoes. Helen watched in horror as Henry managed only two tottering steps before falling and striking his head on the gazebo's unyielding stone bench. Her brother died two days later of a fractured skull.

Before the year ended, eight-year-old William and baby Teddy had joined Henry and all the others in the graveyard. Out of seven Kimball children, only Helen lived.

Helen listened to her mother's cries of grief and longed to bury her face in her mother's bosom and mourn with her, weeping not only for her dead brothers and sisters but for herself. How could she even begin to explain her terror of being the next one to die? The minister spoke of heaven as a place of eternal rest and peace, but Helen didn't want to float among the weightless clouds with willowy, transparent angels. She wanted to remain a child of the earth, like Jimmy, whose strong brown body radiated health and life. She feared being placed in a casket, being lowered into a grave, and weighted down with a thick stone marker more than she feared anything else.

But every time Helen tried to find refuge and consolation in her mother's arms, her mother pushed her away as if afraid to love her lone surviving child, afraid of losing her, too. Helen's father sent her to boarding school as if the sight of her reminded him of all the children he'd lost.

When Helen came home each summer, she saw Jimmy laboring in the yard with his father. He'd grown tall and strong, his limber body barely able to contain the vitality that surged through him. Helen's life seemed ephemeral in comparison, as if she walked on tiptoes, afraid to run for fear of falling, afraid to breathe for fear of catching a deadly cold, afraid to live for fear of dying. Her mother looked at her without seeing her, convincing Helen that she was already transparent and ghostlike, soon to join her siblings in the graveyard.

As Helen sat outside one summer day, reading Joseph Conrad's *Lord Jim*, Jimmy halted as he passed by with his push mower and asked, "Is that a good book?"

"Yes, would you like to borrow it? I'm nearly finished."

"That would be great. Thanks." He continued his labors, striding up and down the lawn with the mower, but she was aware of him now in a way that made her feel strange and shivery. The urge to talk to him eventually overpowered her concentration, and she laid down the book and went inside to ask Cook for some lemonade. She carried a glass of it outside to Jimmy.

"Thanks," he said, wiping his forehead on his arm. "I haven't seen you around in ages, Helen. Where've you been hiding?"

"I've been away at boarding school."

"You like it there?"

"It's okay. I get homesick sometimes. I suppose you're on holidays from school, too?"

Jimmy smiled sadly and said, "Yeah, permanent holidays. I had to quit school last year to go to work."

"Here, with your father?"

"Only on Saturdays. I do yard work and odd jobs for other people the rest of the week." He lifted his chin to drain his glass, and when he lowered his head again, his dark eyes met hers. Helen had to resist the urge to tenderly brush her fingers across his cheek and feel the dark stubble of new whiskers along his jaw.

"You once told me you liked school. Do you miss it?" she asked. He considered her question for a moment, and she saw him disguise his sorrow behind a crooked smile and an easy shrug.

"My family needs the money. Besides, there's nothing to stop me from studying on my own, is there?"

"I have dozens of books you can borrow, if you want."

"Sure. That would be great."

Helen watched for him every Saturday morning after that, ready with a stack of books to lend him, including all of her brother Henry's old schoolbooks. By the time she left home for college, she had fallen in love with Jimmy Bernard. Helen didn't know enough about romantic love to recognize it as such. She only knew that he had exerted power over her since the first time she'd seen him from her bedroom window, drawing her to him in some mysterious way. No one looked at her the way Jimmy did—as if she were truly alive and as beautiful and vibrant as he was, not a fading ghost.

"I don't like you talking with that boy—the gardener's son," Helen's father said the summer after her first year at Vassar College. She had been following Jimmy along the hedgerow as he trimmed it, discussing President Taft, when her father arrived home from the bank in his new motorcar. He had summoned her inside. "Unless you've suddenly developed an interest in horticulture, you have no business hobnobbing with the hired help. You have nothing in common with those people."

"That isn't true. Jimmy is very intelligent and knows a great deal about—"

"*Jimmy?*" He made a face to show his displeasure. "I certainly hope that boy isn't on a first-name basis with *my* daughter."

She didn't tell him that he had called her Helen ever since they were children. An idea had begun to form in her mind, and she couldn't help blurting it out. "He is perfectly capable of doing college-level work and pursuing a professional career. All he lacks is the financial means. If there were some way we could loan him money—perhaps the money that would have educated Henry—"

"Don't you dare mention my son in the same breath as him!" her father exploded. "It's that daredevil boy's fault that I lost Henry."

"It was an accident—"

"Don't contradict me. Stay away from him, understand? You're excused."

Helen did as she was told, but she raced up the stairs to stand at her bedroom window, watching Jimmy as she had the very first time. She would need to be cautious from now on whenever she talked to him, taking care that her father didn't see them together.

But even as she looked down on the yard, her father emerged from the house and beckoned to Jimmy. He hurried over, hedge shears in hand, and she saw him nodding in understanding as Helen's father spoke to him. She wondered if her father had changed his mind. Maybe he would see for himself how bright Jimmy was and would offer him a loan for a college education.

But when her father finished speaking to him, Jimmy strode to the shed to put away the shears. He never came to the Kimball house again.

———

"I'll drive you home," Helen told a very subdued Rosa the next morning. "Mr. and Mrs. Voorhees might be relieved to learn where you spent the night."

"Thanks, Helen. I owe you one."

"I'd prefer if you didn't mention it."

Helen stopped at the cemetery to visit her parents' graves after taking Rosa home. The sky was granite gray, and a bitter wind blew straight off Lake Michigan and through Helen's coat. She walked across the grass to the elaborate grave marker and sat down on one of the curved stone benches. Her family's name—KIMBALL—was so prominent, so deeply etched in the stone that it seemed to shout in the quiet cemetery.

This monument and the enormous empty house were all that remained of the once-proud Kimball family. She gazed at her parents' graves and the six smaller ones surrounding theirs, but she didn't grieve. Memories of her lost brothers and sisters had faded over the years, until it seemed that all she remembered of them were these tombstones and grassy plots. Her family always seemed to have lain here: her sisters Beatrice, Ophelia, and Blanche. Her brothers William, little Teddy, and the only healthy sibling she'd ever had, Henry J. Kimball III, dead nonetheless at the age of twelve. Beside Henry's grave was an empty plot reserved for Helen. But who would stand here and mourn when her turn finally came?

Helen's earliest memory was of standing in this graveyard,

holding her weeping mother's hand as they'd buried Beatrice. The day before, Bea's small white casket, like all of the others, had rested in the mansion's dreary parlor, a room that to this day Helen rarely entered.

She had stumbled upon a newspaper article not long ago, describing a fatal inherited disorder that had been newly named in the 1930s. The symptoms of cystic fibrosis were familiar to her, the same ones her siblings had suffered. But giving the disease a name hadn't done much good as far as Helen could see. There was still no cure. Nor did it help to rage at God and question His ways as her mother had done all those years. God did what He pleased in spite of our angry questions. It was why Helen wanted nothing to do with Him.

On the drive home, Helen's thoughts shifted from her doomed family to Rosa Voorhees, for some reason. She hoped the foolish girl would heed her advice and reconcile with her in-laws. Family life was so complicated. Virginia Mitchell was another example. Ginny had worked at the shipyard for more than two months, and her hapless husband still had no idea. He seemed to travel on business a lot, but even so, one would think he'd pay a little attention to his wife's comings and goings. Last night Rosa had compared herself to Helen, but the person Helen had the most in common with was Jean Erickson. Jean was so remarkably single-minded for a young girl. If only there were some way Helen could sponsor Jean's college education without it appearing to be charity. Jean would hate accepting charity.

Helen realized what she was doing and nearly slammed on the brakes. She was starting to get involved with the other women's lives! She could not allow that to happen. She would suffer too much loss when circumstances changed—as they surely would. The war couldn't go on forever. A teaching position would eventually become available. The other women would disappear from her life.

The wisest course, she realized as she parked her car in the garage, was to remain separate from everyone, to never give away her heart so she would never risk losing it. To remain *aloof*, as Virginia

Mitchell had become so fond of saying. But that meant living the way Helen did now—alone.

Even so, better to be aloof and alone than to have your heart ripped in two.

CHAPTER 12

★ *Jean* ★

Jean arrived home from work on Monday morning to find a letter from Russell. She could scarcely contain her excitement as she ripped it open. When she read that he had made arrangements to come up to Stockton on the weekend to see her, she swung her startled nephew off his feet and waltzed around the kitchen with him, singing, "Russell's coming! Russell's coming! I'm so happy I could dance!"

"How's he getting here?" Patty asked. She had seated the baby in his high chair and was spooning applesauce into his mouth.

"He has a ride as far as South Bend. He's taking a bus the rest of the way." Jean swooped her other nephew through the air, grinning at the sound of his laughter. The baby pounded on the tray of his high chair, adding to the noise.

"Where's Russell going to stay?" Patty asked.

"Here. He doesn't mind sleeping on our couch."

"Sorry. No can do."

"Are you joking?" Jean set her nephew on the floor again, ignoring him as he clamored for more.

"No, I'm serious. It isn't right. It would give Russell the wrong idea."

"Oh, come on, Patty."

"This is my house and I won't allow it. It's for your own good, Jean. Don't flirt with temptation."

"More, Jeannie, more!" her nephew begged.

"No, my turn," his brother insisted. "Dance with me, Jeannie!"

Patty raised her voice so she could be heard above the shouting. "Men have funny ideas, Jean. I can't have Russell sneaking up to your room in the middle of the night."

"Russ wouldn't do that!"

Patty's face wore the superior look that Jean hated. "You don't know men very well, little sister."

"I know Russell!"

"Sorry, but he can't stay here. Ma would tell you the same thing. You'd better make other arrangements. Hey! Stop hitting your brother!" When Patty turned to separate the two older boys, the baby grabbed the bowl of applesauce and flung it onto the floor. Now Patty and all three kids were yelling. Jean had had enough. She stormed upstairs to her room, wishing she could scream along with them. Patty had been crabby all week, ever since learning that her husband would be sailing on a convoy from England to North Africa soon to join the fighting. Even so, she didn't have to take it out on Jean and Russ.

She thought about Russ—and her sister's ridiculous decision— all the next day at work, but she couldn't come up with a solution. She was still distracted when the workday ended, and she headed to the women's locker room to change out of her coveralls. She didn't notice the knot of men standing in her path until it was too late.

"Well, well, look who's coming," one of them said with a smirk. "She's a tall drink of water, isn't she, boys? A regular Amazon woman!"

"You're heading to the wrong locker room, pal," another one said. He grabbed Jean's arm and shoved her toward the door to the men's locker room. "If you want to boss people around like a man, then that's where you belong."

"Get your hands off me! Get out of my way!" Jean wrestled out of his grasp.

"Ooo, we're terrified."

"What're you gonna do, beat us up?"

Jean was too furious to reply, afraid she would cry. She finally managed to push past them, but one of the men called her a terrible name before the locker room door closed behind her.

She didn't want to be a man, she wanted to be what she was—a woman. But she got a glimpse of herself in the mirror as she headed to her locker and hated what she saw. Jean had always towered over other women, and now, with her short hair, shapeless coveralls, and angry face, she certainly didn't look very feminine. The thought of Russ seeing her this way brought tears to her eyes.

Rosa stood at her locker, changing out of her work clothes. Even when she wore baggy coveralls and had her long hair pinned up and covered by a kerchief, no one would ever mistake Rosa for a man.

"Long day, huh, Jean?" Then she noticed Jean's tears. "What's the matter?"

"Nothing." Jean wiped her eyes with the back of her hand. "You wouldn't understand. You're so pretty and feminine.... I wish I could be more like you. The girls in my family are all hardworking farm women, and we don't have the time or the know-how when it comes to fixing ourselves up."

"You mean wearing makeup and things like that?"

"Exactly. Whenever I put on lipstick, I look like a little girl play-ing dress-up. And my hair is hopeless," she said, running her hands through it. "That's why I wear it pulled back all the time. I don't know what else to do with it."

"You could knock 'em dead if you wanted to, Jean. You got a pretty face, and I saw your figure that one time. I bet your blond hair would look great in a pageboy."

"In a what?"

"It's a hairstyle. You comb it straight and smooth and turn the ends under—like Marlene Dietrich wears hers." Rosa reached up to comb Jean's hair around her face with her fingers. Jean couldn't see what she looked like, but Rosa's smile of approval spoke volumes. "There. That's better already. I could show you how to set it in pin curls at night so it would turn under."

"That would be great! My boyfriend is going to hitch a ride up here on Saturday to see me—"

"And you want to look nice for him," Rosa said, nodding. "Hey, I'm in no hurry to get home, are you? Want to go downtown and get some lipstick and stuff?"

"Okay—but I don't want to look overdone."

"You won't. I'll make you into such a bombshell, your boyfriend will get on his knees and propose the minute he sees you."

"That's the last thing I want!" Jean said.

"Oh yeah, that's right. You got your heart set on going to college. Beats me why you'd want that."

Jean finished changing, and she and Rosa left together, taking the bus downtown. Jean splurged on the cosmetics Rosa picked out for her, along with some bobby pins to set her hair. She even let herself be talked into buying perfume.

"Men like it when a woman smells nice," Rosa told her.

"Really? Where I grew up the smell of manure overpowered everything else."

"You wait and see. I'll bet your fella notices right away. Dirk used to say I smelled good enough to eat." Rosa's last few words came out choked. Her bottom lip trembled.

"You miss your husband a lot, don't you?"

Rosa could only nod. But when she finally got her tears under control she said, "Can I ask you something—if it's not too nosy? Ginny's always saying I ask nosy questions."

"Go ahead. I'll tell you if it's too personal."

"How come your boyfriend isn't off fighting in the war? Is he a cripple like Mr. Seaborn?"

"No, he's a farmer." Jean looked away. She felt ashamed but didn't know why. Russell wasn't a draft dodger—and she was grateful that he wasn't in danger. So why did she feel this lingering doubt whenever someone mentioned his draft status?

"Can't farmers fight?" Rosa asked.

"Sure, but then what would we eat?" Jean laughed, trying to

make light of it. "The government decided that food production is necessary for the war effort, so farmers get an exemption if they want one."

"I sure wish Dirk was a farmer," Rosa said with a sigh. "But then I guess I never would've met him."

They finished shopping and rode the bus back to Jean's house. Rosa gave her a quick lesson on how to use her new makeup and set her hair. Jean couldn't help smiling when she saw the results in the mirror. She looked like a different person—a very feminine person.

"Bring everything with you tomorrow," Rosa said as she was leaving, "and we'll practice some more after work."

"Thanks a million, Rosa. See you then."

"Well, look at you," Patty said when Jean slid into her place at the dinner table. "You auditioning for a part in a film?"

Jean made a face. She was still smarting over Patty's refusal to let Russell sleep on their couch and didn't ask her sister what she thought of her new look.

"Listen, Patty," she began, deciding to give it one more try. "I've been racking my brain all week, trying to think of a place where Russ can stay. Stockton doesn't have any hotels, and the town is packed with people who've moved here to work at the shipyard. Housing is a huge problem. Can't he please stay here?"

Patty started shaking her head before Jean finished her sentence. "Sorry. It's out of the question." Jean didn't speak to Patty for the rest of the evening.

The next morning, Earl Seaborn stopped Jean as she hurried in to work. "You sure look nice today, Jean. Is your hair different?"

"Yeah. Thanks."

She had practiced applying just a little bit of her new makeup before work and hadn't covered her new hairstyle with a kerchief yet. She could see the admiration in Earl's eyes as he looked her over and hoped she would get the same reaction from Russell. Thinking of him and Earl at the same time suddenly gave Jean an idea. She paused in her march to the locker room and turned back to Earl.

"Hey, do you have a minute? I have a problem."

"Sure. What is it?" He looked so concerned—and so hopeful. Too late, Jean realized how inconsiderate it was to ask him for anything, let alone a question that concerned Russ.

"Never mind."

"No, tell me." He held on to her arm to keep her from leaving.

"This is really awkward, Earl . . ."

"Just spit it out."

"My . . . um . . . my boyfriend is coming up to see me this weekend. Do you know of any place in town where he could spend the night?" Earl released her arm. He went very still. Jean could see that he was controlling his emotions, trying not to let them show on his face.

"He could bunk with me," he said quietly.

"I can't ask that."

"Why not? I thought we were friends. Friends do favors for each other."

"But I wasn't fishing for an invitation when I asked you the question. I thought maybe you knew of a rooming house or a place that took boarders. I figured you must have stayed somewhere when you first got here. I don't know the town very well yet."

"He's welcome to my sofa."

"I can't accept—"

"Why not? It's just for one night, right? He's not going to start freeloading or anything, is he?"

"That's very kind of you." How many times had she told him that?

"Yeah, that's me—Mr. Nice Guy." Was he hurt and trying not to let it show? Or was she reading too much into it? "I live on the corner of Main and Vine," he told her, "in that big gray house that they turned into apartments. Have your boyfriend drop by when he gets here and I'll give him a key."

"How can I ever thank you?"

He managed a grin. "I'll think of something."

Jean waited for Russell at the station on Saturday, barely able to contain her excitement. When he finally stepped off the shiny silver bus, a duffel bag slung casually over one shoulder, she thought she would burst with happiness. She had forgotten how tall he was, how strong and straight his back and shoulders were. His tanned, muscled arms hung at ease by his sides as he looked all around for her. Anyone who saw him could tell that Russell Benson was a man who loved the land, a man who wasn't afraid of hard work.

"Russ! Over here!" She waved but he didn't recognize her at first. Then his face lit up and he hurried over, weaving powerfully through the crowd the way he had when he'd played basketball in high school, dodging opponents to make a lay-up shot. He lifted Jean in the air and whirled her around as if she were as weightless as a basketball, then set her down on the sidewalk and kissed her, just like a scene in a movie.

"I had to change buses two times," he said when he finally pulled away, "and that was after my ride dropped me off in South Bend. It took forever! Mmm, you smell nice. You look different, too."

"Is 'different' good or bad?"

"It's terrific! You look like a film star. I'll bet the guys at work make passes at you all the time."

"Hardly! You don't need to worry about them. The men at the shipyard can't stand working with women. Most of them are very threatened by any female who can do the same work that they do."

"Come here," he murmured as he took her into his arms again.

Russ made her feel feminine, protected. She loved the fact that he was so strong and steadfast and hardworking. They had begun dating in high school, and they fit into each other's arms like hand and glove. He was also one of the few boys in school who was taller than she was.

"I figured you'd be hungry, so I'm cooking dinner for you tonight," she told him.

He grinned and bent to touch his forehead to hers. "Just the two of us?"

"Sort of. My sister promised to let us have the kitchen after she feeds the kids. You want to walk home or take a bus?"

"No more buses. I need to stretch my legs."

"That's what I figured. We'll walk over to where you'll be staying tonight so you can get the key and drop off your bag."

He placed his hand on her shoulder, stopping her. "I thought I'd be staying with you. I don't mind sleeping on your couch."

"I know. That's what I thought, too, but Patty said no. It's her house." Jean shrugged helplessly. "Sorry."

She could tell by Russell's expression that he was annoyed, but he held his tongue. It was another thing she liked about him—no temper. Russ was what they called "the strong, silent type."

"So where am I staying?" he asked as they crossed the street.

"With my boss, Mr. Seaborn. I asked him if he knew of a rooming house, and he said that you could stay with him."

"I hope he doesn't have a house full of kids."

"He isn't married."

Russ looked at her, frowning. "Just how well do you know this guy that he would make this kind of offer? How old is he?"

Jean had never known Russ to act jealous before, and it surprised her. "I don't know—six or seven years older than us. Mr. Seaborn had polio when he was a kid," she quickly explained. "He's crippled, so the army classified him as 4-F and won't let him serve." Jean felt a pang of guilt for describing him that way, knowing how much it would hurt Earl if he heard her.

She and Russ walked arm in arm to Earl's apartment and rang the bell. Earl winced when Russell shook his hand—and it wasn't even Earl's withered left one. Jean saw them sizing each other up and she felt sorry for Earl. He couldn't fill out a shirt the way Russ did, with his broad shoulders and wide chest. And Russ was three or four inches taller. Jean could imagine Earl thinking, *No wonder Jean won't date me. I can't compare.*

Earl's apartment was small and neat, consisting of a sitting room and a bedroom. "Can I offer you some coffee or a soda pop?" he said as he showed them the tiny efficiency kitchen behind a folding screen.

"No, thanks," Russ said. "You got a spare key for me?" He seemed to be in a hurry to leave and didn't even try to make polite conversation. He circled his arm around Jean's waist and held her close as they walked away, staking his claim on her.

For the rest of the afternoon and evening, Russell's only goal seemed to be to get Jean alone. They decided to go to a movie after supper, but he wanted to sit in the balcony and neck all the way through it. She couldn't have said what the film was about.

"There isn't much to do in town," she said afterward, "but I know a place where we can go dancing."

"I don't dance, remember?" Russell said.

"Yeah, I remember. I guess I was hoping you'd learned how. I could teach you, if you want me to." She smiled up at him, but he shook his head. "Okay, then, what's left? It's too cold to go for a walk. Want to go back to the house?"

"Sure. You think your sister is asleep by now?"

They cuddled together on Patty's sofa, aware that she was still awake and padding around upstairs. Russ wanted to continue necking, but Jean pointed to the ceiling and shook her head.

"How's your father's farm doing?" she asked.

"The same," he said with a shrug.

"Oh, I just got a letter from Johnny. He's at Mac Dill Field in Florida now, training to be a gunner on a B–26. He said that—"

"I really don't want to talk about John."

Jean gaped at him in surprise. "But you and John are best friends—" He cut off her words with a kiss. She wondered if it embarrassed him to talk about Johnny because he had enlisted and Russ hadn't. When the kiss finally ended, she decided to change the subject.

"My job at the shipyard is really challenging. And I've got the nicest girls on my crew. They—"

"No offense, Jean, but I didn't come all the way here to talk about your job." All he wanted to do was smooch. Jean was beginning to think that Patty had done the right thing to send Russ away for the night.

When he stopped necking long enough to come up for air, Russ said, "By the way, I've got some good news. I wanted to tell you in person, not in a letter. They're hiring more workers at the old furniture factory in town. They got an army contract to make parachutes or something. Why don't you come home and work there? We could be together all the time."

"But I like my job. I'm a supervisor and everything."

"So? Maybe they'd let you be a supervisor at the parachute factory, too. I miss you, Jean. I wish I could see you every weekend."

"I miss you, too."

She started kissing him again in an attempt to change the subject, but as soon as Russ pulled away he said, "Give them your two weeks' notice and come home, Jean."

Something about the way he said it made it seem as though he was ordering her, not asking. She thought about Ginny's domineering husband and resisted the idea of giving in. What made Russ think he could call the shots? She didn't want to lose him, but how could she hang on to him and still keep her independence?

"I'm not sure I want to start all over again with a new job," she said. "We're about to launch the first ship that my girls and I ever worked on."

"That's about the hundredth time you mentioned your girls. What about you and me?"

Jean knew she didn't want the pressure of a relationship right now. If she moved back home it would be only a matter of time before Russ would start pushing for marriage, and her dream of going to college would go up in smoke. She would hate to lose Russ to another girl, but it was much too soon to get so serious about each other.

"Do you ever go out with other girls back home?" she asked.

"No, of course not. I belong to you. Why? Do you have another guy?"

"No, I swear. There's nobody."

"Then what's holding you here? Why not work in a factory closer to home so we can be together?"

"Well, Patty needs my help, for one thing. Bill's fighting in North Africa now. And I worry about the girls at work—"

"Sounds like you worry more about them than me."

"Russ, I don't want to argue." She sighed and twined her arms around his neck. "I'll figure out how to get home one of these weekends and look into a job at the factory, okay? Who knows if they even need electricians?"

"So what if they don't? Can't you do some other job?"

"Would you want to do another job besides farming? I'm trained to be an electrician. And I'm good at it."

"Don't be difficult, Jean."

"I'm sorry . . . I don't want to fight. Our time together is much too short."

"You're right about that."

She settled comfortably in his arms again, determined to enjoy their brief time together. But when she kissed Russell good-bye at the bus station the next day, she felt unsettled—almost relieved to see him leave—and didn't know why.

CHAPTER 13

★ *Virginia* ★

Ginny paused as she entered the factory floor on Monday morning, taking a moment to bask in the hum of activity all around her. Out of this chaos of scattered parts, clanging machinery, and earsplitting noises, completed ships emerged. It amazed her.

"Whatcha looking at?" Rosa asked, coming up behind her.

"I don't know," she said, smiling. "Everything! I remember feeling so overwhelmed by the immense scale of it all on my first day here—weren't you? And now just think! We're a vital part of it!"

"Yeah, it's a nice feeling."

"I can't imagine a more beautiful sight than seeing a ship we wired move down the assembly line to the next phase, suspended from the ceiling by those enormous chains. And what could be more exciting, more challenging, than to see another ship being moved into place, ready for us to tackle?"

"Boy, you're sounding real poetic today." Rosa laughed and linked arms with Ginny as they walked to their workstation. Not only was a new ship waiting for them this morning, but Mr. Seaborn was, as well.

"Congratulations, ladies. I've been reviewing our production figures, and your team has the best record of all our electricians. You've wired and installed all of your circuits in record time and you've never held up production. Great job! You deserve to be proud of yourselves."

Rosa gave a whoop of joy. Ginny couldn't resist hugging Jean. Even Helen quietly clapped her hands. Ginny did feel proud. And the friendships they had forged really meant something, too. They were accomplishing real work, not wasting time with silly card games and social one-upmanship.

"We owe all our success to you, Jean," Ginny told her later that day as they all gathered around the lunchroom table. "You're an inspiring leader."

Rosa poured coffee into her Thermos cup and lifted it in salute. "Three cheers for Jean! We should go celebrate."

"Thanks." Jean's fair cheeks turned pink as she blushed.

"You look different lately," Ginny told her. "Your hair is different. I like it that way. And I like your makeup, too."

"Thanks. Rosa helped me. My boyfriend came up to visit me last weekend—"

"Yeah, how'd everything go?" Rosa asked. "If I'm not being too nosy."

"It went well. I miss him already."

"What does he look like? You got a picture?" Rosa asked.

Ginny peered over her shoulder as Jean showed them a snapshot. "He's very handsome," she said. "You'd better think twice before you marry such a handsome man. You'll always be worrying about other women. Better an average-looking one who stays home, in my opinion."

"Russ is a real homebody," Jean said with a sigh. "In fact, he wants me to get a factory job closer to home, and I'm not sure I want to. I love my job here. He has me so confused. What do you do when you like someone and want to be with him, but you like your independence, too?"

"I know exactly how you feel," Ginny said. "Since I started working here, it's the first time in my life that I've ever felt independent—except maybe for the few months I spent in college before I met

Harold. It's going to be very hard to give all this up when the time comes."

"When your husband finds out?" Rosa asked. Ginny nodded.

"I don't know how you've managed to keep it a secret this long," Helen said.

"Well, Harold goes out of town a lot. And when he is in town, he's so busy at the office that he just comes home to eat and sleep and then goes back again. The family dog is the only one who's noticed that I'm working," she said, trying to laugh. "Rex misses me so much that he follows me around like a shadow whenever I'm home. He even lies down with his head on my feet when I'm ironing or washing dishes. I guess Rex is a lot more observant than Harold."

She felt herself getting emotional and was grateful when Jean changed the subject. "What kind of work does your husband do?" she asked.

"He's an engineer. He gets factories up and running. I don't know much more than that because he never wants to talk about his work. He says I wouldn't understand. I know he started getting really busy when the war began in Europe and President Roosevelt announced the Lend–Lease program. His company must have helped hundreds of factories retool for defense contracts by now."

"How come he didn't get drafted?" Rosa asked.

"The government decided that his job is necessary for the war effort. They hired Harold's firm to oversee things and make sure everybody meets their quotas on time. He works very hard."

"So do you, Ginny," Jean said. "When you stop and think about it, you're working two jobs—here all day and then your usual work at home. I don't know how you're able to do it all."

"I just keep going from the time I get up in the morning until I go to bed at night," she said, exhaling.

"Is it getting to be too much?" Helen asked.

"I can manage. I mean, before, with the boys in school all day, I felt like I wasn't doing anything important. What does it matter, really, if you have a spotless house? This work is so much more important. I just don't care anymore if my furniture is a little dusty or there are streaks on my windows or the kitchen floor isn't perfectly waxed. I want to help win the war."

"That's how I tried to explain it to Dirk's father," Rosa said. "Why should I waste my time cleaning all day when I can make ships to help Dirk and all the other boys? Wolter Voorhees can't understand that there's no such thing as men's work and women's work in times like these."

"How are things going with Dirk's parents?" Jean asked.

"They're still mad at me, even though I stayed home like a good little girl last weekend and twiddled my thumbs." She jammed the lid onto her Thermos, as if to emphasize her point, and gave it a twist. "I'll tell you what, though: I was so bored I wanted to cry."

"Where is your husband stationed again?" Helen asked.

"Virginia. He'll finish his Navy Corpsman training in March, then he'll probably be shipped overseas to North Africa or the Pacific. I get scared just thinking about it."

"My sister Patty's husband is fighting in Algeria," Jean said. "She doesn't talk about it much but I know she worries about him. We also have five brothers who are scattered all over the place in three branches of the service. Every time we hear a news bulletin we're reminded of one of them."

"Your poor mother," Ginny said. "I only have two sons, but I know how I would feel if they were stationed overseas."

"That's a very large family with five boys and two girls," Helen said.

"That's not even half of us!" Jean laughed. "There are twelve boys and six girls altogether."

"Holy smokes!" Rosa said. "Eighteen children? Are any of them twins?"

"Just my brother Johnny and me. He's in the air force. My brother Dan was at Pearl Harbor when it was attacked, and now he's out in the Pacific somewhere. Peter is stationed in Iceland, Rudy is in New Guinea, and Roy's latest transfer was to Monterey, California."

"Your poor mother!" Rosa said, shaking her head. "How did she cope with all them kids?"

"She loved and welcomed every one of us into the world. If anyone asks her about having so many children, she always says, 'There are so many things that are worse than having children.'"

"That's beautiful," Ginny said. "I'd have as many children as I could, too, if it were up to me."

"We came one right after the other," Jean said, "from the time Ma got married at age eighteen until the youngest was born seven years ago. My oldest sister is twenty-nine."

"Your mother must have had remarkably healthy babies," Helen said. "My mother gave birth to seven children, but I'm the only one who survived to outlive her."

"Oh, Helen! You really are all alone." Ginny caressed her shoulder in sympathy.

"Don't you have to wonder sometimes why God gives eighteen kids to one mom and only one to another?" Rosa asked.

Helen slammed the lid of her lunchbox with a bang. "I stopped trying to figure out God a long time ago," she said.

Helen's bitter tone surprised Ginny. She was even more surprised a moment later when Helen added angrily, "And I certainly don't understand why God allowed the disgusting Germans to throw the entire world into turmoil for a second time. We should have done away with every last German after the Great War."

Ginny could only stare at Helen in surprise. She had practically spit out the word *German*. "I was only ten years old when that war ended," Ginny said, "so my memories of it are vague. I had two uncles who fought, and I remember seeing them in their uniforms—"

Ginny stopped. Helen was at least fifteen years older than she was. Maybe she had lost someone dear to her in the war. Ginny was trying to think of a delicate way to ask when Mr. Seaborn strode up to their table, interrupting them.

"I came to warn you ladies so you won't get nervous. We've got some army people coming to tour this place after lunch to see how things are going. Just ignore them and keep working. They're evaluating the management end of things, not the workers."

"Don't worry, we won't let them *intimidate* us," Ginny said. "After all, they're just people doing their job the same as we are, right, girls?"

Later that afternoon, Ginny glanced up briefly when she saw Mr. Seaborn leading a group of men in uniforms and dark suits up and down the production line. She returned to her work on the ship's deck, fifteen feet above the factory floor, concentrating on an especially tricky wiring job. Suddenly she heard a familiar voice speaking her name in utter astonishment.

"Virginia. . . ?"

She looked up from her work, her heart pounding. Harold stood at the foot of the ladder below her, staring wide-eyed. Fear surged through her like a jolt of electricity.

"Virginia?" he repeated breathlessly.

The screwdriver slipped from her limp hand. She felt boneless.

"You know him?" Rosa whispered.

"M-my husband."

"Oh boy! The jig is up," Rosa breathed. "Just stand your ground, Ginny. You'll be fine." She patted Ginny's back.

She wasn't fine. Ginny watched in horror as Harold climbed three rungs of the stepladder, looking up at her in disbelief. Mr. Seaborn and the other men watched from a distance. It seemed as though everyone in the entire factory was staring. She'd never felt more *intimidated* in her life. Her hands shook so badly she couldn't even pretend to work.

"What are you doing here?" Harold asked.

"She's screwing this gauge to the console," Rosa told him. "It's the oil-pressure gauge."

"But . . . but that's impossible!"

"Yeah, it's tricky until you get the hang of it," Rosa chattered on. "But Ginny does it the best of any of us. Right, Jean?"

"Virginia, answer me!" Harold said. "What are you doing here?"

"I'm working . . . like Rosa said. I . . . I can't talk to you right now, I have work to do. And so do you." She turned away and sank down as low as she could, wishing she could disappear entirely. Tears blurred her eyes. She had to fold her hands into fists to control the shaking.

"Hey, he really is good-looking," Rosa whispered. "For an older guy, that is."

"Is he still there?" Ginny asked.

"No, he went back with the others. He's gone."

Gone. The word shuddered through Ginny as if echoing through an empty room. Harold was gone. She covered her face to hide her tears. Her stomach rolled as if the ship she was on had been launched into a hurricane. Her thoughts were as jumbled as the wires that she labored to connect, and she had to rush to the ladies' room twice, afraid she might lose her lunch. Good thing her shift was nearly over because she couldn't concentrate on her work. Jean seemed to understand and didn't pressure her.

Harold had seen her here, working!

He was every bit as handsome as Rosa had said, with his dark hair and square, dimpled chin. Ginny loved him, and now she was going to lose him, just as she'd always feared. She couldn't remember why she had ever taken this job.

"You poor girl. Can I do anything to help?" Rosa asked as they punched the time clock at the end of their shift. "Want me to come home with you in case he decides to slug it out with you?"

"We don't fight that way, Rosa. But thanks."

No, Harold fought with cold disapproval, withdrawing his love and tossing barbed, angry words at her. In many ways it was crueler than fists.

Ginny started cooking pork chops and macaroni and cheese for dinner as soon as she got home. Harold arrived two hours later, walking past her as if she were invisible. He didn't speak a word to her during the meal. The boys seemed to feel the tension and picked at their food. Ginny couldn't force down a single bite.

She stayed in the kitchen all evening, waiting like a condemned prisoner on death row. Harold wouldn't discuss things until the boys were asleep, determined not to let them overhear their parents arguing. Even then he wouldn't raise his voice. She wondered if she should get out the two ticket stubs she'd found in his pocket and ask him about them. She decided that she really didn't want to know the truth.

In the meantime he was snubbing her. Ginny wondered briefly if there was a more sophisticated word she could use in place of *snub*, but she was much too upset to worry about her vocabulary. After two and a half months she was only beginning to understand why she had needed to work at the shipyard and why she had taken the job in the first place. She could never explain her reasons to Harold, even if she had an entire dictionary full of words.

She returned to the kitchen after putting the boys to bed, knowing that Harold would come out and speak with her when he was ready. She found herself praying as she swept the kitchen floor, *Please, God, I don't want to lose him. . . .* Then she wondered if the terrible fear she felt was what Rosa and Jean and all the other women whose loved ones were in the military felt every day of their lives.

At last Harold rose from his chair in the living room to stand in the kitchen doorway. He had his arms folded across his chest.

"I have never been so mortified in my life," he said quietly.

Ginny was trembling from head to toe. She forced her gaze to meet his. "Why?"

"*Why?* What a humiliating way for me to find out about your secret life!"

"I tried to tell you that I've been working at the shipyard—dozens of times. You were always too busy or you weren't really listening to me. You were *aloof*, Harold."

"How long has this been going on?"

"I started training at the shipyard last September, right after the boys started school, and I've been working as an electrician for two and a half months now."

"Well, whatever your little game is, Virginia, it's over. You're quitting tomorrow."

She slowly shook her head. "No." She spoke the word softly, and her voice shook, but she meant it.

"What do you mean, 'no'?"

"I don't want to quit. I . . . I'm not going to quit. And it's not a game."

"I won't have you working in a shipyard, of all places. You're a wife and a mother. *My* wife! You have responsibilities here—responsibilities that you've obviously been shirking. No wonder things have been slipping around here. No wonder you're doing the ironing and sweeping at all hours of the night, and there's no supper on the table when I get home."

"You still have plenty of clean clothes to wear, and all your meals are—"

"What about the boys? What have you been doing with them while you're running off to work?"

"They've been getting themselves to school in the morning. They're fine without me for twenty minutes before I get home. You're always telling me I smother them."

"What about Christmas vacation next month? Are you planning on leaving them here alone all day?"

"I . . . I'll work something out." But Ginny hadn't thought that far ahead, and at the moment she had no idea what she would do. Harold wasn't listening anyway.

"I've worked hard to establish a reputation in this community," he told her. "I won't have my wife tarnishing it by working like a common laborer. A shipyard is no place for a woman. The work is too heavy, too dirty, too dangerous for a woman."

"Have you bothered to look at any of the assembly lines in all of those factories you visit? I'll bet more than half of the workers are women. In fact, I work right alongside Allan's second-grade teacher, Helen Kimball." He stared at her as if she were talking nonsense.

"Helen Kimball isn't my wife. You are. I don't want you near all those coarse men, hearing their foul language. Why would you do such a stupid thing without consulting me first?"

"Because I knew what you would say—the same things you're

saying now. But I needed to do something that matters. I'm bored and lonely and I hate staying home all day, ironing your shirts and making your supper and getting nothing in return but a peck on the cheek—not even a word of thanks, Harold!"

"Nobody thanks me for all the work I do." She groaned in frustration and turned away. "I'm not finished, Virginia. And don't think you can turn on the waterworks and get me to change my mind."

"I wouldn't dream of it." Ginny was too angry to cry. She had never argued with Harold this way, had never contradicted him in her life. She had lived to please him, in fact. But she was tired of being afraid of him. Intimidated by him. They should be a team, like the girls at work, not servant and master. She thought of her new friends and summoned courage from them: from Helen Kimball, starting a new job at her age; from Rosa, leaving her home in Brooklyn to move in with strangers; and most of all from Jean, so young yet knowing exactly what she wanted in life. Ginny was tired of walking on eggshells around her husband, working so hard to please him when he never made a single move to try to please her. Enough was enough.

"Well, I'm not going to change my mind, either," she said, speaking with quiet conviction. "I'm going to continue working at Stockton Shipyard."

He stared at her in astonishment. "What has gotten into you, Virginia?"

"My name is Ginny! I've told you a hundred times that I want to be called Ginny, not Virginia! Why don't you ever listen to me?"

"Are you having a nervous breakdown? Should I call the doctor?"

"Listen to me! I make thirty dollars a week, Harold. For the first time in my life I have money to spend that didn't come from you or from my father. I earned it myself. Do you have any idea how good that feels? Do you want to know what I've been spending it on? Last week I bought the roast beef that we had for Sunday dinner. I bought Allan a new pair of shoes for school, and I bought the new lipstick that I'm wearing—that you never even noticed!"

"That's my point, Virginia—"

"It's *Ginny!*"

He made a face to show his exasperation. "I've worked hard to make sure that no wife of mine would ever have to work—especially in a place like that. I make a good living. I'm well able to support my family."

"I don't *have* to work, Harold—I *want* to work! Why can't you understand that? I need to know that there's more to Ginny Mitchell than just somebody's wife or mother."

"Where are you getting these foolish ideas?"

"They are not *injudicious* ideas. Look here ..." She pulled the newspaper article out of the drawer and pointed to the headline. "It says, 'Millions of Women Must Be Shifted to War Work.' I'm one of them."

"You're being ridiculous. That's meant for other women, not you."

"Why not me?"

"Because you have a family!"

"You mean the two sons that I'm not supposed to mother anymore? They're the reason I can't quit? What sort of a future will they face if the Nazis and the Japanese aren't stopped? I listen to world events and I feel threatened and helpless. The attack on Pearl Harbor seemed so close! Most of Europe has been conquered, the Japanese have overrun the Pacific—and I'm sitting home dusting the furniture? Collecting tin cans and cooking fat?"

"It's a man's job to protect his wife and family. That's why I'm working so hard to get the factories up and running, making arms and ammunition."

"I want to help, too. I want to do something to win back the life we had, to make the world safe for our sons so they never have to fight in a war."

"You're a God-fearing woman, Vir—" He caught himself, but she knew he was about to say *Virginia*. "You know that the husband is supposed to be the head of the household. I want you to quit this job tomorrow and put our home back in order. That's all I'm going to say about it. I'm going to bed." He turned off the radio on his way through the living room and stomped upstairs.

Ginny didn't know what to do. He had ordered her to quit, and she didn't want to. She was so frustrated and angry with Harold that for the first time in their married life she slept on the couch instead of with him. It was also the first time in her married life that she had ever defied him. She cried herself to sleep.

The next morning she was up before he was, her clothes wrinkled from sleeping in them all night. She was standing at the stove scrambling eggs when Harold came downstairs dressed in his suit and tie. He sat down at the table and ate in silence. Dark circles rimmed his eyes, and she wondered if he had slept as poorly as she had. When he finished eating and stood to leave, she turned to face him.

"I love you, Harold."

He closed his eyes for a moment. "Then do what I've asked, Ginny. Give up this ridiculous idea and get our household and our family back in order."

"Do you love me?" she asked shakily.

"Of course I do."

Tears of relief filled her eyes. She wrapped her arms around him, hugging him tightly, resting her head on his chest. After a moment his arms circled her, stiffly at first. But she snuggled against him and felt him relax.

"I have to go to work," he said with a sigh.

"Wait." She didn't release her hold on him. "If you love me, then my happiness should be important to you. And working at the shipyard makes me happy."

"That works two ways," he said coldly. He peeled her arms away and freed himself. "Isn't my happiness important to you, Virginia?" He jammed his hat onto his head and stalked out.

CHAPTER 14

★ *Jean* ★

Jean rose earlier than usual for work the next morning, certain that she would have to take time out to see the personnel director, Mr. Wire, and ask him to replace Virginia Mitchell. Jean changed into her coveralls in the locker room, punched her time card, and was reading the day's work orders on her clipboard when Earl Seaborn called her aside.

"You got a minute, Jean? I was wondering what was going on yesterday between one of your electricians and that government engineer? I couldn't hear what they were saying."

"Mr. Mitchell is Ginny's husband."

"So? What's the problem?"

"He didn't know she worked here until he saw her yesterday."

"Oh boy. I can imagine what that did to his pride, finding out that way." Earl's insight surprised Jean. He had zeroed in on the problem in seconds—pride. "You think Mr. Mitchell will cause problems for her?" Earl asked.

"Yeah, I do. He's evidently one of those husbands who thinks a woman's place is in the home. I sure would hate to lose Ginny, but I have a bad feeling that he isn't going to let her come back to work."

"Mr. Mitchell is going to be observing here for a few more days. How about if you and I go talk to him?"

"You would be willing to do that, Earl?"

"Sure. Come on."

They found Harold Mitchell pacing outside Earl's cubicle, clipboard in hand, waiting for everyone else to arrive. He glanced noticeably at his watch as Jean and Earl approached, as if silently rebuking Earl for not being in his office on time. Jean agreed with Rosa that Mr. Mitchell was handsome, yet his somber, unsmiling expression marred his good looks. He might have been carrying the weight of the world on his shoulders. His unapproachable manner was such a stark contrast to Ginny's warm, tender heart that Jean wondered what had drawn them to each other. Maybe it really was true that opposites attracted like the poles of a magnet.

"Mr. Mitchell, could we have a word with you?" Earl gestured to his cubicle, and the three of them entered the tiny room. Earl closed the door, shutting out some of the noise. He nodded to Jean to begin.

"It's about Ginny—"

Mr. Mitchell held up his hand to stop her. "Excuse me, but my wife and my personal life are nobody's business but mine."

His words were so cold and abrupt that Jean felt as if he'd slapped her. She knew then that they weren't going to get through to him. They may as well leave. But she had underestimated Earl.

"You're right, Mr. Mitchell, your personal life isn't our business," he said calmly. "But Mrs. Mitchell is my employee, and—"

"She shouldn't be. Virginia never should have taken this job in the first place."

"I disagree. You're in a better position than anyone to know the importance of production schedules and what happens when quotas aren't met. The truth is, America can't hope to keep up with the demand for arms and equipment unless women step up and take the jobs that men have vacated."

"A shipyard is no place for a woman," Mitchell said. "This is men's work."

Earl kept his composure, refusing to back down. "That was the thinking in the past, I know. But women like your wife and my colleague, Jean Erickson, have shown that they are quite capable of doing so-called men's work—and they do it very well. We have women welders and mechanics—and women electricians, like your wife."

Jean could tell by Mitchell's glaring, tight-lipped expression that his mind was firmly closed. "Are you finished?" he asked coldly.

Earl shook his head. "No, sir, I'm not. The government hired you to come here and make sure this shipyard runs at full production, right? You know how important it is to finish enough landing craft for the invasion of Europe when it comes. Well, I'm telling you that if your wife quits, our production schedule is going to suffer."

Jean finally found her voice and jumped in to help him. "Ginny is one of our best electricians. She knows her job and does it exceptionally well. It would take me weeks to train her replacement—if I could even find one."

"That's right," Earl added. "We have a dozen other vacant positions waiting to be filled. This war won't last forever, Mr. Mitchell. The sooner it's over, the sooner things can go back to the way they were and you can have your wife back."

"Ginny doesn't want to do this work for the rest of her life," Jean said. "But we really could use her help for the duration."

Mr. Mitchell stared at them in icy silence until Jean grew very uncomfortable. "Now we're finished," she said. He opened the door and walked out.

"I'd better go catch up with him," Earl said.

"Earl, wait. I hope he doesn't take it out on you for speaking up."

"There's nothing much I can do about it if he does," he said with a shrug, "except let it roll off. I really don't care if he likes me or not."

"At least we tried."

Earl smiled mischievously. "Oh, I'm not done trying. I've just begun. I plan to point out all of our finest female workers to him today—welders, mechanics, carpenters, maintenance workers, painters. If he's going to hang around me for a couple of days, he's going to get a front-row seat to my lecture on what a great job women war workers are doing."

Jean couldn't help smiling in return. "Thanks for being willing to stick your neck out. It's awfully nice of you."

Jean walked across the vast expanse of factory floor, dodging around workers and tool chests and ships in various stages of construction. When she finally reached her workstation, there was Ginny, wearing her coveralls and tool belt, ready to go to work. She looked tired and shaken, but she was here. Helen and Rosa hurried over to talk with her, too.

"Hey, no black eyes?" Rosa asked. "Your husband sure looked mad yesterday. I thought for sure he would beat you up or something when you got home."

"If he ever tries it, Ginny, call the police," Jean said. "Men aren't supposed to beat up women."

"Some of the men in my mother's life didn't think twice about beating on her," Rosa said with a shrug.

"I'm surprised he didn't tell you to quit," Helen said.

"He did," Ginny said quietly. "I took your advice and made up my own mind. That's why I'm here."

"Is he okay with that?" Rosa asked.

"No. He's very angry with me. I . . . I don't know what's going to happen. . . ."

Jean could see how scared Ginny was, how close to tears. "Let's get to work," she said. "Let's show these government inspectors what we can do." She assigned everyone a task and ended up working alongside Rosa all morning.

"I learned something today," Jean told her. "I never want to marry a husband like Harold Mitchell."

"Yeah, some men think they own their wife."

"My father never treated my mother that way, so I guess I assumed all husbands were like him. Now I'm starting to wonder what kind of husband Russ will be."

"How's things going with him, anyways?"

"I don't know. When he was here, I sort of told him that I would try to come home and look for a job. It was in the heat of the moment, I guess you could say. But I don't really want to quit, Rosa. So now I'm wondering how he'll react if I change my mind and stay here at the shipyard."

"If he makes you choose between him and your job, what are you gonna do?"

Jean shrugged in reply, concentrating on the wire she was connecting.

"Boy, I'm sure glad that Dirk didn't tell me to quit, 'cause I wouldn't of done it."

Jean looked up from her work and gazed down the long production line for a moment, deep in thought. "When we were talking to Ginny's husband this morning, Earl said that life would go back to normal when the war ended—but I don't see how it ever could. Ginny's life as a housewife will never be the same now that she's gained self-confidence working here. And I sure don't want to be a housewife after the war."

"But what else is there?" Rosa asked. "All the men are gonna want their jobs back when they come home, right? And you don't want to be all alone like Helen, do you? With no husband?"

"I want to go to college and have a career first, but of course I want to get married someday. Some of the men around here call me ugly names, implying that I want to be a man—I don't! I like being a woman. But why does life have to be so confusing for us?"

When their shift ended and it was time to go home, Jean pulled Ginny aside on her way out. "If there's anything I can do to help, please let me know," she told her.

"Well, I might have another problem in a few weeks. . . ." Ginny sounded dazed and numb. Her husband hadn't beaten her physically, but she seemed beaten down nonetheless, her newfound confidence bruised.

"What's wrong, Ginny?"

"The boys will be getting out of school for Christmas vacation in December. Harold asked me last night what I planned to do about them, and I didn't know what to say. I know they can't stay home alone all day. I'm going to need a baby-sitter, but we don't have any relatives who live close enough to help."

"Do you want me to ask my sister Patty if she'll watch them? She could use a little extra spending money at Christmastime. And she loves kids."

"Would she do that for me? Doesn't she have some little ones of her own?"

"Three of them. But Patty handled ten or eleven younger siblings when we were growing up, so I'm sure she can handle your two boys."

"I'd be so grateful, Jean."

"I'll ask her and let you know tomorrow."

Jean walked outside to a cold, gray afternoon and falling snow. It already covered the grass and had begun to accumulate on the streets and sidewalks. She waited at the bus stop with dozens of other women, finally giving in to the blustery weather and paying the bus fare rather than walking home. She had promised Patty that she would stop at the grocery store to pick up a few items, so she got off in downtown Stockton and crossed the street to the A&P.

The store was crowded as usual at this time of day, with other working women like herself hurrying to get their shopping done before the supper hour. Jean wished the store would stay open later now that so many women worked. But judging by the Help Wanted sign that had hung in the storefront window for weeks, the A&P was probably too shorthanded to extend their hours. Everyone knew you could make more money at the shipyard than as a store clerk.

Jean quickly perused the crowded aisles and found all the items on her list. As she stood in line at the register, she heard a familiar voice behind her. "Hey, Jean, have you figured out how these stupid ration books work?" She turned to see Earl Seaborn in line behind her, a book of ration stamps in one hand and a pile of groceries expertly balanced between his crippled left arm and his chin.

"I don't have a clue. I'm just going to hand my ration book to the clerk and let her figure it out. My sister Patty usually does all the shopping. I offered to help her today because the weather was so nasty and the baby has a cold. By the way, how did it go with Mr. Mitchell today?"

Earl grinned. "If looks could kill, I'd be a dead man. I think he figured out my not-so-subtle sales pitch for women workers in about two minutes. That didn't stop me, of course. And unless he's more stubborn than I thought, he couldn't help but admire the beautiful seams some of our female welders showed him."

"Do you think it made a dent in his thinking?"

"Probably not. He'd better change his attitude, though, because things aren't going to be the same after the war. It's obvious that women are capable of doing the same work as men. And it's obvious that they deserve fair treatment and fair pay—not to mention respect."

"True, but change comes slowly, Earl. After we talked to him this morning, I realized that women have only been allowed to vote for twenty-two years. That's not a very long time. There are probably a lot of husbands like Ginny's who still haven't adjusted to women being allowed to vote, let alone taking over men's jobs. Those guys are going to want things to go back to the way they were after the war."

"Does that include your boyfriend? Is he going to want to settle down and get married to a traditional wife after the war?"

Jean looked away, unable to meet Earl's gaze. She had wondered the same thing just this morning while talking to Rosa. "Russ and I are too young to talk about marriage. Besides, he knows that I plan on going to college."

The line moved forward, and Jean placed her handful of items on the counter, making space for Earl to set down his items, too. He unloaded them smoothly, obviously used to his one-handed balancing act.

"Don't you want children?" he asked her.

"Of course I do—someday. I just don't want them now. And I don't want eighteen of them like my mother. What about you, Earl? What are your plans after the war? Marriage? Kids?"

"I'd like to get married, but I doubt if I ever will. Not too many women are on the lookout for a crippled husband."

"Listen, Earl—"

"I'm not feeling sorry for myself, just facing facts. Who wants to wake up in the morning beside a man with a withered hand and a leg brace?"

Jean had noticed that he kept his left hand in his pocket nearly all of the time. She couldn't say whether his withered hand repulsed her or not because she'd never taken a good look at it, not wanting to stare. But she wasn't going to let him get away with such a pessimistic attitude.

"What about all the men who will lose limbs in the war?" she asked. "I'm sure that the women who love them will stand by them no matter what."

Earl shook his head. "Some women say they'll stand by their man and they mean it. Most change their tune when they're faced with the reality of it. The truth is, a lot of marriages aren't going to survive the war. A lot of people can't handle anything less than perfection."

As Jean handed her ration book to the clerk and paid for her groceries, she remembered comparing Earl to Russell and judging Earl unfavorably. Was she the kind of shallow woman he was talking about?

It was almost dark and snowing hard when Jean walked out of the store. She stood on the sidewalk for a moment, trying to decide whether to spend more money on another bus fare or walk home and get her feet wet. Earl came up behind her once again.

"Can I give you a ride home? My car is right over there."

She turned to him in surprise. "I didn't know you could drive." Jean regretted her words as soon as she'd spoken them. Earl wasn't very good at hiding his emotions, and she saw that she had hurt him. "I'm sorry, Earl. I didn't mean that the way it sounded. . . ."

"That's okay," he said with a sigh. "Yes, I drive. I had the clutch pedal on my car modified. And I have a special knob on the steering wheel."

"Earl, I'm so sorry."

"Stop apologizing, Jean. You're making it worse. I can't stand pity. I'd much rather have people talk honestly about my handicaps and ask questions instead of avoiding me or ignoring me because I make them uncomfortable. That's the reaction I usually get. People don't know what to say or they're afraid of saying the wrong thing, so they act as if I'm invisible. Then there are the ones who see that I'm crippled and assume that I must be retarded, too."

His car was parked close to the store. She followed him to it and he opened the passenger door for her. "Get in. I'll brush the snow off." He set his grocery bag on the backseat and took a moment to clear the snow from the front and rear windows. He wasn't wearing gloves, and when he finally slid behind the wheel and started the car, his hands were red with cold. He blew on them to warm them.

Earl drove slowly and carefully through the slippery streets, the windshield wipers swishing, the snow dancing in a chaotic flurry in the headlights. He leaned forward, concentrating on the road. The town looked like a Christmas card, dusted in a layer of white. They rode the short distance through Stockton like polite strangers.

"This is my first winter here," Jean said, searching for something to talk about, "but it seems awfully early for a snowstorm."

"People say the reason we get so much snow is because we're close to the lake."

"I know Lake Michigan isn't far," she said, "but I keep forgetting that it's there. I hardly ever get out of town."

"You probably haven't seen it when it's frozen, have you? It looks beautiful. I'll drive you there sometime."

They slid safely to a stop in Patty's driveway a few minutes later. Jean exhaled, unaware that she had been holding her breath while Earl navigated the slippery streets.

"Let me carry your groceries inside for you," Earl offered. Jean didn't protest, knowing that Earl probably needed to be chivalrous. He managed the sack of groceries well with one hand, but the frozen sidewalks were treacherous, and Jean saw the dragging print his left foot made in the snow. They walked into the kitchen to the aroma of baking bread.

"Wow! Something sure smells good," Earl said.

"Thank you, kind sir," Patty said with a grin. "The bread just came out of the oven, and I made a pot of pea soup to go with it." The baby was perched in his usual place on Patty's hip, as comfortable as a cowboy in the saddle. Patty was as adept as Earl was at doing things with one hand. He set the bag of groceries on a kitchen chair, since there didn't seem to be another uncluttered place to put it, then turned toward the door.

"Well, see you tomorrow, Jean. Bye, Patty."

"Whoa!" Patty said, stopping him in his tracks. "It's snowing pretty hard out there, mister. You don't want to go back out in that, do you? Stay for supper, Earl."

"No, I really couldn't . . ."

"Oh, come on. Take your coat off. Have a seat." Patty was already setting another soup bowl on the table for him, much to Jean's dismay. "I made enough soup for an army. It seemed like that kind of a day. And how can you say no to fresh bread?"

"It does smell awfully good."

"Sit down, then. Hang up his coat for him, Jean. I hope you bought more oleo-margarine, because we're o-u-t. Boys! Supper!" Patty yelled. The two older boys thundered out to the kitchen and climbed onto their chairs, glancing shyly at Earl. "Billy, Jr. and Kenny, say hello to Mr. Seaborn. He's your Aunt Jeannie's boss." Neither boy spoke nor moved.

"We should have company more often," Jean said. "Maybe we'd get a little peace and quiet at the dinner table." The peace was short-lived. Earl liked kids, and Jean's nephews quickly warmed up to him, especially after he produced a nickel for each of them from behind their ears.

"They miss their father," Patty said. "Bill used to roll around on the floor and wrestle with them."

"How long has your husband been away?"

"It will be a year in January since he enlisted. He signed up right after the baby was born, a week after Pearl Harbor. He was home on furlough in June before sailing overseas to England. Now he's in Algeria. At the rate this war is going, he won't recognize his own kids by the time it's over."

"Will you make a snowman with us?" Kenny asked Earl.

"I'd love to," Earl said. "But we'll have to wait until there's a little more snow on the ground, okay?"

Jean recalled that Russ hadn't wanted Patty or her children around, then wished she could stop comparing him with Earl. There was no logical reason for it.

"What's wrong with your hand?" Billy, Jr. asked.

"Hey! Don't be rude," Patty chided.

Earl smiled. "It's okay. I'm used to it." He looked right at Billy when he answered him, treating him like a person. "I caught a disease called polio when I was younger, and it made the muscles in my hand and leg weak."

"Does it hurt?"

"Not at all."

Only on the inside, Jean thought.

Earl turned out to be a gracious, attentive dinner guest, giving Patty a chance to talk and laugh and relax. Jean knew it was what her sister needed, and she felt guilty for avoiding Patty and the kids so much.

"Let me help with the dishes," Earl volunteered when they'd emptied the soup pot and Patty had excused the boys from the table.

"I'll take you up on your offer the next time you come to dinner," Patty said. "My guests always get the night off the first time they eat here."

"Are you sure I can't help?"

"Positive."

"And you'd better get going before you get snowed in," Jean said, peering out of the kitchen window. Earl came and stood beside her, gazing out into the darkness where the steadily falling snow was visible in the headlights of passing cars. Jean had the unsettling feeling that he had stood close to her on purpose. Even more unsettling, she liked having him near her. "Aren't your groceries still in your car?" she asked. "They're going to freeze."

"Yeah, I think you're right," he said, turning away. "I'd better go. Thanks for giving me a little taste of home, Patty. I enjoyed the dinner, the kids, your company. I needed this. See you tomorrow, Jean."

She filled the sink with soapy water after Earl left and began washing the dishes while Patty scrubbed pea soup from the baby's face and his high chair.

"He likes you, you know," Patty said. "It's pretty obvious."

"We're just friends."

"Right. That's why he looks at you with eyes like melting chocolate."

"He knows all about Russ. In fact, Earl let Russ sleep on his sofa when he was here—after you kicked him out."

"Must be nice to have two guys falling for you. And you don't have to worry about either one of them going off to fight in the war."

"Listen, Patty. I don't want Earl falling for me. But how can I discourage him without hurting his feelings? You were no help, by the way, inviting him to dinner."

"Why don't you like him? Is it because he's a cripple?"

"No, of course not!" She set a bowl on the drain board with a loud clatter. "Earl is a very nice guy who'll make some lucky woman a wonderful husband. But it isn't going to be me. For one thing, he's too old for me. And for another, I already have a boyfriend."

"Russell the Muscle," Patty said sarcastically. She raised her arm and flexed her biceps like a weight lifter. "Are you sure you're not just a *teeny* bit put off by Earl's deformities?" she asked, holding her thumb and forefinger an inch apart.

"Of course not! They're barely noticeable. But please, Patty, tell me how I can discourage him."

"I can't advise you because, frankly, I don't think you should discourage him. He seems like a very nice man—unlike Russ Benson, who couldn't wait to banish the boys and me from his presence so he could get you alone."

"Russ and I hadn't seen each other in months."

"And remember what a gentleman Earl was to escort Rosa home the night she got so drunk? He could have taken advantage of her, you know. A lesser man certainly would have."

Jean could have added the fact that Earl had gallantly confronted Mr. Mitchell for Ginny's sake. "I already admitted he's a nice guy," she said, "but I'm just not interested in him. Please don't invite him to dinner or anything else, okay? I certainly don't need him over here on the weekends making snowmen."

"Okay ..." Patty said with a shrug, "but it's your loss."

Jean was beginning to wonder if she was right.

PART TWO

1943

"Use it up,
Wear it out,
Make it do,
Or do without."

★ ★ ★

(WARTIME POSTER)

CHAPTER 15
February 1943

"President Roosevelt submitted a budget of $109 billion dollars to the U.S. Congress, calling for 125,000 new planes, 75,000 new tanks, and 35,000 anti-aircraft guns to be manufactured in the coming year."

★ *Helen* ★

Helen started up her father's huge old car in the parking lot at the shipyard, revving the engine to warm it. Rosa Voorhees slid into the front seat beside her while Virginia Mitchell and Jean Erickson climbed into the backseat, slamming the heavy doors. Working in the shipyard had been a drastic change for Helen, but she never imagined all of the other changes her new job would trigger. She was breaking all of the rules she had adhered to over the years and becoming more and more involved in her co-workers' lives. How had this happened? Why hadn't she kept her usual, safe distance?

It was one thing for Rosa, Jean, and Ginny to become close friends over the last six months, but how had she allowed herself to become so entangled? Here they were in her car—in her life! Who knew that an innocent gesture on her part would lead to this? Helen had overheard Ginny making baby-sitting arrangements for her boys during Christmas vacation and had silently cheered. Harold Mitchell would have one less excuse to force his wife to quit working. But another problem had immediately surfaced.

"I'll have to figure out how to get them over to Patty's house before work every morning," Ginny had said. "We only have the one car—and I wouldn't know how to drive it even if Harold did let me take it. I wish winter hadn't come so early this year. It makes waiting at the bus stop such a problem, and the boys can't ride their bicycles—"

"I'll drive the boys for you," Helen had found herself saying. The other three women looked at her in surprise. "Well, I have to drag that monstrous car out every morning anyway, and you don't live very far from me, Ginny. I could drop your children off and pick up Jean—if you would like a ride, too, Jean."

"Yes, thank you," Jean said. "And Rosa lives right around the corner from me."

"Of course," Helen said, stifling a sigh. "Why not Rosa, too?" Helen had been shuttling everyone to and from work ever since. With cold winter weather settling in, it had seemed only natural to continue driving after the Christmas vacation.

Helen put the car into gear, pulled out of the parking lot and onto the street, and listened to the other women talk about the men they loved. As always, she thought of Jimmy Bernard.

"Why do relationships with men have to be so complicated?" Jean was saying. "It's so hard to know what to do. Russell keeps pressuring me to get a job closer to home, and I don't know what to tell him. I got another letter from him yesterday, and I can tell he's losing patience with me."

"I'm the wrong person to ask," Ginny said. "I can't make up my own mind half the time. But do you love him?"

"I'm not sure. How do you know for certain that you're in love?"

"Oh, you'll know it when you feel it," Rosa said. She swung around on the front seat to face them. "It's like you're only half alive when he isn't with you, and when he is with you, you feel so happy you could just explode. When I'm with Dirk, I can hardly breathe sometimes."

Helen recalled feeling that way, but the memory brought sadness, not joy.

"I felt like I couldn't breathe once or twice the weekend Russ was here," Jean said, "but I don't think it was what you mean, Rosa. To tell you the truth, I felt a little . . . claustrophobic. He wanted to swallow me up, and I wanted to keep part of me for myself. Does that make any sense?"

"Yes, I know exactly what you mean," Ginny said. "That was one of the reasons I needed to take this job—so the real me wouldn't get swallowed up. But I also feel the way Rosa does. I love Harold so much it scares me sometimes. I couldn't live without him. That's why I worry so much that he'll find another woman. But even if you do love your boyfriend, Jean, he shouldn't consume you to the point where you lose yourself."

"Albert would have swallowed me whole," Helen said. She didn't realize she had spoken aloud until Rosa turned to her in surprise and said, "I thought the guy you loved was named Jimmy?"

Oh dear. Helen had done it again. She simply had to curb this embarrassing habit of speaking her thoughts out loud. She took a moment to brake at a stop sign, looking both ways for cars, then accelerated through the intersection. But she could only delay answering for just so long. They were all looking at her, waiting. Of course Helen would have to explain herself.

"The man I loved *was* named Jimmy. Albert was the man my father wanted me to marry, but . . ."

"But you didn't love him?" Rosa finished.

"No," Helen said quietly. "No, I didn't." They waited, as if expecting more, but Helen had said everything she was going to say.

"I really don't want to move back home," Jean said after a moment. "I want to stay here and work at the shipyard. But I like Russell an awful lot and I don't want to lose him. It's such a hard choice. How will I know if I've made the right one?"

"Sometimes you don't know until it's too late," Helen said.

"And that's the problem," Jean continued. "I don't want to find out too late. I know that when we do get married someday, Russ is supposed to be the boss—"

"Who says?" Rosa interrupted. "Why does the man get to be boss?"

"Well, for one thing it's what the Bible says," Jean told her.

"Oh, the *Bible*." Rosa's tone was sarcastic. "I could've guessed. Hey, hasn't anybody figured out that the Bible is way out of date? Dirk's father is always reading it at the dinner table, going on and on about donkeys and lost sheep and cloaks, and a bunch of other stuff nobody cares about. The world has changed, you know. None of us have sheep or donkeys anymore. And who in their right mind wears a *cloak*? But Wolter Voorhees still makes sure that everybody follows the same old rules. He's head of the household, and don't you forget it."

"The husband is the family's leader," Jean insisted, "but he's not supposed to dominate everybody. I mean, Roosevelt is the leader of our country, but he's not a brutal dictator like Adolf Hitler, is he? The Bible says a husband should love his wife and give his life for her. I think it's similar to the way my sister Patty's husband, and your Dirk, and my twin brother, John, are risking their lives to save the people they love."

"But that's what's causing the problem in my case," Ginny said. "Harold honestly believes he *is* saving me. He says the shipyard is no place for a woman because the work is too dangerous and the men use coarse language and so on."

"Ha!" Rosa huffed. "With all the racket going on in there, who can hear anything at all—let alone coarse language?"

"Harold Mitchell needs to give up his old-fashioned ways of thinking," Helen found herself saying. She could no longer remain quiet. "His reasons sound more like excuses to me. He's probably afraid you'll discover new things about yourself by working."

"I already have," Ginny said. "I've learned that I'm stronger than I thought I was. Smarter than I thought, too," she added with a smile.

"As for *your* decision, Jean," Helen continued, "you're the one who has to live with it every day. If you choose the job that you honestly think is best for you, your young man should want the same thing for you, shouldn't he?" Helen pulled the car to a halt in front of Jean's house, and she turned around in the driver's seat to face her.

"Yeah, I know you're right," Jean said as she opened the rear door. "It's just so hard to explain these things to Russ in a letter. I can tell when he writes back to me that he doesn't get what I'm saying. Anyway . . . thanks for the ride. See you all tomorrow."

As Helen drove the few short blocks to drop off Rosa, she thought about Jimmy Bernard again, and she suddenly remembered how convinced he had been that he was acting in Helen's best interests. It was so easy to give advice to others, she thought. So hard to see things clearly when love interfered with reason.

After Rosa said good-bye and got out of the car, Helen made her way across town to Ginny's house, driving by instinct, barely aware of what she was doing as her thoughts took her back to the past. She pulled into the Mitchells' driveway a few minutes later, wondering how many stop signs she had inadvertently cruised through.

"Helen, I just want to say how much I appreciate your wisdom," Ginny said as she climbed from the car. "I've learned so much from you these past months."

"Thanks," she mumbled. The only thing Helen knew was that she'd been a fool for allowing herself to get involved in the other women's lives. And they were even bigger fools for heeding any advice she had to offer after the mess she'd made of her own life.

She pulled out of Ginny's driveway again and headed downtown to the bank. Minnie's granddaughter was coming to clean the mansion on Saturday, and Helen needed some cash to pay her. But as she drove past the town library and saw the quaint stone building blanketed in snow, her vision suddenly grew blurry with tears. She pulled into a parking space at the curb, unable to drive any farther. What was happening to her?

The other women were to blame, she thought as she fished in her pocket for a handkerchief. Hearing them talk of love and choices had brought the past to life for Helen. And then seeing the library where she had once worked, covered in snow like a cottage in a fairy tale . . . She blew her nose, wishing she could roll back time and make a different choice.

Helen remembered the aching restlessness she'd felt after graduating from Vassar College and returning home to Stockton. She saw the same symptoms in Rosa Voorhees and knew that if she had been raised the way Rosa had, Helen likely would have lived the same bohemian lifestyle that Rosa did. But Helen was a Kimball, with duties to her parents and to the community. Working as a librarian was one of them. It was a respectable job for a young woman of means and easily acquired when Helen's father donated money to the building fund.

Her father had other plans for Helen, as well, including her courtship with Albert Jenkins. Albert had arrived at one of the many elegant dinner parties her parents hosted, back when the house had been staffed with servants, and he quickly became a regular fixture. The son of one of the bank's partners, Albert was well-mannered, affable, intelligent. He had traveled abroad and, unlike Jimmy, had a university degree and an affluent, pedigreed family. He was a third or fourth cousin of Helen's mother, who seemed to adore him far more than Helen did. If anyone had bothered to ask, Helen would have described Albert as tame, bland, and boring.

She had limited experience with men, having attended a women's college, and had no one with whom to compare Albert except Jimmy Bernard. But whenever Helen did, it was like comparing a calico house cat to a Bengal tiger, a candle to a bolt of lightning.

It hadn't taken Helen long to realize that what little independence she had in life would be quickly swallowed up by her marriage to Albert Jenkins. Her future would be all about his work, his life, his climb up the ladder of success. Her role would be to help him ascend, to be the woman behind the man. The world would view her as Mrs. Albert Jenkins, never Helen. But her parents expected her to marry Albert, so she proceeded down that path in proper, boring fashion, too closely bound to the Kimball family tree to protest.

Then one snowy February evening, Jimmy Bernard walked back

into Helen's life. She had been working alone on the only evening that the library was open when she'd heard the front door creak open, felt a gust of cold air, and heard someone stomping snow off his boots. She looked up from her desk to face Jimmy. She was so surprised that she stood up without knowing why, then found that her knees were too weak to support her and promptly sat down again.

"Helen Kimball," he said with a look of awe. "I do believe you're even more beautiful than the last time I saw you."

Jimmy was no longer a boy but a handsome, dynamic man, so alive and vigorous that his body seemed too insufficient to contain all of him. If he had leaped over her desk and pulled her into his arms, she never would have let go of him again. There were no two ways about it; she was still in love with him.

"Jimmy ..." she murmured. "W-what are you doing here?" A slow smile spread across his face.

"Well, I thought I might check out a couple of books, if that's okay with you."

"Yes, of course! But how are you? Where have you been? What have you been doing these past few years?"

"Nothing much," he said with an easy shrug. "Still working at odd jobs and things, still trying to do some reading in my spare time. I figure the only way I'll ever get to travel the world is through books."

They talked for more than an hour, long past the time when the library should have closed. When she realized how late it was, Helen reluctantly turned off the lights and locked the door. Jimmy walked with her to her car, carrying the stack of books she had helped him choose.

"Wow! Is this yours?" he asked when he saw her two-seater roadster.

"My father bought it for me for a graduation present, but it's all mine."

Jimmy walked all the way around it—twice—admiring it. "It sure is a beauty. I've never even driven a car." He laughed, making light of it.

"Want to learn? I'll teach you. We'll practice when the snow melts and the roads are clear. It's hard enough to get around in the snow, let alone learn how to drive in it."

"It's a deal!" he said with a grin, and Helen found herself hoping for an early spring.

She started the engine and put the car into gear, then pressed the accelerator and let out the clutch. The car didn't move. She could tell by the frenzied whirring sound the rear tires made that they were spinning uselessly, stuck in a snowdrift.

"Helen! Whoa!" Jimmy shouted above the racing engine. "Let me put these books down and I'll give you a push." He walked around to the rear of the car, directing her as he shoved all of his weight against the bumper. Within a few minutes she was free.

His gesture seemed like a metaphor for her life. Helen had been stuck in a rut, her wheels spinning, her emotions frozen. Then Jimmy came along and jolted her out of it.

Nothing was the same after that. She saw how boring her life had become, every day the same, her job monotonous, her boyfriend tiresome and self-absorbed, her parents cold and distant. But after spending less than an hour with the man she loved, Helen had been propelled out of the snowdrift and back into a world of excitement and passion.

She watched the door at the library every Wednesday night after that, waiting expectantly, hoping Jimmy would walk through it. On nights when he did, Helen's world had color and fragrance and joy again. They laughed together. She could no longer recall what had been so humorous, but when she thought of those evenings with Jimmy Bernard, she remembered laughter.

In the spring, Helen kept her promise to teach Jimmy to drive, secretly meeting with him in the evenings or on Sunday afternoons when she wasn't with Albert Jenkins. Jimmy mastered the art of driving on his very first lesson, but they continued to meet, driving out to the state-owned property on Stockton Lake, exploring the deserted back roads and woods.

Helen loved him. It was as simple as that. The hours that they spent together were the only ones that mattered in her life. Their time apart was spent waiting, counting the days and hours and minutes until she would see him again. She believed that he loved her, too, but Jimmy always kept a respectful distance whenever they were together, as if well aware that she was beyond his reach.

Helen became obsessed with seeing him. He made her feel so alive. She could barely stand to say good-bye to him and return to her family's dreary house where everyone seemed to be waiting to join Helen's siblings in the cemetery. Without Jimmy in her life, Helen might truly die. She picked him up behind the lumberyard at the edge of town as often as she could, sliding over into the passenger's seat so Jimmy could drive. They drove only as far as the lake, where they would sit together in the car, talking for as long as Helen dared to be gone.

"If you could afford an education, what would you want to study?" she asked him one afternoon. They had parked in their favorite spot, a grassy clearing that faced the lake. Jimmy sat behind the wheel.

"I wouldn't want a job that would keep me inside in an office all day, I can tell you that," he replied. "It's so beautiful out here, isn't it?"

"Would you want to study nature, then? Biology or maybe geology? Or how about astronomy? Then we could come out here every night and study the stars together."

He turned to face her, his dark eyes somber. "Helen. It's pointless to ask. It won't ever happen. I am who I was born to be—and so are you."

She looked away, refusing to accept the truth. "I don't want to be that person," she said. "I didn't choose to be a librarian. When I graduated from college I wanted to teach school, but Father said it was beneath me."

"You're twenty-one, aren't you? An adult? Why don't you do what you want to?"

"I can't defy my father. He arranged for my job at the library. . . .

He's also arranging for me to marry Albert Jenkins," she added quietly.

"Who's he—besides being the luckiest man in the world?"

"He works at my father's bank. He's from a good family. Wealthy, of course. I think he's a distant relative of my mother's or something."

"Your father is right," Jimmy said. "That's the sort of fellow you should marry."

Helen turned to look at him again, surprised by the conviction in his voice. Jimmy's hands rested on the steering wheel, and the sudden impulse to touch him, to feel the warmth of his touch in return, became too strong for her to resist. She took one of his hands in hers. It was rough with calluses, nicked and scarred, and so stained from heavy labor that no amount of scrubbing could get it clean. She lifted his fingers to her lips and kissed them over and over.

"But I'm in love with you," she whispered.

There. She had said it, admitting the truth to him for the first time. He slid his fingers to her cheek, then took her face in both of his hands, forcing her to face him.

"I know, Helen. I know. And even though it's impossible, I love you."

He ran his hands over her hair, then down her neck and shoulders. His touch defined her, brought her alive, made her aware that she was made of flesh and blood. Helen had never been kissed before, but the need to feel his lips on hers was equally overwhelming. She leaned toward him, kissing him first. Jimmy never would have dared. But he drew her into his arms and returned her kiss with the same passion that she had always loved in him.

How wonderful it was to be held! Her family had never been generous with their affection, keeping one another at arm's length. Albert might take her elbow when he escorted her or she his arm. He held her lightly when they danced, at a distance. But to feel Jimmy's strong arms around her, the warmth of his body close to hers, his breath in her ear, was the most beautiful experience of her life.

"I love you, Helen," he whispered between kisses. "I love you . . . I love you."

"I want to spend my life with you," she murmured in return. "Let's run away!"

He stopped kissing her and leaned back to face her. "You know that's not possible."

"Why not?"

"Look at us! I can't ask you to give up everything you have—your wealth and your position in this town, your education. And I can't support you on what I earn. I don't want you to live where I do. You have to be who you were born to be. I don't ever want to change you or drag you down into my life."

"If my father accepted you and made you part of my life, would you marry me?"

"We both know that isn't going to happen." He gently removed her arms from around his neck and reached down to start the car. "I think we'd better go back."

Helen spent the next two days reliving Jimmy's kisses, thinking about their next meeting, longing to be with him again. She was so removed from everyone and everything around her that it came as a complete surprise one evening to find herself seated at her father's dinner table with Albert Jenkins and his parents, hearing them discussing plans for her engagement party. Helen panicked. She had to stop them.

"Father, please . . . May I speak with you in private for a moment?"

"Of course not. Don't be rude, Helen, we have guests."

"But I'd rather not speak—"

"If you have something to say, let's hear it. If not, don't interrupt."

She swallowed, knowing that once she spoke the truth she could never turn back. "I can't marry Albert. I . . . I'm in love with Jimmy Bernard."

Helen's mother gasped. Her father scraped back his chair and stood. "Will you excuse us, please?" he asked their guests. His face burned with suppressed anger as he marched Helen into his study. As soon as the door closed her father exploded. "How dare you say such a foolish, inconsiderate thing in front of our guests?"

"But it's true. I don't love Albert, I love Jimmy—"

He slapped her face, cutting off her words. Tears came to her eyes as she rubbed her stinging cheek.

"You will never speak of that boy again! He's nothing! You're a Kimball!"

"If you won't accept him, then we'll run away. We love each other."

"Don't threaten me, Helen. And don't try to call my bluff, either. I don't care if you are my only remaining child—the day you walk out of that door with the gardener's boy will be the last day you'll ever set foot inside my house."

"Are you forcing me to choose?"

"There is no choice to make! I'm doing what's best for you. That boy will never amount to anything. Albert Jenkins can give you the world. Your children will be part of the family business. They can make something of themselves."

"Jimmy could make something of himself, too, if you would accept him and help him get an education."

"You're a Kimball. That means something in this town."

"It's a name on a monument in the graveyard!"

For a moment, her father looked as though he might slap her again. Helen feared she had gone too far. When he finally spoke, his voice trembled with anger. "There will be one more name on that monument if you run off with him. You'll kill your mother. Do you want her death on your conscience for the rest of your life? That Bernard boy already killed your brother."

"He did not! It was—"

"It was his fault that Henry died! And if he runs off with you, he'll be responsible for killing your mother, too. Stay away from him, do you hear me?"

Helen fled from the study and ran upstairs to her room, unable to finish her dinner or face Albert Jenkins.

For the next few months she continued to lead a double life, attending dinners and elegant parties with Albert, who had been willing to attribute her foolish words to bridal jitters, and sneaking away to see Jimmy in the secluded woods beside the lake. But now she lived in fear, constantly looking over her shoulder, worried that someone would see them together and tell her father. She and Jimmy both knew they couldn't continue this way, but Helen was helpless to stop. She needed to see him, to be with him, no matter the cost.

They talked endlessly about her dilemma whenever they were together, how she was torn between her loyalty to her family and her love for him. They found no solution.

"I'm all they have left," she moaned. "If they lose me it will kill my mother."

"If only I had an education, a better job—"

"I don't care about the money. I would be happy living in a hut if I had you. But I'm all that my parents have left."

"Helen, you need to forget about me and marry Albert Jenkins."

"I can't. I can't live without you."

They were sitting in Helen's car late one Sunday afternoon in their usual spot by the lake, filling up on stolen kisses, when they heard another car coming down the deserted road. When it halted and the dust settled, she recognized the county sheriff—and he recognized her. He climbed from his car and stood beside Helen's open window.

"Good afternoon, Miss Kimball." He tipped his hat.

"Good afternoon, sheriff." She felt the heat rush to her face. It must be obvious from her disheveled hair and flushed face that she and Jimmy had been kissing.

"Are you okay? Is that boy bothering you?"

"Of course not! We're old friends. I'm teaching him to drive."

"You should know better than to be alone with someone like him, Miss Kimball. And you should know your place, boy. You get out of that car and get on home."

Helen opened her mouth to protest, but before she could speak, Jimmy scrambled from the car and strode into the woods without looking back. She felt herself trembling with anger and humiliation.

"You should know better, Miss Kimball. Better be mindful of whom you associate with from now on."

Even if Helen could have found the words to say, she was afraid to say them, afraid the sheriff would report the incident to her father if she did. "I'll be careful," she mumbled.

"And you really shouldn't be driving around on these old dirt roads, Miss Kimball. This area isn't open to the public."

"I wasn't aware of that."

"Okay, then. Now you are. Good day."

The sheriff climbed back into his car and drove away in a cloud of dust. Helen couldn't seem to move. As she sat there, shaken and furious, Jimmy walked out of the woods and slid quietly into her car again. He kept his head lowered, as if too ashamed to face her.

"We'll find another place, Jimmy. We won't let that ignorant sheriff—"

"No, Helen," he said quietly. "We're all done. I can't put you through this anymore. It's costing you too much. The sheriff never would have talked to you that way if it hadn't been for me. We need to end this, one way or another."

"How can I choose between my family and you?"

He took her shaking hands in his and gently kissed her fingers. "It's not an ultimatum, Helen. I love you. I want this torture you're putting yourself through to stop."

"But I want to be with you."

"I want that, too. But I also want you to have beautiful things, to live in a luxurious home, to travel the world if you want to. I don't ever want you to know sadness or fear or hunger. But I can't give you the kind of life I want you to have."

"I don't care about any of those things. I want to run away with you."

He shook his head as he kissed her hands again. "But most of all, Helen—most of all—I don't want you to have regrets for the rest of your life because you caused your family pain. I know what that feels like. Hardly a day goes by that I don't think about your brother and how it was my fault that—"

"But it wasn't your fault! It was an accident!"

"Not in your father's eyes. And I don't want to be to blame for taking you away from your family. I'm so afraid that you would hate me for it one day."

"I don't know what to do!" she wept.

"Then I'll make it easy for you," he said softly, "and for myself. Because the only way I can ever stop seeing you is to leave town."

"Jimmy, no!" She threw her arms around his neck, clinging to him. "That's not the answer. I'll think of something—I promise!" He slid out of her arms and opened his car door. "Wait! Where are you going?"

"We both need some time to think," he said. "I'll walk back to town."

"Jimmy, no! Come back!" But he jogged into the woods before she could stop him. It was the first time they'd ever parted without arranging their next meeting, and Helen made herself sick for the next few days worrying about him, waiting to hear from him, wondering what he'd meant and what he was planning. She had promised him that she'd find a solution, but there didn't seem to be one.

As she was closing the library the following Wednesday night, Jimmy walked in. "Are we alone?" he asked, glancing around. Helen nodded. He set the pile of books he was carrying on the counter and gripped her shoulders, holding her at arm's length. "I've enlisted," he said quietly.

"Jimmy, no!" She tried to break free, to hold him in her arms, but he was too strong for her.

"I can get training for all sorts of things in the army. This is my chance to better myself, to see the world, to make a better life."

"But there's a war going on over in Europe! What if America gets drawn into it? Jimmy, you can't enlist!"

"I already have. I can't bear to see you suffering anymore. It will be easier for both of us if I leave town."

"No, it won't!" She fought against his grip, furious with him, desperate to make him change his mind. "I can't live without you!"

"Yes, you can," he said softly. Tears shone in his dark eyes. "You're more vibrant and alive than any woman I've ever met. Don't you know that's the reason I fell in love with you?"

She finally broke free and threw herself into his arms, pleading with him, begging him to change his mind. He didn't reply. Tears rolled silently down his face. Helen took his face in her hands and kissed him, certain that the force of her love would convince him to stay. But when their lips finally parted, he freed himself and held her at arm's length again.

"This is the hardest thing I've ever done in my life. I love you, Helen Kimball. Don't ever forget that. But it's time to say good-bye."

"Jimmy, please don't leave me!"

"I have to," he whispered. "Good-bye."

It was as if the sun had set on that Wednesday night and had never risen again. Helen lived each day in a haze of grief, willing herself to stop thinking of him, to stop feeling such terrible pain, to stop living.

A month later, Helen's father hosted a lavish party to announce her engagement to Albert Jenkins. The mansion glowed with lights, and the ballroom came alive with whirling guests and elegant music. They set a date for the wedding and toasted their future with champagne.

Helen resigned from her job at the library, presumably to make wedding plans, but the truth was that she couldn't control her grief each time the door opened on Wednesday night and someone other than Jimmy Bernard walked through it.

Now, as she sat in her car twenty-five years later, she saw the lights in the library shutting off. It was closing time. Helen had been sitting here for nearly an hour. The bank would be closed by now, as well.

Jean Erickson had asked all the women at work how to reach a decision, but Helen realized that she didn't have an answer for her. Helen hadn't been the one who'd made the decision years ago. Jimmy had made it for her. Maybe the answer was that we don't always get to choose. Maybe life or God or other people do all the deciding for us.

She drove home to her huge, empty house and all the worthless wealth her father had left her. Back to a life without love, without Jimmy.

CHAPTER 16

★ *Rosa* ★

Rosa didn't need to see a clock to know that her shift at the factory was nearly over. She could always tell by how tired everyone looked, especially Helen, as the afternoon dragged on. Rosa would begin to feel a sense of anticipation, wondering if there would be a letter from Dirk waiting for her at home. Today she and the others were just finishing up and putting away their tools when Mr. Seaborn came over to their workstation. He was usually so cheerful with his boyish grin, but one look at his face and Rosa could tell that something was wrong.

"You look like you bet a week's pay on a losing horse," she told him.

"I'm afraid I have some very sad news. Mr. Wire, our personnel manager, just found out last evening that his son Larry was killed in action in Guadalcanal."

"Oh no!" Ginny cried. "How awful! That poor man."

"Larry Wire was once a student of mine," Helen said. "He was such a bright boy. It doesn't seem possible that he's gone. What a tragedy." Her words sounded prim, but when Rosa looked at her face, she thought she saw pain in Helen's eyes.

"Do you have any information about a memorial service?" Jean asked. "I'd like to attend. And maybe we could all pitch in to send him flowers or something."

"I'll let you know as soon as I hear," Mr. Seaborn promised.

The ladies talked about it some more as Helen drove them home. "If all of us are planning to attend the memorial service, maybe we could go together," Ginny said. "After all, Mr. Wire hired all of us at the same time."

"Yeah, I want to go, too," Rosa said. "Mr. Wire was real nice to me the day he hired me. And he was so proud of his son. Him and Dirk were friends. They played baseball together and everything." She had to stop before she choked up. Even though Rosa had never met Larry Wire, his death seemed too close to home. If it could happen to Dirk's friend, it could happen to Dirk.

The snow was falling steadily when Helen dropped Rosa off at home. "I seen more snow during my first winter here than in all the years I lived in Brooklyn," she complained.

"And this is only February," Helen reminded her. "There will be plenty more of it before spring arrives. I'll see you tomorrow."

"Yeah, thanks for the lift." Rosa stepped out of the car into a deep drift. Between the lousy weather and the sad news about Larry Wire, she felt pretty blue as she shuffled up to the house. She sure could use a drink to cheer herself up. She missed Dirk so much she ached inside. Maybe there would be a letter from him.

Tena Voorhees was waiting by the kitchen door to greet her. "There you are! I have a little snack all ready for you and I just made a pot of tea." Tena always seemed so happy, as if she had a bottle of hooch hidden away to keep herself going. Dirk must have gotten his smile and cheerful disposition from his mother. "How was your day?" Tena asked.

"Sad," Rosa said, remembering. She set her lunchbox in the kitchen sink. "We got some bad news today. Our boss, Mr. Wire, found out that his son was killed."

"Not Larry Wire? He was a friend of Dirk's."

"Yeah, that's the one. Mr. Wire told me he played ball with Dirk. He was a marine." Rosa got a lump in her throat again just thinking about it. Tena had tears in her eyes, too. Her smile had disappeared.

"Dirk will be so sorry to hear it."

"Do we have to tell him?" Rosa asked. "I mean, I don't want him getting depressed or anything."

"I think it would be better if he knew, don't you, Rosa? I'll tell him the next time I write to him. And I can send him the newspaper article. It's sure to be in the paper. There have only been a handful of boys from Stockton who have died, but the newspaper always puts their pictures on the front page."

"Doesn't it scare you?" Rosa asked in a hushed voice. "I mean . . . to think about it happening . . . to Dirk?"

"Yes. Yes, it does. Oh, Rosa!" Tena pulled Rosa into her arms, holding her tightly. Rosa hugged her in return as if hanging on for dear life. Maybe Tena needed to be held as much as Rosa did. And maybe she was just as scared for Dirk as Rosa was, in spite of everything Mr. Voorhees said about Dirk being in God's hands.

A moment later they released each other. Tena dried her eyes on her apron, and Rosa sat down at the table to eat the applesauce cake that was waiting for her.

"Before I forget," Tena said, "you got a letter from New York today."

"New York? Wasn't there one from Dirk?"

"No, not today. I'm sorry."

"Why're you apologizing? It's not like it's your fault or anything."

Tena handed the envelope to her, and Rosa saw immediately by the handwriting that it was from her mother. Rosa had written to Mona last fall to tell her she'd arrived safely, but she had never heard a word in reply until now. The letter was brief, one paragraph. The gist of it was that Mona's boyfriend had moved out, so Rosa could return home if she wanted to.

Rosa looked up from the letter as she ate the last bite of cake, gazing around at her husband's boyhood home. It still felt strange to be here in this spotless house. She didn't belong. Now was her chance to get out of Stockton, away from Dirk's parents and their stupid rules. If she returned to New York she could have fun again. Go to dances and parties.

"I hope it isn't more bad news," Tena said as she poured Rosa another cup of tea.

"No, it's from my mother."

"She must miss you," Tena sighed.

"Yeah, I guess." But if Mona missed Rosa, she hadn't said so. More likely, she couldn't afford to pay the rent all by herself now that her boyfriend was gone. Rosa stuffed the letter back into the envelope and pushed her chair away from the table.

"Rosa, wait. I have a little favor to ask of you. I am hosting the Ladies' Missionary Society here at our house tomorrow night. We decided to meet in people's homes during the winter months to save money. That way, we won't have to heat the great big church hall, you see? And so the meeting is here at our house this month. I thought I would make some cake for refreshments, and maybe some punch to drink because coffee is so hard to get and so is sugar . . ."

She seemed to be rambling on and on. What did she want from Rosa? Tena finally came to the point.

"I was just wondering . . . If you aren't busy tomorrow night, could you help me? Wolter is going to make himself scarce for a few hours, and I could really use your help serving the punch and things. I know you don't enjoy the meetings at church very much, but this is a little different since it will be here. . . ."

"Yeah, sure. I'll help you."

Rosa didn't know why she had agreed. She'd only been to one meeting of the Missionary Society, and it had bored her to tears. Maybe it was Tena's kindness with the cake and tea every afternoon. Or maybe it was the hug they had shared. For a few brief moments Rosa had felt something from her mother-in-law that she had never felt from Mona. Even in her letter Mona seemed to have an ulterior motive for inviting Rosa to come home. She wished her mother was like Dirk's mom, but Rosa knew better than to hope Mona would change.

"Thank you so much, Rosa. I know the other ladies are eager to get to know you better—"

"Get to know me!"

"Why, yes. You're our Dirk's wife. And this will be a wonderful way to do it."

Getting to know her hadn't been part of the bargain. Rosa had only agreed to serve punch and cake, not get all cozy with everyone. She hurried off to her room, and the more she thought about tomorrow night's meeting, the more scared she felt. Why had she said yes? It was a stupid idea. If the other ladies ever did get to know her— the real her—they would die of shock.

The afternoon suddenly seemed dark and depressing again. Rosa needed a drink. To make matters worse, when Wolter arrived home he was waving a copy of the newspaper with a picture of Larry Wire on the front page. Larry looked so happy and carefree, smiling as he posed in his marine uniform. Rosa could easily picture him and Dirk as teammates, buddies.

All evening long, Rosa felt so antsy she could have climbed straight up the wall, across the ceiling, and down the other side. If only Dirk had written a letter today. She knew he had stuff to learn and lots of work at the hospital to keep him busy. But if she worried about him this much when he wasn't even in danger, what would it be like when they shipped him overseas?

The letter from her mother still nagged at her, too. Should Rosa move back to Brooklyn? She had saved up more than enough money for a train ticket, but she really liked her job and all the ladies she worked with. If only she knew what to do.

When the evening news report came on the radio, telling all about the war, Rosa could no longer stand being cooped up in the house. She leaped up from her chair.

"I gotta get some air."

Wolter gave her a dark look as she grabbed her coat and boots from the closet. She knew what he was thinking.

"I won't be long," she said, staring back at him. He still hadn't given her a key to the house. He could lock her out again if she stayed out too late—and he would do it, too.

Lively music blared from the Hoot Owl as Rosa approached, but she kept walking, resisting the urge to go inside. She wouldn't hang out there anymore. She *wouldn't!* But she needed a little something to calm her nerves after the day she'd had. She'd promised herself that she wouldn't go to bars anymore and hang out with other men, but there was nothing stopping her from buying a little bottle of something and drinking it at home, was there? She had to cheer herself up somehow. Wolter would never even have to know. She hurried over to the liquor store on the next block.

"What can I do for you, sweetheart?" the proprietor asked. She was his only customer. Judging by his red nose and sagging belly, he looked like he sampled his own wares on a regular basis.

"I hear that vodka doesn't leave a telltale smell on your breath. Is that true?" she asked.

"Sure is. You gonna drink it all alone, sweetheart? That would be a crying shame."

Rosa had always enjoyed flirting with men. It was harmless fun, and she liked the attention. It would have cheered her up to have a few laughs with this old guy, but Larry Wire was dead and tonight she was afraid to tempt fate. What if God decided to punish her by taking Dirk?

"My husband is in the navy," she said primly. "I plan on drinking alone until he comes home again." She paid for the vodka and left. She knew she had done the right thing by not flirting, but it didn't stop the loneliness.

She made herself a screwdriver when she got home. Tena always kept a bottle of orange juice in the refrigerator. Rosa sat in the living room with her in-laws, listening to the radio and sipping her drink until it finally helped her relax. But as bedtime approached she realized that she would have to find a place to hide the rest of the bottle. She had agreed to let Tena clean Dirk's bedroom for her and change her bedsheets. Tena washed Rosa's laundry every week, too, ironing it and folding it and putting it away in the closet and bureau drawers. Rosa couldn't hide the bottle in any of those places.

After her second screwdriver—or was it her third?—Rosa decided to search the pantry for an empty bottle or jar to hide the rest of the vodka. She teetered out to the kitchen and looked around.

"Do you need something?" Tena called from the living room.

"Nope. Just rinsing out my glass." She let the water run for a minute and tiptoed into the pantry.

A handful of empty canning jars stood on the shelf, but how would Rosa explain why she kept a jar of clear liquid in her room? Then Rosa saw Tena's home-canned peaches floating in clear syrup and they gave her an idea. She took a jar from the shelf and carefully poured the syrup down the sink drain, then she refilled it with the vodka. If she drank a little more, the rest would fit in the jar perfectly with the peaches. She screwed the lid back on. Rosa could hide the empty vodka bottle in her coveralls and throw it away at work tomorrow.

But now another problem arose. How would she explain why she was keeping a jar of peaches in her room? It was so hard to think clearly after drinking all those screwdrivers, but Rosa finally decided to put the doctored peaches back on the pantry shelf behind all the others. She pulled a tube of lipstick out of her pocket and made a tiny red mark on the lid so she would know which jar was hers, then went to bed. It was the happiest she'd felt all day.

Rosa had a terrible headache the next morning when Helen picked her up for work. "You don't look well," Ginny said. "Do you feel okay?"

"I'm just tired." Rosa decided not to tell them about the vodka, but she did want their advice about moving back to New York. "I got a letter from my mother yesterday. Her boyfriend moved out— you know, the guy who tried to make a pass at me? She said I could come back home and live with her again if I wanted to."

"Do you want to?" Ginny asked.

"I don't know. What do you guys think I should do?"

"I'm sure you must miss your mother," Ginny said, caressing Rosa's shoulder. "Have you asked Dirk what he thinks?"

"No, but he'll probably want me to stay here. He wants me where it's safe. He was really upset when they spotted that German submarine off the East Coast. And then they arrested those German spies outside New York, remember?"

"You haven't talked much about Dirk's parents lately," Jean said. "How have you been getting along with them?"

Rosa thought of Tena's embrace, the snacks waiting for her each day, her neatly laundered clothes. Then she remembered the stern look Mr. Voorhees had given her when she'd gone out last night.

"I don't know," she said with a shrug. "I still don't feel like I belong there. Mr. Voorhees doesn't say much, but he looks at me with daggers in his eyes—like I better not make one wrong move, or else. I like my job, though. I used to think about changing to the graveyard shift so I wouldn't ever have to see him, but I like working with all of you gals."

"We would miss you if you did decide to leave," Ginny said. Jean nodded in agreement. Helen was watching the road and didn't say anything.

"The thing that makes Mr. Voorhees the maddest is that he wants me to come to church—but I'd rather sleep in on Sunday. I usually go, but only because I'm afraid God will punish me and take Dirk away if I don't."

"God doesn't do things like that," Jean said. "I don't know where you got that idea, but it's wrong."

Rosa would have liked a little more reassurance, but Helen pulled the car to a halt outside the factory, and everyone climbed from the car. "Hey, you still haven't told me what I should do—go back to New York or stay here?" Rosa said as they walked into the building together.

"I can't advise you," Ginny said, "because I don't know what it's like for you back home. My advice is to do what Dirk tells you to do."

"I disagree," Jean said. She had been walking in front of Rosa, but she turned around to face her. "I say do what your heart tells you to do."

"No, Rosa must think of her future," Helen said. She stopped walking and Rosa did, too. "Sometimes the thing that's easiest to do now isn't what's best in the long run. What would you like your future to be?"

"With Dirk, forever."

"Then choose the course that most likely will lead to that future."

Rosa thought about going home to New York all day as she assembled wire harnesses, but she couldn't decide what to do. *"What would you like your future to be?"* Nobody had ever asked her that question before.

When Rosa arrived home from work that afternoon, the kitchen smelled wonderful. "How was your day?" Tena asked. "Would you like a snack?" She saw Rosa eyeing the dessert that was cooling on the countertop and said, "No, no, dear. That is for tonight." Rosa remembered the Ladies' Missionary Society meeting and wished for the hundredth time that she hadn't agreed to help. "All the ladies just love my peach cobbler," Tena said with a smile.

Peach cobbler? What if Tena had used the wrong jar of peaches? What if she'd dumped all of Rosa's precious vodka down the drain? No, she couldn't have. Rosa had moved the jar to the very back of the shelf. There were probably a dozen other jars of peaches in the pantry that Tena could have used. The odds were in Rosa's favor that the spiked jar was still safe. Even so, she wanted to check and make sure as soon as she could. She would need to drink a shot or two beforehand to get her through the meeting.

"Rosa, dear? Are you okay?" Tena asked.

"Uh ... yeah. Sorry ... I was just thinking about something else."

"There is a little bit of applesauce cake from yesterday if you want it."

"No, thanks. I'll save my appetite for later."

"Oh, and you got a letter from Dirk."

Rosa couldn't help smiling at the news. Tena smiled with her.

"You go on in the bedroom and read it alone, dear. I'll call you when dinner is ready. We will have to eat a little early so we can get the kitchen cleaned up before the meeting."

By the time Rosa had read Dirk's letter for the third time, she was floating on air. Maybe she wouldn't need the vodka after all. Dirk loved her. He missed her. He had promised to kiss her for a month straight, without stopping, when they were finally back together again. He would never let her out of his sight. He was crazy about her. They would be happy forever.

She was setting the table for dinner when Tena said, "Would you get me a pint of green beans, please, from the pantry? Take one from the back of the shelf. I always like to use up the older jars in the back first."

Oh no. Rosa went into the pantry, dreading what she would find. She had shoved her jar of peaches to the very rear. She picked up one jar after the other, searching for the telltale dot of red lipstick on the lid, but the jar was gone.

She swore to herself. What a waste of perfectly good booze, down the drain! Now Rosa had no way to fortify herself for the dreaded meeting. She snatched up a jar of green beans for her mother-in-law, feeling sick inside.

As the time for the meeting drew near, Rosa grew more and more nervous, watching the clock. While they were washing the supper dishes, Tena fetched her punch bowl and cups from the basement and had Rosa wash them, too.

"I already made the punch," Tena said. "It's in the refrigerator, but I thought it would look nicer in the punch bowl. We need something to cheer us up on a dreary winter night, eh?"

Rosa nodded, wishing she had a shot of vodka to cheer her up. Down the drain! Boy, what a waste!

Tena started getting all fluttery as the time approached. Wolter set up extra folding chairs in the living room for the ladies and unfolded a card table for the society president to use as a podium. Rosa carried the punch bowl to the dining room table and set out dessert plates and forks and napkins. She watched as Tena filled the bowl with punch.

"Will you taste it for me, dear? I want to make sure it's sweet enough."

Rosa did. "It's very good. And plenty sweet enough."

"Oh, good. I changed the recipe a little bit, you see. Sugar is so expensive these days that I decided to use the syrup from the jar of peaches instead."

Rosa nearly dropped her cup. "Y-you mean . . . you put the liquid from the peaches . . . in the punch?"

"Yes. Does it taste okay?"

Rosa nodded, biting her lip. She didn't know whether to laugh or cry. She would get her nip of booze, all right—but so would all of the other women! Should she warn them? She didn't want to get Tena into trouble. But if she spoke up she would get herself into trouble. And where would they get more punch ingredients at this time of night? Rosa was trying to decide what to do when the doorbell rang.

"That must be our first guest. You stay here and serve the punch for me, will you, dear? Make sure everyone has enough."

It was too late to do anything now, even if Rosa had known what to do. She filled her own cup to the top and quickly drained it to fortify herself while she waited for all the women to arrive. She could hear them in the other room, cooing like pigeons in Central Park.

It didn't take long for Rosa's head to start spinning. Oh yes, she knew without a doubt which jar of peaches Tena had used. Rosa felt a giggle bubbling up inside her. She hadn't spiked the punch, Tena had!

The ladies paraded into the dining room like stuffy old hens with their beaks in the air. Rosa handed them plates of peach cobbler and glasses of punch as they filed past, then she followed them into the living room, where they all sat down to eat. She watched as the first lady took a sip, then another one did. Would anyone notice? Before long, the peach cobbler was gone and most of the women had drained their glasses.

"This punch is very good, Tena," the president, Mrs. Edwards, said. She had a figure like a pickle barrel and usually wore a pickle-puss to match. But she was smiling tonight.

"Thank you," Tena said. "I changed the recipe a little bit. I hope it's sweet enough."

"Oh yes. It's wonderful," everyone agreed. "Is there more?"

Rosa jumped up and hurried into the dining room as they all lined up for refills. One old lady, Mrs. Turner, was already a little tipsy after only one glass and had to be helped out of her chair. Rosa watched as Mrs. Turner gulped her second cup and wondered if she would have to be carried home on a stretcher. The thought made Rosa giggle. A lot of the women seemed to be giggling. Everyone hung around the dining room table happily sipping punch until the president decided it was time to start the meeting.

They all took their places in the living room again, which now seemed uphill from the dining room. Mrs. Edwards tried to stand at her makeshift podium and nearly fell over, taking the card table with her.

"Whoa! Who rocked the boat?" she asked. Everyone thought that was very funny. Mrs. Edwards decided to remain seated. "I now call this meeting to odor ... I mean order." She banged her gavel on the table, chuckling. "Order in the court! Order in the court! ... I always wanted to say that." The ladies laughed some more.

"You're a hoot, Elmira!" Mrs. Turner said in her creaky voice.

"I know. That's what my husband always says whenever we ... never mind. I think we're supposed to read the minutes or something, aren't we?"

The society's secretary began shuffling through her papers, searching for them. "They're here somewhere. Wait ... Where did I put my glasses? Oh dear!"

Rosa remembered filling the secretary's glass at least three times and knew what the real problem was.

"Oh, fiddle-faddle!" the secretary finally said. "You were all here at the last meeting. You know what we did."

"Yes, and a very fine meeting it was, as I recall," Mrs. Edwards said, banging her gavel for no apparent reason. "I move that the minutes be accepted as read."

"I second it," old Mrs. Turner shouted.

"Sold to the lady in the red dress!" She banged the gavel two more times. "Now the treasurer's report . . ."

"Oh, who cares about money," the treasurer said. "We have a whole bunch of it." She slurred her words so that *bunch* sounded like *bunsh.* "On with the meeting, Elmira!"

"Yes . . . well . . . For the life of me, I can't remember what we were supposed to discuss—can any of you?"

"Knitting for the soldiers," Mrs. Turner shouted, holding up a bag of yarn and knitting needles.

"Right! Okay, then . . . Do any of you feel like knitting?"

"I feel like having more punch," the treasurer said.

"I'll get it. You sit tight." Rosa jumped up to wait on the ladies, refilling everyone's cup. "I don't even know how to knit," she said as she handed the president a fresh glass. They all laughed—for no reason that Rosa could see. They were such a merry bunch of women, almost as much fun as the guys down at the Hoot Owl.

"Tena tells us that you're an Italian girl," Mrs. Edwards said. "Such a romantic language. Will you say something for us, dear?"

"*Que buon giorno,*" she said in an exaggerated accent. "*Ciao, come stai?*"

"So musical!" Mrs. Edwards hiccuped. "Did you speak Italian at home, dear?"

"Nah, I learned it on the street. The old-timers didn't speak English very good, so if you stole an apple or something from their fruit stand they would chase you halfway down the block, screaming at you in Italian. I know a lot of those kinds of words."

The ladies thought this was hilariously funny. Their laughter egged Rosa on. She imitated an angry grocer, spewing out a string of Italian words that would have turned their hair white if they had understood her. Instead, they applauded.

"If you went to the bakery or the butcher shop," Rosa said, "and one of the old geezers waited on you, you'd better know how to say 'bread' or 'pork chops' in Italian or you'd go away empty-handed."

"How interesting," the secretary said. Then a look of concern crossed her face. "Should I be taking minutes?"

Rosa spewed out a few more phrases, and the president babbled gibberish in imitation, banging her gavel to peals of laughter. Rosa felt like Bob Hope warming up to his audience.

"One time," Rosa continued, "a friend of mine brought his dog over when he came to visit me. We sat around talking all day and pretty soon the dog got hungry, so we decided to go down to the butcher shop and buy him some dinner—the dog, not my friend. Anyhow, the butcher shop was packed and the old Italian geezer was waiting on everybody, and he wasn't in no mood for English. So I told my friend how to say 'meat for a dog'—*cibo per cani*—while I ran over to the deli to get us some dinner. I told my friend, 'If the old guy doesn't understand, tell him *molto buon prezzo*.' That means 'very cheap' in Italian.

"I was only gone a few minutes, but when I came back I could hear a commotion inside the butcher shop—ladies gasping, and the butcher shouting in Italian, 'This? Is this what you want?' He had caught the little stray dog that always hung around in the back alley, and he was holding him up in the air, saying, '*This?*' My friend was grinning from ear to ear and saying, '*Sì! prezzo*—very cheap meat!' I thought one of the old ladies was going to faint dead away.

"I said to my friend, 'What did you ask for?' and he says, 'Just what you told me to say.' Only, he got it mixed up, see, and instead of saying meat *for* a dog, he was saying meat *of* a dog. The butcher had a cleaver in one hand and the dog in the other, and he was real eager to make a sale. The other customers were all screaming and swooning.... Well, that poor little dog didn't know how close he came to being turned into chopped meat before I cleared everything up."

The churchwomen laughed so hard at Rosa's story they had tears in their eyes. One woman was nearly on the floor. "Tell us another story!" Mrs. Edwards begged.

"Okay. Anybody want more punch first?"

By the time the evening ended, Rosa decided that it was the most fun she'd ever had at a church meeting. She liked these women.

Everyone was so cheerful tonight—except for Mrs. Turner, who had fallen sound asleep—but even she looked happy. She was snoring like a motorboat, but she woke up with a start when the president decided to end the meeting with a rousing version of "When the Roll Is Called Up Yonder." The ladies stood, arms around one another's shoulders like bosom buddies, and sang for all they were worth.

"Great meeting, Tena," they shouted as they staggered off into the night like sailors on shore leave. Rosa had to agree. Tena was still humming as they washed the punch cups and dessert plates.

"I don't understand that song about the buns," Rosa told her.

"Buns? What are you talking about, dear?"

"You know, that last song everybody sang before they left . . . about eating buns over yonder."

Tena laughed out loud. "Oh, Rosa! Not buns, *rolls*! 'When the *Roll* Is Called Up Yonder.' I think it's supposed to be a roll call, like the army has every morning. Only it's up in heaven!"

They were still laughing when Wolter returned home. He stood in the kitchen doorway, gazing at them in surprise.

"Tena? Have you been drinking?"

She wiped her eyes with a corner of her apron. "Don't be silly. We had a meeting of the Ladies' Missionary Society. The punch is all gone, but I saved you some peach cobbler."

Wolter looked from Rosa to Tena, suspiciously. "No, thanks. I think I'll put away the chairs and go to bed."

When he disappeared into the living room, Rosa and Tena turned to each other. A giggle bubbled up inside both of them.

"'Meat of dogs,'" Tena said. "'Very cheap!'" And they both laughed until their sides ached.

CHAPTER 17

★ *Virginia* ★

Ginny stood by the huge open factory doors with the other women from her crew, bundled in her coat and scarf against the wintry air. Excitement shivered through her as she gazed up at the magnificent landing craft that was about to be launched.

"Isn't that the most beautiful sight you ever seen?" Rosa asked above the noise. She slipped her gloved hand into Ginny's and squeezed it. "I feel like dancing!"

"Yes—and it's *our* ship."

A government official climbed the steps to a wooden platform and cracked a bottle of champagne against the hull to launch the first landing craft that Ginny's team had ever completed. Slowly the ship began to move, sliding majestically into the river.

"There she goes!" Ginny cheered.

"What a waste of good champagne," Rosa said with a moan. "They could of at least given us a sip or two, wouldn't you think?"

"I feel giddy enough without it," Ginny said with a laugh. "Wow! It's so beautiful! And it's all ours!" She pulled a handkerchief from her coat pocket. What a thrill! And she had played a part in it. "The only feeling that can compare with this is when my sons were born. I guess this is a birth of sorts, too."

Rosa put her fingers in her teeth and gave a deafening whistle.

Ginny clapped and cheered along with all the other workers. Two-thirds of them were women.

"Look at us!" she crowed. "Before the war, no one ever would have believed that our so-called 'weaker sex' could do this kind of work. I certainly wouldn't have believed it. I was afraid to make a simple decision without consulting Harold first."

"And now you helped build that ship," Rosa finished. "It floats and everything."

"It might even help the Allies win the war. I'm so proud of myself I could burst."

"Hey, isn't that your husband over there on the platform?" Jean asked. "I think he's looking for you."

"He is? Where?" Ginny wasn't nearly as tall as Jean, even standing on her tiptoes. She craned her neck as the ship moved farther away, then spotted Harold with the other dignitaries. He was looking her way, scanning the crowd. She smiled and raised her arm in the air to wave. He turned away.

"Maybe he didn't see you," Jean said when she noticed Ginny's tears.

"No, I'm sure he did."

"Don't let him spoil your moment," Rosa said. "If you had quit working last fall when he wanted you to, you never would have seen this ship being launched."

"I know, I know. Yet I hate the distance that has grown between us. We've become *estranged*."

Ginny had searched her dictionary and thesaurus to find a word she could use to talk things over with Harold. She had been practicing what she wanted to tell him, waiting for the right moment. "Harold, I don't want to remain *estranged*," she would say. The word was a fitting one. It meant, *"to turn away in feeling or affection; to keep oneself at a distance."* It was exactly what Harold had been doing for months—what he was doing right now.

The women made their way into the lunchroom after the launching and sat down at the table to unwrap their sandwiches. Jean talked about the fierce fighting that was taking place in North Africa. "My sister Patty is worried sick about her husband," she told them. "He's right in the thick of things. I don't know what she'll do if something happens to him."

"She'll go on living," Ginny said, "even though she won't feel like it. There are other ways to lose your husband besides the war." Everyone turned to stare at her.

"Is he walking out on you?" Rosa asked.

"Not yet. But I'm so afraid that he might. We still live together, but Harold and I have been *estranged* ever since he found out about my job. I wish I knew what to do to get back together with him— besides quitting. After today, I'm more determined than ever not to do that."

"How did you win him over the first time you met?" Rosa asked. She opened a container that held a delicious-looking piece of peach cobbler.

"We met at a dance at my college sorority house. Harold's fraternity was invited. I wore a brand-new red dress, and Harold said that I lit up the room. We danced together all evening—and neither of us ever dated anyone else again."

"You're still a very lovely woman," Jean said, polishing an apple on her sleeve. "Maybe if he saw you all dolled up—"

"Yeah! How about if you bought a *new* red dress?" Rosa asked.

"Good luck," Helen said. "I don't know if any of you has been shopping lately, but there's not much of a selection to choose from these days. Most of the dress factories have retooled to make uniforms. Besides, the best fashions used to come from Paris, and the Germans have put an end to that, stomping all over the city like the pigs that they are."

Ginny and the others sat in silence for a moment, as if waiting for the air to clear after Helen's bitter words. "Maybe I should get my hair done," Ginny finally said. "I haven't had time to get a permanent wave in months."

Jean ran her fingers through her blond hair. "That might work," she said. "Before my boyfriend came to visit me, Rosa helped me do my hair and pick out some new makeup. But you always look pretty,

Ginny. Your husband would have to be blind not to notice."

"I've got it!" Rosa said, snapping her fingers. "Nothing gets a man's attention faster than when he sees *other* men giving you the eye."

"You mean I should try to make him jealous?" Ginny asked. "I don't think I could do that."

"I think I know what Rosa means," Jean said, "and you wouldn't have to flirt or anything. When Russell met Mr. Seaborn, he suddenly got very possessive of me. And I hadn't done a thing. It seems like whenever a man sees other men giving you the eye, then he notices you, too."

"And don't forget perfume," Rosa added. "No man can resist you when you're wearing his favorite perfume."

Their excitement grew contagious. Maybe their ideas really would work. "I think I know the perfect time to try it," Ginny said. "One of my friends from the Women's Club invited Harold and me to a cocktail party this Saturday. I wasn't going to go because I don't have much in common with that crowd anymore—but maybe I should go and try out all of your ideas."

"I'm sure Patty will watch your boys if you want her to," Jean said. "I'm going to Indiana this weekend to see Russ, but Billy, Jr. and Kenny have been begging to have 'the big boys' over to play again."

"You and your husband can have the whole house to yourself," Rosa said with a mischievous grin.

Ginny couldn't help smiling, too. "Harold always feels romantic after he's had a cocktail or two. I just hope I can convince him to go to the party. Most of Harold's friends from that crowd are away in the service. The only husbands who are left are older than he is."

"Well, I wish you luck," Helen said, rising to her feet. "But I expect you'll have a difficult time reconciling, no matter how many new dresses you buy. Your husband was cut from the same stubborn mold as my father, and he always had to be the boss. He refused to give in until he had his way. I hope I'm wrong, but I just don't see

Harold Mitchell ending this estrangement until Ginny quits her job."

"I hope you're wrong, too," Ginny murmured, but she saw the truth in what Helen had said.

Ginny went all out getting ready for the party. She didn't have time to shop for a new dress—her appointment at the hairdresser had taken hours—but she applied her makeup carefully and chose a dress that Harold had admired on her in the past. She made sure she was ready on time, too, knowing how much he hated to be late. But his cold expression didn't soften when she came downstairs looking her best. Harold barely glanced at her. Maybe he was blind, but surely his nose worked, and she had lavished on the perfume, following Rosa's advice. His reaction—or lack of one—disappointed her. She retrieved her coat from the closet, but he didn't help her with it.

Then, just as Harold opened the door to leave, he halted. "Let me ask you something, Virginia. Did everybody except me know that you were working at the shipyard?"

"I didn't tell anyone, Harold, not even Betty Parker next door. But she knows now. She found out during Christmas vacation when the boys told Tommy that they were going to a baby-sitter's. And if Betty Parker knows—"

"The whole world knows. That's just great."

They drove to the party in silence. Ginny began to wish that she had never accepted the invitation. Helen Kimball was probably right; this idea would never work with a man as stubborn as Harold. Now Ginny would have to spend the next several hours trying to hide their strained relationship from everyone else at the party.

"Ginny! It's so *good* to see you," Gloria, their hostess, gushed as she met them at the door. "It's been so *long* since anyone has *seen* you. We *all* miss you at the women's club. There's a meeting next week, in fact. Will you be there?"

"I ... um ... I won't be able to make it," Ginny said. Gloria probably knew perfectly well that she was working at the shipyard.

They made their way inside, and once again, Harold made no move to help Ginny with her coat. "Should I put my coat in the bedroom, Gloria?" she finally asked.

"Yes, and then you two go hunt down my husband—he's handing out the drinks. Poor Harold looks as though he could use something to cheer him up."

Harold disappeared into the crowded living room with a sullen expression on his face while Ginny walked down the hall to deposit her coat. The bedroom window was open a crack for fresh air, and she fought the urge to climb out of it and run home. All of the self-confidence she had gained during the past six months seemed to be dissolving rapidly.

When she returned to the party, she stood in the living room doorway for a long moment, searching for Harold. The women outnumbered the men, but even among the few, he stood out: He was the only man his age who wasn't wearing a uniform.

The party was in full swing, with the lights dimmed and the radio playing music in the background above the sound of laughter. Two serving girls in black uniforms and white aprons walked around with trays of appetizers. Gloria's husband presided over a cartload of drinks. Harold had plunged right in, cocktail in hand, joining a group in the corner that was discussing the war. Ginny went to his side, tucking her hand in the crook of his arm, content to listen quietly as he talked about the North African campaign and tank warfare.

Everything seemed to be going well until the radio began to play the newest song craze, "Rosie the Riveter." Betty Parker shushed everyone so they could listen to it. When it ended she announced, "The Stockton Women's Club has our very own 'Rosie,' right, Virginia?"

Ginny smiled nervously as everyone turned to stare at her. "Well, I don't actually rivet anything. I'm an electrician—"

"At Stockton Shipyard! Can you imagine?" Betty's tone conveyed shock, not respect.

"No, I *really* can't," Gloria said. "That's an *awful* place, with the *worst* sort of men working there."

"It's a wonder the men can do any work at all," Gloria's husband said, "with pretty girls like Virginia running around the place."

Ginny smiled nervously as she glanced at Harold. He looked furious, not jealous.

"I could use a refill," he said, holding up his empty glass. "Excuse me." He slipped away from the group, but Gloria held Ginny's arm, keeping her captive.

"I see that women who work at the shipyard still get their hair done," she said. "And is that a new dress you're wearing, Virginia?"

"No. And I got my hair done for the party," she said, "not work. I have to wear a kerchief at the shipyard and baggy coveralls that—"

"Everyone knows why the younger girls take jobs like that—to meet men," Betty said. "What are you there for?"

Ginny had to raise her voice to be heard above their laughter. "I'm there to build ships." She looked around for Harold, wishing he would come to her defense. He knew the critical need for workers. She felt like a criminal locked in the stocks so everyone could throw rotten fruit at her. But Harold's withdrawal hurt more than their taunts.

"We have to win this war," she said. "None of us is safe from Hitler and the Japanese. I'm only doing my part."

"I suppose you think we *aren't* doing our part?" Betty asked.

"No, that's not what I meant at all—"

"What would happen to America's children if every woman abandoned her responsibilities at home and went gallivanting off to work?"

"But my sons are in school all day—"

Gloria laid her hand on Ginny's arm. "*Surely* you don't plan to *work* this summer when they're home from school?"

Ginny didn't bother to reply. It was none of Gloria's business what she did this summer. Ginny wondered if the club women had always been this catty, and if so, why she hadn't quit sooner. If she had known they would attack her and make her feel ashamed, she never would have come tonight. She tried to remember how proud she'd felt as the ship—her ship—had been launched. It seemed like ages ago. She looked around for Harold, but he had disappeared.

Eventually the others grew tired of ribbing Ginny, and the

conversation changed to another topic. She was able to drift away and go in search of Harold. She found him in the den with Ruth Harper, one of the younger club women whose husband was away in the navy. They stood very close to each other, talking and laughing. Ruth was flirting with Harold, and Ginny was horrified to see that he was flirting right back.

Ginny fled to the bathroom. The evening was a total disaster. She closed the toilet lid and sat on the seat so she wouldn't have to see herself in the mirror as she struggled to control her tears. She would have no way to repair her makeup if it all washed away, and she didn't want to face further humiliation if everyone saw she'd been crying.

A long time later, with her tears under control, Ginny rejoined the party. She looked at her watch and saw that she would have to stay at least another hour before she could politely leave. She didn't bother searching for Harold, knowing it would be better to avoid him since he seemed determined to hurt her feelings. She drifted from group to group, not saying much, watching the clock until it was time to go home. She could understand why Rosa tried to drown her sorrows with alcohol, but every time the host offered to refresh her drink, Ginny politely refused.

She sighed with relief when the first person bade everyone good night and left the party. She hurried to the bedroom to retrieve her coat, then searched for Harold. She found him in a corner of the living room, dancing with Ruth. He was holding her much too closely. When the song ended, he kissed her on the cheek. He seemed surprised when he looked up and saw Ginny.

"Why do you have your coat on?"

"Because I'm ready to leave. I'm sorry to steal your dancing part-ner, Ruth. By the way, where is your husband stationed again? I know you told us at the women's club, but I forgot." She felt pleased when Ruth's cheeks turned pink.

"He's in New Guinea."

"New Guinea. That's right. Let's hope the war ends soon so he can come home to you and the kids, right?"

Through an act of sheer will, Ginny managed to keep herself together as she and Harold thanked their host and hostess, said good-bye to everyone, and left the party.

"Are we supposed to pick up the boys?" Harold asked as he started the car.

"No. They wanted to spend the night at Jean's house." Ginny had planned it that way so she and Harold would have the house to themselves, but she already knew that the romantic evening she had hoped for would never come to pass. She was furious with Harold. And judging by the silent car ride home, he was equally furious with her. When they finally walked through the kitchen door, she could no longer hold back her tears.

"You were flirting with Ruth Harper just to hurt me, weren't you?"

Harold yanked his tie loose. "I wasn't flirting. She reminded me of you—the way you used to be."

"Are . . . are you going to divorce me?"

"Don't be ridiculous! I don't want another wife, I want the one I married back!"

"I haven't gone anywhere, Harold. I'm right here."

"You know what I mean. I want things back the way they were. I remember when we used to have people over like Gloria and Al did tonight. We used to do things together on Saturdays, too. Now you're up to your neck in housework every weekend and every evening instead of sitting with me and listening to the radio. You fall into bed exhausted every night."

"That's because this country is fighting a war. Doesn't anyone care that Hitler and the Japanese are trying to take over the world? I don't understand how Ruth and Betty and all those other women can go on living as if nothing has changed."

"I want things back the way they were, Ginny."

"For your sake or for mine?"

"If you're implying that my motives are selfish, you've got a lot of nerve. I let you have your own way for the past six months, hoping you would get it out of your system and come to your senses and stay home. Or else that you'd tire yourself out and finally quit. I'm losing my patience."

"Why didn't you defend me tonight? You know how important the war industries are. And you know how badly they need women workers. Yet you didn't say a word about any of those things. They were mocking me, Harold."

"They were mocking me, too!" he said angrily.

"How? No one said a single word against you."

"You should have heard what the men were saying behind your back. The implication was that I had lost control over you. That my household was in chaos."

"That isn't true. This household isn't in chaos."

"You know what I think, Virginia? I think you went to work because you're ashamed of me for not fighting."

"What? That's not true—"

"You're always rubbing it in my face, how you're working to help to win America's freedom—as if I'm not."

"How can you say that? Your work is vitally important! That's why the government gave you an exemption."

"I was the only man under forty who wasn't in uniform tonight. Do you know how many questioning looks I get every day? How many snide comments I hear wherever I go? I get strangers coming up to me and asking, 'Where's your uniform, Bub?'"

"Oh, Harold . . . I had no idea."

"Several men implied that we must need the money, that my business must be on the rocks since I had to send my wife out to work to support my family. How do you think that makes me feel? And then there's the fact that you're working in a shipyard, of all places! What kind of a man gives his approval to a job like that? They know me well enough to know that I wouldn't want my wife working there—so what kind of a husband lets his wife rule the roost?"

"A patriotic husband, one who wants to stop the Nazis and the Japanese. A man who loves his wife and gives her freedom."

"You had all the freedom in the world when you were home all day running our household."

"Not to do what I wanted to do. You don't want to have any more children, you won't let me mother the two we have—what else can I do to feel useful? Do you even care how good I felt when I watched that ship being launched the other day? I had played a part in it!"

"The life I've given you isn't enough?" he asked quietly. "This home? Me? I'm not enough for you?"

Ginny didn't reply. She didn't know the answer. She watched her husband turn his back and walk away, aware that they were even more *estranged* than ever before, and she made up her mind to resign from her job on Monday morning.

CHAPTER 18

★ *Helen* ★

"*What?* They can't do that!" Helen tossed the Saturday morning newspaper down on the kitchen table in disgust.

"Something wrong, Miss Helen?"

She looked up in surprise. Used to living alone, Helen had forgotten that Minnie's granddaughter, Thelma, had come to clean the house today.

"Did you read the morning paper, Thelma?"

"Not yet."

"It says that the government is setting up an internment camp to house German prisoners of war at Stockton Lake, of all places! Listen to this: 'The site has been chosen to be one of several branch camps under the control of the Army's Sixth Service Command at Fort Custer.' Well, I'm not going to sit by idly and allow this to happen. They can't bring those filthy Germans here!"

"Them prisoners got to go somewhere, don't they?" Thelma asked. She was a pretty, soft-spoken girl, about the same age as Rosa Voorhees, and a very hard worker. She had begun cleaning the moment Helen had let her in the door—sweeping, dusting, mopping, scrubbing—and she hadn't let up since.

"Well, I certainly don't want any Germans here," Helen said. "As far as I'm concerned, they should be sent to a deserted island some-where."

"You know, there's people feeling that way about us colored folk, too. They don't want us living in their towns or going to their schools."

Helen looked at Thelma in surprise. "I've heard that's true down south, but surely not up here?"

"Up here, too, Miss Helen. I graduated from high school over in Detroit, then took an electrician's course and got me a first-class certificate. But I couldn't find a factory job in Detroit or anyplace else. That's why I'm still cleaning houses."

"Did you apply at Stockton Shipyard?"

"Yes, ma'am, I sure did. They're saying there's no openings right now."

"That's absurd. Earl Seaborn is always complaining that we're shorthanded. I'll talk to him about it first thing Monday morning."

"Thank you, Miss Helen. I'd sure appreciate you putting in a good word for me. But I don't think it's gonna help. Not unless the color of my skin changes between now and Monday morning."

"Do you really believe there's racial discrimination here in Stock-ton?"

"I know there is, Miss Helen."

"Well, I'll talk to Earl Seaborn and see what I can do. And you can be sure that I'm going to speak to someone about the German prisoners, too. In fact, I think I'll go downtown right now and speak with the mayor." She rose from the table and headed toward the front closet to fetch her coat. She was still a Kimball, and her name still wielded power in this community. She had known the mayor, Archie Walton, for years.

The front doorbell rang, interrupting Helen's momentum. She yanked it open and found Rosa Voorhees on her front porch again.

"Rosa! Now what?"

"I got to thinking about what you told me," Rosa said, talking as if she and Helen were already in the middle of a conversation. "How I should figure out what I want my future to be? But you said your father forced you and Jimmy to break up because he didn't like him, and that got me worrying about Dirk's father. What if he tries something like that?"

"My situation was completely different from yours, Rosa."

"But I know his father doesn't like me, and—"

"What about Dirk's mother? Didn't you say you were getting along better with her?"

"I guess so, most of the time. But Mrs. Voorhees is like two different people. We get along okay when it's just the two of us, but she would never, ever go against her husband. She does whatever he says."

"Look, it's too cold to be standing here with the door open. Come in." Helen knew she sounded ungracious, but she had neither the time nor the patience for Rosa's problems. Helen let her in as far as the front hall, but she didn't offer to take Rosa's coat. "Listen, Jimmy and I never had a chance to get married. But you're Dirk's wife. I can't imagine that his parents would try to change that."

"But what if Dirk changes his mind? What if he decides that his father is right and that I'm no good for him? What if he starts seeing me the way his father does, and—"

"Rosa, Rosa . . . when I said to think of the future, I never meant that you should imagine all the bad things that might happen."

"I can't help worrying. Dirk and me didn't get to know each other for very long before we got married. It was kind of a quick thing. To tell you the truth . . . we were both a little drunk the night we decided to elope."

Helen suppressed a shudder. This was dreadful. She didn't want to hear about Rosa's private life, and she certainly didn't feel qualified to give advice. Why had Rosa come here, of all places? Then Helen remembered that Ginny had planned a special night with her husband this weekend, and Jean was going home to Indiana. Was it simply that Helen was the only person left?

"Sometimes I wonder if Dirk sent me home because he wanted me to learn how to be like his mother. Maybe he hopes I'll be the kind of wife that she is, but I know that I can't ever be. She makes bread and soup from scratch, and the only soup I can cook is the kind that comes in a can. I thought all bread came from a bakery until I seen his mother making it."

"Does Dirk talk about things like that in his letters? Is he pressuring you to be more domesticated?"

"No, and I'm afraid to bring it up. I hardly ever talk to Dirk about his parents, and I sure don't tell him that me and his father aren't getting along. I want to change and be the kind of person his mother is, but I can't. I try and try and I just can't be any different."

"I don't know what to tell you, Rosa," Helen said with a sigh. She wished she knew how to get rid of her.

"Dirk is nearly finished with his corpsman training. He's going to be shipped overseas to where the war is in March. . . . And I'm just so scared!"

Helen saw Rosa's lower lip tremble and feared that she would start crying like she had the last time. How on earth would Helen comfort her if she did? Thankfully, Thelma interrupted them as she made her way down the hall with the roaring vacuum cleaner. She shut it off in surprise when she saw the two of them near the front door.

"I thought you left for downtown, Miss Helen."

"I'm on my way. Thelma, this is Rosa Voorhees. We work together at the shipyard. Rosa, this is Thelma King."

"Nice to meet you," Rosa said. "Hey, Helen, if you're going downtown, can I hitch a ride with you?"

"If you'd like." Helen didn't want to know what business Rosa had in downtown Stockton. She simply wanted to drop her off somewhere and be rid of her.

Rosa talked on and on about Dirk as she and Helen walked out to the garage, as they climbed into the car, and as they drove downtown and parked near the village hall. Helen was only half listening as she marshaled all of her arguments against the internment camp. She barely noticed that Rosa was still following her until she walked into the mayor's office and his secretary said, "May I help you ladies?"

"Yes, I'm Helen Kimball. I'd like to speak to Archie—Mayor Walton—if he has a moment." She was ushered into his office a few minutes later with Rosa still tagging along behind her. The plump, balding mayor sat behind his desk with his shirtsleeves rolled up, teetering dangerously on the hind legs of his chair. He plopped forward, then stood and straightened his necktie as they entered.

"Helen! How are you?" he asked, offering her his hand. "What brings you here on a cold Saturday morning?"

Helen decided not to complicate matters by introducing Rosa. Who knew what that girl was likely to say? "I came because I was appalled by what I read in the newspaper this morning, Archie. A prisoner of war camp in Stockton? We simply cannot allow it."

"I know, but—"

"Those German soldiers will be a danger to our community. What can we do to stop this?"

He sighed and sank back onto his chair, gesturing to the two seats in front of his desk. "Nothing. Believe me, Helen, I already asked. That's state-owned land out there. It's out of my control."

"Couldn't we petition someone at the state level, then? I would be happy to get the community mobilized. I'll even take the petitions door-to-door myself if I have to."

"Won't do any good. The deal has already been made over in Lansing. The state officials did promise me, though, that only common soldiers would be assigned here. No Nazi Party members, no officers, no troublemakers of any kind."

"Oh, come on, Archie. They're *all* troublemakers."

"Well, I think there must be a lot of young German boys who wound up being drafted without any say in the matter. I'm sure they just want the war to end so they can go home to their families—at least, that's what the state promised me."

"There are no *good* Nazis and *bad* Nazis—a German is a German!"

He seemed taken aback by her vehemence. After a moment he said, "I appreciate your concern, but I have much bigger fish to fry. Our town has been growing so rapidly with the shipyard and all, that

I can't keep up with all the problems. Do you know our population has tripled in just one year's time? Housing is an issue, and so is rising crime. With so many other concerns, I just don't have time to fight this prisoner-of-war thing. If you want to do it on your own, go right ahead. And if you think of anything I can do, let me know. Believe me, I don't like it any more than you do, but my hands are tied."

"When is the next town board meeting?"

He consulted his calendar. "Two weeks from today."

"Put this issue on the agenda. I'll be back." Helen stalked from his office, mumbling, "This is absolutely unacceptable. Germans are loathsome creatures. . . . I hate them all!"

"Do you hate me because I'm Italian?" Rosa asked as they walked to the car. "We're fighting Mussolini and the Italians, too."

"Of course not. You were born here. Those prisoners are native Germans. And I find it very hard to believe that any of them are innocent. They allowed Hitler to come to power, didn't they?"

"Yeah, I guess so." Rosa seemed shocked by Helen's fervor, too. Why wasn't everyone outraged by the POW camp? "Where can I drop you off, Rosa? Your house?"

"Are you going back home?"

"No, I'm going to drive out and look at that property, see how far along the project is. Maybe it isn't too late to stop it."

"Can I go with you?"

"I suppose." For the life of her, Helen couldn't understand why Rosa was tagging along like her shadow. She retrieved her car, and the two of them headed out of town.

How long had it been since she'd driven out to Stockton Lake? Helen couldn't recall, but she did remember the hours and hours she'd spent out there with Jimmy. Memories of him seemed to be popping up, unbidden, ever since she'd started working at the shipyard. To be driving out here now under these circumstances seemed like an enormous injustice. Bringing German soldiers to Stockton was bad enough, but to let them live in the very woods that Jimmy had loved so much seemed an outrage.

It never occurred to Helen as she drove out of town that the back roads might not be plowed. But as she turned off the county highway and saw that the private road to the lake had been cleared recently, she realized that the project had probably been well underway before the newspaper reported it. Her huge car bounced through ruts and potholes, rattling Helen's teeth and causing Rosa to hang on to the grab bar for dear life.

They finally pulled to a halt in a plowed area at the end of the road. Two state-owned trucks were already parked there. Beyond a half-finished barbed-wire fence, the clearing resembled a military camp with three bunkhouses, toilet buildings, an elevated water-storage tank, and several smaller buildings, all covered with a clean blanket of snow. The only sign of life was a curl of smoke that rose from what must be the cookhouse.

"Looks to me like it's already built," Rosa said.

"They put this camp together during the Depression," Helen told her. "It was another idiotic idea our government had. They built all this in 1933 as an emergency resettlement camp to get the bums off the streets of Chicago. The idea failed, thankfully. We didn't want the bums hanging around our town any more than the people in Chicago did. But hoboes seem tame compared to Nazis."

She shut off the car engine to conserve gasoline. In the winter stillness, Helen heard the faint rustle of leafless branches, the distant call of birds. The snow lay sparkling in gentle drifts.

"It's real pretty out here," Rosa said in a near whisper.

"Yes, it is. This camp seems especially obscene to me because I used to come out here with—" She stopped. She was talking too much. Rosa didn't need to know her personal affairs. But she had already said too much.

"With Jimmy?" Rosa asked.

Helen nodded reluctantly. "I taught him how to drive out here on these roads. Of course, they were just dirt roads back then. This was always such a beautiful spot, overlooking the lake."

"Did you used to sit here and neck?"

"Rosa! Honestly!"

"Whoops. I did it again, didn't I? Ginny says I always ask questions that are too nosy. I'm sorry."

"Apology accepted."

"I would be scared to sit way out here in the woods at night with wild animals and things. I'm a city girl. But it's real pretty here in the daytime. I could see sitting here with a cute guy and . . . talking . . ."

"I may be a spinster, Rosa, but I'm not completely ignorant of the birds and the bees. If you must know, Jimmy and I did spend time out here kissing. But we spent time talking, as well, about all sorts of things. Jimmy was a very intelligent man and he thought deeply about life."

Helen watched a row of clouds shift and change as they blew across the sky above the lake and remembered how much Jimmy enjoyed talking about God and his faith. He had read every book in the Stockton Library on the subjects of theology and religion—not that there were many to choose from. Helen remembered one discussion in particular as if it had happened yesterday. Jimmy had spoken with such passion as he'd talked about Jesus' love for all the social misfits, and he was impatient with Helen's church for not modeling Christ to the underprivileged people in town, calling it a social club, a place to dress up and be seen.

"If I were searching for God," he had said, "I'd be more likely to find Him out here than in your church."

"That's a very pagan concept, you know," Helen replied, "saying that God is in nature."

"That's not what I mean at all, Helen. These woods are His handiwork. Creation shows us what He is like: imaginative, extravagant, generous. We can learn things about God when we study what He has made."

"What do you learn from the fact that wild animals attack and kill each other out here? Even the tiniest mosquito is bloodthirsty."

"That's man's fault, not God's. Adam's sin caused all of that. But can't you see the order and beauty and creativity behind creation?

And the love, Helen. The sheer love God displays in the blue sky and glorious clouds."

"The clouds also bring thunder and lightning—and floods."

"I used to be afraid of thunder when I was a kid, but my father would hold me in his arms so I wouldn't be scared. I think God is like that. Bad things happen to us because we live in a fallen world. But if we have God's arms around us, we can get through anything without being afraid."

"I can't imagine crawling onto my father's lap," Helen said, "much less having him comfort me."

"Maybe that's why you see God the way you do. In your mind He's like your father: controlling, stern, someone whose favor you need to earn."

"I can't help it," she sighed. "God does things that I honestly can't understand—like allowing all of my siblings to die."

"My mother suffered from consumption for as long as I can remember," Jimmy said. "That's why I quit school—to help earn money for doctors and sanitariums and medicine. But when she died a few years ago, I didn't blame God. Death is a consequence of Adam's sin. It's part of living in a fallen world. Yet Jesus says we should look after the sick and the needy if we're His people. Take care of the orphans and the poor. I think maybe He allows all these tragedies to happen in our lives to give us a chance to show others His love."

Helen was remembering the intent look in Jimmy's dark eyes, the passion in his voice, when Rosa interrupted her thoughts.

"You been quiet an awful long time. Did I say something wrong again?"

"No, you didn't say anything wrong."

Helen sighed. Why had this mixed-up, misplaced girl come to her of all people? Could it be as simple as Jimmy made it sound? Had a misfit like Rosa come into Helen's life to give her a chance to put Jimmy's words into practice? If so, then Helen was failing miserably, acting just as stern and unloving as her own father had.

She viewed Rosa through the same ungracious lenses that her father had viewed Jimmy.

"I was just remembering some things, Rosa."

"About him? About Jimmy?"

"Yes. And wishing I could talk with him just one more time."

"I know what you mean," Rosa said in a teary voice. "Sometimes I'm so afraid that I'll never see Dirk again. . . . If anything ever happened to him, I don't know what I would do."

For the first time all morning, Helen really heard what Rosa was saying. It didn't matter why she had chosen to come to Helen, or why she had been following her all over town; Rosa had come to Helen with her loneliness and fear—and that was all that mattered. Helen turned to Rosa and looked into her beautiful, sorrowful eyes and suddenly knew exactly what advice to give. "Is there some way you could see Dirk before he ships off?"

"I wish I could. We been talking about it in our letters, but he won't get enough time off on his furlough. It would take so long to get here from Virginia that by the time he did, he'd have to turn right around the next day and go back. They need him overseas really bad, as soon as his training is finished."

"Can't you go to Virginia to see him?"

"I want to, but won't I lose my job? I don't think they'd give me that much time off to travel and everything, would they? And if I just up and went, I'd be afraid they wouldn't let me come back to work again. I couldn't stand to be at Dirk's house all day with nothing to do. I suppose I could go to New York and live with my mother, but—"

"Let's talk to Jean on Monday and see if she can arrange a leave of absence for you. The other girls and I will work extra hours if we have to. If we skip lunch every day, the three of us can put in three extra hours of work."

Rosa's eyes swam with tears. "You'd really do that for me?"

"Of course. I think it's important that you see Dirk before he ships off."

"That would be a dream come true! I'd give anything to see Dirk again."

Helen turned away and started the engine, worried that Rosa might try to embrace her. "I can't promise you, Rosa, but I'll do my best to make it happen." She would also talk to Jean and Mr. Seaborn about hiring Thelma King.

Helen realized that she was breaking all her own rules again, getting involved in other people's lives. But as they drove back into town, she had a feeling that Jimmy would applaud her for it.

Rosa was so excited about going to see Dirk that she seemed to bounce on the car seat without any help from the ruts and potholes. Helen dropped her off at Dirk's house, a very different girl from the woebegone Rosa who had shown up on her doorstep two hours ago. Once again, Helen thought about Jimmy and wondered if things would have been different if she could have seen him one last time.

The mansion sparkled when she returned home and smelled wonderfully of lemon oil. Thelma was rubbing it into the railing and banisters in the front hallway.

"How'd you make out with them German prisoners, Miss Helen?"

"Not very well, I'm afraid. By the way, are you married, Thelma?" She had no idea what had made her ask that question.

"No, but I have a boyfriend. We plan on getting married soon as he comes home. He got drafted into the army."

"I suppose the draft gets every man, sooner or later, rich or poor ..."

Even rich men like Helen's fiancé, Albert Jenkins. The memory came back to Helen as clearly as if she were watching it on film. She had been standing right here in the front foyer the day Albert came to tell her that he'd been drafted. America had just entered the Great War.

"I came over to ask you what you thought, Helen," Albert had said. "Should we move up our wedding date or wait?"

"Let's wait."

She hadn't even taken time to think it over, and she saw that her quick response had hurt him. Worse, she had probably looked relieved. The world was at war, the future was uncertain, and Albert must have hoped she would say, "Let's get married right now!" It would have been the natural response if she had loved him.

"May I ask you something?" he said gently. "Is it true what you told your father the night we talked about our engagement—that you're in love with someone else?"

She looked away, staring into the dreary parlor where all her siblings' coffins had lain, one right after the other. "It was true," she replied. "I was in love. But it's over now."

"What happened?"

"What difference does it make, Albert?"

He rested his hand on her shoulder. "We're engaged to be married, Helen. Don't you think I have a right to know?"

"It never would have worked between Jimmy and me," she said with a sigh. "Our backgrounds were too different. He lived a simple life. I'm well-off, educated ..." She played with the topaz engagement ring Albert had given her, an heirloom from his grandmother.

He lifted her chin so they faced each other. "Are you still in love with him?"

"Albert, I'm sorry. . . . I met him long before I met you. People can't help who they fall in love with."

"I want to know what really happened between the two of you. I think you owe me that much." When she didn't reply, he asked, "Did it have something to do with your father?"

Helen nodded. "My father disapproved of him. He said I had to choose between my family and Jimmy. He vowed to disown me if we married. I told him I didn't care about his money, and I didn't. But then he said that if we ran off it would kill my mother—and I was afraid he was right. I'm the only child she has. . . . Jimmy didn't want me to have to make that decision, so he left."

Albert was silent for a long moment, gazing at her. The clock on the mantel in the parlor ticked loudly. Helen hoped she hadn't hurt his feelings.

"It sounds to me like your father ended the relationship, not you," he finally said.

"My parents had seven children. All of them are dead except me."

"But you deserve to be happy, Helen—and to be with the man you love. If your father is willing to disown his only child over it, then he deserves to be alone. And if your mother pines away with grief when you're still alive and well and married to someone you love, then that's her fault, not yours. Your parents have no right to manipulate you or choose your future for you." He was silent for another moment, then asked, "Do you think it's too late to change your mind?"

"You mean about our wedding?"

"No, I meant for you and this other man. But I guess it concerns us, too. If you're going to spend the rest of your life with me, I want it to be your choice, not your father's."

He gazed at her for a long time as if trying to read her mind. Or maybe he was searching for a sign of affection or hope. She knew he wouldn't find one. "You're a good man, Albert," she said softly.

He sighed. "We'll postpone the wedding, then, until I come back."

He left disheartened, and Helen felt sorry for him. But she couldn't get Albert's words out of her mind. Was it too late for her and Jimmy?

If her siblings' brief lives had taught her anything, it was that life was short, happiness fleeting. Helen's mother derived no joy from life, and Helen seemed headed for the same fate. What good was all her father's money if she was miserable? And what good would it do to please her parents if she was unhappy for the rest of her life? Albert was right: Her parents were responsible for how they reacted to Helen's choices. She wasn't.

Again she wondered if it was too late for her and Jimmy. Helen still loved him. And if he still loved her, then they should be together. Why should she waste her life trying to please others?

With a burst of hope and joy, Helen decided to write to Jimmy right away—tonight. She would tell him that she loved him and wanted to spend the rest of her life with him. For the first time since she'd kissed him good-bye, she felt truly happy.

Unwilling to wait until Joe Bernard came to work in the yard in the morning, Helen jumped into her car and drove to his house on the edge of town. She would get Jimmy's address, then write and tell him that she had finally made up her mind. It wasn't too late for them.

Jimmy and his father lived in a ramshackle neighborhood near the lumberyard. Surely Helen's father could afford to pay Joe better than this for all the hard work he did. Was Father that stingy? Because of him, Jimmy had been forced to quit school and go to work to pay for doctors and medicine for his mother. At that moment, Helen hated her father.

The Bernard house was small and in need of a coat of paint, but flowers filled the well-tended front gardens and window boxes. Helen wondered if Joe Bernard had planted them for his wife. He came to the front door after she'd knocked, with a look of surprise—or maybe fear—on his face.

"Evening, Miss Kimball."

"Good evening, Joe. I was wondering . . ." She was suddenly at a loss for words. Did Joe know that she and his son were in love? How much had Jimmy told his father? She cleared her throat and started again. "I was wondering if I could have Jimmy's mailing address. I'd like to write to him."

"I hear that you're engaged to be married, Miss Kimball."

It wasn't reproach that she heard in his tone, but uncertainty. What should she say? How much should she tell him? Helen decided on the truth. He deserved that much.

"I am . . . that is, I *was* . . . engaged. But I'm in love with your son and he loves me. I want to write to him and find out if it's too late for us. I want to ask him if he'll take me back."

"We're simple people, Miss Kimball. Poor people." He lifted his hands, gesturing to the crumbling front porch before letting them fall to his sides again.

"Money shouldn't matter if two people love each other, should it?"

"It's more than just the money, Miss Helen. Your people and mine ... well, we come from two different worlds. It would never work—"

"Jimmy and I love each other, Joe. We can make it work."

He seemed to wrestle with his thoughts for a long moment. "Come in," he finally said and held the door open for her. Joe Bernard was not the kind of man who would argue with his boss's daughter.

The air was very warm inside the house and had the stale odor of boarded-up rooms and unopened windows. The furnishings were worn, the wood floors bare. The house had the grimy, cluttered look of a womanless home. Could she live here? Was she certain? Her father would surely disown her. *"Don't call my bluff,"* he had warned. Once Helen informed him that she was marrying Jimmy, there would be no turning back. She closed her eyes and imagined Jimmy's arms around her and knew she wanted to spend the rest of her life with him, no matter where they lived.

Joe retrieved a pile of letters from the kitchen table and bent over them, copying the address for her onto a piece of paper. "Here you go, Miss Kimball." His face wore a sorrowful look as he handed the paper to her. Was he afraid for his son?

"I love him, Joe. That's all that matters."

"Miss Helen? ... Miss Helen?" She came out of her reverie as Thelma called to her. "You were a million miles away, Miss Helen."

"Yes, you're right, I was. I'm sorry. By the way, the house looks wonderful. Thank you for doing such a fine job."

"You're welcome, but I ain't finished with everything yet."

"I know. And as much as I'd hate to lose you as my cleaning woman, I'm going to speak with Mr. Seaborn on Monday about getting you a job at the shipyard."

CHAPTER 19
February 1943

"Allied forces capture Guadalcanal, in the Solomon Islands, after heavy fighting."

★ *Jean* ★

Jean's boyfriend hadn't exaggerated when he'd described the grueling trip between his farm and Stockton. Jean found out firsthand when she left town on the early morning bus one Saturday in February and spent a long, cramped day trying to get home to Indiana. Three times she changed buses, waiting in dirty, overcrowded stations, but she would have changed a dozen times for the chance to see her twin brother, Johnny, again, home on furlough before the air force shipped him overseas. She could hardly wait.

As the familiar scenes of her hometown came into view at last, Jean found it hard to believe that more than a year had passed since John left home for boot camp and she had moved to Stockton. Before the war they'd never been separated for more than a day and had never celebrated their birthday apart. She sat on the edge of her seat as the bus pulled into town, eager for her first glimpse of him. She spotted Russ instead, looking tall and handsome, and realized how very much she had missed him. And there beside him was Johnny! He looked so different in his air force uniform that she might not have recognized him among all the other soldiers if Russ hadn't been standing alongside him. Johnny's girlfriend, Sue, clung to his arm.

Jean grabbed her belongings and bolted off the bus. Russ ran to greet her first, lifting her into his arms. He kissed her in the parking lot in the frigid February air, not caring who saw them, and every mile of the weary journey had been worth it.

"Oh, Russ! It's so good to see you!"

"I'm never letting you out of my arms again."

They kissed once more as the bus roared off to its next destination, enveloping them in diesel fumes. Jean barely noticed the cold or the smell. She finally held Russ in her arms.

"Hey, save a hug for me," her brother said as he sauntered up to them. Russ released her, and Johnny pulled her into his arms, whirling her in a circle.

"You look wonderful, Johnny," she laughed. "You've grown up!"

"Yeah, you too. Is that what happens when you leave home? Look at you all dolled up. You look like a city girl, not a farm girl."

"I'm still the same underneath." She turned to Johnny's girlfriend, who had hurried forward to reclaim him again. "Hi, Sue. How are you?"

"Great, now that Johnny's home."

Sue wrapped her arms around him, as if determined to hold on to him every moment that she possibly could, and some of Jean's happiness turned to worry. Johnny had written to say that Sue wanted to get married while he was home on furlough. Jean had mailed a quick letter back to her brother on the same day.

We're going to college after the war, remember? she had written. *You'll have plenty of time to get married after we graduate and get jobs.* She hoped he had heeded her advice. But before she could ask, Sue flung out her left hand to display the tiny diamond ring on her finger.

"Look what Johnny gave me. We got engaged last night." Sue's eyes shone with happy tears.

"Congratulations," Jean said. "Have you set a date?" She hoped she sounded more enthusiastic than she felt.

Sue looked up at Johnny. "Not until after the war. Right, Sweetie?"

"That's right. We gotta take care of Hitler first." They gazed at each other with so much love in their eyes that Jean was astounded to discover that she was jealous.

"Okay, let's get going," Russ said. He picked up Jean's suitcase with one hand and wrapped his other arm around her waist as they walked to his truck. Jean loved the warm, solid feeling of having Russ beside her, the smell of sunshine and fresh air on his wool coat. Johnny fell into step with them, taking Jean's other arm, and the world felt right again.

"We'll see you back at the house, okay?" Johnny said when they reached the parking lot. "Dad loaned me his car."

Jean watched him climb into it and drive away with Sue and wondered why she didn't feel happy for them. Instead, she felt betrayed by Johnny for getting engaged.

"Hey, there . . . Remember me?" Russ suddenly asked. She turned to him and he bent to kiss her again before helping her into his truck.

"Boy, I thought I'd never get here," she told him as he started the engine. "I don't know how you ever fit in those bus seats, Russ. I felt squished, and you're even taller than I am." The town flashed by, unchanged, as they drove down Main Street. Funny, but it no longer felt like home to Jean.

"Don't go back to Stockton, Jean. Stay here," Russ said.

She looked at him in surprise. "What about all my clothes and things?"

"Your sister can mail them home to you."

"I can't just quit my job," she said with an uneasy laugh.

Russ brushed a strand of her fair hair away from her face as he paused at the town's only stop sign. "Why not? I was hoping you already had quit. Haven't we been talking about it in our letters for months and months now?"

"I need to land another job first before I quit this one."

"Well, then I've got great news," he told her, downshifting into

first gear. "I talked to one of the managers at the old furniture factory here in town, and they're hiring new workers. He's going to be
in his office today if you want to fill out an application. I thought
we could go there first thing."

Jean felt a prickle of irritation as he turned the truck in that
direction. She didn't like to be pressured. "Can't I go home and see
my family first?"

"The guy will only be in his office until three o'clock—and it's
after two now. Besides, why waste gas driving all the way out to your
farm and back again?"

"Oh, all right," she said with a sigh. "I guess we may as well go
there first." She didn't want to be difficult, and besides, the factory
was here in town.

The dreary brick structure looked like something from the nine-
teenth century instead of the twentieth. They entered through the
front door, and Jean glimpsed rows and rows of sewing machines on
the factory floor. It wasn't nearly as noisy as the shipyard—or as
exciting.

"Did you say they make parachutes now?" she asked Russ. He
nodded. "Then I don't suppose they'll have much use for trained
electricians." They made their way to the manager's office and asked
for an application form. Russ waited patiently, jingling the truck
keys, while Jean filled it out.

"We have several openings for seamstresses," the manager told
her as he looked over her application. "I see you already have factory
experience—that's good—even if it's not behind a sewing machine.
The job is yours if you want it. When can you start?"

"Monday morning," Russ said. Jean made a face at him.

"I'll let you know," she told the man. "Thank you."

"I don't understand why you're hesitating," Russ said as they
returned to his truck.

"I need to figure out a few things first—like when I can move
home and how I'll get back and forth to work every day. You know
how far out of town my parents live. It's not like I can hop on a bus
to work."

"It sounds to me like you're looking for excuses."

"I'm not. But one thing you need to learn about me is that I like to take my time making decisions."

He shrugged in response.

The flat, barren farmland lay frozen beneath a layer of snow as they drove out of town to Jean's parents' farm. After living in Stockton for the past nine months, she had forgotten how much she loved the open spaces and vast stretches of sky. She could see her father's barn and the jumbled outbuildings surrounding the house from a quarter of a mile away.

Then she was home again, snug in the farmhouse kitchen with its aroma of woodsmoke and bread dough, enveloped in her mother's sturdy arms. "Welcome home, Jeannie!"

"I've missed you, Ma."

"You look beautiful, honey. So grown-up. Have you done something different with your hair?"

"I got a new haircut. Do you like it? Rosa, a girl from work, has been giving me advice."

"You look like a film star."

Jean's father and three of her younger brothers tromped in from the barn to greet her, carrying the wonderful fragrance of cows and hay.

"Boots off, fellows," Jean's mother ordered. The shoes thumped onto the floor into an untidy pile, and the kitchen quickly became an ant colony of activity with laughter and hugs and greetings.

Jean's father looked older than she remembered, and tired. He probably missed his older sons' help on the farm. He sat down at the kitchen table, and Ma sliced into a freshly baked crumb cake and poured coffee.

"So what's the latest news of my vagabond brothers?" Jean asked.

"Never thought I'd have sons traveling all over the world," her father said proudly. "One in New Guinea, another roaming around somewhere in the South Pacific, Peter's still in Iceland, and now Johnny's heading off to England. Who would have thought?"

An hour flew past as Jean talked and laughed with her family.

Then she noticed that Russell was growing restless, rising from his place at the table to pace near the door.

"What's the matter?" she asked him. "You look like you're late for an appointment."

"I want to show you something before it gets dark. Can I steal her away for a while, Mrs. Erickson?"

"Sure, go ahead," Ma urged. "You young people need some time to yourselves."

Russ drove Jean toward his father's farm several miles away. But he bypassed the brick farmhouse and parked his truck along the side of the road a quarter of a mile down the lane. They climbed out and crunched through the crusty snow to a little island of woodland surrounded by cornfields. It was on one of the very few hills in this part of Indiana. When they stopped walking, Jean savored the frozen winter silence that fell all around them.

Russell took Jean into his arms and kissed her, then said, "This piece of land is mine. My father said I could build a house on it when we get married someday."

Jean's heart raced with happiness—and fear. "It's beautiful! I would love to live out here with you. But we're a little young to talk about marriage, don't you think?"

"Maybe. But someday we'll be ready. Tell me, which way do you want the front door to face?"

She laughed and kissed him again. "I don't know ... what do you think? Facing the sunset, maybe?"

"Mmm. That's a good idea. Then we can sit out on the front porch and admire it every night." He kissed her again, a long, lingering kiss that warmed Jean to her toes. "Now that you're moving back home," he murmured, "we can start planning our future. The war can't last forever, you know."

The ripple of fear returned. She hoped Russ wasn't going to propose. Jean wasn't ready to get engaged like Johnny and Sue. "Don't forget, I still have four years of college ahead of me," she said quickly. She saw a sudden flash of irritation in Russ's eyes. "What's wrong?"

"I thought maybe you'd given up on the idea of college by now."

"Why would I do that?"

"I don't see what you need college for. We're going to live on a farm. You always said you didn't want to be a teacher."

"I don't."

"Then why waste four years of your life?"

Waste? Jean drew a deep breath, searching for the words to explain how she felt. She couldn't find any. "We were so happy a minute ago, Russ. Let's not ruin the few hours we have together by hashing this out right now, okay? We'll have lots of time to talk about things like this if I move back home."

"*If* you move home?"

"You know what I mean. I need to think things through before I decide. Please, just give me a little time and some space to do that, okay?"

"Whatever you want, Jean." He took her hand as they walked back to his truck, but she could tell by his stiff shoulders and out-thrust chin that he was angry. Thankfully, Russ never stayed angry for very long. By the time they drove back to Jean's farm his good nature had returned. "See you later," he said as he left to help his father with the evening chores.

Johnny arrived home a few minutes later, and Jean spent the rest of the afternoon with him, reminiscing about their childhood and high school years, laughing about the pranks they'd played with their older brother Danny. Their younger brothers sprawled across the living room rug like puppies, listening to their stories as if it were a radio program.

"Not a day goes by that I don't think about all our brothers and worry about them," Jean said, turning serious. "Now I'll be even more worried with you off to war, too."

"Save your worries for Danny, not me," John said, laughing. "He was the one who was always falling out of trees and breaking an arm or a leg, remember?"

Jean nodded, but she couldn't manage a smile at the thought of

Johnny fighting a war. "Do you know when you'll be leaving?" she asked.

"We sail from New York next week. They say it takes ten or eleven days to cross over."

"You better watch out for German submarines," one of their younger brothers said somberly. "They like to sneak up and sink our ships, you know."

John ruffled his hair. "Okay, buddy. I'll be on the lookout."

Jean's stomach twisted at this grim reminder. She wondered if Johnny also felt unnerved by the danger, in spite of his calm facade. She longed to ask him, to talk candidly with him, but Ma called them to dinner and the moment passed as they were quickly caught up in the family maelstrom.

"So you'll be flying aerial missions over the continent?" their father asked as they sat down around the dinner table.

"Yep, that's what I signed up for. I told you when I enlisted that I wanted to bomb Hitler and the Nazis, remember?"

"From what I've read about them," their father said, "I've come to believe that this is much more than a political war—it's part of the age-old battle between good and evil."

"Satan has taken control of that man," Ma added as she passed Jean a bowl of mashed potatoes, "and he has to be stopped."

"I know," Johnny said. "I always wanted to do God's work, and I'm convinced that this is it. I don't want to think about what the world will be like if we lose."

"We won't lose," Ma said firmly. "Right is on our side."

"How does it feel to be playing such a huge part in history?" Jean asked him.

"You're doing your part, too, Jeannie, building ships."

"It doesn't seem like enough. I mean, I'm not risking my life or anything."

They were still seated at the table after dinner, talking about the war, when Russ returned from helping his father with the farm chores. "What are we doing tonight?" he asked them.

"Sue wants to go dancing at that new serviceman's club," John said.

"Yes, please, let's go," Jean said. She stood, taking Russ's hands. "You don't have to dance if you don't want to. We can just sit and talk or listen to the music. Please? I'd like to spend time with Johnny while I can."

"It's not because of the dancing," Russ said, making a face. "All the guys will be in uniform except me."

"Does that bother you?"

"I get tired of explaining to people that farmers are needed for the war effort, too. Soldiers have to eat, you know."

"I know, I know," Jean soothed. "But can't you just ignore them for one night? Please?"

He shook his head, refusing to budge, and Jean couldn't help wondering if Russ felt guilty, deep down, for not enlisting. How must it feel to watch his best friend go off to war, while he stayed home where it was safe? She thought of Earl Seaborn, so eager to do his part that he'd tried to enlist in three different states before being turned down each time.

"Okay, we'll go someplace else," Johnny said. Jean tried not to pout.

In the end, the four of them decided to sit around Sue's house in town, talking until well after midnight. Sunday, when Jean had to catch the bus back to Stockton, came much too soon.

"We haven't had enough time to talk, Ma," Jean complained as she ate breakfast with her mother on Sunday morning. Her suitcase was packed again and standing beside the door. "Russ will be here any minute to take me to church, then I have to go straight to the bus station."

"Maybe next time," Ma said. "Do you want me to fix you an egg to go with your pancakes?"

"No, thanks.... Ma, Russ wants me to move back home for good. I applied for a job as a seamstress at the old furniture factory yesterday. They already said they'd hire me."

Ma turned from the stove to face her. "You're always welcome home anytime, you know that. But are you sure that's what you should do?"

"I don't know. I really miss Russ when I'm in Stockton, and when we're together I don't ever want to leave him again. But I like my job at the shipyard. They've given me a lot of responsibility, and I've made new friends there." Jean shredded her pancake with her fork as she talked. "Most of all, I really enjoy my independence. I'd hate to give it up. But I don't think Russ understands that. I don't know . . . what do you think I should do?"

"You're asking the wrong person, Jeannie. You need to ask God. He has a plan for your life, you know, and that should be all that matters, not what I think or what Russell thinks or anyone else."

Ma opened the lid to the cast-iron cookstove and nudged the fire with a poker. She hefted the scuttle, and coal rattled noisily as she poured in more. Then she closed the lid again with a clang. The familiar sounds reminded Jean of her childhood and all the happy years she'd spent here. But as much as she loved being home again, she realized that she was a different person now, a grown woman, an independent woman, in charge of a crew of electricians at a shipyard. She wasn't sure she wanted to move back home.

"I did pray about what to do before I left here and moved to Stockton," she said, "and it seemed like God worked everything out for me to move away. I'm able to save a lot of money for college, plus I can help Patty out until Bill comes home."

"Has God told you something different now?"

"The only thing that's different is that I think I'm in love with Russ."

"That's wonderful, honey. If he loves you, then he'll want God's plan for your life, too. Excuse me a second. . . ." Ma walked to the bottom of the stairs and hollered, "Boys! If you don't get a move on, you'll be going to church hungry and in your pajamas!"

Jean smiled at her mother's familiar threat. None of her siblings had ever arrived at church in his pajamas, but one or two of the dawdlers had been forced to change into his clothes in the car. Ma returned to the kitchen and gave Jean her full attention again.

"I'm sorry. Go on."

"It surprised me that Johnny bought Sue an engagement ring," she said quietly.

"Why is that, honey?"

"Russ and I have been dating for the same length of time, but we're not ready for that kind of a commitment. Watching Sue and John together yesterday, I kept wondering if there's something wrong with me. How come I'm not in a hurry to get married and have babies like all the other girls my age?"

"Maybe you haven't fallen in love yet. Or maybe God has different plans for your life."

"It seems like the desire to go to college gets stronger over time instead of fading away. Johnny and I were planning to go to school together, but I don't understand how that's going to work if he's getting married."

"Did you ask him? You know, there comes a time when twins have to lead separate lives, honey."

Jean nodded, but she didn't like the idea. "Russ still doesn't understand why I want to go to college."

"Does Russell have dreams for his own future?"

"I don't know ... probably." Jean thought of the house that he was planning to build on the wooded hill.

"Would Russ want you to talk him out of fulfilling his dreams?"

"No ..."

"Then he owes you the same consideration. And I know you've been dreaming of college for a long time. At any rate, it sounds like you two have a lot of things to work out. It will be good practice if you do get married. The willingness to compromise, to put the other person's needs ahead of your own, is the foundation of a good marriage."

"We'll work it out. I love Russ, and I know he loves me."

Jean heard his truck tires crunching on the gravel driveway and stood to put her dishes in the kitchen sink. "This whole weekend went by much too fast, Ma. I spent more time sitting on buses than I did at home."

"I know, Jeannie. It went too fast for me, too." She drew Jean into her arms for a hug. "Letters aren't the ideal way to talk to each other, but I guess they'll have to do for now. You be sure to write and tell me what you decide about changing jobs."

Any other Sunday, the morning church service seemed to drag, but today it was over much too quickly. Jean said good-bye to her mother and father and brothers in the churchyard before climbing into the truck with Russ and Johnny to go to the bus station. They barely had enough time to say good-bye before Jean's bus arrived. Russ kissed her as if they would never see each other again.

"Please move back home, Jean," he whispered. "I miss you so much."

Jean remembered Rosa saying that she felt only half alive when she wasn't with the man she loved, and Jean thought she finally understood what Rosa meant. "Okay. I'll hand in my two weeks' notice at the shipyard on Monday."

Russ grinned. "I'll be waiting for you."

She exhaled, relieved that the decision had been made, and turned to her brother. "So. I guess it's time. It was worth the long trip to see you again. You're still my best friend, you know."

"Since the beginning," he replied.

She looked up at him, as tall and as blond as she was, and couldn't bring herself to say good-bye. It sounded so final.

"I hate this stupid war," she said.

"That's why I'm gonna go over there and end it."

"Would it do any good to tell you to be careful?" she asked. Tears choked her voice.

He laughed and pulled her into his arms for a hug. "See you later, Jeannie," he said softly, and Jean knew he didn't want to say good-bye, either.

"Yeah. See you later, Johnny."

On Monday morning, Jean crowded into Earl Seaborn's cubicle at work with the other crew chiefs for their monthly review meeting.

She had spent a restless night planning how she would break the news to Earl and to the women on her crew that she was resigning, yet she still wasn't sure what to say.

Earl began by reading a list of all the departments that had fallen behind during the past month, and he spent a few minutes encouraging the chiefs to do better. Then he congratulated the departments that had met or exceeded their quotas. Jean was thrilled to hear her crew named among the highest achievers. She was the only woman crew chief on the 7:00 A.M. to 3:00 P.M. shift, yet her all-women team had fulfilled their production quotas for two straight months. She knew she had a right to feel proud. Her elation lasted only a moment. Would she feel this glorious sense of accomplishment as a seamstress in the parachute factory? Why had she promised Russ that she would move home?

Jean had planned to give Earl her two weeks' notice as soon as the meeting ended, but he seemed so preoccupied with other matters that she decided to wait until after work to tell him. Besides, there wouldn't be as many people hovering around to overhear her, particularly Doug Sanders and the other men who habitually harassed her. If they learned she was quitting, they might accuse her of not being able to handle the pressure.

Rosa, Ginny, and Helen were waiting for Jean at their workstation. "I've got good news," she told them. "Our crew met all of our production goals for a second straight month!" As she listened to them cheering and congratulating one another, she felt like a traitor for deserting them.

"We'd better get to work," Helen said finally. "After all, we want to keep up the good work."

When the lunch break finally came, Rosa started talking first. "Hey, how'd the big date with your husband go?" she asked Ginny.

The joy that had filled Ginny's face a moment ago vanished. "It was a disaster. Harold is still *aloof*, and now we're more *estranged* than ever. I need to give my two weeks' notice," she said, turning to Jean. "I hate to do it, but I can't have Harold mad at me this way."

Jean opened her mouth to speak, ready to give Ginny a hundred reasons why she shouldn't give in to her husband's pressure, but the words died before she uttered one of them. Hadn't she been ready to do the very same thing? Russ had pressured her to quit, and they weren't even married yet. In the end, Helen Kimball was the one who spoke first.

"Before you offer your resignation, Ginny, there's something we need to discuss. Rosa's husband is getting a brief furlough next month before he gets shipped overseas, and I think we should help her go to the naval base in Virginia to see him."

Her request astounded Jean. Helen was the last person she would expect to show concern for Rosa. Ginny was the one who usually mothered everyone.

"Do you think we could all work extra hours or something," Helen continued, "so that Rosa could have some time off? Before you respond, let me quickly tell you that my cleaning woman, Thelma King, is a qualified electrician. She has a first-class electrician's diploma from a school in Detroit. She said that she already applied for a job here, but they didn't have any openings at the time. I wondered if we could get her to fill in for Rosa on a trial basis, and maybe she could be hired full time later on to replace Ginny if everything works out?"

"I'll have to talk to Earl—Mr. Seaborn—about all this," Jean replied. "And to Mr. Wire, of course. But I don't see why not." Jean would wait until Rosa returned before she resigned. But why did she feel such regret at the thought of leaving and of someone else taking her place? "Have your friend come in and fill out an application," she told Helen.

"She already filled out one. It should be on file. But I'll tell her to fill out another one if you think it will help. And what about getting Rosa a leave of absence?"

"I want to help Rosa, too," Ginny added. "I'll be glad to work overtime or during lunch hour or anything else I have to do. That poor girl needs to go see her husband."

"I agree," Jean said. She could easily delay her own resignation for a few more weeks until Rosa came back. That would also give her time to train Thelma King. Jean had grown fond of Rosa and wanted to help her be with the man she loved. When she thought of Mr. Wire's son dying so young, she knew she would never forgive herself if something happened to Dirk Voorhees and she hadn't helped Rosa see him one last time.

"I'll talk to Mr. Seaborn right after work," Jean told them. "I promise to do everything in my power to get Rosa some time off."

"And I changed my mind about resigning," Ginny said. "I'm so happy for you, Rosa. I hope you get to go see Dirk and that you have a wonderful time."

After her shift ended, Jean waited in Mr. Seaborn's office to speak with him, but now it was for a different reason than she had intended this morning. Management didn't work shift hours, and when Earl finally arrived, almost an hour after Jean's quitting time, he looked tired and discouraged. She was glad she wasn't handing him her resignation.

"What's up, Jean? Sorry if I kept you waiting."

"Rosa's husband has finished his medical corpsman training and is being shipped overseas next month. Do you think we can help her get some time off to go see him?"

"It would have to be without pay."

"I don't think she cares about pay. And I might be able to get a temporary replacement for her. Helen knows a woman who already has an electrician's diploma. She might not need much training. Do you think we can get her to fill in for Rosa? Are they hiring new workers?"

"We always need skilled workers. What's her name? Have her come in and talk to Mr. Wire tomorrow. And I'll ask about the leave of absence, but it should be okay."

Jean felt happy for her friends as she began the long walk home; Ginny was staying, Rosa was going, and Helen's friend might be getting a job. Then she remembered that her own plans to resign had been postponed, and she knew she needed to write to Russ right away. Surely he would understand that Jean was needed here for another month.

I went to work this morning, she wrote in her letter that night, *intending to give my two weeks' notice, but I'm afraid there has been a change of plans. I need to help Rosa, one of my workers, go see her husband before he is shipped overseas. If I resign now it will affect production. I'm so sorry, Russ. I can't leave for at least another month. It would be irresponsible. Please have patience with me for a little while longer so I can help out my friend.*

At work the next day, Earl called Jean aside. "I went to bat for Rosa and got her some time off. But you'd better brace yourself for more harassment if you fall behind in your quotas. The two shifts that come after yours will have to pick up the slack, and some of those workers won't be too happy about it. Just so you know. I sure hope Rosa decides to come back to work once her husband ships out."

"What about Helen's friend? Can't she fill in for Rosa while she's away?"

"I talked to Mr. Wire about her. He said he'd look over her file. I guess Helen Kimball went to see him, too, and applied a little pressure."

Jean was so busy at work that a week went by before she realized that Russ had never answered the letter she'd written. At first she made excuses for him, blaming it on the post office or on too much farm work. But when two weeks passed without a letter from Russ, she could no longer fool herself. His silence had to be deliberate. He must be angry with her for not quitting immediately and coming home. She thought she understood how Ginny Mitchell felt, working against her husband's wishes and becoming *estranged,* as Ginny put it.

The night before Rosa's last day of work, Jean fled to her room after supper to write yet another pleading letter to Russ, begging him to understand, to have patience. She pictured the little grove of trees on the hill where he wanted to build a house for her, and she couldn't stop her tears. *"If he loves you,"* her mother had said, *"then he'll want God's will for your life."* Jean knew that helping Rosa see her husband had been the right thing to do. If only she could convince Russ to see it that way, too. Tears splotched the writing paper as she searched for the right words to convince him.

Above the ruckus that her nephews were making downstairs, Jean heard someone knocking on the front door. She held her breath as Patty answered it, always afraid it would be a dreaded telegram about Bill. A moment later Patty called to her.

"Jean? Someone's here to see you."

Jean had the wild thought that it was Russ, coming in person to hog-tie her and carry her home to Indiana. She jumped up and went to the dresser mirror, dismayed by how disheveled she looked. She quickly combed her fingers through her hair, but there was nothing she could do about her red, swollen eyes. She tucked in her blouse and hurried downstairs. Earl Seaborn stood near the door. Jean didn't know if she was disappointed or relieved that it wasn't Russ.

"Did I come at a bad time, Jean? Are you all right?" He eyed her teary face with concern.

"Yeah. I'm fine . . . it's nothing."

"You sure?" She nodded. "Listen, Jean, I thought I'd better come over and tell you this news tonight before you found out at work tomorrow."

"Oh no. Please don't tell me that Rosa's leave of absence fell through."

"No, it's about Helen Kimball's friend—Thelma King." Jean felt a surge of relief. "She has been hired to work at the shipyard, probably because Helen Kimball applied pressure. But she won't be working in your department and I think I know why. Were you aware that Thelma King is a Negro?"

"What? No . . . what difference does that make?"

"I'm so furious about this that I . . . I can hardly talk about it without raising my voice and throwing things. They gave Thelma King a job in maintenance. *Maintenance,* Jean! I found out that she really does have an electrician's diploma from a trade school in Detroit—I saw it in her file when Mr. Wire stepped out of the room for a moment. The only reason I can think of why she wasn't hired for your crew is because she's a Negro. All of the electricians and other skilled workers at the shipyard are Caucasian; all of the maintenance workers are Negro."

"Earl, that's terrible! I can't believe it!"

"I don't want to believe it, either. I really like Mr. Wire. I don't know if this decision came from him or from someone higher up. But no matter where it came from, it stinks! I just thought you should know."

"Have you told Helen Kimball?"

"Not yet—because I really don't have any proof that it is a racial thing. I wasn't supposed to see Thelma's file. Technically speaking, there isn't an opening for an electrician on your crew because Rosa is coming back. And I'm afraid if I make a fuss, Thelma King will lose her new job in maintenance. She says she's thrilled to be working in any department. They promised her that she might be able to work her way up."

"But you don't believe it?"

"I'll be watching to see what happens when there is an opening for an electrician."

"Are you going to fight for her?"

"You bet I am! This isn't right, Jean. I know how it feels to be discriminated against. But at least my handicap is a physical one. The only 'handicap' Thelma King has is the color of her skin. You bet I'll fight for her!"

"I admire you for that."

"Sorry. I guess I got a little carried away. Thanks for letting me get it off my chest—I'll see you tomorrow."

"Earl, wait," she said as he turned toward the door. "Would you like to stay awhile? Have a soda or something?"

The frown left his face for the first time since he'd arrived. He smiled faintly. "Yeah, that would be great."

CHAPTER 20
March 1943

"The U.S. government announced that meat rationing will begin this week."

★ *Rosa* ★

Rosa watched through the window as the train crawled out of Stockton, and she wondered how she would ever sit still all the way to Virginia. She was so excited she wanted to crawl out of her skin! She told herself to be patient, that she had a long journey ahead of her, but it was hard to stay calm when Dirk was waiting for her at the end of the trip. Dirk! She would finally hold him in her arms again and never ever stop kissing him. How could she help being excited?

It seemed like she'd already spent a hundred years waiting in the Stockton train depot for the trip to begin. Dirk's parents had insisted on driving her to the station—with plenty of time to spare, of course. Mr. Voorhees always had to arrive at every function at least an hour or two early. He nearly wore out the platform once they got there, pacing up and down, looking at his watch a hundred times until the train finally arrived.

Neither of Dirk's parents had seemed happy for her when she'd told them she was going to Virginia for Dirk's furlough. Mr. Voorhees got all grumpy and agitated, as if he didn't like the idea of them being together. *"Too bad,"* she wanted to say. *"We're married and there's nothing you can do about it."* Mrs. Voorhees seemed embarrassed by the idea of a second honeymoon. That's why it had surprised Rosa when they offered to take her to the train station in downtown Stockton. They'd surprised her even more by waiting with her until the train arrived. Tena had packed a hamper for Rosa with enough food to feed everybody on the entire train.

"Please, give my love to Dirk," Tena whispered as she hugged Rosa good-bye.

"I will," she promised. But she had a whole bunch of her own love to give him first.

Eventually the train picked up speed and steamed into South Bend, Indiana, a few hours later. Rosa switched trains to catch the "Lakeshore Special," which headed across northern Indiana and Ohio to Buffalo, New York, then journeyed across New York State during the night to Albany. There she changed trains again, going south to New York City. With only an hour layover in Grand Central Station, she didn't have enough time to visit her mother. Instead, she changed to a third train headed south to Philadelphia and Washington and eventually to Norfolk, Virginia, where Dirk was stationed.

Every time the train chugged into a station, Rosa saw crowds of people greeting one another or bidding each other a tearful good-bye. Soldiers were always granted boarding preference, and the other passengers had to squeeze in around them in the remaining seats. She always chose one beside a woman, if she could. Dozens of men in uniform tried to flirt with Rosa, but she refused to give them the time of day.

"I'm a happily married woman," she informed them, "on my way to see my husband."

Along with sailors and soldiers, hundreds of women crowded the stations, trying to reunite with their husbands. Rosa talked to several of them on the long trip and learned that some, like her, were visiting their husbands at their military bases. Others had been living close to a base to be near their husbands and were now returning home after the men had been sent overseas. The whole world seemed to have been turned upside down and shaken hard, with people cruelly torn away from their loved ones. Rosa wondered how long until it would all be over and life returned to normal.

By the time the train neared Dirk's base, Rosa felt tired and wrinkled and grubby from sleeping on train seats for two straight nights. The tiny washroom in the coach was filthy from overuse, but she took her time primping and applying her makeup and perfume, wanting to look and smell her very best when she saw Dirk.

Rosa's heart speeded up as the train finally pulled into his station. She yanked the window open, braving the cool March air to hang out of it and scan the mobbed platform. Even in a sea of uniforms, Dirk was easy to spot, so tall and fair-haired and handsome in his uniform.

"Dirk!" she yelled. "Dirk, over here!" At first he didn't hear her above the noise, so she put her fingers in her teeth and whistled. He turned his head at the sound and his face lit with joy.

"Rosa!" He dodged between people, running toward the train, jogging alongside it until it finally halted.

Rosa wished she could shove her suitcase out the window and climb out behind it, but she waded into the crowded aisle, hefting her suitcase and the food hamper, and pushed her way forward. She was so impatient to get off that she wanted to knock all the people down and climb over them to get to Dirk.

At last she reached the door and leaped down from the train and into his arms, dropping her baggage to the ground. Dirk hugged her so tightly she thought she might pop open. It felt wonderful—wonderful! The crowd buffeted them as they stood on the platform kissing, but she didn't care. She was back in his arms and that was all that mattered.

"Hey, don't cry, beautiful lady," he said when he finally looked into her eyes.

"I can't help it! I love you so much, Dirk! Let's get out of here and go to the hotel."

"Honey, you read my mind," he said with a grin.

Oh, how she loved his smile and the way it made his eyes crinkle—she loved everything about him! She clung to him as he picked up her suitcase and the basket of food and led her out of the station to the street. She didn't intend to let go of him for three whole days.

"I started looking for a hotel room as soon as you wrote and told me you were coming," he said as they walked. "That's when I found out that every hotel and rooming house within miles of the naval base is filled to capacity. I've been working night and day, begging everybody I met, trying to find us a place to stay. Finally, one of the ensigns had mercy on me and told me about a family who sometimes rents out a spare room in their house. It's not very fancy, and you'll have to share the family bathroom . . ."

"I don't care! Can you stay, or will you have to go back to the base at night?"

"I'm staying with you, honey. I have a three-day furlough. We can be together night and day for the next seventy-two hours."

"I'm not letting you out of my sight for one minute of that time. I might even stay awake all night so I can keep looking at you."

"Oh, Rosa . . ." He pulled her into his arms again and kissed her. Neither of them cared that they were standing in the middle of the sidewalk alongside a busy street.

"Let's splurge on a taxi," Dirk said when he came up for air. "A bus will take too long."

Rosa put her fingers in her teeth and whistled for one, too impatient to politely flag one down. She loved him so much she could hardly breathe.

They went straight to their rented room, and for the first twenty-four hours they never left it. If someone had asked Rosa what the room had looked like she couldn't have described it. They foraged for food in Tena's basket whenever they got hungry but finally had to leave when the food ran out. They walked a few blocks to a cozy Italian restaurant on the boardwalk that their landlady had recommended and sat side-by-side in a dark booth with a candle on the table. They ordered Chianti and spaghetti.

"I want to hear all about your work, Dirk. Tell me what you learned to do in corpsman school—unless it's too gory." He laughed and kissed her.

"A corpsman usually helps the ship's doctor. But there aren't always enough doctors to go around, so a smaller ship might have just a corpsman. If we get into a combat situation, I'll be giving basic first aid—applying compress bandages and splints, disinfecting with sulfa powder, injecting morphine, and so on. We try to stabilize the patients until they can get to a surgeon onboard a hospital ship."

"Will you see wounded men who are all bloody and banged up?"

"If I'm assigned to a war zone, I will. We're taught emergency measures—how to stop the bleeding and deal with shock and trauma. But don't worry, Rosa, battles aren't fought every day. In between times, I'll be doing a lot of routine stuff, like handing out headache pills and dealing with seasickness. I've also learned how to take care of guys who've had too good of a time on shore leave."

"Do you like your job?"

"Yeah, I do. I've learned a lot of interesting things."

They hadn't talked about Rosa's job, and she was afraid to mention it, afraid he might want her to quit the way Ginny's husband and Jean's boyfriend were always nagging them to do. But the need to know finally outweighed her fear.

"Can I ask you something, Dirk?"

"Sure, honey."

"I like my job at the shipyard a lot, but your father said that if you told me to quit he would expect me to obey you. And your mother said you were a lot like him—" She stopped when Dirk laughed out loud. "What's so funny?"

"Rosa, honey, I may be a lot like my father in some ways, but I don't think I would ever dare tell you what to do."

She slammed down her water glass with a bang. "What's that supposed to mean?"

Dirk gently rested his hand on top of hers. "It means that one of the reasons I fell in love with you was because of your fiery Italian temperament. Why would I ever want to change you?"

"But I can't cook like your mother—in fact, I can't cook at all. And I can't clean house the way she does, either, or bake bread."

He laughed again and pulled her close, holding her head against his shoulder. "If I wanted all of those things I'd live at home for the rest of my life and never get married. I want *you*, Rosa."

"It's just that . . . I never had a home like yours. I don't know how—"

"I know you didn't, honey. You told me all about it when we first met. That's my gift to you—to be the kind of husband who works hard so you can have the home you deserve. I love you more than I ever imagined I could love someone, Rosa. Just return that love. That's all I'll ever ask from you."

She couldn't imagine a love like that, couldn't imagine that someone would want to give so much and ask only for her love in return. She felt another wave of guilt for going to bars, laughing with other men, dancing with them and getting drunk. Dirk's father was right: If she loved Dirk, she wouldn't do all of those things. As she held Dirk in her arms, Rosa silently vowed to change, to be the kind of wife he deserved. She sniffed as her tears fell, and Dirk held her away from him for a moment to look into her eyes.

"What's wrong, Rosa?"

"I want it all so bad, Dirk! I never cared about much of anything before. I just lived day by day, I guess you could say. But I know what I want now—you, our life together. And I'm so afraid!"

"Our lives are in God's hands. All we can do is pray."

Rosa gazed at him in astonishment. They were the same words his father had spoken. "I don't remember you talking about God when we first met back in Brooklyn."

"Didn't I? I guess I had too many other things on my mind." He began kissing her neck, sending chills all over her. "We'll have a lifetime to get to know each other, honey."

"Can I ask you something else?"

"Umm-hmm," he murmured.

"I been going to church with your mother and father, and I was wondering . . . Is all that stuff as important to you as it is to them?"

He stopped kissing her and sat back, thinking before he answered. "That's a good question. It is important to me—but in a different way than it is for them, I think. They took me to church all my life, and I do believe everything the Bible teaches. I know Jesus

died for my sins. But it has always seemed like my parents' religion—
you know what I mean? Once I got away from home and started
seeing new things and meeting all kinds of people, I had to grow up
and take a good look at my Sunday school faith for the first time. I
guess I had to decide if it's important to me or not—and I've discovered that it is. I admit it scares me to think about being shipped
overseas. They say there aren't any atheists in foxholes. I know I'll
keep praying—and I hope you'll be praying, too. I meant it when I
said that our lives are in God's hands."

"I'll keep going to church with your folks if you want me to."

He traced his finger down her cheek. "Only if you want to go,
Rosa, not because anyone is making you. Your faith has to become
your own, just like my parents' faith had to become mine."

They left the restaurant and went to a dance at a serviceman's
club near the base. Rosa loved to dance—fast, slow, and everything
in between. But tonight she wanted every song to be a slow one so
she wouldn't have to leave Dirk's arms. He seemed so different compared to the other sailors and soldiers—fun-loving and a great dancer, but never rowdy or crude. He never used bad language around
her, like the men at the factory or the Hoot Owl did, but was always
a gentleman, pulling out her chair for her and opening doors. He
was also the most handsome man in the room.

She hadn't known Dirk very well when they'd eloped, but now
that she'd met his parents she could see things in him that she hadn't
noticed before. How he bowed his head to pray before he ate. How
he treated women and older people with respect. How clean and neat
he was, picking up after himself and never leaving a mess for her in
the bathroom.

Rosa felt so peaceful and calm when she was with him. It was
one of the things that had attracted her to him, but she hadn't
known how to put it into words when they'd met. She only knew
that she felt at rest when she was with him, as if Dirk had found the
key to the motor that had always run, nonstop, inside her and had
gently, firmly, shut it off. Maybe it was contentment. Rosa felt content.

During the day they walked along the beach, holding hands. The spring air felt cool, but they sat on the sand and snuggled beneath a blanket they'd borrowed from their room. Rosa had found what she'd longed for all her life, and she was terrified that she would lose it. She'd never thought about death before, but now it consumed her thoughts. She looked out at the huge ocean and shuddered to think that Dirk would be crossing it soon, going into danger, facing submarines and torpedoes and bombs and bullets.

"Are you too cold?" he asked when he felt her shiver.

"No, I'm scared, Dirk. I can't imagine you out there on that cold, deep water in a boat that the Nazis could try and sink."

"Tell you the truth, I can't, either. It seems so peaceful here on land."

"Do you know where you're going to be sent?" she asked. He nodded. "You do? Where? Why didn't you tell me sooner?"

He sighed. "I didn't want to talk about it because then it might start to seem real. I've been assigned to a marine battalion that's headed to the Pacific Theater. They're going to try to win back the Philippines and all the other little islands over there."

Rosa was silent for a long moment, trying to let his words sink in. "My friend Jean has two brothers in the Pacific, one in New Guinea and the other in the Solomon Islands. I guess you'll be helping them fight the Japanese, huh?"

"I guess so."

"Those battles seemed so far away whenever Jean talked about them, and I never paid much attention to the news—but I sure will now. When I'm building a ship I always imagine that I'm making it for you. I know that's silly, since I'm building landing craft for the army, not the navy or the marines. But all the men who'll use my ships are somebody's sweetheart, somebody's son or brother or husband. I want everything I do to be just perfect, so I try to do the very best job I can, every single day."

"I'm proud of you, Rosa. I can't imagine such a beautiful, feminine little gal like you doing a man's job like that, but I'm real proud of you." He held her tightly for a moment, then said, "You know what I noticed these past few days? You're even more beautiful than I remembered."

"That's about the hundredth time you told me that," she said, laughing. "You sound like a broken record."

"I meant it every time, too. I can't wait until this war is over and I can come home to you every single night."

"Maybe we can buy us a nice little house. I been saving all my money and most of yours—after I give some to your folks for room and board every month. Where do you want to live?"

"With you, honey. That's where."

They kissed for a while, but when Dirk pulled away and looked at her, Rosa could tell he was worried about something.

"Tell me," she said.

"When I trained in the hospital wards, I saw some of the men who'd been sent home already—the casualties. So many of them had horrible wounds, Rosa—arms and legs missing, terrible burns ... I think I'd rather die quickly than come home to you like that."

"Dirk Voorhees, don't you *dare* talk that way!" She punched his arm as hard as she could. "I don't care how many arms and legs you got, I don't want to live without you!" A wave of emotion overpowered her and she broke down and cried in his arms, harder than she had in years. He held her, soothed her.

"Do you really think you could still love me if I wasn't all in one piece?"

"That's a stupid, stupid question! How could you even ask a question like that? Just come home to me, Dirk. *Promise* me that you'll come home!" Their eyes met. He had tears in his, too.

"I promise," he said solemnly.

Much too soon, Rosa had to leave him again. Dirk rode with her to the train station and they stood together on the platform, holding each other until her train arrived.

"I was hoping it would be too full and I wouldn't be able to get a ticket," she said. "Then I could have a little more time with you."

"Not much more, I'm afraid. I have to report back to the base in . . ." He looked at his watch. "In exactly three hours and forty-two minutes."

"I'll take whatever time with you I can get."

He went onboard with her to carry her suitcase and the basket, stowing them in the luggage rack for her. Dirk was so tall he had to duck his head to keep from hitting it on the doorframe. When he turned to take her into his arms, Rosa knew they had finally run out of time. They stood in the crowded aisle, hugging for as long as they could.

"All aboard," the conductor shouted.

"I don't want you to go to war!" she wept. "I'm so scared!"

"I'll be back, Rosa. I promised you I'd come back, remember? Wait for me."

He kissed her one last time, then ran down the aisle and jumped off the train as it began to move. Rosa hung out of the window, reaching for him. Dirk grabbed her hand and jogged alongside for as long as he could, their fingers clutching.

"I love you, Rosa! I love you. . . ."

Then she could no longer hang on to him as the train steamed off into the night.

CHAPTER 21

★ *Virginia* ★

Ginny walked through the back door after work so exhausted she could have lain down on the floor beside Rex and fallen asleep. The week had been a long one with Rosa away. Ginny and the others had worked through lunch hour every day, trying to meet their work quotas. Now she dreaded all the chores that awaited her at home, but at least she wouldn't have to cook an elaborate supper tonight; Harold was away in Washington all week. Good thing, too, because the government had begun rationing meat this month, and Ginny didn't have the time or energy to wait in a long line to buy her allotted amount. She and the boys would be content with tomato soup and toasted cheese sandwiches. Speaking of the boys, the house seemed unnaturally quiet.

"Hello . . . I'm home," she called. Rex was waiting near the door to greet her, panting happily, his hindquarters wagging along with his tail. But aside from the sound of the dog's toenails dancing on the linoleum, the house was silent.

She usually found the boys sitting at the kitchen table when she arrived home or else listening to the radio in the living room. She walked down the hall to the bottom of the stairs and called again.

"Anybody home? Allan? Herbie?"

No reply.

She returned to the kitchen and gazed out the window into the backyard. The shed door stood open. That's probably where they were. She stuck her head out the back door to call to them, and Rex shot past her, bounding into the yard to do his business. He acted as if he'd been waiting a long time. The boys knew they were supposed to let him out as soon as they got home. Had they forgotten?

She went outside to search for them, but they weren't in the shed. The wagon was missing, and the usually tidy shed appeared as though someone had been rooting around inside it. Maybe the boys had gone door-to-door in the neighborhood to gather newspapers. It was one of their projects for the Boy Scouts, but they were supposed to wait until she got home. They had been involved in a lot of projects with their scout troop, collecting scrap metal and tin cans, used rubber items, and household fat. Allan could recite all the statistics: "One shovel has enough metal in it to make four hand grenades," he would tell their neighbors. "And one pound of fat drippings makes one pound of black powder for bullets. Old nylon and silk stockings can be turned into parachutes and tow ropes for gliders. . . ." And on and on he would go, just like a radio commercial.

Ginny had assigned the boys more chores to do around the house, too, such as drying the dishes, taking out the garbage, and running errands to the store for milk or bread. She had handed her sons a lot of responsibility since taking the job at the shipyard, but never before had they gone off without asking her permission. She stood in the middle of the yard, trying to decide where they could be. Something about the kitchen hadn't looked quite right. They knew they were supposed to clean up their breakfast dishes before going to school, but their dirty cereal bowls and juice glasses still had been on the table.

She hurried back inside and noticed that the usual pile of coats and schoolbags was missing from the back entryway. So were their lunchboxes. Allan and Herbie were supposed to empty them out after school and put them in the sink.

Where could the boys have disappeared to? This was the first time she had ever come home from work and not found them here.

Ginny felt her anxiety level rising, but she told herself to stay calm. Maybe they had gone next door to the Parkers' house. She hurried across the yard and knocked on their back door. Betty answered it.

"Hello, Virginia. What brings you here?"

Ginny drew a deep breath, trying not to look as fearful as she felt. "Hi, I was wondering if my boys are over here?"

"No. Why? Are they missing?" Ginny recalled Betty's words at the cocktail party about irresponsible mothers gallivanting off and abandoning their children and knew she was blushing.

"So it seems. Do you think Tommy might know where they are?"

"Tommy . . ." Betty called. "Have you seen the Mitchell boys this afternoon?"

Tommy walked into the kitchen, shaking his head. "Allan wasn't in school today. I figured he was sick."

Ginny went cold all over. *Not in school?* Both boys had been fine when Ginny left for work this morning. Now she was the one who felt sick.

"Is there anything I can do?" Betty asked.

Ginny forced herself to smile. "No, thanks. I'm sure they can't be far."

Ginny wasn't sure at all. She fought panic as her imagination ran wild. The town had grown so quickly since the war started, with all sorts of strange people moving here. Could someone have abducted the boys on their way to school? The thought made her queasy.

Of all the times for Harold to be out of town. Ginny didn't know what to do. She hurried back home and searched the house, checking their bedrooms to see if they'd left a note for her. She didn't find one. Her heart had begun to race the moment Tommy Parker said Allan hadn't gone to school, and it couldn't seem to stop. What should she do? Who could she call?

She suddenly thought of Helen Kimball. Helen had years of experience with children. Maybe she would know where to look. Ginny's hands shook as she dialed Helen's phone number. Her voice shook, too, as she explained that her sons were missing.

"What should I do?" she asked. "Should I call the police? The hospital?"

"I don't think you need to panic," Helen said calmly. "Young boys have played hooky since schools were invented. They usually show up safe and sound eventually. But I can understand why you're worried. Listen, would you like me to drive around and see if I can find them?"

"Oh yes. Please. I don't have a car and Harold is out of town."

"Did you try calling Jean's sister? Doesn't she baby-sit for them sometimes?"

"That's a great idea. Thank you."

But the boys weren't at Patty's house, either. "Do you have any idea where they could be?" she asked Patty. "Did they ever say anything to you that might give a hint where they'd go?"

"I can't think of anything, but I'll get out the baby carriage and have a look around the neighborhood and the park. Jean can run down to the drugstore. They liked to go there for ice cream and *Superman* comics. Maybe someone has seen them."

Ginny hung up the phone, then paced the hallway, trying not to panic. She couldn't believe that Allan and Herbert would deliberately skip school. Where on earth could they be? She decided to call the school to see if their teachers could offer her any advice.

"We've been trying to phone you all day," the school secretary said after Ginny identified herself. "No one was home. You're supposed to call the office if your children are ill."

"Yes, I know. I . . . I'm calling to explain that my sons are missing. I always leave for work in the morning before they leave for school, and . . . and it has never been a problem before . . . I mean, for all the months that I've been working. B-but when I got home today they were gone."

"Well, neither Allan nor Herbert came to school. I'll have to report them as truants. It will be an unexcused absence on their permanent record."

"I don't care about that! Didn't you hear what I said? Aren't you concerned that they're missing?"

"Perhaps you should phone the police, Mrs. Mitchell, instead of the school."

The police? She couldn't seem to catch her breath. Ginny saw Helen Kimball's car pulling into the driveway as she hung up the phone and ran to open the front door for her.

"Oh, I'm so glad to see you!" Ginny couldn't help hugging her. "I . . . I just don't know what to do!"

"I had an idea on the way over here. Who is Allan's best friend?"

"Tommy Parker. He lives next door. He said he hasn't seen Allan all day."

"Best friends usually know a lot more than they let on. They promise each other, you see. Swear each other to secrecy and so on. Let's go see if he knows something he isn't telling."

"Will you talk to Tommy and his mother for me?" Ginny asked as she led Helen across the yard to the Parker house. "I'm so intimidated by Betty. She turns up her nose at my job, and she practically came right out and told me once that I was an unfit mother for abandoning the boys and going to work. I'm sure she thinks this is what I deserve."

"What utter nonsense!" Helen charged up the porch steps and knocked on the door. Betty looked quite surprised when she opened it and saw Helen.

"Miss Kimball? What are you—?"

"I'm helping Ginny find her boys. She and I work together at the shipyard."

"*You* work there?"

"You sound surprised. Why is that?"

Betty began to sputter, taken aback by Helen's question. "Well, I don't know . . . I . . . I mean . . ."

"Because I'm old? Or because I'm a Kimball? Or is it because you think I'm too well-educated to work in a place like that?"

"No, no, I didn't mean to imply—"

"The reason I work there, Mrs. Parker, is because our nation is at war, and I felt it was my patriotic duty to do my part. But this is hardly the time or the place for this discussion. I wonder if I might speak with Tommy?"

"Yes, of course. Please, come in.... Tommy!" she called. He looked frightened when he saw Helen.

"Could I have a word with you, please, Tommy?" She drew him aside, leaving Ginny and Betty alone.

"I know you think I'm a terrible mother, Betty, but I love my boys—" Betty started to interrupt but Ginny quickly said, "No, just let me clear up a few things. I went to work because I wanted to, not because we needed the money, not because of any problems between Harold and me, not for any other reason than to help win the war. I know everyone's gossiping about me behind my back. I used to hear the ladies gossiping all the time when I was a club member, and I got tired of all that. So I went to work, and I met Helen and two other really wonderful women there. Building ships isn't something I want to do for the rest of my life, but if it will help bring an end to the war, then I'm willing to sacrifice my time. I'm telling you this, Betty, so you can tell all the other ladies. When you wag on and on tomorrow about how unfit I am and how I lost my sons, be sure to tell them that I'm also an accomplished electrician now."

"You've changed, Ginny."

"I know. The old Ginny never would have had the courage to tell you this to your face, would she?"

Before Betty could reply, Helen returned with Tommy. He looked more subdued than Ginny had ever seen him.

"Tommy has agreed to come with us—if that's all right with you, Mrs. Parker. He's going to show us where he and Allan and Herbert have been constructing a fort down by the river."

"Tommy isn't allowed down by the river," Betty said. "He wouldn't—"

"Perhaps you could discuss that with him when we return," Helen interrupted. "But for now, it seems that he *has* been going down to the river and that he does *indeed* know where the boys might be. I'll drive him home when we're finished."

Tommy climbed into the front seat of Helen's car with Ginny

and pointed the way. They drove the few blocks to the river in silence.

"You can stop right here," he finally said. Helen parked the car near the curb, and Tommy led the way down into the ravine. Patches of snow still dotted the woods, and Ginny's feet sank into the soft, muddy ground. She was glad she still wore her work shoes and coveralls. Tangled brush, faintly tinted with spring green, lay on either side of the narrow path.

Then, at the bottom of the riverbank, Ginny saw a mound of scrap lumber and tree branches. Beside it was the boys' wagon. And their lunchboxes.

"Allan? Herbert?" she called breathlessly. Herbie stuck his head out of the hut, and Ginny's knees went weak with relief. "Oh, thank God!" she breathed. She turned and hugged Helen again, mostly to keep from fainting. "How can I ever thank you?"

"No need. I'll drive young Tommy home and return for you."

"Thank you, Helen. Thank you so much!"

Helen turned Tommy around and they began climbing back up the path as Ginny descended the rest of the way to the bottom on shaking legs. Both boys crawled out of the hut, looking worried as they watched Ginny pick her way down the ravine toward them. They exchanged nervous glances, then hung their heads, guilt written all over their faces. Ginny didn't know whether to yell at them or hug them when she finally reached them. She decided to do both at the same time.

"Do you have any idea how worried I was?" She squeezed Allan in a bear hug that made him grunt. "I've been frantic!"

"We were planning on getting back before you got home from work, but I guess we lost track of the time," he said.

Herbie looked conscience-stricken. He was trying not to cry. "Are we going to get a spanking?"

"Oh, you're in much worse trouble than a mere spanking. You played hooky from school!"

"Are you going to tell Dad?"

"Of course I am. I have to—you know that. Why did you do such a stupid thing?"

"Tommy Parker says that a bunch of Nazi soldiers are coming here to Stockton any day," Allan said. "We needed a hiding place, and we were running out of time so we had to skip school and finish our fort before they come."

"Those men are captured prisoners of war. They don't have any guns or weapons. Besides, they'll be in a prison camp way out by Stockton Lake, not here in town."

"What if they escape and come here?"

"They'll be very well-guarded, Allan. And if one ever does escape, the guards will track him down with dogs long before he reaches town."

"This is gonna be a bomb shelter, too," Herbie said.

"A bomb shelter! What do you need a bomb shelter for?"

"'Cause if the airplanes come and bomb our house, we'll need a safe place to hide."

"Herbie, nobody is going to bomb us. The war is thousands of miles from here."

"But they bombed Pearl Harbor," Allan said. "And they bombed London and all those other places. One of the newsreels showed how the Nazis always bomb factories that make stuff for the war."

"We made room for you to hide in here with us, Mom, in case they bomb your factory."

It astonished Ginny to learn that her bright, responsible sons had been so afraid of Nazi soldiers and enemy bombs that they had played hooky from school to try to protect themselves—and her. Why hadn't they shared their fears with her? The war had certainly turned her own life upside down, but she'd never realized how much it had upset theirs. She didn't know how to reassure them, but she had to try.

"I know that everything seems different from the way it was a year ago. I wish we didn't have to hear so much about the war every time we turn on the radio. I'm sorry if you've been worrying about it, but you should have talked to your father and me. We would gladly do whatever we could to—"

"Why do you have to leave us and go to work all the time?" Allan asked. "I wish you could be home again."

Ginny was speechless. Was that what their disappearing act was all about, a cry for her attention? Or was Allan cleverly manipulating Ginny, using her guilt to wiggle his way out of trouble?

"Start walking," she said. "Let's go. Up the bank."

Herbie led the way up the hill, and Allan followed behind Ginny with the wagon. Her knees still shook, making it difficult to climb the steep slope. She reached the top out of breath and waited beside the road for Helen to return with the car. What would she ever have done without Helen? Ginny would have had the police out searching by now while she was home having a nervous breakdown. Who knows how long it would have taken the police to find them?

"Let's put the wagon in the trunk," Helen said when she arrived.

"Would you mind doing me a favor?" Ginny asked her. "Could you drive us to the shipyard?"

Helen didn't question why but simply nodded. They drove across town, following the curving river road, and pulled into the factory's parking lot. Helen and Ginny still wore their identification badges, but Ginny didn't think they would need them. She led the boys around to the back of the parking lot where they could see one of the nearly completed ships inside the huge, open bay doors, waiting to be launched.

"That's one of the ships Miss Kimball and I worked on," she told them. "It's a landing craft that can go into shallow water and ferry soldiers from place to place. When it's finished, it might be used by the marines to help fight the Japanese in the Pacific Islands, or maybe it will carry soldiers to the European mainland to fight the Nazis when the time is right."

"It's big!" Herbie said.

"You made that, Mom?"

"Not all by myself. It takes hundreds of people, working all day and all night to build one. But Miss Kimball and I helped. I'm building ships so we can win the war. I'm doing this for you, so the Nazis and the Japanese won't ever come here to hurt us."

"Tommy Parker says that men are supposed to work in factories, not women. He says it's the dad's job."

"That was true before the war, but so many men went overseas to be soldiers that there aren't enough of them left to work in the factories. That's why I decided to work. If all the mothers stayed at home, who would make ships and tanks and guns? I'm not the only mother who is working, you know. There are a lot of others, too."

The boys stared at the ship as if awestruck. "I'll bet it's fun to make something like that," Allan finally said.

"It's hard work—but you're right, it's very satisfying. Your father's work is even more important than mine is. This is just one factory. He keeps dozens and dozens of factories running smoothly."

"Are you still going to tell him we played hooky?"

"Yes, Herbie. But I think you should tell him the reason why."

"Could I work here, too?" Allan asked. "I'd like to help."

"I'm afraid you're too young," Ginny said as she herded them back to Helen's car. "But I know something else you can do to help. It said in the newspaper that everybody on the home front should plant victory gardens this spring. If we all grow our own vegetables, then the food that the farmers grow can be sent overseas to our soldiers. Do you think we could do that?"

"Yeah. Sure."

Ginny thanked Helen once again when they reached home, but it would have taken an entire dictionary full of words to tell her how truly grateful she was.

"I'm glad I could help," Helen said simply.

Losing the boys had been the last straw, Ginny decided as she opened a can of soup for their dinner. It was bad enough having Harold upset with her, but now the boys were upset with her, too. She couldn't have her family in turmoil any longer. She would have to resign as soon as Rosa returned so things could return to normal here at home. It would be a relief not to have Harold angry with her anymore, but she felt sad at the thought of spending the long, lonely days at home again. She wouldn't go back to the women's club. Ginny supposed she could find something else to do, but she'd miss the satisfaction of seeing a completed ship. Housework was never finished.

"I know it has been hard on you with me working," she told the boys at dinner. "I don't ever want to lose you again, so I think I'd better resign from my job. I was going to quit a few weeks ago, but Rosa Voorhees needed some time off to see her husband before he was shipped overseas, so I decided to work for a little longer. But now, after today, I can see that I'm needed at home."

Allan stared down at his bowl, stirring his tomato soup in slow circles. She wondered what he was thinking. He surprised her when he finally looked up and said, "I don't want you to quit, Mom."

"Do you mean that?"

He nodded. He looked so much like his father when his expression was somber. "Who's going to build ships if you quit?" he asked. "I don't want to lose the war, because then the Nazis really will come here."

"What about you, Herbie? What do you think about me working?"

"I'll try not to be scared anymore when you're gone. I want you to make more ships, too."

She stood and went around the table to hug each one. "If you're really, really sure," she said, "then maybe I'll think about it some more before I resign."

CHAPTER 22

* *Helen* *

"And so Helen saved the day," Ginny said as she finished telling Rosa and Jean about her runaway sons. They sat around the lunch table, relaxing after a busy morning's work.

"I think you're exaggerating just a bit." Helen tried to brush the accolades aside, uncomfortable being cast as the heroine. "Your boys would have turned up eventually without my help."

"But not before I would have had a nervous breakdown," Ginny said. "You can't imagine how frightening it is to have your children go missing until it happens to you. The world suddenly seems so huge and dangerous—your children so small and vulnerable."

Helen sat back and opened her Thermos of soup, determined to quietly listen and not comment as she and the other women ate their lunches. The aroma of tuna fish drifted out as Ginny unwrapped her sandwich.

"Ever since this trouble with my boys," she said, "I've been try-ing to decide if I should resign. My entire family has been affected by my decision to work, and I feel so selfish for putting them through grief just so I can have my own way."

Helen noticed that Jean had been unusually quiet today. Her lunch sat untouched. She hadn't seemed her buoyant self for several days, but now she looked up at Ginny with a worried expression on her face.

"Could I ask a favor, Ginny? Could you please keep working for just a few more weeks until I can train someone else? Because after I train your replacement, I'll need to train someone to replace me."

"Replace *you*?" Ginny asked. Jean nodded, blinking back tears. "Oh, Jean, why?"

Jean leaned forward, speaking softly, as if unwilling to let the table full of men alongside them overhear. "I've been waiting until you got back, Rosa, so we wouldn't be shorthanded. But I need to move back to Indiana."

"You can't leave us!" Rosa said. "We need you!"

"You're wonderful at what you do," Helen said. "Why would you want to resign?"

Jean re-wrapped her uneaten sandwich and pushed it to one side. "When I went home to visit Russ, he had arranged for me to apply for a job at a factory in town. He wants us to be together so badly, so I told him that I would move back home. Then I found out about Rosa needing a leave of absence, so I wrote and told him I was staying another month until she got back."

"That was awful nice of you," Rosa said. "I'm sorry if I kept you away from the guy you love."

"That's just it," Jean said, her tears finally spilling over. "I'm not sure if Russ still loves me or not. He hasn't answered any of my letters since I wrote and told him I wasn't coming home right away. I think he's really, really mad at me."

"I know how that feels," Ginny murmured.

"Me too," Rosa added. "Not with Dirk but with his father. He sure can dish out the silent treatment when he's peeved."

"The only way I can make it up to Russ is to quit and go home. But I suppose Ginny wants to resign so she can patch things up with her husband, too. Maybe we should flip a coin to see which one of us gets to quit first."

"Now wait just a minute, Jean," Helen said. "I don't think you and Ginny should let other people manipulate you this way. I never had a husband or a boyfriend telling me what to do, but my father certainly did—even after I became an adult. He used anger and threats to control my life, and I was foolish enough to let him. I wanted to please him, just like you and Ginny want to please the men you love, but I ended up losing everything that was dear to me. You might be paying a very steep price for your compliance."

"But what if I lose Russ?" Jean asked.

"Good riddance! Don't you see that he's using emotional black-mail to get his own way? Ginny, your boys tugged on your heart-strings by running away. And your husband is manipulating you into quitting by withdrawing his affection. Now Jean's boyfriend is doing the same thing—refusing to answer her letters, refusing to concede to her very simple request to wait a few weeks so she could help Rosa. All of these men are going to pout and maneuver until they get their own way—and you think *you're* being selfish, Ginny? Rubbish!"

"But my household is in turmoil, and it was my decision to work that caused it."

"I don't believe that, either. Albert was right when he told me that people are responsible for their own choices. Harold and Russell are *choosing* to be miserable; you aren't causing it. There are plenty of other husbands, like Rosa's, for instance, who are very happy that their wives are helping out with the war effort."

"Who's Albert?" Ginny asked, looking confused.

"He's the guy Helen's father wanted her to marry," Rosa said before Helen could reply.

How had she allowed his name to slip out? Helen hated it when everyone knew the details of her personal life. Next thing you knew, one of them would ask why she'd never married him.

"It doesn't matter who Albert is," Helen said quickly. "The point is, he was right. We all know that our jobs are important to the war effort. We all know that we aren't acting selfishly by working here. If Russ and Harold and Ginny's two sons want to make themselves miserable over it, that's their choice, not yours."

"My mother said I should ask God what to do," Jean said. "Ma told me He has a plan for my life—but it's so hard to know what that is."

"Well, I'm certainly not about to speak for God," Helen said. "As far as I'm concerned, God derailed my plans as thoroughly as my father did." She sat back in her seat and crushed saltine crackers into her soup to signal that she was finished dispensing advice. But Jean wouldn't let her withdraw.

"Then what do you think I should do about Russ?" she asked. All of the women looked at Helen, waiting.

"Since Russ is the one who stopped writing," she found herself saying, "then he obviously should be the one who takes the next step and restores the lines of communication. If he chooses to break up with you simply because you helped a friend, then good riddance to him, Jean. You're obviously a much better person than he is. I wouldn't want to be married to him if that's how he behaves. But if you give in and go running home to him, then he'll do this sort of thing every time he wants his own way."

Jean stared at her as if this was a brand-new idea.

"My father manipulated and bullied everyone to get his own way," Helen continued. "In the business world and at home. I'm sorry I didn't have the wisdom to see it back when it might have made a difference in my life. I'd hate to see you and Ginny make the same mistake." She returned to her lunch, quickly downing the remainder of her soup, eager to end this conversation. She stowed the empty containers in her lunchbox and snapped it shut.

"Now, if you'll please excuse me," she said, rising from the bench, "I need to gather some more signatures for my petition before the lunch hour ends." She gazed around at the other tables, trying to decide where she had left off yesterday, then strode to the nearest table.

"Excuse me for interrupting your lunch, but might I have a moment of your time? Are you aware that the government has created a German prisoner of war camp just outside our community, near Stockton Lake? If you are, and if you're as outraged by it as I am, I'd like to ask you to consider signing this petition, demanding that the government remove these dangerous prisoners immediately."

Helen was able to gather a dozen more signatures before the lunch whistle blew, then a few dozen more from workers arriving for the evening shift. After work, she drove to the elementary school where she'd once taught to gather still more signatures. Oddly enough, the teachers she had worked with for so many years seemed like strangers to her and she to them. She had wanted it that way at the time, determined to avoid personal entanglements like the ones she was currently mixed up in at the factory. She had eaten lunch in her classroom every day and shunned the teachers' lounge during recess. Now the other teachers listened politely as she explained her petition, but her visit evoked no warm greetings or inquiries about when she might return to teaching.

By the end of the week, Helen counted over one thousand signatures. Surely that would impress the state officials. Before the war, a thousand names represented a sizable percentage of Stockton's population. She hurried home to change her clothes, then drove downtown to deliver the petitions to the mayor's office. He teetered on his chair as usual, his sleeves rolled up and tie askew. As he thumped his chair forward onto all four legs, Helen marveled that the two hind legs didn't break off beneath his weight.

"Well, Helen, I understand you're still determined to stop the internment camp," Archie said before she'd spoken a word. He smiled at her look of surprise. "I've heard all about those petitions you've been circulating all over town. My sister-in-law works at Lincoln School, you know."

"You've heard correctly. I've collected pages and pages of signatures—well over a thousand. Now, can we please do something about those disgusting Nazis?"

"The first batch of prisoners is already living out there, Helen."

"I don't care. They can pack up and leave just as easily as they came, can't they?"

"I suppose that's true.... Okay, then. I'll bring this issue up at the town board meeting later this week. The other members and I will draft a letter and send your petitions to the state. I'll call you when I get a response."

Helen waited two weeks. In the meantime, Ginny and Jean seemed to have heeded her advice, because neither one of them had resigned yet. Now that spring was here, the women spent every lunch hour talking about planting victory gardens.

"Mr. Voorhees already had a garden before the war," Rosa told them. "But he dug up even more of the yard and is making it even bigger. I hope he don't think that *I'm* gonna work in it."

"My sister wants to plant one, too," Jean said, "but I told her it's too much work. We were raised on a farm, and I've had my fill of hoeing and weeding."

"Well, I really wanted a victory garden," Ginny said. "I thought it would be a wonderful experience for the boys, but Harold didn't go for the idea. I still think I'd like to grow a few tomatoes, though. Are you going to have a garden, Helen?"

"I've been considering it."

"Have you seen her yard?" Rosa asked the others. "She could grow enough food to feed the whole town!"

Helen was at home one evening, gazing out at the backyard, wondering if she could get anyone to help her with a garden, when the mayor telephoned.

"We finally got a response, Helen. Someone from the state is going to come and talk to us about the internment camp this Saturday. They've invited you and me and all of the town board members out there to tour the facility. They'll try to answer our questions and concerns."

"You sound as though you don't think it will accomplish anything."

"You're right, I don't. I told you from the get-go that the decision had already been made and that my hands were tied. The camp is on state-owned land, outside the town limits."

"I'll be there on Saturday, Archie. Thanks for including me in the invitation."

"It's the least I could do after you collected all those signatures."

Helen arrived at the mayor's office on Saturday morning for the excursion to the internment camp, ready to do battle. She was the only woman. She knew all of the town board members who were going along, but she was surprised to see Mr. Wire from the shipyard. They parked their cars outside the barbed-wire enclosure and waited for an armed guard in a U.S. Army uniform to let them through the gate. The government had built guard towers overlooking the camp since the last time Helen had visited with Rosa, but otherwise, the place looked much the same.

Once inside, Helen felt her stomach turn in revulsion when she saw the Germans. Some three hundred prisoners milled around in the warm spring sunshine, clothed in blue uniforms with the letters PW stenciled on their backs and trousers. The men appeared so ordinary. Who would ever think that they had unleashed such horror on the world—twice! Two dozen of them worked to cultivate a square of land that looked as though it was going to be a garden. They turned over the earth with spades and used hoes to break up the clods.

"I'm surprised they're allowed to have hoes and shovels," Helen told the guard. "Things like that could be used as weapons."

"Our guns are loaded, ma'am." He lifted his rifle to emphasize his words, offering Helen a close-up look. The dark, satiny steel— or whatever it was made from—looked sinister to her. She couldn't imagine a gentle young man like Jimmy or Albert carrying one of those guns, much less firing it. Nor could she imagine boys like Dirk Voorhees and Larry Wire and all the others she had taught in school toting weapons. She felt her anger rising as she walked with the mayor and the others to the warden's office.

"How did the world's leaders ever allow the Germans to engulf the world in a second war?" she asked aloud. "We should have killed all of them the first time."

The board members crowded into the warden's office, which was little more than a hut. Helen listened with mounting unease as the state official introduced one of the blue-clad prisoners to everyone.

"I'd like you to meet Meinhard Kesler. His English is very good, so we've put him in charge of the other prisoners and assigned him the task of interpreting for us."

Kesler extended his hand in greeting to all of the men, but Helen folded her arms across her chest in refusal. The German was in his fifties, a slightly built, unassuming man with short, graying hair. Helen would have expected a Nazi officer to be stern and severe, but this prisoner had a friendly smile and a gentle expression in his blue eyes. He looked more like a kindly shopkeeper than a ruthless Nazi. Helen wouldn't let herself be fooled by him.

"You seem a bit old to be a common soldier," she told him. "The state specifically promised us that no officers would be sent here."

"I am neither, ma'am." His voice was soft, his English strongly accented. "The Nazis make me a soldier because they need me in their army to fix the ... how do you say? The connections—the wires and so forth. My age does not matter to them, only my skills."

"I'm going to let Meinhard lead the way," the state official said, "and take us on a little tour of our camp facilities."

They followed him outside into the brisk spring air, crossing the grassy compound to enter the first of three wooden bunkhouses. The spartan interior housed rows of iron army cots and mattresses, all neatly made up military style with green woolen blankets. A wood-stove sat in the center of the bunkhouse, but there was no fire in it today. Helen saw very few personal items aside from the usual toiletries and writing paper. A radio stood on a homemade table near the window.

"We are getting up at five-thirty in the mornings," Meinhard explained, "when they blow for us the whistle. And we must be putting out the lights in the nighttimes at ten o'clock."

"These look like decent accommodations to me," Helen said. "In fact, they're much like the bunkhouses our own American soldiers live in during basic training. It seems you and your fellow prisoners are being treated rather well. Wouldn't you agree, Herr Kesler?"

"Oh *ja*. I do agree, ma'am. So do my men. In truth, some of them are saying this kindness shows you Americans are weak. But most of my men, like me, are grateful."

When they had looked the place over, Meinhard guided them out of the building and across the compound to the mess hall. The nearly windowless building held rows of wooden tables and benches and another unlit stove. A crew of prisoners worked in the kitchen in the rear, but no aroma of cooking food drifted out.

"The noon meal is usually something simple," the state official explained, "like bologna sandwiches and a beverage. But we give the prisoners breakfasts and evening meals that are always hot, nutritious, and filling. Right, Meinhard?"

"Ja. It is not bad food. Some are saying it is better than when we are in the German army. But you will see no large bellies," he said, gesturing to his own thin waistline, "or . . . how do you say? Two chins." The mayor and board members smiled at his little joke, but his attempt at humor annoyed Helen.

"The mess hall also serves as a classroom," the warden added. "Tell them about it, Meinhard."

"We have two of the men who were teachers in Germany, and they are giving school lessons to whoever wants them. Some men have never learned to read and write or do the arithmetic. I am teaching English—even though mine is not so good."

"Miss Kimball, here, is a schoolteacher," the mayor told him.

"Ah, you are a teacher? Maybe you would come sometimes, and teach English classes with me? You see for yourself what we are like."

"Never." Helen's reply was quick and cold. "I'm trying to get this camp closed, not join your fun and games." The group fell silent for a moment, apparently stunned by her reaction. Finally, the state official cleared his throat.

"The mess hall is also where the prisoners hold religious services on Sunday. It was Meinhard's idea to instigate these services, right?"

He nodded. "We must lead them ourselves, since we have no one who is a minister. We are welcoming a priest or minister from your town, if he likes to come."

"Over here is the camp canteen," the warden said, leading the way. He unlocked the top half of a double door that opened to reveal a small storage closet packed with a variety of items. "Before you accuse us of coddling the men, you need to know that the canteen is required by the Geneva Convention. We sell cigarettes, beer, candy, toiletries—things like that. Each prisoner gets an allowance of ten cents a day in canteen coupons to spend any way he likes. He can earn eighty cents a day by working in a labor detail."

Helen turned away, shaking her head. "Remind me to read up on the rules of the Geneva Convention," she whispered to Archie. "I find it hard to believe that prisoners of war are supposed to have comforts like beer and candy, don't you?"

"It's news to me, Helen. I'll admit it sounds strange."

"How would you describe a typical day, Meinhard?" the state official asked as they emerged into the yard again.

"Dull," he said with a faint smile. "Every day is the same as before. After we work, there is not much to do. We play ballgames or hear the music on the radio or read one of the books we have—but the books are few."

"Well, what do you expect?" Helen blurted. "You're a prisoner, not a guest at a summer camp."

"Exactly right," the state official said. "Life here consists of regular hours, regular meals, and lots of hard work. Whenever they aren't working, the men are locked behind barbed wire."

"What do you mean?" the mayor asked. "Aren't they locked in here all the time?"

"Well, now that spring is here, those who volunteer for a work crew are being sent out to do farm labor. We already have crews weeding onions and trimming fruit trees for local farmers. But don't worry, we always send an armed guard with them. The prisoners are never allowed out of his sight. And they return to camp at night."

"Do they get paid for their work?" Mr. Wire asked.

"Yes, but their earnings will be credited to their accounts, and they'll be reimbursed by their own governments after the war ends. They receive the same wages as other farm workers in this area. As I'm sure you gentlemen know, there is a critical need for laborers with so many of our own local boys in the military. This POW camp is doing area farmers a service."

"When we are at home, many of us are working on the farms or in the factories," Meinhard added. "The men know this work and they like to be doing it. They are not bad people, you see. Just young men who are given a gun into their hand and ordered to kill the enemy. So they must."

"No one in this camp is a member of the Nazi Party," the warden explained. "Party members are separated from the rest and sent to more secure prison camps. Every now and then a POW camp will get an S.S. member, but I'm told that they are so hated by the other prisoners that they've been known to have 'accidents' if we put them in with regular soldiers. We've never had S.S. members here at our facility, though. We've had a few problems—men fighting amongst themselves and so on—but after a few days of eating bread and water, losing their privileges and allowances, and being confined to the camp, they've always straightened out."

"I understand you work at the shipyard, Mr. Wire," the state official said. "I'd be interested in talking with you about adding prisoners to your labor force."

"We can always use more help—"

"Wait! You would trust them not to sabotage something?" Helen interrupted.

"I don't see why not," Mr. Wire said.

"They would be supervised every minute and their work carefully inspected," the state official explained. "American prisoners are doing forced labor in European factories, so it's only fair that we put their people to work here. Tit for tat. Otherwise, it is going to be like a summer camp for them out here."

"It already is," Helen grumbled.

Meinhard led the group over to the garden area, where the prisoners were digging, and named all the different vegetables the men wanted to grow. "That is all there is to show you," he finished, "unless you like to see the latrine and the showers?"

"I'll pass," the mayor said, laughing. He extended his hand to Meinhard again. "Thanks so much for showing us around. I'm sure the others will agree that this has been very informative."

"Are there any other questions?" the warden asked.

"Just one more," Helen said. "I would like to ask Mr. Kesler if he also fought in the Great War?"

"Ja. I was in the . . . how do you say? With those big guns? The artillery."

"Did you fight against Americans?"

"Ja, of course. In the Argonne Forest."

Helen could barely control her fury. The Argonne Forest was where Jimmy had fought. Her voice shook with emotion as she asked, "Wasn't one war enough for you people? Did you have to start another one so that even more young men and innocent civilians would die? You don't deserve a place half as nice as this—any of you!" She didn't wait for a reply but turned and strode back to the gate. She had no more questions for Kesler or anyone else.

Helen didn't say a word on the way back to town. She could tell that the tour had soothed the other men's concerns, and their reaction infuriated her. Mr. Wire and one of the board members were even discussing the idea of employing prisoners as factory workers.

"I'm very sorry to see that you were right, Archie," she told him when they arrived back in town. "The prisoners will likely be our neighbors for the duration. That doesn't mean I'm giving up, however. You can bet that at the first sign of trouble—an escape or any other incident—I'll be clamoring to get rid of them once and for all."

By the time Helen returned home, it was late in the afternoon. The fresh air and hiking had tired her. Today was Thelma's day to clean the house, and she would be finishing up by now and waiting for her pay. Thelma had insisted on cleaning Helen's house once a month even though she now worked in the maintenance department at the factory five days a week. Helen was happy to hire her, but the girl must be exhausted.

"Your friend is here to see you, Miss Helen," Thelma said as soon as Helen walked through the kitchen door. "I hope it was okay for her to come inside and wait for you."

"My friend?" Helen couldn't imagine who Thelma meant. Then

Rosa appeared in the doorway to the den, her dark hair curling around her pretty face, her sultry lips bright with lipstick.

"Hi. I got something I want to ax you."

Helen stifled a groan. She was in no mood for Rosa Voorhees. "What now?"

"You told us how you wanted to teach kids who didn't have advantages and things? Well, that was me. I guess you can already tell by how I talk, huh?"

"Rosa, I had no right to correct your grammar—"

"Hey, I know I got mad before when you did it, but now I want you to correct me. I want to learn to talk better. And also—please don't tell them at work—but I never got my high school diploma, either. I really could use your help learning everything. Ever since I got back from Virginia, I been trying to change. I want to learn to cook all Dirk's favorite dishes and I want to stop drinking all the time and I want to finish high school. Do you think you could help me graduate?"

As tired as Helen was, the teacher in her rose to the challenge. "I would be very happy to help you, Rosa. There's a state examination you can take, and if you pass it you'll receive a high school equivalency diploma. It's considered just as good as the other kind. I'd be happy to help you prepare for it. You're a bright young woman, and I don't think you'll have any problem passing with a little hard work."

"When I write to Dirk I want to use good grammar and spelling and things. He writes such beautiful letters describing everything to me."

"They must be good ones. I've seen you reading them during work breaks."

"I been keeping all of them so he can look back and read them someday and remember everything he done."

"He *did*."

"No, *I* did. *I* been keeping them and—"

"Rosa, I was correcting your grammar. You should say, 'Everything he *did*, not everything he *done.*' And you should say, 'I *have* been keeping' . . . not 'I *been.*'"

Rosa raked her fingers through her glossy hair. "How am I ever going to learn all this?"

"I'll get some materials for you. We'll go over all of the sections that are on the exam, one by one. I know you can do this, Rosa. Heavens, you learned what to do at work in no time at all—much more quickly than I did. But in the meantime, I'm quite certain that Dirk is so thrilled to get your letters that he doesn't care one whit about your grammar or spelling."

"Can I ax you something else?" Rosa's pronunciation made Helen cringe, like fingernails on a chalkboard.

"Yes, but please *ask* me, Rosa, don't *ax* me. It's much too painful."

"Okay. What I want to *ask* you . . . well, I'm worried because everyone keeps saying Dirk is in God's hands, and I don't know much about God—especially about what His hands are like. Everywhere I go it seems like everybody's praying for all the people they love, yet good men are still dying in the war—like Mr. Wire's son. What happened? Didn't they pray right or something?"

"I'm the wrong person to ask these questions," Helen said quickly. "Let's just stick to questions about arithmetic and grammar."

"But I remember you told us at work how all your sisters and brothers died, so I figured you must know a lot about it."

"Yes . . . well, when they died I was told simply to accept it as God's will."

"How did you do that?"

Helen knew that her own response to the losses in her life had been to pull away from other people the way her mother had, to stop loving so she wouldn't be hurt again. But Helen couldn't advise Rosa to do that, even if—God forbid—something did happen to Dirk. It would be a terrible shame if grief drove this vibrant young girl to stop living.

Helen started to speak, then stopped, remembering how Jimmy

had once said the same thing about her. *"You're more vibrant and alive than any woman I've ever met. . . . Don't you know that's the reason I fell in love with you?"* Helen knew she was no longer that same woman.

Rosa stood wobbling on her high heels, waiting for words of advice. Instead, Helen changed the subject. "Where is Dirk stationed again?"

Rosa's pretty face grew somber. Her wide, dark eyes glistened. "He's with a battalion of marines in the Pacific Ocean. I looked the place up on a map in the newspaper, but I can't pronounce it. He has to follow the marines ashore when they land on the beach and set up an aid station in case anybody gets wounded in the attack. But what I want to know is, who takes care of the corpsmen if they get wounded?"

The knowledge of what Dirk Voorhees faced made Helen shiver. She'd been given too much to absorb for one day. "Maybe the corpsmen take care of each other. Listen, Rosa, it's too late in the day to start any lessons. I'll hunt down some materials to use, and I'll let you know when we can get started, okay? Right now I have to pay Thelma and . . . and then maybe you can catch a bus across town with her, get to know her."

Helen couldn't seem to herd everyone out of the door quickly enough. For once, she longed to be alone. She never should have asked about Dirk Voorhees and learned what a dangerous position he was in. The marines seemed to get the worst of every battle. What would that poor girl do if he were killed? How would she cope? How did all the other wives and mothers and sweethearts cope with the terrible losses of war? That had been Rosa's question, but Helen didn't know the answer. She supposed some people turned to God, but Helen had derived as little comfort from Him as from her own father.

Once again, Helen's thoughts turned to Jimmy. Rosa's fears and her questions about God had brought him immediately to mind. So had Meinhard Kesler, of course. Helen could easily imagine Kesler peering across enemy lines at Jimmy, taking aim with his cursed artillery. Jimmy had answered Helen's letter, writing to her from France to tell her that his 93rd Infantry division had been assigned to fight as part of France's Fourth Army in the Argonne Forest. For some reason, she suddenly had the urge to unearth his letter from the drawer in her vanity and read it again.

She hurried upstairs, admiring the beautifully polished handrail that slid beneath her fingers, the gleaming banisters that Thelma had painstakingly dusted. Motes of dust still swirled in the sunbeams from her bedroom windows, stirred up by Thelma's hard work. Helen sat down on the vanity seat and dug the letter out of the bottom drawer.

The address on the envelope was Joe Bernard's. Helen had asked Jimmy to send her letters to his father's house, fearing that her own father would intercept her mail if it came to the mansion. She remembered the day that Joe had given it to her, pulling it from the pocket of his overalls after he'd arrived to work in the yard. Helen had been waiting anxiously for Jimmy's reply. Then on a warm summer day, with locusts buzzing and sparrows hopping through the tree branches, this letter had finally arrived. She had taken it into the gazebo to read it, opening it with shaking fingers.

Now, twenty-five years later, the envelope was yellow and brittle with age. Helen smoothed her fingers over Jimmy's writing. His hands had touched this. He had licked the envelope shut. She studied his neat printing and the care he'd taken with her name, then her vision blurred with tears.

She couldn't read it now. Not after meeting that German soldier today. Besides, Helen already knew by heart what Jimmy had written.

She placed the letter back in her vanity drawer and dried her eyes.

CHAPTER 23
May 1943

"President Roosevelt issued an executive order today forbidding government contractors to discriminate on the basis of race."

★ *Rosa* ★

Rosa walked through the factory doors with Jean into the bright spring sunshine.

"Hey, you taking the bus home today, Jean?" she asked.

"No, I think I'll walk. I need to save every nickel I can. Why don't you walk home with me, Rosa? It's a gorgeous day."

"Nah, I gotta get home. I'm waiting on a certain letter from Dirk. He writes to me almost every day, but our letters keep crossing in the mail. I wrote and told him about something special, and now I'm waiting for him to write me back."

"Maybe another day, then."

"See you tomorrow, Helen," Rosa called as Helen pedaled past them on her bicycle. Helen lifted one hand from the handlebars in a halfhearted wave. "Hey, here comes my bus," Rosa said. "I gotta run."

Rosa shoved her way through the crowd at the bus stop the way she'd learned to do in New York. Her feet ached from standing all day, and she made up her mind to get onboard fast and get a seat, no matter how many people grumbled at her. The bus rolled away from the shipyard with a hiss of air brakes and a cloud of diesel fumes, jammed to capacity.

It seemed to take forever to get home. When she finally neared her stop, Rosa pulled the cord above the bus window and elbowed her way down the packed aisle to the door. She broke into a slow jog for the last half block, hurrying up the sidewalk and into the kitchen. Her mother-in-law stood waiting at the door with an envelope in her hand.

"You got a letter from Dirk," she said cheerfully. "I did, too, but I already read mine. You go ahead and take it to your room, then you can come out and have a little snack."

Rosa's stomach rose right up to her throat at the mention of food, as if she had just crested a hill on the Coney Island roller coaster.

"No, thanks, not today," she said on her way to her bedroom. The thought of food, not to mention the smell of it, made her feel like puking. She sat down on the bed and slit open the envelope with a nail file.

> *My darling Rosa,*
>   *When I read your news that we're going to have a baby, I let out such a whoop of joy that five marines came running to see if I was okay. Now I have two reasons to finish up this war and come home. I only wish I could see you, all rosy and pregnant. I'll bet you're more beautiful than ever. . . .*

He had written more, but Rosa's tears of joy and relief fell so fast that she couldn't see. Dirk wanted their baby! She'd had no idea how he would react, since they had never talked about having babies. She'd been afraid to find out. Rosa's own father had been so angry when he'd learned that Mona was expecting that he had left home, saying he didn't want a baby messing up his life. Ginny's husband didn't want any more children, either, even though Ginny still did.

Rosa's joy was short-lived as her other fears began to soar. What if she was a terrible mother? What if Dirk got killed? She covered her face and sobbed.

"Rosa?" Tena tapped on her door. "Is everything all right, dear?"

"Yeah," she sniffed. "I'm okay." She pulled a clean handkerchief from her dresser drawer and blew her nose. Now that Dirk knew about the baby, Rosa wanted to tell the whole world. She dried her eyes and went out to the kitchen.

"You've been crying, Rosa."

"I don't know what's wrong with me, Mrs. Voorhees. I'm crying because I'm just so happy . . . and that doesn't even make sense!" She covered her face and started all over again.

Tena wrapped her arms around her. "There, there. It's okay."

Rosa let herself be held. Tena's arms had held Dirk this way when he was a little boy.

"I want you to be the first person who knows after Dirk," Rosa said with a sniff. "I'm going to have a baby, Mrs. Voorhees."

"I know, dear. Isn't it wonderful?"

"How did you know? Did Dirk tell you in his letter?"

"No, it was easy to guess the truth. You always loved your snacks after work, and you used to eat every bite of food in your lunchbox. Then about a month after you got home from Virginia, you suddenly stopped eating. I remember so well how it feels when the smell of food makes you sick. Yes, I had my suspicions." Tena's arms tightened around her. "And, Rosa, I am so very, very happy for you and Dirk."

Rosa started crying all over again. Tena had said home—"*after you got home from Virginia.*" For the first time since she had arrived in Stockton, Rosa felt welcome here. Then she remembered Mr. Voorhees.

"I don't think Dirk's father will be very happy about it," Rosa said. She pulled away from Tena and dried her eyes.

"Men sometimes feel scared when they hear that a baby is on the way. Wolter will be worried about you and the little one, with Dirk so far away. Whenever Wolter is worried about something he acts . . . What is the word? *Gruff.* He acts gruff. But I have known him long enough to know that he isn't mad, he is worried."

"Do we have to tell him?" She slid into a chair at the kitchen table, and Tena sat down beside her.

"He is sure to notice in a few months, don't you think? He might be hurt that we didn't tell him sooner."

"Will you tell him for me? When it's just the two of you?"

"If that is what you want, Rosa. But you don't have to be so afraid of Wolter. He does not mean to act the way he does. You need to let his words . . . how do they say it? Roll over your head." She gestured with her hands to mimic rolling waves, and Rosa recalled sitting with Dirk on the beach in Virginia, watching the breakers crash against the shore. Now he might be on a foreign beach somewhere with the marines, a heavy pack on his back, his boots sinking deep into the sand.

"Are you all right, dear?" Tena asked.

Rosa nodded, wiping her eyes. "I never had a father, Mrs. Voorhees. I mean . . . at least, not one that hung around every day."

"Fathers can be very protective of their children. And when Wolter is worried about the people he loves, he sometimes acts angry."

"In this letter I got today from Dirk, he says he's happy about the baby." Rosa couldn't help smiling through her tears. "I hope it's a boy. Dirk should have a little boy."

For some reason, she would feel better about having a son. Dirk would know how to help raise him and could teach him to play baseball and things. Rosa didn't know how to raise a daughter. A girl might grow up to be wild and independent the way she had. What if they fought all the time like her and Mona?

"Will you teach me to cook?" Rosa asked suddenly. "I mean, when I feel like being around food again?"

Tena reached across the table to pat her hand. "Of course, Rosa dear. I'd be happy to."

"I want to learn how to make all of Dirk's favorite dishes for when he gets home. That way when we have our own little place, he can still eat all his favorite things." And Rosa decided that from now on she would go to church every Sunday—morning *and* evening, whether she liked it or not. It would be good for the baby. Dirk had gone to church all his life and look how good he turned out.

The next day she found Jean, Ginny, and Helen all standing in line by the time clock waiting to punch in. Ginny had the latest copy of *The Saturday Evening Post* and was showing everyone the picture of "Rosie the Riveter" on the cover, painted by Norman Rockwell. "See that, girls? We're famous," Ginny said.

"I hope I don't look like her," Jean said. "Look at that girl's biceps!"

"What did your husband have to say when he saw the magazine?" Helen asked.

Ginny's smile faded. "He doesn't say much at all these days. And I didn't think I should stick this under his nose. Mr. Seaborn was right when he said Harold's pride was at stake."

Rosa couldn't wait one more minute to tell the girls her news. "Hey, guess what? I'm gonna have a baby."

"Oh, Rosa!" Ginny hugged her tightly, the magazine quickly forgotten. Jean congratulated her, and even Helen looked happy about it—as happy as Helen ever looked, that is.

"Will you teach me stuff, Ginny? About babies and things? You're such a good mother."

"I'm hardly a sterling example. My sons played hooky from school and ran off, remember? Harold says I smother them too much."

"But that's the kind of mother I want to be—you know, hugging my kids and playing with them and things. To be honest, I'm scared stiff. Dirk will want me to be a good one—like his mother, not like mine. But I have no idea how to be a good one. Will you teach me how?"

"I would love to." She couldn't resist hugging Rosa again.

"What's going on, ladies?" Earl Seaborn asked, limping over to them. "Good news, I hope?" Jean whispered in his ear. "That's what I was afraid of," he said with a crooked smile. "Listen, you'd better keep it a secret if you want to continue working here. If the rest of the bosses find out, you'll be let go."

"That's ridiculous," Jean said. "Shouldn't it be up to Rosa how long she works?"

"Of course it should be," Helen said, "but society has its unspoken rules. When I taught school, any teacher who was in a family way was let go as soon as the principal found out about it."

Mr. Seaborn put his finger to his lips. "I won't tell if you won't," he said. "And congratulations, Rosa. Children are a wonderful blessing."

"I'm scared of what Dirk's father will say when he finds out. He's mad at me for working here as it is, and I'm afraid this will really set him off. But I'm not gonna quit until I'm too big to fit in coveralls, no matter what he says."

"Mr. Voorhees is from a different era," Earl said gently. "He grew up in a time when it was a man's job to protect his wife and children. Try to see things through his eyes."

"His eyes are always narrow and squinty when he looks at me— like he's shooting daggers out of them. I don't know how he can see good enough to drive." Mr. Seaborn and everyone else laughed. Rosa wasn't sure why, but she joined in anyway.

The happy feeling lasted all morning and Rosa even hummed to herself as she worked. At the end of the day, she walked to the bus stop again with Jean. "Could I sit with you in church on Sunday morning?" she asked. "You always go there and pray for your five brothers in the service, right?"

"There are six of them now. My younger brother Howie just enlisted. And I've been praying for Patty's husband in Algeria, too— although it looks like God answered our prayers now that North Africa surrendered. Wasn't that great news?"

"I want to pray the way you do. And I need to learn how to be good like all the other women at church. I want to change."

"You're no worse than the rest of us."

"Oh yes, I am. I never see you getting drunk at the Hoot Owl and stuff like that."

"I have other faults, Rosa. We all do. But you're welcome to sit with me any Sunday you want to."

"I been sitting with Dirk's folks, but Mr. Voorhees gets upset with me because I can't sit still during the boring parts. He makes me nervous, and then I start dropping the hymnbook and things like that. He has this annoying way of clearing his throat to let me know he's mad, and sometimes it's like he's got a whole pond full of frogs in his throat." She stopped when she saw Jean cover her mouth to hide a smile. "What's so funny?"

"Nothing. I'm sorry. I know it isn't funny."

"The more upset he gets," Rosa continued, "the more nervous it makes me. Last time I got out some chewing gum to calm my nerves, and he just about had a fit because I rattled the wrapper during the silent prayer. I can't do nothing right."

"Well, you'll fit right in alongside Patty's boys. Believe me, when it comes to being fidgety in church, they've got you beat. I'll save you a seat this Sunday, okay?"

"Oh, I guarantee I'll arrive at church long before you do. If Dirk's father isn't there at least an hour early, he thinks he's late. I'll be pulling into the parking lot when you're still in your pajamas eating breakfast. I'll wait for you and Patty."

"Okay, see you there." Jean waved and strode away, her long legs quickly taking her out of sight.

As Rosa stood in the foyer on Sunday waiting for Jean, she began to worry that attending church may not be such a good idea after all. She watched the people streaming through the church doors, and the women all seemed so sweet and soft and good that she wanted to sink into the floor and disappear. Compared to them, her untamable hair and tight, flashy New York clothes made her stick out like a sore thumb. Dirk would fit in real good with these people—sweet, happy Dirk. Why on earth had he ever picked someone like her? Maybe she should wait until after she learned how to be good before coming to church regularly. What if God sent a lightning bolt to zap her or something? She sure would hate it if Jean or her cute little nephews got zapped along with her.

Rosa was thinking about leaving and hightailing it home when Jean and Patty finally arrived. Gosh, those little boys of Patty's sure were adorable. Rosa got tears in her eyes as she thought about holding a little carbon copy of Dirk by the hand and ruffling her fingers through his blond hair.

"Hi, Rosa. Sorry we're so late."

"Do I look okay?" Patty asked. "It's such a job getting three kids ready and keeping them ready that it doesn't leave much time for me. I don't know how our mother ever did it with our huge family."

"You both look fine," Rosa said. They shook hands with the wholesome-looking family who greeted everyone outside the sanctuary doors, and one of the ushers led them to a seat near the back. Rosa flopped down beside Jean, jiggling her crossed legs nervously.

"I have a question already and church hasn't even started. You said I could ask questions, right?"

"Sure. Fire away."

"Well, I see that they're doing that thing with the bread and wine today—"

"Yes, Holy Communion."

"I'm not supposed to eat any of it unless I've been sworn in or whatever they call it, right? At least that's what Mr. Voorhees said."

"The Lord's Table is for believers who have accepted Jesus Christ. It's for Christians of all faiths. I'm sure the pastor would explain what it meant if you want to talk to him about it."

"Maybe when I'm good enough. After I've changed a little more."

"That's not the way it works, Rosa. We're welcome to come to Jesus the way we are. You don't have to be good enough."

"Can I ax—I mean *ask* you another question? Why is everything so tiny? They use those little-bitty cups with hardly a swallow of juice in it and those teeny-tiny crackers with no cheese or anything. Can't they afford bigger ones? Is it because of the war?" She could tell that Jean was struggling not to laugh.

"They're symbols, Rosa. They're supposed to be small. It's not like we're having a meal or anything."

"How long does it usually take for someone like me to learn the language?"

"What language?"

"You know, church language—the one that the Bible is written in? It's almost like English, but it has some really strange words in it like *shalt* and *thine* and *dost*."

"It *is* English." Jean lowered her voice to a whisper as the service began. "Sort of old-fashioned English. I'm sure you'll catch on."

"There's something else I always wondered about," Rosa whispered back, "but I was afraid to ask Dirk's mom. You know how they always have this confession thing? Is that like if you robbed a bank or you murdered someone, you're supposed to come forward and confess? And will they arrest you, or are you immune or something because you're in a church?" She could tell that Jean was trying not to laugh again. Rosa hadn't meant to be funny.

"No, it isn't that kind of confession. Honestly, Rosa, you think of the funniest things sometimes."

"I was always kind of glad that no one stood up and confessed to something. I'd sure hate to be sitting here next to a murderer. But at least then I wouldn't look so bad in comparison."

"We're all sinners, Rosa. We're supposed to confess our sins silently and tell God about all the mistakes we've made this week."

When it was time for the prayer of confession, Rosa was just getting started on all her mistakes when the pastor said, "Amen."

"Hey, I wasn't done," she whispered to Jean. "Is that okay or should I keep going until I'm finished?"

"It's okay to stop when he does."

"I told you I was a lot worse than all of you. They didn't give me nearly enough time."

Rosa liked singing the songs, even though some of the words seemed to be in that old-fashioned English. She liked listening to the organ music, too. It sounded like heaven, especially when the choir sang along in their wobbling voices. It must be what angels sounded like. Then Rosa thought of another question.

"Why do they keep talking about a ghost with holes? Is this place haunted?" Jean had to clap her hand over her mouth to keep from laughing out loud.

"I'm going to need a lot of time to explain the Holy Ghost to you," she whispered when she could control her giggles. "But don't worry, the church isn't haunted. Why don't you write down all your other questions as you think of them, and I'll try to answer them afterward."

Rosa took out a pencil and scribbled questions on her church bulletin all through the service. By the time it ended, there was hardly any blank space left. As everyone filed from the sanctuary, Rosa saw Mrs. Voorhees searching for her. Mr. Voorhees was already heading toward the door.

"I gotta go," she told Jean. "Dirk's father wants his Sunday dinner right away. It's always a big deal at their house. And that's another thing I don't understand—Dirk's father says it's a terrible sin to do any work on Sunday, yet he makes Tena cook a huge meal for him after church. They eat it in the dining room, no less. Tena says she loves to cook, but it still looks like a lot of work to me. Her and me wash the dishes afterward, and nobody in their right mind would say that washing dishes isn't work."

"Gosh, I don't know the answer to that one, Rosa."

"Well, what should I do with all these other questions?" she asked, waving her bulletin.

"Bring them to work tomorrow," Jean said. "I promise I'll try to answer them at lunch."

Rosa went home from church determined to be good all week. She would do everything just right from now on so that God wouldn't punish her by taking Dirk or her baby away. Her life was the best that it had ever been, except for Dirk being gone, and she was so afraid that she would do something to make God mad at her. She had heard the pastor say that Jesus was without sin and that people were supposed to be like Him, but Rosa knew she had a long, long way to go.

They were all sitting at the table, digging into the roast beef and mashed potatoes that Tena had made, when Mr. Voorhees cleared his throat as if about to make an important announcement.

"Tena has told me the news about ... you know. You will be quitting your job now, right?"

"Wrong! I don't see why I can't work as long as my belly doesn't get in the way." She saw him draw back at the word *belly* as if she had uttered a curse word, but for the life of her she couldn't understand why.

"It isn't proper to continue working in your condition," he said, scowling. "Women must stay at home when they are in a family way. There must be a proper period of confinement. They do not flaunt themselves in public."

"Who says so? Is that in the Bible or something?" Rosa was trying really hard not to lose her temper, but she could tell that Mr. Voorhees was close to losing his.

"Decent society says so. How many women do you see walking around like that? And how many do you see working at the shipyard in such a condition? You would be very foolish—and very irresponsible—to continue working in such a dangerous place. You are carrying my son's child, not just your own."

His voice had grown louder and angrier in the course of his speech until he was practically shouting at her. He gripped his fork as if he might use it as a weapon.

"Would anyone like more carrots?" Mrs. Voorhees asked. Rosa could tell by her shaky voice and worried eyes that their argument upset her. *"Let his words roll off,"* Tena had advised, but Helen Kimball said not to allow people to use anger to get their own way. Rosa considered the two women and decided she would rather be strong and fearless like Helen instead of timid and mousy like her mother-in-law.

"Well, this baby is still inside of me, so that makes it mine! This is still a free country, and I got a right to do whatever I want. You're not my boss!" She slid back her chair and stood. "And if that makes you mad, then it's just too bad." Rosa stalked off to her room.

"What about dinner?" Tena called after her.

"I'm not hungry." She slammed the door.

Rosa felt good about standing up to Wolter for all of thirty seconds. That was how long it took to remember that she had promised God she would be good. She was so upset by her failure that she cursed out loud—then realized she had made matters worse! She would run out of time for sure next week when she confessed her sins—if she even went back to church, that is.

How did those sweet little churchwomen do it? How did they manage to sit still and not fight when their fathers-in-law bossed them all around? And how come they didn't think of curse words every five minutes, much less say them out loud the way she did? Being religious was just too hard, Rosa decided. She would never be good enough. Why bother to try?

CHAPTER 24
July 1943

"Following Allied successes in the North African campaign, American airborne troops and British paratroopers have launched a surprise invasion of Sicily."

★ *Jean* ★

Jean pulled a bandana out of the pocket of her coveralls and wiped the sweat out of her eyes for what seemed like the hundredth time. No matter how many fans blew nonstop throughout the building, the production line remained a very hot place to work. The humidity made her hair hang limp, and she gave up trying to style it, wearing it pulled back and tied in a ponytail. She noticed that Rosa had the opposite problem. Her wild, naturally curly hair frizzed up like a lion's mane in the humid air, poking out from beneath the kerchief she wore on her head. It felt like an oven down in the hull of the ship where Jean and the other women worked. Her hands grew so sweaty she could barely hold a screwdriver or manipulate all of the fine wires and tiny screws.

"Let's get out of this hothouse and take a break," she finally told her crew. "We need to drink plenty of water to make up for all the sweat we're losing. I don't want anybody fainting on me."

Helen, Rosa, and Ginny gladly climbed out of the hull and followed Jean to the water fountain, lining up behind several other workers waiting for a drink. They were talking about the war and the invasion of Sicily when Jean noticed an elderly Negro janitor staggering toward them. He stopped suddenly and leaned against the wall as if he was about to keel over.

"Are you all right?" Jean asked, hurrying over to him.

"This heat's getting to me, I guess. As long as this wall don't move, I'll be okay. Give me a second."

"You'd better take a drink of water and cool down."

"Here, you can cut in line in front of me," Helen said.

"I was heading over here for a drink, ma'am, but I see that my water fountain is out of order." He gestured, and for the first time Jean noticed that there were two water fountains, ten feet apart, one marked Whites Only and the other marked Colored. The one that the Negroes used had an Out of Order sign on it.

"But you obviously need a drink," Helen said. "I'm sure they'll let you use this other one."

The man's eyes grew wide. "Oh no, ma'am. I ain't allowed to do that."

"Look, you're about to faint," Helen insisted. "At least let me get a glass and fill it up for you." The janitor held up his hands as he began backing away.

"Thank you kindly, but there's a sink over yonder in our colored bathroom. I'll just head on over there. You ladies don't need to trouble yourselves."

"Hey! What's the holdup?" someone in the back of the line shouted. "Come on, we're thirsty, too!"

As Jean got back in line and waited her turn for a drink, she saw three other Negro maintenance workers approach, then turn away when they saw that their fountain was out of order. By the time she rejoined her crew, Jean was fuming.

"That's just not right. The least they could do is put out a cup for that poor man and all of the others to use."

"There's a cup on my Thermos," Ginny said. "I'll be glad to go get it and put it out for them."

"I doubt very much if any of the colored workers would use it,"

Helen said. "Did you see how intimidated that poor man was? He seemed more worried about causing an inconvenience than fainting."

"I have a better idea," Jean said. "You all go back to work. I'm going to talk to Mr. Seaborn about this."

"Tell him I'll pay to have the fountain fixed myself," Helen said.

Jean found Earl sitting in his cubicle with his shirtsleeves rolled up and his tie loosened. The small fan mounted near the ceiling did little more than push the stifling air around the room and rifle the papers on his desk. He looked up when he saw Jean and smiled. She quickly told him what she had just seen, then finished by saying, "They're human beings, Earl. Surely the decent thing to do is to let everyone use the same drinking fountain until the other one is fixed."

"You're right. May I borrow your screwdriver?" Jean pulled one from her tool belt and followed Earl out of the cubicle. She watched in satisfaction as he took down the Whites Only and the Colored signs.

"Hey! What do you think you're doing?" one of the men in line shouted.

"We can certainly share our water with our fellow workers until both fountains are working," Earl said calmly.

"We're not drinking out of that after *they* do!" someone else said. Several others echoed his feelings.

"Then I guess you'll be the ones who are thirsty from now on," Earl replied.

"Either you put those signs back up or we're leaving."

Earl turned to face them, his shoulders squared. "I don't make decisions based on threats. I'll put the signs back up when the water fountain is fixed."

"Isn't he the union representative?" Jean whispered as she and Earl walked away. She glanced over her shoulder and saw a knot of workers gathering in an angry huddle. No one was lining up for drinks.

"Doug Sanders is not only the union rep, he's also a known troublemaker," Earl replied. "I think he's the one who kept Thelma off your crew. Sanders applied pressure to management and they caved in."

Jean left him to rejoin her crew, then realized that Earl still had her screwdriver. She returned to his office, arriving at the same time as Doug Sanders.

"Hey, Seaborn!" the burly welder said. "There's thirty of us ready to walk off the job right now unless you put those signs back up."

"Don't forget to punch the time clock on your way out, Doug," Earl replied. "No work, no pay."

Doug whirled away and signaled to the others. "Okay! Let's go!"

Jean shook her head in disbelief as she watched more than two dozen workers walk off the job—over a drinking fountain! "You did the right thing, Earl."

He sighed and leaned against the office doorframe. "Maybe in theory. But with production schedules so critical, this is going to hurt us. I'd fire them all if there wasn't a labor shortage."

"You'd better call a plumber—fast!"

When the workday ended, Jean was headed to the locker room with Rosa when she noticed the Whites Only sign on the women's locker room door for the first time. "Did you ever notice this before?" she asked. Rosa shook her head. "Me either. I walked right by it every day and never even saw it."

"Where do the Negro workers change their clothes or go to the bathroom?" Rosa asked.

"I don't know, but I'm going to ask Mr. Seaborn as soon as I change my clothes."

"The Negro workers have to get dressed at home," he said, in answer to her question.

"But what do they do about rest rooms?"

"There's one in the old part of the building—it's the factory's original bathroom. There's only one toilet, and both men and women have to use it. There are two outhouses, too."

"Outhouses! And only one bathroom for all those men and women? That's disgraceful!"

"I'll tell you something else—I submitted a work order to the shipyard's plumbers to fix the drinking fountain, and I found out that it's been broken for more than a week. They've had the work order all that time, but they said it was a 'low priority' job—meaning that they'll get to it whenever they feel like it."

"That stinks, Earl. You should go over their heads and hire a plumber. Rosa Voorhees' father-in-law is one, you know. I'll even take up a collection to pay the bill. Helen Kimball said she'd donate money. She was outraged by this whole business."

"That's an excellent idea." Earl opened his desk drawer and pulled out the telephone directory, leafing through it for the listings for plumbers. "I never noticed this blatant discrimination until I tried to hire Thelma. The trouble is, I don't know how high up this attitude goes."

"Speaking of Thelma," Jean said, "I know Rosa isn't planning to leave for a few more months, but I wondered if we could give Thelma a test run after work—on our own time? If she is already qualified to work, they'll have no excuse for not transferring her. And if she needs a refresher course or something, I'll be glad to train her after work on my own time."

He looked up at her, his brow furrowed in concern. "That's risky business, Jean. You saw the reaction to an integrated drinking fountain."

"What's the worst they could do—fire me? I don't really care if they do. My boyfriend found a job for me in a factory back home. It's not as challenging as this job, but it would be closer to my family."

"We'd miss you. You're a great crew chief." Earl looked away, returning to the phone listings at the word *boyfriend*. Jean felt bad for bringing him up. The truth was, she still hadn't heard from Russ. After hearing Helen's advice, Jean had written one last letter to him, more than four months ago:

I think the world of you, Russ, and I want to be with you forever in that house you're going to build on the hill. But you're the one who stopped writing to me, so I guess we don't want the same things. I've decided to stay here in Stockton, for now. I like my job and I'm very good at it. I have a lot of responsibility at work and my boss says that I could go places. I'm not dating anyone else. I still think of you and wish that things could be different, but I guess that's up to you.

"Let me know what you decide about training Thelma," Jean said on her way out of Earl's office. He mumbled a reply, his face still buried in the phone directory.

Jean arrived home from work to find that Patty's house was even hotter than the factory had been. "The boys and I are going to sleep out on the screened porch tonight," Patty told her. "Want to join us?"

"I might do that. Was there any mail from Johnny or Dan?" Jean no longer asked about a letter from Russ, and Patty had enough tact by now not to tease her about it.

"We both got a letter from Ma," Patty told her. "She said she hung another star in the window now that Howie's off to boot camp. That makes six. Evidently he wasn't the only guy in his graduating class who left right after final exams. In fact, only two boys stayed around to march in cap and gown. Ma said there were so few boys that the girls had to go to Senior Prom with their fathers."

"I'd like to see our dad wearing a bow tie and boutonnière," Jean said, laughing.

"I'd like to see him dancing!"

Jean noticed a strained atmosphere at work as soon as she arrived at the shipyard the next day. She went straight to the drinking fountain before punching in and saw that nothing had changed since yesterday. One fountain was still out of order, and the signs hadn't been rehung.

"Did you see what they did to Earl's office?" Helen asked as they both punched the time clock. Jean's heart rate sped up.

"No. What happened?"

"Go have a look."

Jean couldn't believe the sight. Someone had smashed the window to his cubicle, littering his office with shards of glass. His filing cabinets had been overturned and emptied, his desk upended, and the words *Nigger lover* were scrawled across one wall in red paint. Earl arrived with two maintenance workers equipped with buckets and brooms as Jean stood gaping at the mess.

"It happened last night during the graveyard shift," Earl told her. "Nobody saw a thing, of course. I guess some people aren't too happy about my decision to integrate the drinking fountain."

"Better get a plumber here to fix it—fast."

"I already arranged to have it fixed, but I'm not going to allow these cowards to intimidate me. In fact, I'm more convinced than ever that I need to hire Thelma to take over for Rosa. Are you still willing to help train her? No, don't answer now. Think about it for a couple of days. I'll understand if you've changed your mind."

"I have to admit that the vandalism has me a little scared, but this is one battle that I want to fight. My brothers aren't afraid to confront the enemy, and I'm not going to back down, either. I'll work with Thelma today, in fact."

"Good. I'll set something up with her after work. Is here in my office okay? I figure they've already wrecked it once. There's not much more anybody can do."

Jean's crew talked about the incident at lunchtime and agreed to support Mr. Seaborn if he hired Thelma on their crew in spite of the risks. Later, Helen drew Jean aside and handed her two envelopes.

"I sent away for this information when I was ordering some materials for Rosa. They're brochures for two different colleges. Our troops seem to be making progress in the war, so it's not too early to start thinking about your future studies."

"Thank you," Jean managed to say. She hoped she hadn't appeared too surprised by Helen's thoughtful gesture, but Jean was surprised. When they'd first started working together Helen had seemed so aloof—to use one of Ginny Mitchell's favorite words. In the months since, Helen had warmed up to all of them, even to Rosa.

"One other thing, Jean. I would like to help you train Thelma, if I may."

"Are you sure, Helen? I mean, I could use your help, but you saw how people reacted to the water fountain. . . ."

"Yes, I saw. And that's exactly why I want to make it clear where my loyalties lie. Besides, I was the one who recommended Thelma. I'd like to look out for her."

"Okay, sure. Meet us in Earl's office after you punch out."

After work, Jean assembled some of the equipment and tools that she had used to train her crew members and carried them into Earl's office. It smelled of fresh paint. The mess had been tidied and the words covered over, but the window was still missing from his cubicle. Thelma and Helen arrived after their shifts, ready to work.

"If you're worried about stirring up more hatred after everything that happened, Thelma, I'll understand," Jean told her. "We don't have to do this."

"I'm used to people not liking me," she said matter-of-factly. "It's the way things are when your skin isn't white."

"I never imagined there was this kind of racism here in Stockton," Helen said. "I read about those terrible race riots in Detroit last month, and I could hardly imagine such hatred. And now we have the same thing cropping up here. I suppose I've been sheltered, but even so . . ."

"It's everywhere, Miss Helen. Best thing for a colored person to do is ignore it and get on with life. Best thing for a white person to do is thank God you weren't born colored."

They settled down to work, and within a few minutes Jean saw that Thelma was a very competent electrician. She would fit right in once she became familiar with the ship's electronics. But as they worked, all three of them were aware that they were being watched. Not only were the time clocks and locker rooms close to Earl's office, but many workers seemed to stroll past for no reason at all, as if curious to see what Jean and Helen and Thelma were up to.

They were just quitting for the day, when Earl returned to his office and noticed Jean's college catalogs. "Helen gave them to me," she told him. "One is for Purdue University in Indiana, and the other is for a college here in Michigan."

"I remember you saying that you wanted to go to college after the war," he said, leafing through them. "What did you want to study again?"

"Probably political science or history. I loved my U.S. Government class in high school. My twin brother and I might even go to law school together someday."

"Great! Then you could run for office. We can always use a good, honest politician."

"I'm not sure the world is ready for a female politician. But I loved doing campaign work to help Roosevelt win in the last election."

"You'd also make a terrific judge, Jean. You're a bright woman. I'm sure you could succeed at anything you put your mind to."

"Thanks, Earl."

Jean and Helen worked with Thelma every day for the rest of the week. "You're ready to join our crew," Jean told Thelma on Friday. "All we have to do is wait for an opening."

"I sure appreciate what you and Miss Helen are doing for me, Miss Erickson."

The unrest continued, even after the water fountain was repaired, and Earl received several threatening letters demanding that the Negro workers "stay in their place." Jean knew it was because of Thelma. When she found a threatening letter stuffed through the vent in her locker, Jean crumpled it up and threw it away.

"Can I give you ladies a lift home?" Earl asked as they were leaving the factory on Friday afternoon. Helen and Thelma had come by bicycle, but Jean accepted his offer gladly. The heat wave had continued all week, and she was much too tired to face the long walk home.

She and Earl left the building together, talking about her college plans as they walked across the gravel parking lot to his car. He was about to unlock the doors when two men suddenly jumped out from behind a nearby car, wearing masks. Jean froze in fear.

"It's the two Nigger lovers!" one of the men said. "Let's teach them a lesson." He gripped a billy club in his fist.

"Jean, run!" Earl said. "Go! *Now!*" He gave her a push to get her started, but he didn't run with her.

She glanced over her shoulder as she stumbled back toward the factory and saw that one of the men had started to chase her. Earl sprang sideways to block his path. "Run, Jean!" he yelled again.

Jean's feet felt huge and clumsy as she raced toward the building, dodging between cars. It seemed a long way off. She tried to scream for help, but no sound came out. When she looked over her shoulder again she saw both men attacking Earl. Why wasn't he running from them? They were bigger and stronger than he was, but he stood his ground, fighting both of them so she could escape. Then she remembered that Earl couldn't run. The knowledge that they would pick on a crippled man made Jean so furious that she sprinted into the building with an angry burst of speed. She heard the sound of breaking glass in the distance behind her and knew they were smashing his car windows.

"Help!" she finally screamed as she burst through the door. "Somebody help!" The clamor from inside the factory, along with the vast acreage of the place, seemed to swallow her pitiful voice. "Somebody help us!"

She ran to the nearest office cubicle and screamed, "Call the police! They're attacking Earl Seaborn!"

"What? Who is?" the shift foreman asked.

"Two men! Outside in the parking lot. You've got to help him!"

She ran back to the door, followed by the foreman, a maintenance man, and several of the workers from the production line. Jean sprinted across the parking lot, leading the way, but there was no sign of Earl or his attackers. She ran in the direction of his car and found Earl sprawled in a heap on the ground, covered in blood.

"Earl! Earl!" she cried as she knelt beside him. He didn't move. She was terrified that they'd killed him. The foreman knelt beside her and rolled Earl over.

"He's still breathing," he said. "Somebody call an ambulance!"

A gawking crowd quickly gathered around them. Jean lifted Earl's head onto her lap and stroked his hair. Blood from the gash above his eye stained her slacks, but she didn't care. "Earl! Earl, wake up!" *Oh please, God. Let him be okay.*

It seemed as though hours passed before Jean finally heard sirens. One of the maintenance men ran out to the street to direct the ambulance driver. It halted nearby and a medic leaped from the back of it.

"What happened, miss?" he asked as he listened to Earl's heart with a stethoscope.

"T-two men jumped out from behind his car ... and ... and they started beating him with clubs. This is Earl's car—what's left of it." Every window had been smashed, the fenders and roof dented in.

"Let's get him to the hospital." The medic retrieved a stretcher, and the foreman and one of the maintenance men helped lift Earl onto it and load him into the ambulance.

"I want to go with him," Jean said.

"Are you a family member?"

"No, but I ... I was with him. I saw the men attack him. He protected me."

"You'd better stay here if you were a witness. The police will want to talk to you."

"Tell them I'm at the hospital," she told the foreman. She turned back to the ambulance driver. "Please, I don't want to leave him. He's my friend. Let me come with you."

The driver gestured to the open rear door. "Okay, get in."

Jean climbed into the back of the ambulance, and the driver slammed it shut. The attendant worked on Earl as the vehicle began to move, examining his wounds, applying a compress to stop the bleeding, taking his blood pressure. The ride to the hospital in the speeding van turned out to be a wild one. Jean hung on to the little seat with both hands, the wail of the siren deafening her.

"Is he going to be all right?" she asked above the noise.

"Don't know. Looks like he might have a head injury." He said it so ominously that Jean began to cry. She tried to pray, repeating the words *Please, God . . . please,* over and over. She didn't want to take her eyes off of Earl.

There was a flurry of activity once they reached the hospital. One of the emergency-room nurses made Jean stay behind in the waiting room. "He'll need X-rays," the nurse told her. "It's going to be a while."

"Will he wake up? Why isn't he waking up?"

"We'll know more after the doctor examines him."

"Please come back and let me know how he is!"

Jean found a pay telephone and called Patty to tell her what had happened. Her fingers shook so hard she could barely put the coin into the slot. She had just sat down again to wait when a policeman arrived to take her statement. Jean struggled to gather her thoughts.

"I . . . I work with Earl at the shipyard. Two men attacked him and beat him up. . . . It's because of the colored workers—Earl let them use our water fountain. He has been standing up for them. And he protected me from . . . from the two men."

"Can you describe his assailants, Miss Erickson?"

"They wore bandanas over their faces and hats—ordinary hard hats, like from the factory. They were in work coveralls. Only one of them spoke. He called Earl and me 'Nigger lovers.'"

"Any idea who they could be?"

"I didn't recognize their voices. There must be hundreds of men who work there, and a lot of them aren't happy about integrating. They vandalized Earl's office and sent us threatening notes. And a bunch of people walked off the job because they didn't want to share the drinking fountain."

The whole mess seemed unbelievable to Jean. And now it had ended in violence. She couldn't understand how the policeman could sit there calmly writing everything down. Why wasn't he outraged, as well?

He asked her a few more questions, then left. Jean stood and began to pace, too worried to sit still. Why was it taking so long for the doctor to examine Earl? What if he died? She realized that she didn't know anything at all about his family. Earl was her friend, yet she'd never bothered to ask him about himself. She slumped in the chair and bowed her head to pray. At last a doctor came out to talk to her.

"Are you here with Earl Seaborn?"

"Yes. Is he going to be okay?"

"He has regained consciousness, so that's a good sign. The attackers broke his nose and his left clavicle, cracked three ribs, and fractured his radius. He's badly bruised and has a moderate concussion. We want to keep him overnight because of the concussion and make sure there's no brain swelling. He's going to be pretty sore, but it looks like he'll recover."

"May I see him?"

"If you keep the visit short."

Earl was still in the emergency area behind a curtain, waiting to be transferred to a room for the night. His face was so badly bruised, his nose so swollen, that Jean hardly recognized him. He opened his eyes when she entered.

"Hey, Jean. What are you doing here?" He sounded groggy.

"I was worried about you. Are you okay? No, that's a stupid question. Of course you're not." All her worry and fear suddenly came to a head, and she started crying again. She looked around for a tissue.

"I'm in the hospital," Earl said slowly, "but I don't remember why. They said I got beat up?"

"Yeah. Two guys from work attacked you with clubs. It was because of the drinking-fountain thing and because of Thelma." Jean reached for his hand and held it, stroking it. She realized after a moment that it was the hand he usually kept hidden in his pocket. The other arm was in a cast.

"Hard to believe someone would get violent over a water fountain, isn't it?" he asked. He gave a sad half smile. "Did I at least put up a good fight?"

"You were wonderful! You fought off two of them so that I could get away! The army made a huge mistake when they turned you down. You would make a very courageous soldier."

"It's hardly the same thing."

"No, it's exactly the same thing whether you're wearing a uniform or not. Those cowards have the same attitude that created Hitler and Mussolini. You finally got to fight in the war, Earl. You were
wounded in a battle for someone else's freedom. It's exactly the same
thing."

He smiled slightly and closed his eyes. "I've got a whale of a
headache. I actually saw stars—you know, like in the cartoons when
someone gets whacked on the head?"

"Do you want me to call anybody for you? Your family?" He
shook his head. She could see how weary he was. "I should probably
go. They said you could go home tomorrow. Do you want me to see
if Helen will drive you? Your car is in worse shape than you are."

"After work?" he mumbled.

"Tomorrow's Saturday. I'll come back when you're discharged
and see that you get home, okay?"

"Yeah, thanks."

She was so glad he wasn't dead that she had the urge to bend
over and kiss his forehead. But Earl Seaborn was her boss. She didn't
want him to get the wrong idea and think that she cared about him
in that way. Her eyes filled with tears. She did care—more than she
had ever realized. She gave his hand a gentle squeeze instead.

"I'm so glad you're going to be all right."

"Yeah. Me too."

An orderly entered, drawing the curtain aside. "Okay, Mr. Seaborn, we're going to take you up to your room now."

"See you tomorrow, Earl."

Jean called Helen Kimball as soon as she got home, and Helen
readily agreed to drive Earl home from the hospital tomorrow. When
she called Ginny and Rosa, they wanted to come along, too. They
both offered to cook something for Earl since he'd be helpless for a
while. "That's a great idea," Jean said.

She rose early on Saturday morning to make fried chicken for
him and was transferring it to another container when she heard a
knock on the front door. Thinking Helen must have arrived a little

early, Jean swung open the door, expecting to see one of the girls from work. Instead, Russell Benson stood on her doorstep.

"Hi, Jean."

"W-what are you doing here?"

Russ pulled her into his arms and held her for a long moment. Then he bent to kiss her. "That's what," he said when he finally pulled away. "I missed you, Jean." She fell into his arms again, and he held her tightly, his face pressed against her hair. He let out a deep sigh. "I've been acting like an idiot. I don't want to fight anymore. Do you think you can forgive me and we can try again?"

"Of course, Russ!" She was so happy she started to cry. Jean couldn't believe it! Russ still loved her. He'd come back to her after all these months, after all her tears. They were kissing again when Patty hurried in from the kitchen, interrupting them.

"Hey, is Earl here already? I thought I heard a man's voice and . . ." She stopped in surprise. "As I live and breathe, it's Russell Benson!" Jean's nephews had been running down the hall behind Patty, but they froze when they saw that it wasn't Earl. Russ looked from Jean to Patty and back again in confusion.

"Were you expecting someone else?"

Jean didn't know what to say. The last thing she wanted to do was make him jealous.

Patty spoke first. "Wow, you're a long way from home. Isn't summer supposed to be the busy season for you farmers?"

"I needed to see Jean."

"Then I guess I'll skedaddle. Come on, boys."

"But where's Earl?" Billy, Jr. asked. "I thought you said he was—"

"Let's go out to the garden and see what's ripe. Hey, Russ, maybe you can give us some farming advice later on. Our poor, pitiful victory garden could use some expert help. We'll be out back." Jean heard the screen door slap shut a moment later.

"Why is everybody talking about this Earl guy?" Russ asked when they were alone again. "Isn't he your boss? You been seeing a lot of him?"

"Yes, he's my boss, and no, I haven't been seeing him—at least, not the way you mean. He came over once or twice to play with Patty's boys. They miss their father." She didn't dare tell him that Earl had been attacked at work, or Russ would haul her home in a heartbeat. Jean suddenly remembered that Helen and the others were due to arrive any minute. She peered out the front window just as Helen's car turned into the driveway.

"Can you wait here for a second?" she asked Russ.

"What now? Did you have plans with this guy?"

"It's the ladies I work with. We were going to visit a friend in the hospital, but I'll run out and tell them to go without me. You're more important." She gave him a quick kiss, grabbed the container of chicken, then hurried out to the car. Helen cranked open the driver's window.

"Russ is here," Jean said breathlessly. "He came all this way to ask if we can get back together."

"And are you going to take him back?" Helen asked.

Jean remembered the wonderful crush of his arms, the stubble of his beard when he'd kissed her. It had felt so good to hold him again after all this time. "Yeah. I really, really want to get back together with him. Will you explain everything to Earl? Tell him I'm sorry, okay? And give him this for me." She handed the container of fried chicken to Helen through the open window, and she passed it to Ginny, seated beside her on the front seat.

"Sure, Jean. See you on Monday."

Jean noticed Russ's truck parked in front as she hurried back inside the house. "You drove this time? How'd you get gasoline? Isn't it rationed?"

"My dad has a storage tank. Farmers get unlimited supplies to operate their tractors and things. I traded with some friends—my gasoline for their ration stamps—so I could stop and buy more along the way." Jean had the fleeting thought that what Russ had done wasn't quite legal, but she didn't dwell on it.

"I'm so glad you came. It's wonderful to see you." The summer sun had bleached his hair blond and burnished his face and arms to a deep tan. He looked so handsome! He could play leading roles in Hollywood. "How long can you stay?"

"I promised my dad I'd be back by tomorrow night. Any chance I can bring you home with me? There's room in my truck for all your things."

Oh dear. Jean still wasn't ready to move back home, but she didn't know how to reply without making him angry all over again. Then she remembered Helen's warning about not allowing him to manipulate her with anger. She decided to be honest with Russ right from the start instead of raising his hopes.

"I can't come home with you, Russ. There's too much going on at work. One of my crew members is going to have a baby and I have to train a new—"

"I get the message," he said, holding up both hands. "I didn't come here to talk about work, so let's not."

He pulled Jean close and kissed her again. The sensations that flooded through her were so wonderful that she almost decided to hand in her own resignation along with Rosa's. The attack on Earl had scared her more than she was willing to admit to anyone—even herself. And if Thelma did manage to get hired on Jean's crew, there might be more attacks. But as much as she wanted to be safe and to be near Russ, Jean knew that the battle over hiring Negro workers was well worth fighting. She wasn't a quitter. Earl had stood up for what was right and so would she.

"I'm so glad you came," she murmured as she hugged Russ again.

CHAPTER 25

★ *Rosa* ★

Rosa leaned forward from the backseat of Helen's car as they pulled out of Jean's driveway. "What did Jean say? Why isn't she coming?"

"Apparently her boyfriend drove all the way from Indiana to see her," Helen replied.

"So she isn't coming with us at all?"

Ginny turned around on the front seat to face her. "I gather from some of the things that Jean has said in the past that her boyfriend gets jealous easily."

"I wouldn't have taken him back if it were me," Helen said, almost to herself.

"Me either," Rosa said. "He's got a lot of nerve. He doesn't write for months and months, then he just shows up one day like everything is hunky-dory? That stinks, in my book."

"They say love is blind," Ginny said, smiling faintly.

When they arrived at the hospital, Earl was sitting in a wheel-chair in the lobby with a huge fruit basket on his lap. Rosa winced when she saw how awful he looked—like something from a bad horror movie. His face was black-and-blue and swollen up like a balloon, his nose was bent and crooked looking. The row of Frankenstein stitches above his eye didn't help any, either. One of his arms was in a cast—his good arm, poor guy. Evidently no one had thought to bring him a change of clothes, so he wore the same shirt and trousers from yesterday, torn and stained with blood. Someone had cut the sleeve of his shirt so it would fit over the cast.

"What's the wheelchair for?" Rosa asked. "Is your leg broken, too?"

"It's hospital policy," the gray-haired woman who was pushing it said. She wore a striped volunteer's uniform and thick-soled shoes that squeaked on the linoleum as she maneuvered Earl outside to Helen's car.

"You look terrible," Rosa told him. "They really worked you over, didn't they?"

"What a lovely fruit basket, Mr. Seaborn," Ginny said before he could reply. Too late, Rosa realized that she shouldn't have told him the truth about how awful he looked. Why couldn't she ever keep her mouth shut?

"The fruit came from Mr. Wire and the other bigwigs at the shipyard," Earl replied. Ginny lifted it from his lap so he could climb into the front seat. He moved stiffly, as if he ached all over, and he let out a grunt as he seated himself again. He glanced all around as everyone else climbed in. "Where's Jean?" he asked.

"Some unexpected company arrived at the last minute and she couldn't come," Helen explained. "She said to be sure to give you her best wishes."

"And she made you some fried chicken," Ginny added.

"Was it her boyfriend from Indiana?" Earl asked as Helen started the engine and pulled out of the parking lot.

"Yeah, how'd you know?" Rosa asked.

"Lucky guess."

Rosa heard the disappointment in his voice and had a sudden thought. "You're sweet on Jean, aren't you?"

Ginny laid her hand on Rosa's knee. "Shh, Rosa."

"Was that a nosy question? Sorry. You don't have to answer it, Mr. Seaborn. Besides, I think the answer's pretty clear from your long face."

He gave a short laugh. "Am I that transparent? Great!"

"We were just talking about Jean's boyfriend on the way over here, weren't we?" Rosa continued. "To tell you the truth, we don't think too much of him. None of us has ever met him, but even so ..."

"I've met him," Earl said, "and I don't stand a chance competing against him."

"I may be speaking out of turn, Mr. Seaborn," Helen said, "but you do have one huge advantage over her boyfriend. Jean says you've been very supportive of her college education—and I've heard her say that her boyfriend isn't."

"A lot of good that does me. The guy is built like a statue of Atlas."

"Give Jean a little credit for not being superficial," Helen replied.

"I can think of another advantage you have," Ginny said. "You're with Jean every day and he isn't. You have more opportunities to make a good impression. I know she was very concerned about you after you were attacked. She insisted on riding in the ambulance with you. And she told everyone how brave you were, standing up to your attackers and not running away."

"I couldn't have run even if I'd wanted to," he said quietly.

"Because of your crippled leg?" Rosa asked.

"Rosa ..." Ginny said with a sigh.

"Did I do it again? Gosh, I'm real sorry, Mr. Seaborn."

"That's okay. I'm the one who brought it up."

They arrived at his apartment, and he climbed out of the car very gingerly, holding his arm close to his chest as if his ribs hurt. "Thanks for the lift, Helen," he said when he finally maneuvered to his feet.

"We're coming inside with you," Rosa said. "We all made food for you. Dirk's mother and I made a peach pie. We'll help you carry everything into the house."

"Thanks." It took him a long, awkward moment to fish his keys from his pocket with his withered left hand and unlock the door. Rosa was surprised to see how small his apartment was. He pointed to the counter behind a folding screen where there was a hot plate and space to set down the food and the fruit basket. "That looks like enough food for an army," he said. "I can't tell you how much I appreciate it."

"What you're trying to do for Thelma and the other Negroes is very courageous," Helen told him. "I admire you for standing up for what's right, even when it has cost you so much. You're a good man, Mr. Seaborn."

"Yeah, Jean's crazy for not picking you," Rosa said. She knew by the look Ginny gave her that she'd been too forward again. She wanted to make it up to him. "Mr. Seaborn, can you dance?" she asked him.

"Can I . . . dance?"

"Yeah, I mean . . . with your crippled leg and all—can you dance?"

"Rosa, not now—" Ginny tried to interrupt, but Earl stopped her.

"No, that's okay. I'd rather have people come right out and ask about my handicaps than simply ignore me. To answer your question, Rosa—I probably could dance if I knew how. Why?"

"Because Jean has told me a bunch of times how much she loves to go dancing, but her boyfriend doesn't like to and won't ever take her. If you offered to take her to a dance sometime, you'd have a leg up on the guy—so to speak."

Helen rolled her eyes. "I believe we have meddled in your life enough for one day," she said, opening the door. "Come on, Rosa. Let's allow Mr. Seaborn to get some rest."

"I'll teach you how to dance if you want me to," Rosa said, pausing in the open doorway. "I can make you into a regular Fred Astaire."

Earl laughed. "I don't think Fred Astaire ever danced with a broken arm and cracked ribs, but maybe I'll take you up on your offer when I heal a little bit. Thanks again for all your help."

"You're welcome," Rosa said. "And you take care of yourself, Mr. Seaborn."

CHAPTER 26

July 25, 1943

*"Benito Mussolini has been ousted as 'il duce' and premier of Italy.
Marshal Pietro Badoglio will succeed him."*

★ *Virginia* ★

Ginny tried to forget about all the housework that she was neglecting
at home as she rode the bus to Rosa's house one steamy Saturday
morning in August. She never worked on Sunday, the Lord's Day, so
all of her chores—laundry, shopping, vacuuming, cleaning—had to
be done on Saturday. But Rosa had pleaded with her for help in
getting ready for the baby, and Ginny didn't have the heart to refuse.

Rosa stood on the Voorhees' front steps, waiting for her.
"Thanks so much for coming. I don't know a thing about babies,
and you're a real-live expert!"

"I think you're exaggerating, Rosa. I only have two children.
Now, Jean's mother, with eighteen kids—that's a real expert!"

Ginny greeted Mrs. Voorhees, who was in the kitchen baking
something that smelled wonderful, then followed Rosa to her bedroom. It was obvious from the baseball equipment and school pennants and the shelf full of adventure stories that this was Dirk Voorhees' boyhood bedroom. But Rosa's things were scattered around in
abundance, as well—perfume bottles, makeup containers, high heels,

a brassiere, and silk slip. Piled on the floor were several boxes and bags.

"Dirk's sister gave me some clothes and things that her kids don't need no more, since they're school age already. And Jean's sister loaned me the stuff in those bags. To tell you the truth, I don't know what half of it is even used for, let alone what else I need to buy."

"We'll sort through everything together," Ginny said, "then we'll have a better idea what to shop for. Just think," she said with a sigh, "in only four and a half months you'll be holding a little one in your arms! You're halfway there already."

She sat down on Rosa's bed and opened the first box, pulling out baby-soft undershirts, nightgowns, and receiving blankets. Such tiny little things! Ginny battled her emotions as she sorted everything into piles according to size.

"Does a little-bitty baby really need this much stuff?" Rosa asked.

Ginny cleared the knot from her throat. "You'll be surprised how quickly they grow. It seems like only yesterday that Allan and Herbie could fit into tiny undershirts like these." She held one to her nose and inhaled, remembering how wonderful a new baby smelled.

Rosa pulled out a nightie and studied it as if it might start talking to her. She lowered it to her lap with a sigh. "You know what, Ginny? I'm scared."

"I was, too. I think every woman is afraid the first time. We hear so much about the pain of childbirth and the hours and hours of labor and so on."

"It's not the birth so much as afterward," Rosa said softly. "I never even played with dolls when I was a kid. I don't know anything about babies—like how to pin diapers or fix bottles or anything."

"It's much easier if you skip the bottles and feed your baby yourself. The milk is ready whenever he's hungry and it's always the right temperature. You get to hold him close to your heart.... It's the most wonderful thing. . . ." She couldn't finish.

"You want another baby, don't you?"

Ginny could only nod. The longing felt like a hunger that consumed her from the inside. She had to get hold of herself. She pulled out a handkerchief and blew her nose. "Don't mind me. Maybe it's a good thing that Harold doesn't want any more children or I'd probably end up with as many as Jean's mother."

"She must have been pregnant all her life!"

"Most of it, anyway. Have you felt the baby move yet?"

"I think so. I was sitting in the living room listening to the radio the other night and felt something fluttering inside—like I had butterflies in my stomach or something."

"That's exactly what my babies felt like the first time—like a tiny little hand was waving at me from the inside. But wait until he starts to kick! You'll feel that for sure. It's the most wonderful sensation, feeling that baby moving inside of you. I missed it so much after they were born."

"You *should* have eighteen kids," Rosa said, frowning. "You're a natural-born mother. Why doesn't your husband want any more?"

"I don't know. He never really gave me a reason."

"Can't you talk to him about it?"

"He's still so mad at me for working at the shipyard that he barely speaks to me about anything these days."

"That's what I call carrying a grudge. You been working there almost a year."

"And you know what? I made up my mind to keep working there until he gets over it. Like Helen says, I won't let him use anger to get his own way."

"Atta girl, Ginny!"

They sorted through all the boxes and bags, putting the smallest things on top to use first. Then Ginny helped Rosa make a list of all the other things she would need.

"Dirk's mother has already started knitting sweaters and booties. She said she'd help me sew diapers if I got some cloth. But I was wondering ... is there some other way I can keep diapers on the kid without using pins? I just know I'm gonna stick his little behind and make him cry."

Ginny laughed. "I guarantee you won't stick him—unless he

squirms all around the way Herbie did. I used to warn him that it would be his own fault if he got pricked."

"Did his fanny bleed?" Rosa asked in horror.

"No, because I never did stick him, and you won't, either. But we can practice if you want to. I'm sure Patty would let you diaper her baby, or we can borrow a doll from somewhere. Believe me, if you can learn to solder the circuits on a landing craft, you can certainly learn to diaper a baby."

"It seems like being a mother is a really important job—a hard job. And I don't want to mess things up. Especially with Dirk's baby."

"Motherhood *is* a really big job, Rosa. But—"

She'd been about to say how meaningful and fulfilling motherhood was, but it suddenly felt like a lie. Ginny remembered nursing both of her sons and thinking, *This is what I was born to do, what I'm happiest doing.* But once her children had become independent, she had outgrown her usefulness. Wasn't that why she had gone to work in the shipyard nearly a year ago—because motherhood no longer fulfilled her? She remembered thinking that her family never noticed her, that they no longer needed her except in the same way they needed the refrigerator or kitchen range. She had felt as though she was losing herself. If she was no longer a mother, then who was she?

But how could she tell Rosa that her baby would need her, that his very life would depend on her, not just for nourishment but for protection, nurture, instruction—and then one day he wouldn't need her anymore? That she would have to find something else to give her life meaning?

Ever since Ginny had taken the job at the shipyard, she had begun to grow in new directions. She had looked up the words *growing* and *sprouting* in her thesaurus and had discovered the word *burgeoning*. It meant: *"to begin to grow, as a bud; to put forth buds and shoots, as a plant."* That's what she was starting to do—*burgeon out.* But if Harold didn't want her to be a mother or to have a job, in what other direction could she grow?

"But what?" Rosa asked. She was still waiting for Ginny to finish her sentence. Ginny couldn't tell her all of these things. Rosa would have to learn them for herself. And she would learn them soon enough.

"I just remembered," Ginny said, struggling to change the subject. "I still have the bassinet I used when the boys were babies. I think it's down in the basement at home. It will fit in this little bedroom quite nicely, and you won't have to worry about getting a crib for a while."

"Maybe by that time the war will be over and Dirk will be home, and we can get our own house."

"Let's hope so," Ginny said, smiling.

There was a knock on the bedroom door. "I thought you ladies might like some lemonade and cake," Mrs. Voorhees said from the other side of it. Rosa opened the door, and Tena handed her a tray. Mrs. Voorhees' face softened when she saw the baby clothes spread out on the bed. "Ah, look . . . so precious," she murmured.

"Why don't you stay and have some lemonade with us?" Ginny offered.

"Oh no. I don't want to bother you." She backed from the room and closed the door again, but Ginny had the distinct feeling that Mrs. Voorhees would have stayed with a little encouragement from Rosa.

"This was very nice of your mother-in-law," Ginny said as she bit into the still-warm cake. "You know, I think she would be more than happy to give you advice and to help you with the baby if you asked her."

"I don't want her to know how dumb I am when it comes to babies," Rosa said in a whisper. "She might tell Dirk. And I also don't want her interfering in my life."

"She isn't interfering; it's her way of showing love—like bringing us this cake and lemonade. It must be so hard for her now that her children are all grown—and then to have Dirk leave home, too. There is nothing worse than feeling useless. Believe me, I know. But if you let Mrs. Voorhees help you, she would feel valued and needed."

"She always takes Wolter's side."

"All the more reason to get her on your side. You told us about your mother and how she wasn't a very good one. Why not let Mrs. Voorhees mother you? She seems like a wonderful one. Look how well she raised Dirk."

"He thinks the world of his mom."

"Why not let her be a friend and a mother to you, a grandmother to your baby?"

"She sure bakes good cake," Rosa said, taking another bite.

Ginny went down to the basement as soon as she got home and found the white wicker bassinet she had used for her boys. The sight of it rekindled all of the feelings and emotions that had been stirred up as she'd sorted the baby clothes with Rosa. Ginny dragged it upstairs later that night after the boys were in bed and was on her knees, giving it a good scrubbing, when Harold walked into the kitchen.

"What are you doing with that thing?"

"Rosa Voorhees from work is expecting her first baby. I'm going to let her borrow this if I can get it cleaned up. Rosa's husband is a Navy Corpsman. He's with the marines on one of those Pacific Islands." Harold winced at her words. "That's a really dangerous job, isn't it?"

"I don't suppose it's much worse than any other job in the military."

"Rosa said he's seen some terrible fighting."

"I'm sure he has." He surprised Ginny by sitting down in a kitchen chair to watch her work. He didn't speak again for several minutes, but she could tell that he had something on his mind. She had a sudden premonition that he was going to ask her for a divorce. She stopped scrubbing.

"Is something wrong, Harold?"

"I can't stop thinking about the incident at the shipyard. That was your foreman who was hospitalized, wasn't it? Earl Seaborn?"

"Yes. He's a good man, and he got beat up for doing the right thing. I was shocked that people would create such an uproar over a silly drinking fountain. What difference does it make what color a person's skin is if he's thirsty?"

"Racism is everywhere, Ginny. The war and the need for defense workers have simply brought it to the forefront. President Roosevelt issued an executive order last January banning discrimination, and now the defense industries are supposed to offer jobs to all citizens, regardless of race. He even set up the Fair Employment Practices Commission to implement the order. The shipyard should report this incident to the commission before things get out of hand the way they have in Detroit."

Ginny nodded. Before the war, she had never kept up with current events and would've had no idea what Harold was talking about. But she'd read how twenty-five blacks and nine whites had been killed in race riots in Detroit this summer—and then she'd witnessed racism firsthand at the shipyard.

"It was horrible how all those people got killed in Detroit," she said. "Thank God those men stopped short of killing Mr. Seaborn."

"I visited a factory in Maryland last week, and trouble is brewing there, too. A group of white women walked off the job after management transferred a Negro woman to their department."

Ginny thought immediately of Thelma King. "What happened?"

"The workers are threatening to stay on strike until the factory provides segregated bathroom facilities, even though Roosevelt's executive order requires that they be integrated. It's a standoff at the moment. The War Labor Board is supposed to intervene."

Ginny knew about the plans to hire Thelma to replace Rosa and decided to confide in Harold. Maybe he could offer some advice. "There's a Negro maintenance worker at the shipyard who's a qualified electrician. Jean Erickson and Helen Kimball have already started training her to replace Rosa after she leaves to have her baby. Mr. Seaborn is all set to fight for her, too."

"They're walking a very dangerous line—even if it is the right thing to do."

Ginny rose from her knees and pulled out a chair to sit at the table beside Harold. "Why is there so much hatred in the world,

Harold? There's racism here in Stockton, hatred toward Jews over in Germany, and people out on the West Coast have turned against all the Japanese-Americans. I don't understand it."

Harold shrugged. "I guess it's part of our fallen nature to mistrust anyone who isn't like us. It's tragic when fear leads to hatred and violence."

"Life is much too short to spend it hating other people. I hope we've taught our sons not to judge anyone by what they see on the outside. I pray that they'll grow up without prejudices."

"I do, too." Their eyes met, and Ginny realized with a jolt of surprise that they were talking, connecting. Harold hadn't had divorce on his mind after all.

"We haven't talked like this in a long time," she said softly.

"I know. . . . You've changed, Ginny."

She hesitated before asking, "In what way?" She wasn't sure she wanted to hear his answer.

"You seem . . . stronger. More sure of yourself. More involved in things like this race issue . . . Some men would say those traits aren't very feminine."

"Is that what you think?"

He shrugged again, then fiddled with a loose straw on the bassinet, not meeting her gaze.

"I've learned a lot about myself these past few months," she said. "I found out that I'm capable of doing more than I ever believed I could. I've been growing, Harold—*burgeoning out*. I think that's a good thing, to know myself a little better, don't you? Maybe men prefer women who are weak and helpless, but I'm ashamed of the way I used to let Betty Parker and the others push me around. I used to hear such vicious gossip from the club women and I was afraid to say anything. A year ago I never would have had the courage to speak up for Thelma and the other Negroes at work, but that's wrong. My crew chief, Jean Erickson, isn't even twenty years old and she's leading the way. I want to stand up for what's right, too. I don't want to go back to the way I used to be."

He looked at her and she saw sorrow in his eyes. She wondered if he still wanted the old Ginny back. Once again, the thought occurred to her that he was preparing to leave her.

"I love you so much, Harold. I wish I knew that you still loved me."

"Of course I do. You're the one who is moving away from me, not the other way around. You left our home, you're always working ... Sometimes it seems like you care more about the people at work than you do about the boys and me."

"That isn't true." She reached to take his hand. "If I learn new things about myself, then I'll have more to offer you. I'm becoming a better person. I'll have more to give the boys, too. I showed them one of the ships I built. They said they were proud of me. I wish you felt that way, too."

"I do."

The two words had been barely audible, but they were music to her ears. Ginny knew they were all Harold was capable of. She leaned toward his chair to hug him, and he pulled her onto his lap and kissed her with a passion that had been missing from their marriage for a long time. When he finally pulled away, he rested his forehead against hers.

"Are the boys in bed?" he asked. Her mouth opened in surprise. It was what he always used to ask whenever he felt romantic.

"Yes," she whispered.

"Let's go upstairs." He slid her off his lap, then stood and took her hand. Ginny could have floated up the stairs. She wondered if she would glow in the dark. Maybe things would be different between them from now on.

But on Sunday morning Harold acted as *aloof* as usual. "There's another article about the racial strife in Baltimore," he said as he read a section of the newspaper at breakfast. He lowered the page to face her. "The unrest is bound to spread. While I agree with what Earl Seaborn is doing, it's extremely dangerous. I don't like it that he wants to put a Negro woman on your crew. I wish you would consider quitting, Ginny."

"He hasn't hired Thelma yet. Rosa is going to continue working for a few more months." Harold made a face. "What's wrong?"

"Women don't belong in a place like that, especially if they're in the family way." He folded the paper and stood. But he surprised Ginny by kissing her before he went upstairs to dress for church.

She watched him go, feeling happier than she'd felt in months. Then, as she cleared his breakfast dishes from the table, she suddenly had an astonishing thought: *What if I got pregnant last night?*

Ginny leaned against the sink as she tried to absorb it. Had that been Harold's plan when he'd decided to get romantic? Was he manipulating her, letting her have a baby so that she would finally quit her job?

She was still sorting through her feelings when Allan walked into the kitchen. "What's that thing doing here?" he said when he saw the bassinet.

"It's for Rosa Voorhees, from work. She's going to have a baby."

A rush of joy and hope welled up inside Ginny. Even if those were Harold's motives, she didn't care. She might have another baby! Maybe it would be a little girl this time.

CHAPTER 27

★ *Helen* ★

Sunday had become a very boring day after Helen stopped believing in God and attending church, but tutoring Rosa now helped fill the long afternoons. It surprised Helen to discover how much she enjoyed teaching her. They had spent nearly every Sunday afternoon for the past few months seated at Helen's massive dining room table, studying geometry and geography and grammar.

"It's time to take the examination," Helen told Rosa in August.

"Oh no, I don't think I can—"

"You're ready. You passed this practice test with a score of eighty-nine percent. The equivalency exam is being given next Saturday morning at the high school. I'll drive you there." Rosa sputtered in protest, but Helen remained firm.

On Saturday, Helen hung around outside the school, pacing like an expectant father while Rosa took the exam. "How did it go?" she asked the moment Rosa emerged from the building. She looked like an exotic flower that had wilted under the strain.

"I don't know. Some parts of it were really hard. I had to figure out the volume of a cylinder and I think I messed it up."

"We'll study some more. Don't worry. You can always take it again."

"They wanted to know where to send the results," Rosa said as they walked to Helen's car, "so I gave them your address. I hope that's okay. I don't want Dirk's folks to know how dumb I am."

"Rosa, for heaven's sake. You're not dumb."

"I didn't finish high school."

"There's a big difference between being uneducated and being dumb. Jimmy was uneducated but he certainly wasn't dumb."

"Whatever happened to him? Did he die or something?"

"I'd rather not talk about him, if you don't mind."

"Sorry ... Maybe sometime you could teach me how to stop asking nosy questions. I think Ginny gave up on me."

"Children usually learn manners from their parents."

"Well, that explains it, then. I never had a father, and my mother didn't teach me nothing—I mean anything."

Helen watched the mail, waiting for Rosa's test results. One afternoon a letter arrived from the principal of Lincoln Elementary School. An uneasy feeling writhed through Helen's stomach as she ripped it open. It should have been good news: The school needed a sixth-grade teacher for the coming fall. The principal wanted Helen to call him right away if she was interested. But the unsettled feeling persisted.

A teaching position. Helen could teach again.

She called the school and set up an appointment for tomorrow after work. She would come home and change her clothes, then drive to the school. "We're eager to fill this position right away," the principal told her, "before classes start. We know how highly qualified you are."

But after Helen made the appointment, she felt as though she were walking around in lead shoes. Why should that be? She should be jumping up and down with excitement at this opportunity. Her career was in teaching, not working in a shipyard. She had enjoyed tutoring Rosa, hadn't she? And she was good at it. Helen didn't understand why there was even a question in her mind about returning to Lincoln School—but there was. Where had it come from?

Helen pondered these questions all evening and slept restlessly that night. It was the same anxious, dreamless sleep she'd experienced when her parents had been ill and she had awakened dozens of times to listen to the dreary old house creak and groan. In the morning she rose before dawn and paced the floor as if waiting for a loved one to return home. By the time she left for work at the shipyard, she felt exhausted. The day seemed endless.

At five minutes to four that afternoon, Helen parked her bicycle in front of Lincoln Elementary School. The two-story brick building looked as solid and uninspiring as always. The principal was waiting for her in his office, and they chatted about the war and the fall of Italy's dictator for a few minutes before he suggested that she visit her sixth-grade classroom on the second floor.

"You might want to look over the textbooks you'll be using. Take them home with you, if you'd like."

Helen plodded dutifully up the squeaky wooden stairs, even though she knew the classroom well. The school smelled of disinfectant and floor wax, scents that would evaporate quickly once the students arrived with their sweaty bodies and bologna sandwiches. The building was clean and ready for fall, the desks sanded, the floors polished, the chalkboards scrubbed, the erasers cleaned. Helen walked into the classroom that would soon be hers and looked around at the bulletin boards waiting to be decorated, the textbooks waiting to be distributed, the desks waiting to be filled. She thought of all the young minds waiting to be shaped and felt weary before she even began. She leafed through one of the teacher's manuals on her desk, but the pages may as well have been blank.

Why couldn't she get excited about returning here? She had fought so hard to become a teacher, defying her father, who'd considered teaching a commonplace profession, far beneath a wealthy, Vassar-educated woman. She had been forced to battle the prevailing notion that it was a father's duty and right to make decisions for his unmarried daughter.

"It's a new world, Father," she'd told him. "I'm a grown woman, capable of making my own decisions. It isn't up to you to choose where I'll work or who I will marry; it's up to me."

She had successfully broken through barriers in her life and in society's way of thinking—the same way Ginny Mitchell was now fighting the notion that a woman's place is in the home. The way Jean Erickson would fight stereotypes to study something other than nursing or teaching. Even Rosa was doing battle, fighting against her upbringing to get a high school diploma and choosing to continue working when she was nearly five months pregnant.

The schools hadn't been integrated when Helen had begun to teach, and she'd further outraged her father by teaching in a one-room schoolhouse in rural Michigan. Her students were nearly all Negroes, children of tenant farmers and migrant workers, children who deserved a good education, too, she'd believed. She had encouraged them to get as much schooling as they could, to reach for the sky. Many of them had, and Helen was proud of them all. She had moved to Lincoln School not by choice, but because the rural ones eventually consolidated. Helen had loved teaching. Why did she hesitate now?

She closed the classroom door and went downstairs. In a few weeks the other teachers would arrive and put their rooms in order. Helen recognized most of the names stenciled on the doors, but she didn't know any of these people very well. She had always remained aloof, to use one of Ginny Mitchell's favorite words.

Helen smiled fondly when she thought of the girls from the shipyard—then she caught herself. How had she allowed herself to become so fond of them? She suddenly realized which emotion she had felt last night when she'd been unable to sleep: loneliness, something she hadn't felt for a long time. She would miss Jean and Ginny and, yes, even Rosa. Helen would be lonely again after she quit. In that case, she had better quit right now before the ties tugged any tighter, before she ended up getting hurt.

The principal had a contract ready when she returned to his office. "It's pretty standard. You've seen one just like it before. Do you have any questions?"

Helen couldn't bring herself to sign it. "May I take it with me? I'd like to give it some more thought. I'll let you know tomorrow."

She found the envelope with Rosa's examination score in the

mailbox when she returned home. Helen could hardly wait to bring it to work tomorrow. She spent another restless night thinking about the decision she needed to make, trying to imagine herself standing in front of the chalkboard in the sixth-grade classroom. She dreamed of Jimmy Bernard.

Before punching the time clock the next morning, Helen took Rosa aside and gave her the envelope with the test results. They both held their breath as Rosa opened it. "I'm scared to look," she whispered.

"It doesn't mean anything, Rosa. Don't let a test score tell you who you are." Helen watched as she pulled the letter from the envelope and scanned it.

Rosa let out a squeal of delight. "I passed!" She hugged Helen, jumping up and down. Helen felt Rosa's baby like a hard little ball between them. "Look! Ninety-two percent!"

Helen forced back happy tears. "That's excellent. You have a right to be proud, Rosa."

"You helped. I couldn't of done . . . I mean I couldn't *have* done it without you."

Helen held Rosa at arm's length and met her gaze. "Listen, I don't want to hear you putting yourself down or acting inferior anymore, understand? You're a bright young woman. As good as the next person. Shall we tell the other ladies?"

"I really want to, but I think we should wait. Ginny is pretty upset today. I saw her crying in the locker room."

"Oh. Then we'll wait for a better time." Ginny's problems were none of Helen's business, she told herself. But of course Rosa thought everyone's business was her own.

"I did the nosy thing and asked Ginny what was wrong," Rosa whispered. "She said she'd been hoping that she was pregnant, but she just found out that she's not."

"That really isn't our business," Helen told her.

"But Ginny is my friend, and I figured that if she's happy, then I'm happy—like you and me when I got this good news. And if she's sad, then I'm a little sad, too. Wouldn't you have felt bad if I had flunked? Ginny wants a baby so bad, you know."

"Yes, I know."

"Then if we're friends, why is it nosy to—"

"We'd better punch in, Rosa. We have a lot of work to do."

Helen watched the clock all day, thinking about her decision, wondering if she should sign the teaching contract or not. Who knew how long it would be before another teaching position opened up? Near the end of her shift she saw Mr. Seaborn escorting a solider and a crew of blue-clad prisoners from the interment camp along the assembly line, the letters PW stenciled conspicuously on their backs.

"What are they doing here?" she asked Jean Erickson.

"Earl told me that some German POWs might be coming to work here. Mr. Wire has been negotiating all the details with the state officials. He said that a lot of the prisoners worked on area farms this summer and they did a good job. We sure could use the extra help here. We're falling behind on our quotas."

"They make me nervous. How can we be sure they won't sabotage something?"

"The crew chiefs will have to inspect their work, I guess."

Helen made up her mind to come early and help Jean double-check all their work if any of them got jobs as electricians. Then she remembered that she wouldn't be working here much longer. Once again, the thought made her feel a little sad.

As Helen stood in line behind Rosa to punch the time clock at the end of the day, the Germans and their guard suddenly halted a few feet away from her. The English-speaking prisoner, Meinhard Kesler, was among them. To Helen's dismay, he recognized her.

"Good day," he said with a shy smile. "You are Miss Kimball, right?"

She didn't reply. It galled her that he was here instead of behind barbed wire, and she was appalled that he would have the nerve to speak to her.

"Yeah, she's Helen Kimball," Rosa said, butting in. "How'd you know?"

"We met before when she comes to visit our camp. They tell me you are a schoolteacher, Miss Kimball, yes? I did not know you are working in a factory."

"She is a teacher—and a good one, too," Rosa replied. Helen turned her back to punch her time card, then walked away. Rosa caught up with her a moment later.

"Hey, what's the matter? Why didn't you want to talk to that guy?"

"I have nothing to say to him. I toured his camp because I was trying to get it closed down. I wanted him and all the rest of them out of Stockton, remember? Unfortunately, they're not only still in town, they're here in our factory."

"Mr. Seaborn says they might work here from now on."

"That infuriates me!" she said, turning on Rosa. "They won't allow honest, respectable colored people like Thelma to work in production, but they'll allow Nazis? That's absurd!"

"But Mr. Seaborn said—"

"Excuse me, Rosa. I don't mean to be rude, but I need to go home." She needed to cool off before she snapped at Mr. Seaborn or Mr. Wire the way she was snapping at poor Rosa. And she could no longer delay her decision about the teaching contract.

Helen felt much more calm by the time she arrived home. The contract lay waiting for her on the coffee table in the den. Beside it was a pile of newspaper clippings she'd collected that mentioned some of her former students who were away at war. Four of them had been killed in action already, including Larry Wire. It seemed like a lot of casualties for a small town like Stockton.

Helen remembered taking the job at the shipyard to support young men like them and to do her part for the war effort. She had helped fight the war by working there—not only against the Nazis and the Japanese, but she had fought for equality for the Negro workers. She had started all the unrest in the first place by recommending Thelma, so it seemed wrong to stop fighting for her now. And for her other friends, as well.

Helen would need to help Jean keep an eye on the German prisoners, she told herself. She needed to help Ginny remain strong and not give in to her husband's pressure. And Rosa still needed Helen's guiding hand, too, even though she'd passed her equivalency test. All of them would need to work together with Earl Seaborn to help Thelma get the job she deserved. How could Helen desert everyone now when the battle had just begun? It would mean another year at the shipyard, maybe more. Who knew how long the war would last? In the meantime, Helen's friends needed her.

Her friends. Yes, that's what Jean and Ginny and Rosa and Thelma and Earl were—her friends. Helen might be making a huge mistake, but she tore the teaching contract into pieces.

CHAPTER 28
October 1943

"American Fifth Army troops occupied the city of Naples, Italy, today."

★ Rosa ★

Rosa forgot all about teaching Mr. Seaborn to dance until he called her aside after work one day. "I'd like to take you up on your offer of dancing lessons, if you really meant it. I'd like to learn how."

"Oh, wow! Are you gonna ask Jean out?"

"Maybe ..." he said shyly.

"Sorry, that was none of my business. But that's great news, Mr. Seaborn! I'll be glad to teach you!" Excitement raced through Rosa until she could hardly stand still. Not that she cared about her boss's love life, but the lessons would give her an excuse to go out on the town—and with a really nice man, too. It wouldn't be a date, because Mr. Seaborn would never make a pass at her. He liked Jean.

"How about Friday night?" she asked. "Come pick me up at Dirk's house, and we'll go to that dance hall they have for servicemen."

"Well ... I don't know. I'm not sure I want to be seen in public when I'm just a beginner."

She waved her hand to brush away his concerns. "Hey, it'll be so crowded in that place nobody will even notice you. We can start with a slow dance. The worst you can do is stomp all over my feet, and nobody will notice that except me."

Rosa took her time getting spruced up on Friday night as if she were going on a real date. She was so excited to be going someplace fun, even if it was with her boss, that she tried on three dresses before choosing a bright red one. Her clothes were getting very tight now that her pregnancy had started to show a little bit more. Mrs. Voorhees had helped her rip out some of the seams and re-sew them.

When Rosa emerged from her bedroom, all dolled up and wearing high heels, Mr. Voorhees threw his newspaper aside and nearly leaped out of his chair. "Where do you think you're going?" He looked like a junkyard dog that had finally snapped his chain.

"It's none of your business where, but if you must know, I'm going to a nightclub with my boss, Mr. Seaborn. He wants to learn how to dance."

"I'll bet he does!"

"What's that supposed to mean? You calling me a liar?"

"Please, please . . ." Tena begged. "Don't fight . . ."

Wolter ignored her. "Have you no shame at all? You are a married woman with a husband overseas. You have no business going out to a nightclub, especially in your condition. You'll ruin your reputation."

"For your information, I'm helping a friend from work learn how to dance so he can win the girl he loves."

"You should care more about your husband than these people from work."

"You find fault with everything I do. There's just no pleasing you, so why should I even try?" Rosa grabbed her purse and stalked from the house, banging the door shut. She waited outside on the street for Earl, pacing up and down the sidewalk. When he finally arrived, she flopped down in the front seat beside him and slammed the car door. "Boy! Some people!"

"What's the matter? Am I late? Didn't you say eight o'clock?" He kept the car in neutral, idling in the driveway.

"No, you're okay. I got in a fight with Dirk's father. He just about called me a liar when I told him where I was going and why.

He says I should be ashamed and that I'll ruin my reputation. He always says stuff like that, and I'm sick and tired of it! Boy, if there was an apartment I could rent in this stupid town, I'd move out tonight!"

"You know, he might be right," Earl said quietly. "Maybe it's not such a great idea for me to be going out with a married woman. I mean, what if somebody from work saw us together? They might get the wrong idea."

"You taking his side?"

"No, but I do see his point, Rosa. He doesn't know me from Adam. I'm sure he's just looking out for you."

She huffed in anger, upset that no one sympathized with her. "But I really, really wanted to go dancing," she said, trying not to cry. "And you're such a safe, harmless guy to go out with because you won't try to make a pass or anything."

"Thanks—I think. Listen, Rosa, I have another idea. You have a radio at home, don't you? Or a record player? How about if you teach me to dance right here at your house? Would your in-laws mind? That way they'll see that you're telling the truth about me, and I'll still get my dance lesson. Who knows? It might even be fun."

"It won't be nearly as much fun as going out someplace. I was looking forward to it so much. I haven't been out in ages and ages."

"I understand. But I wouldn't feel nearly as self-conscious if we stayed home. Please?"

He really was a sweet guy. And she'd sure show Dirk's father how wrong he was to jump to conclusions. "Okay, come on in," she said with a sigh.

Earl turned off the engine and followed Rosa inside. Mr. Voorhees looked as if a belly dancer had just jumped out of his birthday cake when Rosa led Mr. Seaborn into the living room. Mrs. Voorhees looked worried, as if expecting another argument.

"This is my boss from work, Mr. Seaborn," she told them. "He's the guy who wants dance lessons. And these are Dirk's parents, Mr. and Mrs. Voorhees," she told Earl.

Wolter stood up to shake hands. "How do you do. Aren't you

the fellow from the shipyard who was attacked? They had a story about it in the newspaper. Did they ever catch those two men who did it?"

"No, and I doubt they ever will. Please, call me Earl. Rosa told me you had some ... uh ... concerns about our going out tonight. I understand how you feel, Mr. Voorhees. I hope you don't mind, but I suggested that Rosa could teach me here, with a radio. Would that be okay with you?"

"That would be fine." Wolter looked so pleased he actually smiled for once. Was it because he'd gotten his own way? Well, he may have succeeded in getting Rosa to stay home, but she refused to put on a show for him by dancing in the living room.

"Come on. Let's go out in the kitchen, Mr. Seaborn." He helped her push the table and chairs out of the way, and she hauled Dirk's old phonograph from his bedroom, along with the stack of hit songs she'd bought with money from her paycheck.

"I'm kinda nervous—can you tell?" Earl asked. "Good thing I'm not in public or I'd be stepping all over you and snapping your dainty little toes like pretzels."

Rosa sorted through her records, picking a good, slow song to begin with. This wasn't as much fun as going to a nightclub, but it beat sitting home all alone. She pulled Mr. Seaborn to his feet as the music began to play and showed him how to hold her. He seemed embarrassed about his withered hand, the one he usually kept in his pocket, so Rosa decided it would be best not to say anything about it.

Earl learned quickly, and after the third song, Rosa told him, "You can try holding Jean a little bit closer, if she'll let you."

"How will I know that? Should I ask her?"

"No, just try it once. Believe me, she'll let you know if she wants to get close or not. And I still say she's pretty dumb if she doesn't fall for you."

"It's a question of chemistry, Rosa. People are either attracted to each other or they aren't. Can you really put your finger on what made you fall for Dirk?"

"Well, yeah. It's because he's so ... He's ..." She tried to talk, but her throat tightened as her tears started to fall.

"I'm sorry, Rosa. I didn't mean to upset you."

"You didn't. It's just that I miss him so much! And this song always makes me cry. It makes me wish that the war would hurry up and end so Dirk could come home. Sorry—I'm dripping all over you." She grabbed a dish towel and wiped her eyes, leaving a smear of mascara on it.

"Maybe you should play a different song." He sat down on a kitchen chair to wait while she pulled the needle off the record and looked for a different one.

"You know, Jean held my hand that day I wound up in the hospital," he said quietly. "That's a good sign, isn't it?"

"It's a great sign!"

"I sound like a love-struck teenager. How pitiful is that? I'm twenty-seven years old, and I've seen a lot of girls come and go—in high school, here on the job, and when I was in business college in Cleveland—but I've never met one as wonderful as Jean."

"I hope you win her heart, Mr. Seaborn. I really, truly do." They danced to three more songs until he was relaxed and at ease leading Rosa around the tiny dance floor. She decided it was time to try a faster song. "Okay, we're going to speed things up. Just listen to the rhythm of the music and then start moving to it. That's it ... Good!"

He would never be able to cut up a dance floor the way Dirk did, mainly because of his crippled leg. But Earl had a good feel for the beat and he got the hang of it quickly. They fell onto their chairs, laughing, when the song ended.

"You're no Fred Astaire yet, but any girl would be happy to dance with you," she told him.

"Thanks," he said, puffing. "That's hard work. How long until I'm any good?"

"You know what? If a girl likes to dance as much as Jean does, she won't care how good you are. She just wants a guy who's willing to take her out someplace—trust me."

"Can I ask you something?" he said, turning serious. "Do you really think I'd ever stand a chance with Jean?"

Rosa hesitated. Ginny was trying really hard to teach her to think before she spoke. She liked Mr. Seaborn and wanted to encourage him, but she didn't want to get his hopes up too high, either. She knew that Jean didn't see Earl in a romantic way, only as a friend. Besides, Jean was still stuck on her boyfriend from Indiana.

"You'll never know unless you try," Rosa finally said. "And right now you got nothing to lose, really—but everything to gain, right?"

"Yeah, I suppose so. Will you do me another favor, Rosa? Please don't say anything to Jean about these lessons—or about me liking her."

Rosa gestured as if zipping her mouth shut. "My lips are sealed, Mr. Seaborn. Cross my heart and hope to die."

He lifted her hand and kissed it the way a gentleman would. "Thank you, kind lady. And thank you for the lesson. I think I'm going to need a few more, right? How about the same time, same place, next week?"

"Fine by me."

Earl stuck his head into the living room to say good-night to Mr. and Mr. Voorhees and to thank them for letting him use their kitchen. Then he left. He sure was a nice guy. If only Jean would open her eyes and see what was right beneath her nose.

———

On Monday, Rosa brought her church bulletin to work, as usual, filled with all the scribbled questions that she needed to ask Jean. She pulled it out of her lunchbox during the break and slapped it down on the table with a sigh.

"I'm getting nowhere with all this stuff. The more I learn about how good I'm supposed to be, the more I feel like quitting. Now the minister says I'm supposed to let people push me around? Uh-uh. Somebody lays a hand on me, I give it right back to them—pow! I'll never make it into heaven."

"That's not exactly what the minister was talking about," Jean said. "Turning the other cheek is an attitude of the heart. It doesn't mean we should let people push us around."

"It did when I went to church," Helen said. "That's why I stopped believing in God." Rosa stared at her. So did all the others. It was as if Helen had thrown a bucket of ice water over all of them, shocking them into silence. "I'm sorry," Helen said, rising to her feet. "I didn't mean to say that out loud. If you'll excuse me, I'll sit someplace else so you can continue your discussion."

"No, don't go," they all said at once.

"We can talk about other things," Ginny said. "Please stay." But Rosa couldn't remain quiet.

"You mean you used to believe in God and now you don't? Why not?"

"It's none of our business," Ginny said quietly. "Helen doesn't need to tell us unless she wants to."

Helen sank down in her seat again. "I'm sorry. I shouldn't have spoken at all," Helen said. "Please continue your conversation and I'll sit here quietly and listen. Go ahead, Rosa. Ask Jean your questions."

"Now I forgot what they all were," she mumbled.

"Your questions all come down to the same thing," Jean said quietly. "You keep insisting that you have to be good enough before God will accept you, and I keep trying to explain to you that none of us are good enough on our own. We come to Jesus the way we are and then He changes us."

"But none of the other women in church are as bad as me," Rosa said. "They're all so nice and good—like a big, happy family. The people in the Bible were all goody-goodies, too. I'll never belong in a church."

"Whoa, hold on," Jean said. "There is a list in the Bible of some of the women in Jesus' family, and believe me, they were not all nice, sweet women. There was a woman named Rahab who was a prostitute and worshiped false idols, and she even spied on her own people. But the minute she decided to trust God, He accepted her."

"Is that for real?" Rosa asked in surprise.

"Yep. She converted and became part of His family. In fact, Jesus was one of her descendants."

"Jesus' ancestor was a prostitute?"

"Yep, many generations removed, of course. Maybe that's why He had a heart for sinners and outcasts. And then there's an entire book in the Bible about his ancestor Ruth. She was an outsider who left her family and her homeland and married into God's family."

"Just like me with Dirk."

"I know of another woman in the Bible who wasn't perfect," Ginny said. "Her husband died, but she wanted a baby so badly that she tricked her father-in-law into sleeping with her. I know it's wrong to trick my husband no matter how badly I want a baby. But Tamar was even worse—she tricked her father-in-law. Can you imagine?"

"No! Never!" Rosa said in horror. "He couldn't have been like my father-in-law. He's a regular Mr. Holy!"

"But Tamar's father-in-law was supposed to be 'Mr. Holy,'" Jean said. "When he slept with Tamar, he thought he was sleeping with a prostitute—and he knew that what he did was wrong."

"That's disgusting!" Rosa said. "I thought the people in the Bible were all goody-goodies. It's a wonder God didn't zap them with a lightning bolt or something."

"He not only didn't zap them," Jean said, "but Tamar's son was one of Jesus' ancestors, too. Tamar was His great-great-whatever-grandmother."

"Tell her about Bathsheba," Helen said quietly. They all looked at her in surprise, then Jean nodded in agreement.

"Helen is right. Bathsheba was a married woman who supposedly knew God's laws, but she had an affair with King David—who should have known better, too. When she got pregnant, David arranged to have her husband killed so they could get married."

"Are you kidding? This stuff is really in the Bible? You'd think they'd clean it up or something to make their heroes look better."

"But that's proof that it's authentic, don't you think?" Jean asked. "If they were making up fables, they would doctor up all the important people's stories. God forgave David and Bathsheba, and

Jesus is their direct descendant, too. His family members are far from goody-goodies, Rosa. You don't have to wait until you're good enough to come to Jesus. He takes us the way we are and He changes us. God adopts us and becomes our Father."

Rosa sighed. "Maybe this would be easier to understand if I had a father. I don't really know what one is supposed to be like, so how can I understand God? Now I'm stuck with Dirk's father, and he has so many rules and opinions, I can't keep track of them all. He's always criticizing me, and he doesn't want me to have any fun at all."

"I used to think God's rules were like that," Ginny said. "Then I had children of my own, and I realized that the rules I give my boys are for their own good, so they won't get hurt. I think it's the same with God. We hurt ourselves, not Him, when we break His laws."

"Which way of life was better, Rosa?" Jean asked. "The way you lived in Brooklyn, with nobody watching out for you, or here with a family and guidelines?"

"Well, my life is not so much of a roller-coaster ride here. The only thing that would make it happier is if Dirk came home."

"Mr. Voorhees isn't being mean or trying to judge you," Ginny said. "He's just being a typical father. When he says you shouldn't work, for instance, it's because he's worried about you and the baby. Harold wouldn't want me to work, either, if I were pregnant. That's just the way men are. They like to be protective."

The lunch whistle blew, and they had to end the discussion. But Rosa had two new thoughts to ponder as she worked that afternoon: Jesus' family wasn't perfect, and Mr. Voorhees was only acting like a father.

A father? She'd never had one.

Then Rosa thought of a third thing to ponder: Why didn't Helen Kimball—who was so wise and so strong—believe in God anymore?

CHAPTER 29
November 1, 1943

"American Marines in the Pacific Theater have invaded Bougainville,
the largest of the Solomon Islands."

★ *Jean* ★

Jean watched Rosa pull an enormous sandwich out of her lunchbox and unwrap it. Judging by the amount of food she ate every day, Rosa might be having triplets. Yet she still looked petite and shapely even though her baby was due in one month. All she had to show for it was a little bump the size of a soccer ball, hidden inside a very baggy pair of coveralls. No one had ever imagined that Rosa would get away with working until her eighth month of pregnancy.

"It's hard to believe this is my last week working here," Rosa said after swallowing a huge bite of her sandwich. "I'm sure going to miss all you guys."

"Well, of course we'll visit you and your baby," Ginny said. "Just try to keep us away—right, girls?"

"Of course . . . Absolutely . . . You bet," everyone chorused.

"You'll let us know as soon as the baby is born, right?" Ginny asked. Rosa nodded, her mouth too full to talk.

"And we want to know all about Dirk, too," Jean said. "We'll be praying for him."

"It's so hard not knowing exactly where he is," Rosa said. "He's not allowed to say in his letters, and if he does let something slip, the censors cut the words right off the page. His last letter looked like a piece of Swiss cheese. Dirk's father put all the clues together, and he thinks he's fighting in the Marianas Islands."

"What kind of clues?" Jean asked.

"Well, Dirk said to say hello to Cousin Mariana, but he doesn't have any cousin by that name. So Mr. Voorhees thinks Dirk must be in the Marianas Islands."

"He's in our prayers," Ginny said.

"What about Rosa's replacement?" Helen asked. "Are they going to hire Thelma King?"

"I think so," Jean said. "She's all trained and ready to go. But nobody will ever replace you, Rosa."

That afternoon before Jean left work, Earl Seaborn called her into his office. She could tell by the angry expression on his face that he did not have good news.

"I had a meeting with my boss this morning. I told him that this was Rosa's final week of work and that the wisest approach was to transfer personnel within the company. I told him that Thelma King has done excellent work in maintenance and that she is actually a skilled electrician and deserves a promotion. I fought as hard as I could for her, but I was overruled. They have someone else in mind."

Jean's temper flared. "Don't tell me I'm going to have to train someone new? That will take too much time. And why go to all that trouble when Thelma could start tomorrow?"

"I know, I know. Those were my arguments exactly. Unfortunately for Thelma King, the person they're hiring is also skilled—more so than Thelma, in fact. And he already works here."

"Who is it?"

"One of the German prisoners—Meinhard Kesler. He was an electrical engineer back in Germany."

Jean groaned. "Helen Kimball will quit if he joins our crew. She hates Germans. She'll never agree to work side-by-side with him."

"Why would she hate someone she doesn't even know?"

"I don't know. But remember how hard she worked to get the

POW camp out of Stockton? All those signatures she got on her petitions? She's convinced that the Germans are going to sabotage something. I'm telling you, she hates all of them."

Earl leaned back in his chair with a sigh. "Where's the end to all this hatred, Jean? I've got people who won't work beside Thelma because she's a Negro. Helen won't work beside Kesler because he's a German. Some of the men don't want to work alongside women. Why can't we just see each other as people? Are we really all that different from each other in God's eyes?"

"That's the problem. We don't try to see each other as God sees us."

"Maybe there would be fewer wars if we did."

"This makes me furious, Earl. We both know they would hire Thelma in a heartbeat if she were white. It's racism, pure and simple. Can't we fight this?"

"I tried. I got nowhere. They didn't come right out and say it, but they're worried about causing more unrest here at the shipyard if they hire a Negro. There's a lot of it going around the country these days."

Jean felt defeated. She stood up to leave. "Thanks for trying, Earl." He rose at the same time and hurried to open the door for her.

"By the way, Jean, if you're not doing anything this weekend, I was wondering if you would like to go to a dance with me on Saturday night."

She nearly blurted out, *"You can dance?"* but stopped herself in time.

"It's a fund-raiser for War Bonds," he added when she didn't reply. "I heard they've hired a terrific dance band from Chicago. What do you say?"

Jean hesitated. Russ wrote to her nearly every week now, but it wasn't as if they were engaged like her brother and his girlfriend. Jean had never promised not to date anyone else. She loved to dance, and Russ refused to take her. Besides, Earl was just a friend.

"We would just go as friends," he said, as if reading her mind.

"I promise it won't be a date—unless you'd like it to be?" He smiled hopefully.

"My boyfriend hates to dance."

"Gee, that's too bad. He doesn't know how much fun he's missing, does he?" Earl had a funny grin on his face that she'd never seen before.

"I don't want to lead you on, Earl."

"I understand. You're in love with someone else. We'll just be two friends, sharing a fun evening together for a good cause."

Jean couldn't resist. "Okay. I'll go."

She found herself looking forward to the dance more and more as Saturday approached. It was exciting to have a reason to dress up and use her new makeup and fix her hair. She couldn't remember the last time she'd gone dancing. Before she had started dating Russ, that was for certain.

Jean recognized dozens of people from the shipyard as she walked into the crowded dance hall with Earl on Saturday night. The place seemed to be especially popular with all the young female workers who'd been hired last spring after finishing high school. Jean noticed several of them staring at her and Earl, and she hoped that the rumors wouldn't start flying around the shipyard about the two of them. Maybe this hadn't been such a good idea after all. She took care not to snuggle close to him at their table or hold his hand.

Then the band started to get lively, and she was surprised to discover how much fun Earl was to be with. And he was a pretty good dancer, too, considering his dragging leg. They spent the first hour on the dance floor, never taking a break until the band did. Jean felt exhilarated.

"I haven't had this much fun in a long time," she told Earl.

"Me either."

Jean was in the ladies' room, refreshing her lipstick, when three girls from the shipyard cornered her. "Excuse me, can we ask you a question?" a petite brunette said. "We noticed that you're here with Mr. Seaborn—are you two an item?"

"No, no. We're just friends. I have a boyfriend back home." The girls exchanged glances, smiling. Jean was about to emphatically deny any romantic feelings toward Earl and reemphasize their friendship when one of the girls spoke up.

"Then you wouldn't mind if we dated Mr. Seaborn, would you?"

"He's really dreamy."

"Yeah. And a great guy."

"There aren't too many nice guys left around here with all the men in the service."

"And he likes to dance, too."

Jean was so surprised she could hardly pull her thoughts together. This was the last thing in the world she'd ever expected. "N-no, I don't mind."

"Great! Thanks a lot." The trio exited the ladies' room, giggling.

Jean didn't know what to think. As she walked back to her table, she spotted Earl from a distance and tried to view him through the girls' eyes. He was hardworking, educated, responsible, polite—and quite good-looking. She'd found out tonight that he was a lot of fun to be with and a pretty good dancer, too. He'd be a great catch for any girl. He smiled when he saw Jean and stood to pull out her chair for her.

"I bought us each a soda," he said. "Unless you'd rather dance some more?"

"Yeah, I would." They danced to the next song and were just returning to their seats when the bandleader called for a "ladies' choice." The little brunette Jean had met in the washroom appeared out of nowhere and asked Earl to dance.

"You don't mind, do you?" she asked Jean.

"Um ... no, go ahead." But Jean did mind. The girl was very petite and pretty. The top of her head came to Jean's armpits, making her feel like a hulking Amazon. She watched Earl guide the girl smoothly around the dance floor, smiling and laughing, and was astounded to discover that she was jealous. She had no right to be, no reason to be—but she was.

As the song neared the end, a second girl from the ladies' room cut in on the pair. Earl politely danced through the next song with the second girl. Then the third girl pulled the same trick for a third dance. Jean was fuming. She could easily see her entire evening being sabotaged by these scheming girls—and she had only herself to blame.

She sipped her soda as she watched from a distance, feeling very confused. If she didn't want Earl for a boyfriend, why not stand aside and let him have fun with another girl—or three—who did want him? It wasn't fair to Earl for Jean to stand in their way. After all, she already had a boyfriend, didn't she? She was still trying to decide what to do when the song ended and Earl returned.

"I'm sorry, Jean. I didn't mean to leave you sitting here all by yourself, but they were quite insistent."

"That's okay. I enjoyed listening to the music. You can dance with them some more if you want to."

His dark eyes met hers. "I don't want to. I want to dance with you." He extended his hand to her in invitation, and they walked onto the floor for a slow dance. She noticed that he pulled her a little closer than he had earlier. She let him. It felt so nice to be held tightly, possessively. She felt content in his arms. Then she saw the three girls watching from the sidelines and felt a pang of guilt.

"Your three young dancing partners are eyeing you, Earl. I'll bet they'd go out with you sometime if you asked. They're all very pretty."

"I'm sure they have a lot of nice qualities," Earl said carefully, "but I like a woman I can talk to. And by the way—from one friend to another—they aren't nearly as pretty as you are."

Jean had no idea what to say. She'd grown up surrounded by brothers—sparring with them, teasing them, competing with them. They had always made her feel like one of the guys, and so had Russ, even after he and Jean began to cuddle and smooch. But Earl made her feel different about herself—feminine. And she didn't know how to deal with that. She wished Ginny or Rosa were here to advise her.

Earl gracefully fended off the other girls for the rest of the night and danced only with Jean. They stayed until the band played the very last note, sorry to see the evening end. They talked and laughed all the way home in the car, and Earl escorted Jean to the front door after they arrived—something Russ rarely did.

The porch light was turned out, and she wondered if Earl would try to kiss her. Her heart beat a little faster at the thought.

"We should do this again," he said.

"Yeah, we should. I had a wonderful time." She looked up at him, imagining what it would feel like to have his lips on hers.

He opened the front door for her and smiled. "Well . . . good night, Jean. See you on Monday."

"Good night."

He turned and walked back to his car. Jean didn't understand why she felt so disappointed.

CHAPTER 30

★ *Virginia* ★

Ginny lifted the collar of her coat, shivering as she and Helen stepped from the factory into the cold November air. "I don't know how you can ride your bicycle to work every day when it's this cold," she told Helen.

"I promised myself I wouldn't drive until there was snow on the ground, but I may have to renege. I hope the old beast starts up after all these months."

"I would drive every day if I knew how. I have so many errands to run, and it sure would make my life easier if I didn't have to wait for buses."

Helen stopped walking. "Why don't you learn to drive?"

"I don't have time, for one thing. I work here all day, and I have all of my housework to do on evenings and Saturdays. Besides, I don't think Harold would ever have the patience to teach me."

"I'll teach you."

"Oh, Helen. I would hate to trouble you. And yours is such a beautiful old car. . . . What if I dented it?"

"Good riddance to that monstrosity! Besides, if you learned to drive on that huge old thing, you'd be able to drive any car. I've given lessons before, you know. I taught Jimmy to drive in no time at all, and he—" Helen stopped. She looked away, as if sorry she had divulged so much. She started walking again.

Ginny knew from the snatches of conversation she'd overheard that Jimmy was the man Helen had once loved. The girls at work were dying to know what had happened to him, but none of them dared to ask.

"We'll start tomorrow," Helen said. "I'll bring the car and you can practice driving to and from work every day."

Ginny thought about the prospect of learning to drive all that evening. She was about to *burgeon out* in another new direction! It was on the tip of her tongue several times to confide in Harold as they ate dinner, but she decided not to. What if she turned out to be a failure behind the wheel? She had watched Harold shifting gears and stomping all the pedals, and it seemed so daunting. It would be *injudicious* to tell him about the lessons until she found out if she could get the hang of it.

The next day Ginny sat behind the steering wheel of a car for the first time in her life. "I feel so dumb," she said.

"Listen to me, Virginia," Helen said sternly. "You have to get rid of the notion that you're dumb. All it takes to drive a car are a few lessons and a little self-confidence."

"Harold is Old School," Ginny said with a sigh. "He thinks that driving a car isn't very feminine."

"This belief that women are the weaker sex, incapable of doing things like driving, is pure rubbish. You've already proven that by building ships this past year, haven't you?"

"How did you become so strong, Helen?"

"I had to be strong to stand up to my father. I only wish I would have stood up to him sooner.... I know you're all dying to ask me why I never married. I don't hate men, even though it must sound like it sometimes. I was engaged once. But Albert was my father's choice, and I didn't love him. Love is important in a marriage, don't you think?"

"Yes, very important," Ginny said quietly. She felt all of her fears slowly rising up inside, choking her. She needed to pour them out to someone. "Things have been a little better between Harold and me lately. And he says he still loves me. . . . But every time he travels, I start worrying again that he'll have an affair. I'm trying to become more independent in case he does decide to leave me, so learning to drive is another preparation for that day. I want to be ready in case it happens. Remember the speech Eleanor Roosevelt gave after Pearl Harbor? She said we should always be prepared—"

Ginny paused, struggling to hold back tears. "But I think it will still destroy me if Harold leaves, no matter how much I prepare for it."

Helen was silent for a long moment. "I have no idea what to say, Ginny."

"That's okay. Me either." She drew a deep breath and raised her chin. "Anyway. On with the lesson."

"You're a lot stronger than the Ginny Mitchell who started working a year ago," Helen said. "If the worst does happen, and your husband does find someone else, you'll make it on your own. . . . Although I think Harold Mitchell would be a fool to leave you."

"Thanks," she whispered.

"Now. Push in the clutch and start the engine."

Ginny practiced depressing the clutch pedal and shifting the gears for a few minutes before lurching out of the parking lot. The car hopped like a drunken rabbit, pitching poor Helen forward and backward as Ginny struggled with the clutch.

The driving lessons consisted of traveling to and from work at first, and the hardest thing for Ginny to learn was releasing the clutch and shifting smoothly without grinding the gears or stalling. As she began to improve, they took excursions into town to practice parallel parking, then drove out of town on country roads to build up speed.

"You're ready," Helen announced one Thursday afternoon in December. "You should take the driving test now before the snow flies. We've been lucky so far. We haven't had snow and icy roads yet. But you don't want to wait until spring."

"Oh, Helen, I don't know—"

"I telephoned the licensing office and learned that they stay open an hour later on Fridays. We should go tomorrow after work. Before you have too much time to think about it and talk yourself out of it."

"But what if—"

"You'll need to make arrangements for your boys after school. We'll go there straight from work."

"Are you sure that—?"

"I'm positive."

Ginny felt frightened and unprepared, but she was grateful for Helen's insistence. All the girls at work knew how indecisive Ginny was, but Helen wasn't allowing her any room to back out. They drove to the testing site immediately after work the next day.

"Now, listen to me, Ginny. If something goes wrong and you don't pass the first time, it's not the end of the world. We'll practice some more and you can retake the test."

Ginny realized she was holding her breath. She let it out. "Okay."

"And Ginny—one more word of advice, if I may. You're a lovely woman. A little flirting goes a long way. You've seen how well it works for Rosa."

Ginny stared at her, surprised that Helen of all people would suggest such a thing. "Are you telling me to flirt with the man who gives the test?"

"Why not? Women have been doing whatever it takes for thousands of years."

Ginny laughed, and it seemed to ease her tension. Maybe that had been Helen's plan all along.

The examiner turned out to be a tidy, unsmiling gentleman in his sixties. He climbed into the passenger seat and instructed Ginny to pull away from the curb. She smiled at him, wiped her sweating palms on her thighs, then carefully checked her mirrors the way Helen had taught her before pulling out onto the street. She saw Helen wave to her in the rearview mirror.

The instructor spoke curtly at first, saying little more than, "Turn left ... turn right ... stop here," as he made notes on his

clipboard. Parallel parking worried Ginny the most. Helen's car was
so huge. But she followed Helen's advice and smiled sweetly at the
man each time he gave her a command, and by the time they got
around to parallel parking he had thawed like an ice cube on a hot
stove. He chose a spot with two empty spaces to test her parking
ability, and she slipped the car into it with ease. They arrived back at
the licensing office in no time at all.

"Very good, Mrs. Mitchell," the man said as the car drew to a
halt. "You passed with flying colors." She nearly hugged him. Instead,
she jumped out of the car and hugged Helen.

"I passed! Helen, I passed!" They went inside together to pick
up her brand-new license. Even Ginny's nosy neighbor, Betty Parker,
didn't have a driver's license! Ginny wanted to celebrate. "I can't wait
to tell Harold. He's been away all week but he's coming home this
evening."

"I'm proud of you," Helen said. "Mr. Mitchell should be, too."

Ginny tried to decide how to surprise Harold with the news as
she scurried around the kitchen, making supper before he arrived. But
the moment he walked through the door she could tell by his expression that he was in no mood to celebrate.

"What a week," he groaned as he dropped his suitcase and
shrugged off his overcoat. "I don't know how the government
expects to win a war overseas when they can't even solve our problems at home. This race issue is cropping up more and more, everywhere I go."

"What happened now?"

"Remember I told you about that factory in Maryland where
some of the workers walked off the job after a colored woman transferred to their department? Well, the War Labor Board held hearings
and ruled that she could stay and that the bathrooms had to be
integrated for her. Now seventy percent of the work force has gone
out on strike. Seventy percent! Of course, the Negroes are willing to
cross the picket lines and take over the strikers' jobs, so the whole

place is in an uproar. President Roosevelt is probably going to have to call in the National Guard to cool things down."

"That sounds pretty frightening. And you're in the middle of it all?"

"I'm supposed to make sure the government quotas are met. I'll tell you, I have a feeling that as soon as we win the war overseas, we're going to have a new war here at home. I fail to see how the color of a man's skin makes any difference in his ability to do a job."

"Remember the colored woman at the shipyard I told you about who was all set to fill in for Rosa after she left to have her baby?"

"Whatever happened with her?"

"Jean and Helen had trained her and everything. But management sidestepped the issue and hired a German POW instead. Helen's worried that the German prisoner will sabotage something. She watches him like a hawk."

"You're getting quite involved with all these people, aren't you?" He sounded irritated with her. In fact, his entire mood seemed sour, and Ginny knew he wouldn't celebrate her good news with her. She went to bed without telling him.

"My suit needs to be dry-cleaned," Harold told her at breakfast the next morning. He sat at the kitchen table reading his newspaper while Ginny washed and dried the breakfast dishes. "Everyone smoked during the meetings except me. Can you take it to the dry cleaner?"

In the past, Ginny would have walked or taken the bus to run errands in town. Today she could drive. She was barely able to suppress her excitement as she asked, "Is it okay if I take your car?"

"My car? Take it where?"

"May I drive it to the dry cleaner?" Harold stared at her as if she were talking gibberish. Ginny pulled her new license from her purse and handed it to him.

"Surprise! I learned to drive! See? Here's my new license."

"What? When? ... How in the world did you learn to drive?"

"Helen Kimball gave me lessons in her father's car. She took me to get my test yesterday, and I passed. 'With flying colors,' the man said." Harold stared at her, his mouth hanging open. He looked so shocked that she couldn't tell if he was pleased or not. "Well, say something, Harold!"

"Good for you, Ginny." He surprised her with a smile. Then he stood and pulled the keys from his pocket and handed them to her. "Be careful." Ginny was so happy she wanted to sing.

She went upstairs to get Harold's suit and was emptying out his pockets when she found a folded piece of paper. It looked like a receipt. She unfolded it, guessing that it might be important.

It was a receipt for flowers, dated a week ago. They hadn't been for her.

"Oh no ..." She sank down on the bed as all the strength drained from her legs. Her breakfast rolled sickeningly inside her stomach. "Oh, Harold, no ..." she whispered.

Should she ask him about it? Confront him? He would probably try to cover it up with a lie if she did. Harold was a very skilled poker player. Besides, did she really want to know? If she did confront him, she would have so many decisions to make, and she just wasn't ready to make them.

Ginny folded the receipt and put it in her purse. Then she took the suit and her grocery list and walked to the bus stop. It would be impossible to drive a car with tears blurring her vision.

CHAPTER 31
December 1943

*"After conferring with Prime Minister Winston Churchill and
Russian Premier Joseph Stalin, President Roosevelt expressed
the three leaders' determination to 'work together in the war
and in the peace that will follow.'"*

★ *Helen* ★

As soon as Helen learned that Meinhard Kesler would join their crew
in Rosa's place, she climbed down from the deck of the ship they
were building and went straight to Earl Seaborn's office.

"I am furious!" she told him. "How could they hire a Nazi
instead of Thelma King?" Earl had been seated behind his desk,
working his way through a stack of papers, but he rose when she
entered.

"I understand, Miss Kimball. I'm upset about it, too. I fought as
hard as I could for Thelma, but—"

"I'm not blaming you, Mr. Seaborn, but where can I go? Who
can I talk to about this . . . this . . . injustice! The personnel director?
The chairman of the board?"

"You'll be wasting your breath, I'm sorry to say."

She gave a strangled cry of frustration. "I feel so helpless! I
worked so hard to get those Germans out of Stockton, getting all
those petitions signed—and my efforts did no good at all. Now this!

Jean and I worked with Thelma King, training her, encouraging her. We both know how well-qualified she is. It's so unfair!"

"I feel the same way you do."

Helen remembered the beating Earl had taken because of the Negro workers, and she knew he was telling the truth. "I'm sorry, Mr. Seaborn. I shouldn't be taking it out on you. I just don't know where else to turn. Can't anything be done?"

"I would be busy doing it if there were something."

Helen sank into the chair across from Earl's desk, trying to rein in her temper. He sat down, too. "How can you be certain that these prisoners won't sabotage something?" she finally asked.

"We can't be entirely certain. But the company is getting the prisoners' labor for free, so they're probably willing to take that risk in order to increase their profits."

"I wish I had known this was going to happen. I was offered a teaching position this fall, but I turned it down so I could help Thelma and the others. Now I wish I had accepted it. Who knows how long it will be before another vacancy opens up? And I don't think I want to work alongside a Nazi."

"I'm really sorry, Miss Kimball. I would have warned you if I had known. I was certain Thelma would get the job. I think the unrest over the drinking fountain frightened all the bigwigs."

"Cowards! They did the easy thing instead of the right thing!"

"Hiring prisoners offered them an easy way out, yes. But the warden assured us that Mr. Kesler isn't a Nazi—and he is highly qualified."

"Just so you know, I'll be watching his every move. I hope he gets the death penalty for sabotage if he tries anything."

For the first few days, Helen noticed that Jean assigned jobs to Meinhard Kesler that kept him well away from her. But she knew it was only a matter of time before she'd be forced to work more closely with him, the way she had with Rosa. At least Helen wasn't forced to socialize with him or any of the other Germans during their breaks. A guard took the prisoners to a separate room to eat, and she was able to forget about him for a short time, at least.

On the Monday after Ginny earned her driver's license, Helen announced the good news to Jean as the three of them ate lunch. "Some congratulations are in order. Ginny passed her driving test."

"That's wonderful!" Jean said. "I'm so proud of you, Ginny! I'll bet your husband was, too. Did you show it to him?"

"Yes. He said he was happy for me. He ... he gave me the car keys so I could take his suit—" She couldn't finish. Her shoulders shook as she wept.

"Ginny, what's wrong?" Jean quickly moved to her side to comfort her.

"I'm sorry. It's just that ..." Ginny dug in her purse for a handkerchief and pulled out a folded piece of paper along with it. "I found this in his suit pocket."

Helen leaned across the table to look. It was a receipt from a florist shop. "I gather that the flowers weren't for you?" she asked.

Ginny shook her head. "I don't know what to do."

"I'd stick that paper under his nose," Jean said angrily, "and demand an explanation."

"No, I'm afraid to confront him. I'm not sure I really want to know the truth. I don't think I'm ready to hear it. Maybe if I waited—"

"And let it eat away at you?"

Ginny shrugged. "Maybe it will all blow over. Maybe Harold will get this *philandering* out of his system and come to his senses. In the meantime, I'm ... I'm just not ready to face it."

Helen remained silent. She had no experience in this area and could offer no advice. She would dearly love to punch Harold Mitchell in the nose for hurting his wife this way, but that wasn't the solution, either.

"Let me know if I can do anything," Jean said.

"I will."

Ginny didn't talk about it again, and Helen didn't pry. Asking nosy questions had been Rosa's forte. It was surprising how much Helen missed Rosa. All three of them did. Her name came up at least once a day.

Meinhard Kesler's presence served as a constant reminder to Helen that Rosa was gone and that Thelma had been cheated out of a job. And he also reminded her of the Great War—and Jimmy. She wished she could find fault with Kesler's work so they could get rid of him, but he was excellent at what he did. And he was also unfailingly polite and courteous. He gradually won over Ginny and Jean with his soft-spoken, gentlemanly ways, and they began conversing with him as they worked together. Helen couldn't help overhearing that he was a widower and that he had been assigned to a mobile communications unit in the African desert. He'd been captured a year ago in Egypt after El Alamein.

Helen refused to be taken in by him. Every time he moved within ten feet of her she would quickly step aside. She never spoke to him and would turn her back if he tried to speak to her. She watched him during breaks and after work hours when the others were distracted, but she found no evidence that he was sabotaging the ships. In fact, as they were assembling wire harnesses one morning, Kesler showed Jean a design deficiency in the schematic drawing.

"I think there is a better way to do this. Look here—wouldn't it be easier and more efficient if we did it this way?" He sketched an alternate design on a scrap of paper. "Here, you take this to the—how do you say? To the chief electrician. He will see what I am talking about."

Jean studied it for a moment. "You're right. I will show him. Thanks." Within a few days, the boss told Helen and the others to assemble the harnesses the new way—Kesler's way. Helen couldn't imagine why Kesler would agree to build a ship in the first place since it would be used to attack his own country, much less help redesign it.

As the weeks passed, Helen became aware that Kesler had begun watching her. Her continual rebuffs and the fact that she never spoke to him seemed to bother him. He made several attempts to greet her and draw her into the conversation with the others, but Helen simply turned her back on him every time and walked away. She hoped he would get the hint and stop trying—but he didn't.

One afternoon as Helen worked with him and the others deep inside the ship's bulkhead, he confronted her. The whistle had blown, signaling the end of their shift, but as Helen headed toward the narrow doorway, Kesler blocked her path. Her heart sped up as she tried to go around him.

"You are in my way," she said coldly. "Kindly move."

"Wait—before you go, I . . . I must ask you something." Helen lifted her chin and folded her arms, waiting. "I need to ask you to forgive me," he said quietly.

"For what?"

"For whatever it is that I have done to make you hate me."

She was about to deny that she hated him but realized it would be pointless after her behavior the past few weeks. "Why would you ask for such a thing?" she said instead.

"Because I am sorry for you . . . sorry that you are so bitter."

"You don't know anything about me!"

"I recognize this bitterness because I was once the same. When you came to our camp, you asked me where I am fighting in the first war. I am wondering if someone you love has died in that war."

"That's none of your business!" He infuriated her, yet she felt powerless to push him aside and leave. His voice, his calm manner, and the way his gentle eyes held hers seemed to have a hypnotic effect that she couldn't break.

"Someone I loved also died in that war," he continued. "Not in the fighting, but in the time of starving that followed. My wife and our small son, Heinrich, died of disease and not enough food to eat. Our conquerors did not care. They demanded our money and our food and our land in punishment for starting the war. And so when Adolf Hitler comes with his promises and lies, my country—myself—we all follow him. It is because of our bitterness that we want revenge. You see where this bitterness has led the whole world, Miss Kimball?"

When she didn't reply, Meinhard continued. "That is why I ask you to forgive me. If you do, it will bring the bitterness to an end. It will bring freedom. I wish I had known this much sooner. I never saw it until *Kristallnacht*, when my people turned all their anger against the Jewish people, destroying homes and businesses and synagogues. The week of broken glass, they called it. I am sickened by it. I see my Jewish neighbors being ridiculed, beaten, killed. And I am thinking, 'that is somebody's wife, somebody's child.' I understand them because of my own wife and child. And that is when I know this bitterness must end.

"When this second war begins, they make me become part of it against my will. But the first chance I have, I lift my arms in surrender." He raised his arms in the air to demonstrate. "Enough! Enough bitterness. Enough fighting. I could no longer fight with God. And you see, He is the One that I was most angry with."

"I don't believe in God," she said in a trembling voice.

Meinhard shook his head. "I have met people who truly do not believe in God, and they feel no anger when they see suffering. They are indifferent to it. But you and I are angry. Anger is not indifference. I blamed God because He took my family—but I couldn't get revenge from God, so I turned my rage against other people. I wanted revenge. Someone must pay!"

"You're wrong," Helen said, wanting desperately to believe that he was. "I told you, I no longer believe in God."

"Then why are you so angry with Him?" His eyes were so sorrowful that Helen had to look away. She was unable to reply. "You blame me and my country for your losses, Miss Kimball, and I blame you and your country. But you and I are people, not countries. Did you kill my wife? My child? Would you put a gun to their heads and shoot them or take away all of their food and watch them die? No. Of course not. Neither would I kill someone you love if I met him face-to-face. Wars come from bitterness and hatred. They are started by nations without faces. But wars end, the hatred ends, in the hearts of people like you and me. That is why I ask you to please forgive me."

Helen didn't want to think too long or too hard about what Meinhard was saying. She groped for something to say, desperate to divert him from this terrible, painful subject. "When you came here to work," she said, "when you took this job, you stole it from a woman who needed it—a woman who deserved it. She happens to be a Negro. But what do you care? You Germans believe in the so-called 'Master Race.' You believe that Negroes are inferior."

"I do not believe that," he said flatly. "My Bible tells me that Jesus looks inside our hearts, not at the color of our skin. But please believe me, Miss Kimball. I did not know about this woman. I am sorry for taking her job. . . . If I make it up to her—and to you—then will you forgive me?"

"What do you care if I forgive you or not?"

"God has forgiven me for all the wrongs in my past. He even forgave me for being angry with Him. I want to thank Him by living the best way that I can from now on. I want to make peace with my enemies. I know that you think of me as an enemy . . . and so I ask you once again to please forgive me, Miss Kimball."

Helen slowly shook her head. To answer otherwise would have been a lie. "You ask too much," she said softly.

Meinhard closed his eyes and quietly stepped aside, allowing Helen to pass. As Ginny and Jean followed her up the ladder, she was ashamed to realize that they had heard every word. She punched the time clock and bolted from the building without another word to anyone.

When she arrived home, Helen turned on the radio to distract herself, then spent a half hour scrubbing a perfectly clean kitchen sink—anything to avoid thinking about Meinhard Kesler's words. While she scrubbed, she heard a news report telling how American forces had invaded the Gilbert Islands in the Pacific and was reminded of Rosa's husband. He was stationed out there somewhere. Helen knew the terrible pain and loss that girl would experience if anything happened to Dirk, and once again bitterness toward her enemies blazed in Helen's heart like a furnace. She quickly turned off the radio.

Kesler was wrong. She wasn't angry with God—she didn't believe in God. And why should Helen forgive Meinhard or the Germans or anyone else? He had no right to ask such a thing.

Helen made herself some supper, skimmed through the newspaper, then went upstairs to bed an hour earlier than usual. She couldn't sleep. She found a book to read and curled up in her bedroom chair, desperate to forget Meinhard Kesler and Dirk Voorhees and Jimmy Bernard, desperate to silence all of her raging thoughts.

She awoke at dawn, stiff and cramped from falling asleep in the chair. She nearly called in sick for the first time since she'd started working at Stockton Shipyard but decided not to. She refused to give Kesler the satisfaction of knowing that his words had affected her. Even so, she dreaded facing him.

As soon as Helen reached her crew's workstation, she sensed that something was wrong. Jean was missing, and her clipboard, which always posted their daily work orders, wasn't hanging in its usual place. "What's going on?" Helen asked when Jean finally emerged from a meeting in Mr. Seaborn's office.

"Management is scrambling to issue new work orders. All of the German prisoners quit—just like that." She snapped her fingers. "The warden can't force them to work here, because it's supposed to be voluntary. But every last one of them refused to come back. Meinhard is their spokesman and he wouldn't give a reason why."

Helen's heart speeded up. She knew the reason. Then she realized what else this might mean. "Is Thelma King finally going to work with us?"

"Earl went to get her. She's on her way right now." Jean smiled in triumph, and Helen couldn't help smiling along with her. Finally justice was being done!

Helen was still euphoric when Mr. Seaborn brought Thelma to the harness shop where Ginny, Jean, and Helen were working. Thelma seemed to glow as she took her place alongside Helen to assemble her first wire harness.

"I don't know how I can ever thank you, Miss Helen," she said.

Helen brushed her thanks aside. "Nonsense. I had nothing to do with it. You earned the right to work here."

"But I know that you and Mr. Seaborn and Miss Erickson were all fighting for me. You have no idea how hard it is for us colored folk. We have to fight for things that come so easy to you—like getting a good job and earning decent pay. I'll be able to help out my family now—and maybe I can start saving up to buy us a house after the war."

"Are you married, Thelma?" Ginny asked.

"No, not yet. My boyfriend's in the navy. He's stationed in San Francisco for now."

"And the armed forces are still segregated, aren't they," Helen said bitterly. "They were segregated in the Great War, too. How many years ago was that? Twenty-five? And nothing has changed in all that time."

"Oh, I know there will be plenty more battles to fight before colored people get a fair chance, Miss Helen. But at least we won this fight. And you all helped. I don't know how I can ever thank you."

It wasn't until Helen was driving home that afternoon that she realized the unspoken bargain she had made with Meinhard Kesler. He had quit. He'd convinced all of the others to quit. And now she would have to admit that she'd been wrong about him. She would have to forgive him. She felt the nugget of bitterness burning inside her at the thought of him and knew that she wasn't ready to do it. She had nourished that blackened trophy for twenty-five years, shaping it and polishing it until it glittered like a diamond. What would fill its place if she let it go?

Could Meinhard be right about God, too? Would she be this angry with Him if she didn't believe in Him? Helen parked the car in the garage and slammed the door on her way out. Those were questions she refused to think about.

CHAPTER 32

★ Rosa ★

Rosa clapped her hands until they stung. She would have put her fingers in her teeth and whistled, but she'd never heard anyone else whistle in church and figured it probably wasn't allowed. But seeing all those little kids dressed up as Mary and Joseph and the wise men, and hearing them sing Christmas songs like "Away in a Manger" and "Silent Night," had been just about the cutest thing she'd ever watched.

She felt her unborn baby kicking her in the ribs and she rubbed her tummy, smiling to herself. *Yeah, you'll be singing up there with all the others in a few years, just you wait.* She turned to Ginny and Jean, who were seated in the pew with her.

"Wasn't that the cutest thing? Didn't Patty's boys make darling shepherds?"

Ginny nodded, blowing her nose.

"They did great," Jean agreed, "especially after we took away their shepherd's crooks so they'd quit whacking each other with them."

"Do we get cookies now?" Ginny's son Herbie asked. Her boys had come to the Christmas program that evening, too, to see Jean's nephews perform.

"Refreshments are downstairs in the church hall," Jean told

them. "You can run on ahead and we'll meet you there."

"She doesn't really mean 'run,'" Ginny said, grabbing Allan's shirttail. "Remember your manners." The boys took off at a fast walk, and Ginny helped Rosa to her feet. The doctor had said the baby might come anytime, but meanwhile it was getting harder and harder for her to stand up again once she was seated.

"Uff! Thanks, Ginny. This kid has really been . . . what's that funny word you're always using lately?"

"You mean *burgeoning*?" Ginny laughed. "I think you're the one who has been *burgeoning out*, Rosa."

"Well, I just want this kid *out*! I don't care if he *burgeons* or not." Rosa felt so happy to be with her friends from work again that she would have danced if she could have. She'd missed Jean and Ginny this past month. And Helen, too. "Gee, I sure wish Helen would have come. Then we'd all be together again. I guess she didn't want to come to church because she doesn't believe in God. But how can anyone not believe in God?"

"Maybe it's because of all the losses in her life," Jean said. "I can't imagine losing all of my siblings."

Ginny linked her arm through Rosa's as they followed the chattering crowd downstairs to the church hall. "People sometimes have a hard time understanding God when they're hurt," Ginny said. "They can't understand why He would let them suffer so much pain."

"Ginny and I overheard someone talking to Helen about this at work," Jean said. "He told Helen that deep down she knows God still exists, but she's angry with Him."

"And maybe we'd be angry with Him, too," Ginny added, "if someone we loved died. Jean and I came to the conclusion that the man Helen loved must have died in the first war. What was his name?"

"Jimmy," Rosa said. "She never did tell me what happened to Jimmy—just that they went their separate ways. And I couldn't find out because you made me stop asking nosy questions, remember? But

I always figured he must have died in the war, and that's why Helen hates Germans so much."

"It would explain a lot," Jean agreed.

Rosa gripped the railing as she made her way down the narrow stairs. What if God took Dirk from her the same way? It was a question she tried hard not to think about because it always made her insides feel like somebody was twisting them in knots. To be honest, she would probably hate the Japanese for the rest of her life. But would she stop believing in God? All you had to do was look up at the stars at night or at a baby's face to know God existed.

Downstairs, the church hall was as loud and rowdy as a beer joint. Dozens of overexcited children, including Patty's two oldest boys, chased each other around the room in circles while their Sunday school teachers tried in vain to calm them down. The line for coffee and cookies reached to the bottom of the stairs.

"I'm too beat to wait in line," Rosa told the girls. "How about if you go ahead, and I'll save us a table." She sank into the nearest chair with a sigh.

"Do you want coffee or punch?" Jean asked.

Rosa's stomach rolled at the thought. "Neither one, thanks." She watched the swirl of activity while she waited and imagined Dirk as a little boy running around like all the others. The little girl who'd played Mary was tossing her baby Jesus doll into the air and catching him again. Two little wise men fought over one of the fake gifts they had brought to the baby. Rosa wondered if Dirk had ever played the part of a wise man or a shepherd. Tena had shown her pictures of him all dressed up for church, his blond hair nearly white in the sunlight as he grinned at the camera.

"Is that story really true that they told in the play tonight?" Rosa asked Jean when she and Ginny returned with their coffee and cookies. "Did God really send His Son as a little baby?"

"It's absolutely true," Jean replied.

Rosa frowned. "But all that other stuff about Him being born in a barn with sheep and cows—that part isn't true."

"Yes, it is," Jean insisted. "The Bible says that Mary had to use a feeding trough for Jesus' crib."

"But if Jesus was really God, wouldn't He have been born someplace nice?"

Jean shook her head. "If He had been born as a king in a palace, then the shepherds and the common people never would have been able to get near Him. But anyone can visit a stable. Jesus came for all people, so He had to come from a simple background that everyone could relate to."

"But the shepherds wouldn't have come traipsing in all dirty and smelly with all their sheep, would they?"

Jean smacked her fist on the table. "Yes! This is what I've been trying to tell you for months and months, Rosa. The shepherds came to Him the way they were. You don't have to be nice and clean first."

"God could never love someone like me, though."

Jean exhaled in frustration. "Listen, Dirk loved you the way you were, didn't he? Even though he knew all about your background?"

"I told him everything about me." Rosa felt her face flush as she remembered.

"And he loved you and married you anyway, right? And he gave you a home with his family. He would give his life for you, wouldn't he? And what did he ask you to do in return?"

Tears welled up in Rosa's eyes as she remembered lying safe in Dirk's arms on the beach in Virginia, hearing him reassure her. "He said all he wanted was for me to love him back."

"See? Dirk didn't say, 'Be good first. Clean up your act, then I'll love you.' But now, because of his love, you *want* to be a better person, right? You asked Ginny to teach you to be a good mother. You asked Helen to help you finish your education. You even asked Mrs. Voorhees to teach you to cook all the food Dirk likes, remember? Dirk didn't demand that you do all of those things. And he won't stop loving you if you can't bake pies like his mother. But you want to live a better life *because* he loves you."

"I want to be everything he sees in me."

"That's the way it is with God, Rosa. He loved us before we

were ever good enough. Jesus died for us before we ever deserved it. But if we love Him, we'll want to change. If we tell Him everything we've done wrong, He'll forgive us and take us into His family and help us change. We can't change all by ourselves. He helps us, just like all your friends helped you learn new things."

"I even learned to stop asking nosy questions," Rosa said, smiling at Ginny through her tears. "I think I finally understand. Thanks, Jean. I don't know why I'm crying if I'm happy. I don't know what's wrong with me."

Ginny reached over to hug her, then said, "Here, eat something. You haven't touched your cookies."

Rosa shook her head. "I haven't felt like eating all day. I don't know if it's nerves or the flu. I feel all ... crampy."

Ginny looked at her intently. "When is your baby due again?"

"Any day ..." Suddenly Rosa had the most embarrassing feeling she could ever imagine. She had just wet herself! Her dress and her chair felt very warm and soaking wet. She could even feel water running down her legs.

"What's wrong?" Ginny asked. "You just turned as white as a sheet."

"You know how you told me about all the water that's inside with the baby?"

"Did it just break?"

"It's all over, everywhere! I'm so embarrassed! What am I going to do?"

"You're going to go to the hospital, that's what," Ginny said. Rosa couldn't imagine why she and Jean were smiling. They looked like they'd just won the largest poker kitty of the night. Jean hurried to round up Patty and her kids, and Ginny rushed outside to warm up her husband's car. They acted so excited. All Rosa could think about was who would mop the floor and how would she ever dare to ride in Ginny's nice car without getting the seat all wet?

Ginny took Rosa home first, driving as if she had a car full of loose eggs that she didn't want scrambled. "Change your dress and pack your overnight bag," she told Rosa. "I'll come back for you after I drop off everyone else."

Mrs. Voorhees took one look at Rosa and said, "It's time, isn't it?"

"Yeah, I guess so." Rosa couldn't understand why everyone was smiling at her when she was wet and embarrassed and feeling like something the cat dragged in. Her back hurt, and her stomach felt like she'd drunk too much vodka, and all she wanted to do was lie down somewhere. Tena took Rosa's hands in hers.

"We have never talked about it . . . but would you like me to come to the hospital with you?"

Rosa had never dared to ask Tena to come with her, afraid that she wouldn't want to be bothered with her, like Rosa's own mother. But as tough and as street-smart as Rosa might be in other situations, she admitted to herself that she was scared half to death right now. She didn't want to go through this ordeal alone.

"Would you?" she asked.

"Of course. Let me help you get changed."

Ginny offered to stay at the hospital with Rosa, too, and the two older women settled in with her for a long night. They walked up and down the hospital corridors with her as the hours passed, kept track of the time between contractions for her, and sat at her bedside, soothing her as the labor pains came and went.

"Don't think about how bad it hurts," Tena said as another pain squeezed Rosa like a wringer. "Think about holding your baby soon. Think about what he will look like. When you hold him in your arms, you will be holding a little part of Dirk."

The pain finally eased again. Tena's words had helped. But Rosa still feared motherhood more than she feared giving birth. "You should be having this baby, Ginny, not me. I'm scared I'm going to be a terrible mother."

"Never! Motherhood is all about giving love," Ginny said. "And you have so much love to give. You've worked your way into everyone's heart at the shipyard—even Helen's. I knew her when she was a teacher, and I always felt so sorry for her. She was so *aloof* and alone, *estranged* from everyone. But she opened her heart to you. She talks about you all the time and asks if we've seen you. She said to be sure to call her with the news when the baby comes."

Rosa felt another labor pain start to build, and she groaned as she gripped the sheets, bracing herself. "Only three minutes apart this time," Tena said. "You're getting close." She wiped Rosa's forehead when the contraction finally ended.

"I loved being a mother," Ginny said. "I guess that's why I felt so lost when my family didn't need me anymore."

"You must have done your job very well, then," Mrs. Voorhees said. "Children are supposed to grow up and leave the nest and fly on their own. Of course, we want to hold them close, and we want them to always need us. But that is not healthy for them or for us. Today Rosa's little one will take his first step in outgrowing his mother. Children are their own persons; they are not part of us."

"But do they have to go to the other extreme?" Ginny asked. "I felt as if my family didn't even notice me anymore. They didn't see *me* as my own person. And I didn't know who I would be without my role as a mother. That's why I went to work in the shipyard."

"Mothers give and give and give, unselfishly," Tena said. "We—"

"Not my mother," Rosa said. "My mother only thought about herself."

"That's very sad," Tena said. "She missed out on so much. It is the hardest job there is, to love unselfishly. Mothers are often ignored and rarely thanked. But Jesus said that the most important command is to love God and love others. So that tells me that being a wife and a mother is one of the most important jobs in the world. I am not just serving my family, I am serving God. And only He can make you feel fulfilled."

"I never thought of it that way," Ginny said softly.

"And, Ginny, you are still a mother, even after your children leave home. Later on, their love comes back to you, multiplied. They get married, you see, and their wives become your children, too." Tena looked down at Rosa and smiled. "Then they give you grandchildren. Wait until you see how wonderful grandchildren are!"

Rosa tried to stifle a groan of pain but couldn't. "Tell your grandchild to hurry up! I can't take this much longer. Can't they do something to make it stop hurting?"

The pain quickly became one long, unending flame. Tena gave Rosa's hand a final squeeze before the nurses chased her and Ginny to a waiting room and wheeled Rosa down the hall to the delivery room. Pushing her baby into the world felt like the hardest work Rosa had ever done.

But then came a rush of joy like nothing she had ever felt before. Her son, her perfect little baby boy, lay warm and whimpering in her arms. He had dark hair like her own and a very red face. And the tiniest little hands she had ever seen with fingernails like drops of candle wax. The poor little fella had Dirk's pointy ears, but she loved him anyway. Oh, how she loved him! She kissed him over and over again.

"Thanks for finally coming out," she murmured. "I've been waiting to see you. I'm going to take real good care of you, you'll see."

She would call him Joseph, the name Dirk had picked out. Rosa never imagined that she could love someone as much as she loved Dirk, but her love for little Joseph welled up inside her until it overflowed in tears. He hadn't done a single thing to make her love him yet and had caused her ten long hours of pain. But she loved him. This must be what Jean meant when she said God loved His children enough to die for them.

Joseph was so fragile and vulnerable. He needed Rosa in order to live. And they both needed Dirk. She closed her eyes in exhaustion and prayed.

"God, I have nothing to offer you. But if you take care of Dirk for me, I'll take care of this little baby for you the best way I know how."

PART THREE

1944

*"Courage is the first of human qualities because
it is the quality which guarantees all others."*

★ ★ ★

Winston Churchill

CHAPTER 33
April 1944

*"Allied airplanes have been methodically strafing and bombing
the coast of northern France in preparation for the expected invasion.
Some two thousand planes have taken part."*

★ *Jean* ★

The town of Stockton seemed like a beautiful place to Jean as she
walked to work on a warm spring day in April. But her mood darkened when she opened her locker and found yet another threatening
letter calling her a "Nigger lover." She quickly changed into her work
clothes, then brought the letter to Earl, as he'd asked her to do. As
she neared his cubicle, she saw that it had been vandalized once again.

"Not again," she moaned. The vandalism had happened so often
in the four months since Thelma joined Jean's crew that Earl might
as well give up cleaning it.

"Here's another letter," Jean said, handing it to him. "I found it
in my locker this morning. Is it my imagination or is the racial tension here at the shipyard going from bad to worse?"

Earl gestured for Jean to sit in the chair in front of his desk.
"It's not your imagination. The pressure to get rid of Thelma has
escalated almost daily. First she found threatening letters stuck to
her time card or stuffed among her tools, saying *Whites only* and *Quit
or else*. Then she said that people started jostling her and elbowing

her and tripping her whenever she stood in line at the punch clock, or headed to the lunchroom, or moved through the exit doors when the shifts changed. I warned her never to be alone in the factory or outside on the grounds. I've started meeting her at the door before every shift and escorting her out at the end of the day."

"I don't understand what these troublemakers want," Jean said as she gazed at the black paint splattered on Earl's walls.

"Me either. Integrated washrooms are the big issue in other factories, but ours are still segregated—and we're breaking the law by keeping them segregated, I might add. No one is being forced to work with Thelma, so why all this hatred and venom?"

"I guess it's the only thing some people know," Jean sighed. "I never saw such prejudice back home. Maybe I've been sheltered."

"What about the other two women on your crew—Ginny and Helen? Is this unrest bothering them?"

"If it is, they haven't said anything. Should I go ask them?"

"Better yet, let's have a meeting about it right now, here in my office."

Jean quickly found Helen and Ginny, and the three of them squeezed into Earl's cubicle. "I see someone has redecorated your office again," Helen said, gazing around at the mess.

Earl nodded. "This problem seems to be growing, and I'm getting worried. I'm sure you are, too. I want you to know that if you would like to change shifts or transfer to another crew, everyone will understand."

"I'm not abandoning Thelma," Helen said. "I'm standing beside her. I'll admit that I'm getting tired of looking over my shoulder all the time, but if we quit now, then the racists win. And at least there's one small victory to celebrate. Did you read about the Supreme Court decision in *Smith v. Allwright*? They declared that all-white election primaries are against the law. Negroes must be allowed to vote in them."

"That's great," Earl said, "but why has progress been so slow? Negroes won the right to vote after the Civil War. Why are they still being prevented from voting in 1944?"

"I don't know," Helen said, "but it's outrageous."

"How about you, Ginny?" Earl asked. "We'll all understand if you've had enough."

"I'm not quitting," she said softly.

Her answer surprised Jean. It usually didn't take much to frighten timid Ginny. She barely had the courage to stand up to her husband. "Are you sure?" Jean asked her. "I know you've found threatening letters in your locker, too."

"Yes, I'm sure."

"What about you, Jean?" Earl continued. "Are you certain that you want all this pressure? I know that some of the men were pretty hard on you even before Thelma joined us. And this racial tension is getting serious."

"I've made up my mind not to let them scare me," Jean said. "My twin brother, Johnny, is a gunner on a B-26, flying bombing raids over Germany. He's standing up to a far more powerful adversary than I am."

"And it looks like we're winning over there, too," Earl said. "The invasion of Europe can't be too far off. It's what the soldiers are all preparing for. In the meantime, let's hope we win this racial battle, too. Okay, ladies. I guess you can go back to work."

Jean noticed how quiet Ginny had been during the meeting and drew her aside when they were alone at the tool station. "Are you okay, Ginny? You don't need to stay on my crew just because Helen does. If you feel threatened at all, please let me know."

"No, I meant it when I said I wanted to stand beside Thelma. She's been so brave through all of this." Ginny paused, staring down at her feet. "But these cowards who are harassing us don't even have the courage to confront us face-to-face, and they made me realize what a coward I am. I still haven't confronted Harold about his *philandering*."

"Do you know for certain that he is?"

"No, I haven't found any more evidence, but I never did ask him about the receipt for the flowers." She lifted her chin and drew a deep breath as if summoning her courage. "If Thelma and our soldiers overseas can be courageous, then it's high time I faced things head on, too."

Jean knew that Ginny was doing the right thing, but she couldn't help worrying about how she would ever recover if her husband did leave her for another woman. "Once you know the truth, there will be no turning back, you know."

"I know," Ginny said softly. "So I need to decide what I'm going to do in the event that . . . that he is *philandering*."

Jean squeezed her shoulder. "Good luck, Ginny. You're stronger than you think you are. And you can always turn to your friends."

Jean was still thinking about Ginny's dilemma at the end of the workday when Earl stopped her on her way out the door. "A little birdie told me that you have a birthday coming up next week, Miss Erickson. I was wondering if you would you like to go out dancing again to celebrate?"

Jean wanted to accept his invitation, but she hesitated. "Can I think about it and let you know?"

"Sure." Earl's grin wavered. She had hurt his feelings. He couldn't seem to help wearing his heart on his sleeve, as Jean's mother used to say, where it was plain to see.

"It's not like I'm waiting to see if I get a better offer," she explained. "It's just that you caught me by surprise, that's all."

He laid his hand on her arm. "You don't owe me an explanation, Jean. Let me know when you decide, okay?"

She pondered Earl's offer on the long walk home. The spring day was still magnificent with new buds on the trees and forsythia in bloom. She passed daffodils and tulips in people's yards and was tempted to pick them. What was it about springtime that made her feel like dancing?

Jean had been out dancing with Earl two times, first for the War Bond rally and then on New Year's Eve. Both times, Earl had shown her a good time. On New Year's Eve, as midnight approached, they had stood together on the dance floor, counting down with the rest of the crowd: "Five . . . four . . . three . . . two . . . one! Happy New Year!" Earl had pulled Jean into his arms and kissed her. It had felt so natural—and so exciting—that she'd wanted him to kiss her again. Her reaction had stunned her. What about Russ? She wouldn't like it if he kissed another girl, whether it was New Year's Eve or not. Now she didn't know if she should go out with Earl again.

She longed to confide in someone who could help her sort out her feelings, but she wasn't sure who it should be. Her sister Patty wouldn't be objective because she didn't like Russ. And it would be too awkward to ask Ginny or Helen, since Earl was their boss. She decided to wait and see what Russ had to say in his birthday card. But the week passed without a letter or a card from Russ.

On Sunday—another gorgeous spring day—Jean ran into Rosa at church. Her baby was four months old already and growing fast. Joseph had a head of wild, dark curly hair like Rosa's and chubby, rosy cheeks.

"Look at him!" Jean gushed as she lifted him into her arms. "I've always been fairly immune to cute babies, having grown up with seven younger brothers, but this little guy is special. Even Helen says so—and think of all the children she's seen in her lifetime."

Rosa beamed at the praise. "I know. Helen gave me a camera for a present so I could send pictures of him to Dirk. Hey, want to walk home with us? I've been taking Joey to and from church in your sister's baby carriage now that the weather's nice."

"Yeah, sure. That'll give us time to talk."

Rosa settled Joey in the carriage, tucking a blanket around him, and they started on their way. "You have to tell me all about the gang at work—and about Mr. Seaborn, too."

Jean felt a stab of guilt. She had left Earl's offer dangling all week and knew she needed to give him an answer soon.

"Can I tell you something, Rosa? And can you promise not to tell anyone—not even Ginny or Helen?"

"Yeah, sure."

"I went out dancing a couple of times with Earl Seaborn."

"No kidding? Is he a pretty good dancer?"

"Yeah, he's great—and he's a lot of fun to be with, too. He even—" She paused. Rosa looked like she was about to burst into laughter or song, or maybe dance a jitterbug. "What's going on, Rosa? Why do you have that look on your face?"

"Me? What look?"

"I don't know—like you're up to something."

"I'm just glad to hear you're going dancing. You used to tell me all the time how much you love to dance." Rosa still looked like she had a secret she was dying to share, but Jean went on.

"Well, Earl asked me to go out dancing next week for my birthday, but I'm feeling a little guilty. I have a boyfriend, you know. Russ and I have been together for almost four years and I like him a lot."

"What do you like about him?"

"Well . . ." Jean paused, listening to the carriage wheels thumping on the cracks in the sidewalk. Rosa's question stumped her. Why couldn't she think of a dozen things she liked about him? "He's very good-looking . . ." she began, then realized how shallow that made her sound. She searched for something better. "He's part of me, I guess, part of my past. We've shared a lot of good times together—Russ and Johnny and Sue and me."

Her answer sounded so feeble. Was that the best she could do? Maybe it was because she and Russ had been apart for so long that she'd forgotten what she liked about him. And he wasn't very good at writing regularly. Jean and Rosa stopped at an intersection and waited for the traffic to clear. When they'd crossed to the other side, Jean changed the subject.

"Earl and I are just good friends," she insisted, "and I want to keep it that way. But both times when he took me home I started imagining how it would feel to kiss him good-night. I didn't kiss him, of course, but the thought made me feel so guilty. Like I was cheating on Russ. Have you ever gone out with two different guys at the same time?"

"Oh, sure. Most girls do."

"Is it wrong to be a two-timer like that?"

"Mr. Seaborn knows all about Russ, right? So you're not two-timing him. Did you ever promise Russ that you wouldn't go out dancing with a friend?"

"Not in so many words . . . But Russ never takes me dancing, so does that mean I have to sit home for the rest of my life and never dance again?"

"Of course not! You're too young to give up dancing! These should be the best years of your life. You deserve to have a little fun, be a little independent before you settle down and get married. You're not engaged to Russ, are you?"

"No, but I don't want to do anything to lose him."

Rosa stopped walking and faced Jean, her hands on her hips. "Listen, if he gets sore because you went dancing with a friend—when he won't even take you himself—then I say good riddance."

"But my life would be so empty without him."

The baby had kicked off the blanket, so Rosa tucked it around him again before they resumed walking.

"Russ would be very jealous if he knew about Earl," Jean continued. "But jealousy is a good quality, isn't it?"

"I guess so." They walked a little way in silence before Rosa said, "Can I ask you a question about church?"

"Yeah, sure." Jean was relieved to change the subject, even though she was still unsure if she should accept Earl's offer.

"Mr. Voorhees says I need to have Joey baptized. I've seen them baptizing other babies at church, and the daddy always holds him. I don't think it's right to do it until Dirk comes home, but when I told Mr. Voorhees that I wanted to wait, he got real upset. He says it's important to do it now and I shouldn't wait. Is that true?"

"Gosh, I don't know what to tell you. Joey is your son, so it seems like it should be your decision. What does Dirk say?"

"I don't know. I wrote and asked him, but I haven't gotten any letters from him since the end of February."

A chill shuddered through Jean. "February? That's more than a month ago."

"Yeah, I know." Rosa's voice shook with emotion. "They said in the news that they've been fighting some terrible battles on Iwo Jima and all those other islands. They said the marines are taking all the heat. And Dirk is out there with them . . . somewhere."

Jean groped for words to reassure her. "He probably has so many patients to treat that he doesn't have time to write. And it's probably hard for the ships to get in and out of those war zones with the mail. And who knows? Maybe Dirk's letters were on a ship that got damaged or sunk."

"Yeah, I know. I've been telling myself the same things, but it's so hard not to worry. I've never gone this long without hearing from him before. And in the meantime, Mr. Voorhees keeps nagging me about getting Joey baptized."

"Did you explain to him how you feel?"

"He won't listen. But if I go ahead and baptize him, it'd be like admitting that Dirk might never come home. He *will* come home! He promised me! And I want to wait for him, even if Joey is old enough to walk up the aisle and dump the water on himself. His daddy should be there!"

"Oh, Rosa. I'm so sorry for going on and on about my own silly worries with Russ and Earl. It's all so stupid in comparison—"

"Hey, that's okay. I miss everyone at work so much. . . . It's been nice to hear about your life."

"I know it doesn't sound like much, Rosa, but I'm praying for Dirk—and for you."

"Thanks. I wish I knew how to pray better. I'm no good at it."

"Just talk to God the same way you're talking to me. Pretend you have Him on the telephone or something and just talk. He knows what's in your heart anyway—how scared you are, how worried. But it will help if you tell Him and get it off your chest."

They stopped walking again when they reached Rosa's house. "And Jean? I think you should go dancing with Earl on your birthday."

Jean got a letter from her twin brother on Monday with birthday greetings. Her mother sent a card and a present, along with homemade birthday cards from Jean's younger brothers. Jean shared the birthday cake Patty had baked with the girls at work. All week she waited for a birthday card or a letter from Russ, but when none came she decided to accept Earl's invitation.

He arrived on Saturday night with a bouquet of flowers, then took her to a dinner dance in Kalamazoo. Earl ordered cake for dessert, then pulled a package of birthday candles out of his pocket and stuck them in the cake for Jean to blow out.

"What did you wish for?" he asked as she took her first bite.

"That my brothers would all come home safely. That the war would end."

"We all want that. But what about something for yourself? Do you think you might start college next fall?"

"No, not until the war is over."

"Why not? Is it a question of money?"

"Not really. I've been saving every cent I earn. I'd probably have enough if I worked during the summers."

"Then why wait?"

"I don't know," she said, licking the icing off the candles. "It just doesn't seem right to start yet. This isn't how I planned it."

"But I know how much you've looked forward to college," Earl said, frowning. "Did you change your mind?"

"No, I haven't changed my mind. It's just that . . ." Jean mashed her cake crumbs with her fork as she poured out her frustration. "I had my life all figured out and planned, and then the war ruined everything. Johnny and I were going to go to college together; afterward, my boyfriend and I would probably get married. My family was poor but at least we were whole and happy. Then the Japanese attacked Pearl Harbor, and now six of my brothers are away fighting and in danger—and I feel like I'm not really living. I'm in limbo, working at the shipyard, waiting to get back to the life I planned. Johnny and I promised each other we would go to college together and study like we did in high school. We'd help each other. We're so much alike and we're best friends. He has his girlfriend and I have Russ—but now things just won't be right until the four of us are all together again. Back to normal."

Earl leaned toward her, covering her hand with his. "It's great to have plans, Jean, but don't forget to live your life right now. It's a mistake to overlook today because your eyes are on tomorrow or looking back to the past. When we're always wishing for the past or the future, we miss today. Besides, plans have a way of being changed against our wills. I had plans, too, before I got polio."

"How old were you when you got it?"

"Sixteen."

"Wow. I always thought of it as a childhood disease, for babies. I had no idea."

"I loved baseball. That was my plan, to be a great baseball player. When I look back on the past I can still remember what it felt like to run the bases and slide into home plate. How it felt to swing a bat with all my might and feel it connect with the ball—*whack!* The jolt goes all the way up your arms, and you know you've hit it over the fence. Home run!" Earl leaned back and took an imaginary swing, making a knocking sound with his tongue like a bat hitting a baseball. He gazed into the distance as if watching the ball soar. Then he looked at Jean again, his eyes meeting hers. "But I don't want to live in the past, always wishing I could have it back. I want to live today and do the best job I can with it. I want to work hard, then enjoy a fun evening with a good friend."

"I'm sorry I talked about Russ," Jean said. "That was unfair. I promise I won't mention him again." They finished their dessert and got up to dance. Jean decided to take Earl's advice and put away her thoughts of the past or the future for one evening. She and Earl laughed and talked and waltzed around the dance floor, just the two of them, as the bandleader crooned "Happy Birthday."

"I wonder how he knew it was my birthday," she said, laughing.

At the end of the evening she found herself wondering once again if Earl would try to kiss her good-night. And if she should let him. But as they got out of the car and walked toward the house, she was annoyed to see that all of the porch lights were on, lighting up the yard. Earl would never try to kiss her beneath the glare, for all to see. She felt a stab of disappointment, then guilt for wishing it. What on earth was happening to her?

They walked onto the porch together, and Earl reached for the doorknob. Jean looked up and saw Patty standing in the front window as if she was spying on them. Then Patty beckoned for her to come inside. Earl opened the door, and as soon as Jean saw her sister's reddened eyes and tear-streaked face, she knew something terrible had happened. Jean's first thought was for Patty's husband, Bill, fighting in Italy.

"What's wrong? Patty, tell me!"

"Ma called."

With those two terrible words, Jean knew it wasn't Bill. Patty would have received a telegram if it had been her husband. Something must have happened to one of their brothers. Jean's mind still thought logically, but her heart seemed to have stopped beating. She loved all of her brothers, but her greatest fear was for her twin.

"Oh no . . . Please don't tell me it was Johnny," she whispered. "Please . . ."

Patty nodded. "He's gone, Jeannie."

"NO!" Jean screamed. "Oh, God, *no!*" She would have collapsed, but Earl's arms were suddenly around her, holding her tightly, supporting her weight. "It isn't true! It can't be true!" she cried.

"I wish it wasn't," Patty said softly.

"I'm sorry, Jean . . . I'm so sorry," Earl soothed as she screamed and wept, pouring out her anguish. He led her to the sofa and sat down with her. She clung to him tightly.

"Ma got a telegram," Patty said. "Johnny's plane was shot down on a bombing run."

"Maybe he parachuted out. Maybe he . . . he just got captured or something. . . ."

Patty shook her head. "His plane crashed, Jeannie. Everyone on board was killed."

"No . . . Oh, God, no. It isn't true!"

It couldn't be true. Jean had hugged Johnny good-bye before he'd left for England, and he'd been so strong and happy, so alive. He was too young to die. Today was his twentieth birthday. He couldn't be gone. It was a mistake. Someone would tell her that they'd made a terrible mistake. Or else she would wake up and see that it had all been a horrible nightmare.

Jean knew that this was one of those moments when her life changed forever. She would never be the same. Johnny was gone, and Jean felt as though her own life had been cut short, as well. She didn't know how to start all over. She didn't want to. She had always believed that Johnny would be in her future. And now he wouldn't be.

Everything in her life seemed meaningless as she grappled to accept the truth.

Johnny—her twin, her best friend—was dead. She didn't know how she would ever stop crying.

CHAPTER 34

★ *Virginia* ★

Ginny learned the terrible news from Jean's sister. When she hung up the phone, Ginny sank down at the kitchen table with her face in her hands and cried. It would be hard enough for anyone to lose a brother that way, but Johnny was Jean's twin. Ginny knew from the way Jean had talked about him that the two of them were very close. What a terrible loss. At last Ginny dried her eyes and telephoned Helen and Rosa and Thelma, as she'd promised. The news shocked all of them.

Grief-stricken, Jean didn't come to work for several days, and things at the shipyard didn't seem the same without her. Helen pulled away from everyone, becoming *aloof* again the way she'd been when Ginny had known her at Lincoln School. Ginny had forgotten the old Helen, but this fresh grief brought her back. Ginny, Helen, and Thelma worked hard to fill in for Jean but couldn't meet their quotas without her.

"How's Jean doing? Have you seen her?" Ginny asked Earl when he came to the harness shop where they were working. "I brought a casserole over last night and asked if I could do anything, but Jean stayed upstairs in her room and wouldn't come down. Patty says she isn't eating."

"She wouldn't come down when I went over there, either," Earl said. "She learned a few more details about the crash, and I'm not sure if it made matters better or worse. Her brother's B-26 was flying a late-afternoon mission over Dunkerque in France when it was hit by enemy fire. The pilot lost control before anyone could escape, and it collided with another American plane in the same formation. Both planes went down in the English Channel."

Ginny got such a huge knot in her throat that she couldn't speak. She heard Thelma murmur, "God rest all their souls. . . ."

Earl's voice was very soft. "I guess Jean has lost all hope that the news was a mistake or that Johnny might have bailed out and lived. There won't be a burial, of course, but Jean's family is planning a memorial service for him this weekend."

"That's a good idea," Helen said. She had stood apart from the others with her back turned, so it surprised Ginny that she had spoken. "Otherwise, without a service, it's hard to grasp that he really is gone," Helen continued. "Everyone will keep expecting him to walk into the room and—" She stopped. "I'm sorry," she mumbled, turning away again.

"I offered to drive Jean and Patty to Indiana for the service," Earl said. "I could use some more ration stamps if any of you ladies have extras."

"I'll ask my husband if we can spare a few," Ginny said.

"I'll give you mine." Helen turned and joined them at last. "The weather is warm enough for me to ride my bicycle, and if it rains, it won't kill me to ride the bus."

"I'd like to go to the service with you if there's room in your car," Ginny said. "I'd like to give Jean and Patty my support."

"Thanks. I know they'll appreciate it. And there's room for you, too, Helen. It would make it easier to explain why I have your ration book."

Helen didn't reply. She wouldn't meet anyone's gaze as her fingers idly traced the wires laid out on the board. Ginny knew how much it would cost Helen emotionally to go to the funeral. She would be reliving the deaths of her own siblings. But at last she nodded, agreeing to come.

At the supper table that night, Ginny asked Harold if she could drive his car to Rosa's house. "I promised to keep Rosa up-to-date on how Jean is doing, and I need to tell her about the memorial service. It seems too impersonal to do it over the phone."

"You're taking this death awfully hard, aren't you?" Harold asked. "You didn't even know this boy."

"Jean has become a good friend. All of the women have. I won't be long."

Rosa's baby felt warm and wiggly as Ginny cuddled him, plump and overflowing with life. Holding him made her realize how badly she'd needed the comfort of a child in her arms.

"Look how fat and happy he is!" she told Rosa. "See? Didn't I tell you you'd be a wonderful mother? A baby is God's way of saying He wants the world to continue."

"Joey's good as gold, too. He hardly ever cries."

"How are things with Dirk's father?" Ginny asked. "Jean told us he was giving you a hard time about baptizing the baby. Has he changed his mind?"

Rosa shook her head as she reached to caress her baby's foot. "No. He makes it sound like Joey is going straight to hell and it will be all my fault."

"I can't believe God would do that. You stick to your guns, Rosa. What does Dirk say?"

Rosa bit her lip. "Still no letters from him. It's been two months."

The news worried Ginny, especially after what had happened to Jean's brother. She tried not to let Rosa see her fears. She had enough as it was. "If you ever need to get away from here for a time, you're welcome to come over to my house," Ginny said.

"Are you sure your husband wouldn't mind? How are things with . . . you know . . . with the flowers he bought?"

"I was trying to figure out a way to ask him about that receipt when I heard about Jean's brother. Now I need to wait until I get my emotions under control again. I'm going to a memorial service for Johnny on Saturday—Earl's driving us to Indiana."

"I'd like to come, too. Would there be room for me and Joey?"

"Sure. We'll squeeze you in somehow. We can hold Patty's kids on our laps if we have to."

On the Friday before the memorial service, Jean returned to work. She walked around in a daze of grief, and her tears came often. Whenever they did, Ginny held her in her arms and let her cry. She knew that no words could possibly console her. At the lunch break, Ginny, Helen, and Thelma sat outside on one of the picnic tables that the shipyard provided, but Jean didn't join them. The sun felt warm, the fresh air welcome after spending the morning inside the hull of a ship. The women had the table all to themselves—as they always did whenever Thelma ate with them.

"At least this tragedy seems to have halted the flow of nasty letters," Helen said.

"You're right," Ginny said. "I hadn't noticed until now. Although it's hard to believe that racists would respect someone's grief."

"It worries me that Jean has stopped eating," Thelma said. "I can see she's losing weight."

"Grief is a merciless tormentor," Helen replied.

Ginny hated to leave the sunshine when it was time to return to work, but she followed the other women inside and back to the ship they were building.

"Now, where could my tools have run off to?" Thelma asked, gazing all around their work area. "I thought I left them right here with yours," she told Ginny.

"I'll help you look for them." Ginny searched the tool locker and the entire area where they had been working before the break, with no luck. Then, as she stood on the ship's deck, gazing around, Ginny saw a tool belt hanging from a light fixture above the factory floor. A stepladder still stood in place below it as if to taunt Thelma. Whoever had played this trick on her would be watching, waiting to laugh at her as she climbed to retrieve her tools.

The prank made Ginny furious. She scrambled down from the

deck and strode across the factory floor to the ladder. She wasn't fond of heights, but Thelma was her friend and she didn't deserve this treatment.

Ginny could feel the ladder wobbling as she began to climb—or maybe her knees were shaking. She wondered if she was tall enough to reach the tool belt dangling above her once she reached the top. She might have to stand on the very top step with nothing to hang on to. The idea scared her but she kept climbing.

She was nearly to the top of the ladder, trying hard not to look down, when her foot slipped on one of the rungs. Ginny grabbed the sides of the ladder to catch herself, but they felt slippery, too. She felt herself falling, felt her face smash painfully against the rungs, but she couldn't seem to hang on.

"Help!" she cried out as she lost her balance. But her weight shifted as the ladder tilted sideways, and she felt herself falling helplessly toward the ground. The hard cement floor raced toward her.

Then everything went black.

CHAPTER 35

★ *Helen* ★

Helen was scanning the deck of the ship, helping in the search for Thelma's tools, when she suddenly heard a scream. She looked up, then watched in horror as the ladder Ginny was climbing tilted sideways and crashed to the ground. Ginny landed like a rag doll on the unforgiving cement floor. The ladder landed on top of her.

"God, no!" Helen breathed. "Ginny!" For a split second, Helen relived the terrible moment years ago when her brother Henry toppled from the railing to land in a heap on the gazebo floor. The same helpless horror rocked through her.

She clambered down from the deck, her movements clumsy with fear, and raced over to where Ginny lay motionless. Helen shoved away the ladder and knelt at her side.

"Ginny! Ginny, wake up! Please, Ginny. Please be okay . . ." She lifted Ginny's limp hand and felt a pulse, but Ginny didn't open her eyes.

"Don't move her," Jean said. "Somebody call an ambulance!"

Helen was dimly aware of other people gathering around them. She heard Thelma praying, "Oh, Lord, please help her. Please let her be okay. Please, Lord!"

Helen continued to plead frantically. "Wake up, Ginny. Please wake up." This couldn't be happening. In the past few days, Helen had thought so often of how her brother Henry had died as she'd grieved for Jean and her brother. And now she had witnessed yet another fall—with Ginny.

"Everyone stand back," Earl Seaborn shouted. He crouched beside Helen. "What happened? Did you see what happened?"

"Sh-she took a terrible fall . . . off this ladder. I saw her hit the ground."

"What was she doing on a ladder in the first place?"

"I . . . I don't know. . . ." Helen looked up and saw Thelma's tool belt dangling from the light. The hatred behind the deed shocked her into silence. She could only point to it. Thelma looked up, as well.

"My tools! She was getting my tools! Oh, Lord . . . Oh, Lord!"

Earl pivoted around to examine the ladder, still lying on the floor nearby. "These rungs feel greasy. Could this be deliberate?"

"Oh, Lord," Thelma moaned. "That fall was meant for me!"

Helen could barely breathe. Her pounding heart felt as heavy as a boulder, weighing her down. She remembered feeling the same way after her brother Henry had fallen, wishing she could stop time and roll it backwards and do everything differently the second time.

"Oh, Lord, please help her," Thelma continued to pray. Helen remembered how Jimmy had done the same thing, kneeling on the gazebo floor beside Henry, begging God to spare him.

"Don't touch anything," Earl said. "I'm calling the police. This was premeditated. They're not getting away with this."

"Tell . . . tell the police I'll offer a reward . . . f-for information," Helen stammered. "Somebody knows who did this."

Helen and Thelma each held one of Ginny's lifeless hands as they waited endlessly for the ambulance. Any minute now Ginny would open her eyes and smile her timid smile and apologize for causing so much trouble. She would be fine, and tomorrow morning she would come to work with a new word that she'd found in the dictionary to describe what a clumsy nuisance she was. But Ginny lay on the ground, not moving, and Helen was terrified. Her brother Henry had never regained consciousness.

At last she heard sirens. She released Ginny's hand and stood aside, watching as they loaded her carefully onto a stretcher and carried her away. Then Helen noticed Jean, huddled on the floor, her face white with shock. She had barely uttered a word throughout the ordeal.

"Someone had better take Jean home," she whispered to Earl. "She's in no condition to deal with this. I would drive her, but I don't have my car."

"I'll ask Mr. Wire to drive her," Earl said. He stood and gently helped Jean to her feet.

"Has anyone called Ginny's husband?" Helen asked.

"I'll do that, too," Earl said. "Thelma, you need to wait right here so we can talk to the police." She nodded wordlessly.

"I think I should go meet Ginny's husband at the hospital," Helen said. "He knows me from school. I'll explain to him what happened." Earl agreed, and Helen fetched her purse and lunchbox from the locker room, glad to flee this terrible place.

By the time Helen arrived home and changed out of her work clothes, she had stopped trembling enough to drive her car to the hospital. She begged every emergency-room nurse and orderly she could find for information.

"Mrs. Mitchell is still unresponsive," they finally told her. "She'll need X-rays."

"It isn't a good sign that she's been unconscious for so long, is it?"

"You'll have to speak with the doctor about that. Now please take a seat in the waiting room." Helen wished she could pray.

When Harold Mitchell ran through the hospital doors a half hour later, Helen barely recognized him. The cool, efficient engineer who had toured the shipyard with the army officials and had asked levelheaded questions during his son's parent–teacher meetings had vanished. In his place was a devastated man who looked as though he had lost himself. The same fearful, distracted panic that Helen had seen in Ginny's eyes when she'd lost her boys, now filled his.

"Where is she? What happened?"

Helen told him.

"Oh, God, oh, God, not Ginny. Who would do such a thing? She's such a gentle soul ... I didn't want her to work there, I told her it was dangerous. I ... I don't know what to do!"

Helen could see that Harold Mitchell was too upset to think coherently. "Let's tell the doctors that you're here and ask for a report," she said.

"But how will we live without Ginny? Our boys ..."

"I just remembered! Your boys will be arriving home from school soon. Would you like me to go to your house and stay with them until you've spoken with the doctors?" He nodded mutely. She gripped his arm for a moment and said, "Let me know when you hear something."

Helen drove across town and parked her car in front of Ginny's house, then sat in it, unmoving. She knew, suddenly, that Meinhard Kesler was right. She did believe in God because right now she was furious with Him. For the first time since the attack on Pearl Harbor, Helen prayed. But her silent, angry words were neither submissive nor beseeching.

God, don't you dare take Ginny! It's bad enough that you let Jean's brother get killed, but don't you dare take away this family's wife and mother! She's my friend, God, and you can't have her!

When she saw Allan and Herbert ambling up the street from school with the Parker boy from next door, she reined in her anger and drew a deep breath. What on earth would she say to them? They saw her climbing out of her car as they approached.

"Hello, Allan ... Herbert."

"Hi," Allan said softly. He looked frightened, as if he was about to get into trouble the way he had the last time Helen had shown up at their house. "If you need to see my mom, she's not home from work yet."

Helen felt tears filling her eyes. Rage helped her hold them at bay. "Actually, I'm here to see both of you," she said, swallowing. "Your mother will be a little late today, so I offered to come over and make sure you're okay ... until ... until she ..." Helen recalled Ginny's motionless body and chalky face. She couldn't finish.

"Where is she?" Allan asked.

"She's in the hospital. Sh-she had an accident at work. Your father is there with her, and I told him that I would come here and stay with you until he comes home."

"Is Mommy okay?"

"The doctors were still examining her when I left. Your father will know more when he gets home."

Herbie began to cry. "I want Mommy!"

Comforting him didn't come naturally to Helen, but she knew that Herbie needed it. Ginny was always so affectionate with her boys. Helen reached out, stiffly at first, and put her arm around him.

"It's going to be okay, Herbie. . . . Maybe we should have a snack while we're waiting. Are there any cookies in the house?"

"Mommy made some last night."

"Good. Let's go inside and see if we can find some milk to go with them."

Ginny's oaf of a dog bounded to the door to greet them, leaping all over Helen and trying to lick her face. The boys had chores to do, making sure the dog had water and a chance to run outside in the yard, and soon the distraction of a normal routine seemed to calm everyone. Somehow Helen found a way to keep the boys talking as they ate their snack. She was helping them with their homework afterward when someone knocked on the back door. She opened it to find Thelma and her grandmother Minnie on the doorstep with their arms full of groceries.

"We come to help out," Minnie said. "And we plan on staying here to do all the cooking and cleaning and whatever else needs to be done to help this family for as long as they need us."

"Miss Ginny helped me," Thelma said. "She took this fall for me. Least I can do is show her how thankful I am." The women took over the kitchen and had Ginny's ironing all done and dinner prepared when Harold Mitchell arrived home from the hospital.

"There's been no change," he said numbly. "I thought I'd better come home and talk to the boys." Helen saw tears in his eyes. She watched from the doorway as he took his sons into the living room, then crouched down and gathered them close, an arm around each one. "Your mother is hurt and we have to be very brave," Harold said.

Helen couldn't bear to watch any longer. She excused herself, knowing that the family was in Minnie's capable hands. As she started the car engine, Helen remembered one more friend who should be told about Ginny. She drove across town to Rosa's house with the bad news.

"Helen! Hey, what brings you here?" Rosa had come to the door in a housedress and apron, the baby balanced on one hip. She looked as exotically beautiful as ever. "How's Jean doing? I heard she was taking the news about her twin brother real hard." In all of the turmoil, Helen had nearly forgotten the first disaster.

"Yes. Jean is understandably upset. May I come in?"

"Sure. What's going on?" Helen made Rosa sit down, then perched on the sofa beside her.

"I'm afraid there has been another tragedy. I wanted to tell you in person, not over the phone. Ginny fell at work today and hit her head. They took her to the hospital by ambulance."

"Oh no!"

"It happened right after lunch, and she's still unconscious. I went to her home to look after her boys until Mr. Mitchell came back from the hospital. He said there has been no change. Ginny's still in a coma."

Rosa's wide, dark eyes glistened with tears. "How'd she fall?"

"That ... that's the worst part, I'm afraid. It wasn't an accident. Someone deliberately greased the ladder. They hung Thelma's tools from a light fixture, and Ginny was climbing up to retrieve them for her."

"They did it on purpose?" Rosa stared as if unable to comprehend it. "I need to see Ginny," she finally said. "Are you going back to the hospital? I want to come with you." Rosa scrambled to her feet.

"What about the baby? I don't think they'll allow him—"

"Mrs. Voorhees will watch him. I just fed him, so he'll be okay for a few hours. Let me get my purse from my bedroom."

As Helen waited in the living room, she heard Rosa give the baby to her mother-in-law in the kitchen. Mrs. Voorhees began singing to him in Dutch and he cooed happily in reply. The doorbell rang.

"I'll get it," Helen called. She opened the front door to face two men in U.S. Navy uniforms. The older man wore a chaplain's insignia on his lapel. Helen took one look at their grave faces and shouted, "*NO!* Don't you dare tell me that something's happened to Dirk Voorhees!"

"Are you his mother?"

Oh, God, what are you doing? Helen groaned inwardly. *Please, don't do this to Rosa. . . . Please . . .* Her knees felt so weak she was afraid she would fall over. The chaplain gripped her arm.

"May we come in, Mrs. Voorhees?"

"I'm . . . I'm not Mrs. Voorhees. I . . . I'll get her." Helen reached the kitchen just as Rosa emerged from the bedroom with her purse.

"Who was at the door?" Mrs. Voorhees asked. Helen didn't reply. She couldn't stop her tears. Rosa gripped her shoulders.

"Helen? Helen, what's wrong?" Helen pulled Rosa into her arms and hugged her fiercely. "Did something happen to Ginny?" Rosa whispered.

"You . . . you both need to go into the living room," she finally managed to say. The women paled when they walked into the room and saw the men in uniform. Rosa lifted her trembling hands to her mouth, unable to speak. Helen took the baby from Tena's arms, afraid she would drop him.

"Are you here . . . Is this about our Dirk?" his mother asked.

"Mrs. Voorhees, I'm very sorry to tell you that your son Dirk is missing in action."

"So he isn't dead?" Rosa breathed. The two men exchanged glances.

"We don't know for certain. I suppose there's always a chance that he may have survived and has been taken prisoner by the Japanese. They don't always turn over the names of their prisoners to the Red Cross. But we don't want to give you false hope. There has been fierce fighting in the region and heavy enemy bombardment."

"The moment we know something one way or the other, we'll be sure to let you know. In the meantime, it's probably best to assume—"

"He's okay," Rosa said quietly. "I know he's okay. He promised."

Helen heard the back door open and close in the rear of the house, and a moment later Wolter Voorhees walked in from the kitchen in his plumber's overalls.

"I saw cars out front. Who is—?" He looked from one somber face to another. "Is it my son? Has something happened to my son?"

"I'm afraid he's missing in action," the chaplain said.

"He isn't dead!" Rosa insisted. "He's just missing. He's going to be okay, I know he is." She and Tena clung to each other.

The baby squirmed in Helen's arms, trying to escape. She shifted him around to get a better grip, and when she looked at Wolter Voorhees again she saw tears coursing down his face. First Harold Mitchell had wept, now Dirk's father. Helen's own father had never shed a single tear in front of her, even after the deaths of his children. Mr. Voorhees swiped at his tears, as if impatient with them.

"Please tell me everything you know about my son."

The men sat down to tell their story and offer comfort. Rosa lifted Joseph from Helen's arms, clutching him as if she needed to hang on to him for dear life. Rosa had what she needed to get through this—her family—so Helen tiptoed into the kitchen and quietly let herself out the back door. But she sat in her car for a few minutes, shaking so violently with rage and grief that she couldn't drive.

"I hate you, God!" she cried out in the darkness. "How could you do this to such dear people? How *could* you?" She rested her head on the steering wheel and wept bitter tears for Rosa's husband. For Jean's brother. For Ginny Mitchell.

When she was able to drive, finally, Helen returned to the hospital. Jean and Mr. Seaborn were sitting together in the waiting room. "There's been no change," Jean told her. "Ginny's still unconscious."

"The police finished looking around the shipyard," Earl said.

"They're certain that it was deliberate and that it was meant for Thelma. They have some people in custody that they're questioning. They'll get to the bottom of it."

Jean seemed numb and bereft of tears. "I can't believe someone would want to hurt another person because of the color of her skin," she said softly. Helen hated adding to everyone's sorrow but knew that she had to.

"Something else has happened," she said in a trembling voice. "I just came from Rosa's house. Two men from the navy arrived while I was there and told her that Dirk is missing in action."

"Oh no!" Jean leaned into Earl's arms and wept. Earl stared at Helen in disbelief.

"He might have been taken captive by the Japanese," Helen continued. "They don't know for certain. Poor Rosa is—" She waited until she was in control of her voice and said, "I need to go home, but I'd like to go with you to Indiana tomorrow if you're still going." Earl nodded.

Helen drove back to the house that had never been a home to her, the house she'd always hated. She wished she had never left it a year and a half ago to work at Stockton Shipyard. Why had she ever become involved in the other women's lives? She should have known better. Instead, she'd opened her heart to Jean and Ginny and Rosa, and now the pain she felt for them was nearly unbearable. She hadn't felt such heartache since the day she'd received Jimmy's letter more than twenty-five years ago. That had been the day that her heart had died.

Helen knew she never should have risked loving again. But without love there was only hatred, and hatred had caused the Nazis to rise to power—and Jean's brother's death. It had caused all of the atrocities that the Japanese had committed—and the loss of Rosa's husband. And hatred had caused Ginny Mitchell's fall. Helen had never realized that Negroes faced such terrible hatred, through no fault of their own. She had been blind to the racism, unwilling to believe that it existed in Stockton. She had been so wrong.

And Jimmy had been right.

Helen climbed the stairs to her bedroom and found his letter in the drawer of her vanity. It was the only letter that Jimmy had ever sent to her. The paper felt brittle as she pulled it from the yellowing envelope. She brushed aside her tears to read it.

Dear Helen,

When I got your letter this morning I couldn't believe my eyes. You were supposed to forget all about me and marry that other fellow. Instead, you said that you still loved me. How could someone as beautiful and as smart and as wonderful as you love a nobody like me? It's a marvel that I will never understand.

You also said that you hoped it wasn't too late for us. I wish I could lie to you and tell you that I've found someone else or that I don't love you anymore. That way you would finally forget me and marry your suitor. But I can't lie and I can't seem to stop loving you, so I'm going to try once more to convince you that it will never work for us to be together. I pray that you haven't cut all the ties to your family and your fiancé yet, because I need to tell you what I've experienced since I left Stockton to join the army.

Back home the color of our skin didn't matter to us. I saw you as my beautiful Helen, not as a white woman, and I know that you never saw me as a Negro. But when I joined the army I learned that a lot of people in America can't look past the color of our skin. The U.S. Army is segregated by race, and there is little opportunity to advance or to better myself in any way. My 93rd Infantry is all Negro, and we are treated like ignorant slaves, assigned to unload cargo or dig ditches. We begged and begged for a chance to fight like real soldiers, and the army finally got us off their backs by reassigning us to be part of France's Fourth Army. We're finally going into combat soon in a place called the Argonne Forest.

Please believe me, Helen, when I say that it would be even harder for you and me to be together than either of us ever imagined. It's not only a matter of social class, rich and poor, but a much, much bigger question of race. Your family would reject you if we got married, and you say you don't care. But I've learned that my fellow Negroes probably wouldn't embrace us, either. They would always look at you with suspicion and distrust because of the way other white people have treated them.

Our children might never be accepted by either race. What future would there be for them? Or for us?

I've felt hatred and racism and discrimination every single day since I left Stockton. Some days I can hardly hold my head up underneath it all. I don't ever want you to experience this. I love you too much to take you down with me. Even if I got the best education in the world, I would be refused jobs because of the color of my skin. Nobody would sell me a house in a white neighborhood like yours.

Colored people have to use separate rest rooms—usually outhouses. They have to stand up on buses and ride in colored railroad cars. They have colored hotels and motels—and they're always run-down, flea-bitten places. That's where we would have to spend our honeymoon. We couldn't even use the same drinking fountain or eat at the same lunch counter. I hate being treated this way. I hate feeling degraded and worthless. How can I ask the woman I love to suffer the same treatment? Especially when you deserve to be treated with dignity and respect and love?

I made up my mind to forget you when I left Stockton. I haven't, of course. But you need to forget me. Marry a white man. Live the life you deserve. Be happy. Please don't write to me again, Helen. I won't answer.

Jimmy

Helen refolded the letter and tucked it into the envelope. After what had happened to Ginny Mitchell today, Helen understood Jimmy's words for the first time. Grief poured from her—grief for Ginny, and for Jean, and for Rosa. And grief for herself. She had wasted all these years refusing to love others, feeling rejected, believing that Jimmy hadn't loved her—when all along it had been love that had made him give her up.

CHAPTER 3 6

★ *Jean* ★

Jean's friends said very little as Earl drove them to her home in Indiana for Johnny's memorial service, but she valued their support more than words could ever say. She sat in the front seat between Earl and Helen, while Patty and Rosa rode in the back, trying to keep their four wiggling children occupied during the long drive. Jean's mind felt ravaged from bouncing endlessly between thoughts of Ginny Mitchell to concern for Rosa's husband to grief for her own brother. Three tragedies in a row. She could barely comprehend them, much less deal with them. The effort left her numb.

She ached to see Russell, to have him hold her, comfort her. Yet she couldn't escape the nagging thought that he should have been at his best friend's side to protect him. Why had Russ decided to take a farm exemption and stay home where it was safe, while Johnny had turned down an exemption to put his life at risk?

And why had God allowed all of these terrible things to happen in the first place—to Johnny and to Ginny and to Dirk Voorhees? Why hadn't He answered their endless prayers and watched over His children, keeping them safe? Every time Jean looked at Rosa, she thought of the months and months she had spent trying to convince her that God loved her—and now this! If Jean's own lifelong faith had taken a direct hit by these disasters, Rosa's infant trust in God must be in ruins.

With all the stops for gasoline and one for a punctured tire, Jean didn't have time to go home to the farm before the memorial service. It was nearly time for it to begin when they drove into town. Her eyes filled with tears when she saw Church Street lined with cars. So many people had come to pay tribute to Johnny that Earl would have to drop everyone off in front of the building and park a few blocks away.

"You go ahead. I'll meet you all inside," he told them.

Jean barely heard him. She had spotted Russ standing on the church steps, watching anxiously for her, and she barely had the patience to wait for Helen to climb out of the car first so she could run into his arms. She cried uncontrollably as Russ held her. She heard him sniffling as he buried his face on her shoulder.

"I miss him so much, Russ! What am I going to do without him?"

"I know . . . I know . . ."

They stood that way for a long moment, wrapped in each other's arms. Then Patty said, "Come on, Jean, we'd better go inside."

Ma had saved a seat for Jean and Patty in one of the front rows. Their six younger brothers were there, and all of Jean's sisters, along with her two older brothers' wives. Jean knew that none of them felt the depth of pain that she felt for Johnny, her twin. Then she saw Johnny's girlfriend across the aisle, leaning against her mother for support, and Jean felt a fresh wave of grief and also guilt for meddling. Sue had wanted to marry Johnny before he shipped out, but Jean had talked him out of it. If he had married her, maybe Sue would have his baby to console her, a little piece of him, the way Rosa had Joseph.

The service began. There were prayers and hymns, kind words of remembrance from friends and family members. The pastor gave a short sermon. Someone played "Taps." Jean listened to all of it yet didn't hear a word. She gripped Ma's hand but felt as though none of this was really happening, as though she floated above it all, in a dream. She would wake up soon, and Johnny would come home.

The churchwomen had prepared a funeral luncheon for Jean's family in the church basement. She didn't feel hungry. She walked through the buffet line behind Russ, watching him fill his plate, but took only a dinner roll. She sat beside him at the table and pulled the roll into pieces, barely eating any of it. Afterward, Patty's two older boys squirmed away from the table to chase Jean's other nieces and nephews around one of the Sunday school rooms, laughing and letting off steam after sitting still for so long. Jean wondered when— or if—she would ever feel happy again.

"It was so nice of your friends to come," Patty said, leaning toward her.

Jean saw Helen, Rosa, and Earl huddled at a nearby table, and her anger toward God swelled as she thought of them being forced to endure this grief all over again if Ginny Mitchell died. Or Dirk Voorhees. Jean was furious with God. She had been told all her life to have faith in Him, but today the words seemed meaningless.

"Do you want anything else?" Russ asked as he rose to his feet. "I'm going back for seconds." She shook her head.

Her mother and father weren't eating, either. She watched as they made their way from table to table, thanking their friends and guests for coming. The loss of their son had clearly devastated them, yet Jean saw none of the rage or doubt in them that she felt. She longed to talk to Ma and find relief from all the turmoil in her heart.

The opportunity finally came later that afternoon in the farmhouse kitchen. Jean introduced Helen and Rosa to Ma, and the four of them sat around the table with cups of tea. Ma was the one who raised the issue of faith.

"Our days are known to God from the very beginning," she said, "even before we are born. He knows all about your little one, too." She nodded at Joey, cooing happily on Rosa's lap as he played with a teaspoon.

"Johnny had his whole life ahead of him," Jean said through her tears. "Why did he have to die so young?"

Ma reached across the table for her hand. "Johnny isn't dead, honey. He's still alive, and he'll live for all eternity. God has plans for him, just as he has plans for each one of us, only His plans for Johnny will take place up in heaven for now, not here on earth."

"Dirk's father keeps saying that Dirk is in God's hands," Rosa said, "and that we have to trust Him. But now that Dirk is missing in action, I don't know what to think."

" 'Trust in God' doesn't mean that He won't ever let anything bad happen," Ma told her. "It means that if we know Him, no matter what happens we can still trust His love."

"But I don't get it," Rosa continued. "You and Jean have a lot more faith than I do, yet Johnny still died. Why didn't God protect him?" Jean looked up from her own grief and saw fear and bewilderment on Rosa's beautiful face. Jean closed her eyes as she waited to hear her mother's answer.

"I believe that God has the power to protect my children from all harm. I have faith that He hears my prayers when I pray. But when He doesn't answer them the way I'd like, I still have faith in God's love. He knows far more than I ever will, and I can trust His purposes, even though I can't understand them. Jesus had more faith than any man or woman who ever lived, but His prayer, 'Let this cup pass from me,' wasn't answered. He was God's own Son, yet He died a horrible death, worse than our Johnny's. But Jesus' death had a purpose that no one could have foreseen at the time, even those who were closest to Him. I have faith in God's love. He knows how it feels to lose a beloved Son."

"My sisters and brothers all died when they were children," Helen said quietly. "Six of them. My parents stopped believing in God's love. Then they stopped loving altogether."

"How old were you?" Ma asked.

"I was ten when my last brother died."

"Then you've never known love?"

Helen looked away from Ma's gaze as her eyes filled with tears. "Not from my parents. I fell in love once—and then he wrote and told me that we could never be together. All these years I've believed that he never loved me. How could he, if he would hurt me so badly? I didn't trust in his love. But now I understand what you're saying about God's love, Mrs. Erickson. I should have trusted, even when Jimmy hurt me, that he had acted out of love."

"When tragedies like this happen," Ma said, "we can either draw closer to Jesus, who was 'a man of sorrows and acquainted with grief,' or we can turn away from Him and stop loving so we'll never be hurt again. But when we cut ourselves off from love, we find out what hell is like." Ma reached to take Jean's hand, then waited until Jean looked up at her. "Imagine how much harder it would be to face Johnny's death if you were alone, Jeannie, instead of surrounded by people who love you." Ma nodded toward Helen and Rosa.

The back door opened and Russ came in. He dragged over another chair and sat down beside Jean as if to emphasize Ma's words. "Are you okay?" he asked as he draped his arm around her shoulder. She nodded and leaned against him.

"Would you like some coffee or tea, Russ?" Ma asked.

"Yeah, sure. Coffee." Ma rose to pour him a cup and to replenish everyone's tea.

"This might not be the best time to discuss this, Jean," Helen said, "but I want you to know that I'm sorry for the way I treated Meinhard Kesler. If he wants to come back and work with us . . . I mean, with Ginny in the hospital . . . until she gets better . . ."

"Who's this Kesler guy?" Russ asked. "I don't think you've mentioned him before."

"Yes, I have. I wrote and told you how they hired some German POWs at the shipyard, remember? The government built a camp outside of Stockton for them. A bunch of them worked on area farms last summer to help with the labor shortage."

"It's been hard to get good farm labor around here," Russ said. "I'd hire POWs if we had any. All we have are a bunch of shiftless Negroes coming around looking for work, but I hate hiring them."

"*What* did you say?" Jean turned to him so abruptly that his arm slipped from her shoulders. She stared at him, stunned.

"I'd much sooner hire POWs than Negro migrant workers. They're lazy as all get-out and you have to keep your eye on them every minute. Of course, colored people will live anywhere so they're easy enough to house. They're one step above animals, so they don't mind living—"

"Russ, *stop it!*" Jean said in horror.

"Huh?"

"How can you say such terrible things?"

"Because it's true. Everybody knows that Negroes are shiftless—"

"Get out of my house, Russell Benson! Get out right now!"

"Why? What did I say? Since when do you care about a bunch of Negro migrants? They're not even important."

Jean rose from her seat, so furious she could hardly speak. She battled the urge to slap him. "Get out!" she repeated.

"Come on, Jean, you're getting upset over nothing." He reached to take her hand, but she yanked it away.

"Over *nothing*? One of my dearest friends is lying in the hospital in a coma because someone felt the way you do about Negroes. My friend Earl was beaten with baseball bats by people like you. Now get *out!*"

"Okay! Fine!" He rose, knocking the chair over, and strode from the house, banging the door behind him.

Helen stood and put her arm around Jean to console her. "You did the right thing," she said.

"How could he talk that way? I can't believe I ever thought I loved him. I . . . I didn't know . . ."

"Of course you didn't. Thank God you found out before you married him."

Jean sank down in her seat again, her knees too shaky to support her. Helen righted Russell's chair and sat facing her.

"I know how you feel, Jean. I broke my engagement with Albert, the man my father wanted me to marry, because he was a racist."

"How did you find out?" Rosa asked.

"Albert had been drafted during the Great War and had gone off to fight. I had promised to marry him when he returned, and I knew that he'd be coming home any day. Meanwhile, Jimmy Bernard, the man I loved, had also gone overseas to fight, and I found myself wondering how he had fared. I saw his father working out in our yard one afternoon, so I went outside to ask if he knew when Jimmy would be coming home. Joe's eyes filled with tears. 'He isn't coming home, Miss Helen,' he told me. 'Jimmy died over in France.' We clung to each other, crying. Joe knew that I loved his son, and I knew that Joe had no family to console him. His wife had died, and Jimmy was his only child. That was the moment when my hatred for Germans was born.

" 'The army wrote me a real nice letter,' Joe told me when he could speak. 'Jimmy died on the twenty-sixth of September, 1918. The letter said there'd been a day of real hard fighting, and the 93rd Infantry had fought very bravely. They went into battle with seven hundred men, and all but one hundred fifty of them died. Jimmy's buried over there, and I don't suppose I'll ever get to see where his grave is.'

"I hugged Joe again and went back into the house, trying to comprehend the truth that Jimmy was dead and gone, like all of my siblings. I would never see him again. He had died two months short of the cease-fire on November twentieth. I wanted to be alone, but when I reached the house, there was Albert. He had been watching us from the dining room window, and his first words to me after being separated all those months were, 'How could you hug that filthy old Negro?'

"I explained to Albert that Joe's son had been killed in the war, but Albert looked at my tears and said, 'You're crying for a *Negro*?'

"I could see his revulsion. He didn't want to touch me after I'd hugged Joe, as if I'd become contaminated. I was shocked and disgusted. And furious, just like you are right now, Jean. I pulled the engagement ring from my finger and threw it at him. I told him that Jimmy Bernard was ten times the man he'd ever be. I lost Albert and Jimmy on the same day, so I do understand how you feel. But I made the right decision—and so did you."

Rosa stared at Helen in astonishment. "You never said that Jimmy was a Negro."

"Didn't I?" Helen seemed surprised. "You know, I never saw the color of his skin. I saw his heart. And I loved him."

"I had no idea that Russ felt that way," Jean said. "I feel like I've lost everything."

"I know," Helen said. "I really do. But please don't stop living, the way I did. And don't stop loving, either. I was so afraid of being hurt again that I made a huge mistake and cut myself off from everyone. You have a wonderful family and friends who love you. And you have your faith. Those are all good reasons to go on living."

Jean heard what Helen was saying, but at the moment, with Johnny and Russ both gone, she felt as though her life had ended.

"Why is God turning all my plans upside down?" she wept.

"Do you want your own plans, Jeannie, or what God has for your life?" Ma asked. "His plans are always better, you know, even though it may not seem that way right now."

"I always thought that Johnny and I would go to college together, that we would help each other. Ever since he died I've felt so scared. Like only half of me is here."

"You can do it alone, Jean," Helen said. "Look at all the responsibility you've shouldered at work. You can do whatever you put your mind to. Wouldn't your brother want you to?"

"Maybe you can get a degree in something that'll help you fight for people like Thelma," Rosa said. "I'll bet you could change the whole world, Jean, if you put your mind to it."

She didn't share their confidence. She couldn't believe that she'd been such a poor judge of character. "I never knew Russ was that way," she murmured.

"Earl Seaborn is ten times the man that he is," Helen said. "And Earl had so much confidence in you that he made you a crew chief."

Jean looked up and saw Earl through the kitchen window, talking with her father outside. She knew Helen was right. Earl had been with her through all of this, a rock she had leaned upon. He had protected her from two racists with baseball bats. Yet she had been so enamored with Russ's good looks that Earl's handicaps had repelled her.

She was about to admit to everyone that she had been a complete fool, when Rosa said, "And you know what else, Jean? Mr. Seaborn didn't even know how to dance. He asked me to teach him how, just for you."

The knowledge that Earl would do that for her reduced Jean to tears.

CHAPTER 37

★ *Rosa* ★

Rosa thought that the ride home from Indiana would never end. At least the fresh country air had tuckered out the children. Patty's boys and little Joey fell asleep in the backseat of the car. Rosa closed her eyes and pretended to sleep, too, but the funeral weighed her heart down like a block of ice, disturbing her rest. She had never been to a funeral before, and it had affected her deeply. She couldn't help picturing herself all dressed in black, sitting through Dirk's memorial service, weeping and mourning for him the way Jean and her family had mourned.

Johnny's plane had crashed into the sea, and Jean would never see her brother again. And Helen never got to see Jimmy one last time, either, or the place where he was buried over in France. Rosa thought it would be the worst punishment of all if she never saw Dirk again. What if she couldn't even have his body to bury or a grave she could visit and show to their son?

She was exhausted by the time she got home. Joseph had awakened from his nap feeling cranky. His body felt warm.

"He's a little feverish," Tena told her. "He's probably teething." Tena felt the baby's gums with her finger and showed Rosa a budding tooth that was causing his distress. "If you've ever had a toothache, then you know how he feels."

Rosa couldn't cope. Why did the baby have to be sick on top of everything else? After going to Johnny's funeral, her worry over Dirk had grown to unmanageable proportions, and she didn't know how much longer she could stand the fear and uncertainty. The only way she knew to escape her anxieties was to drown them in a bottle of booze.

"I'm going to take Joey for a walk," she told Tena as she hauled out the baby carriage. "He always likes that. Maybe he'll go to sleep."

"You're going now? At night? In the dark?"

"We'll be fine."

Rosa grabbed the largest purse she could find to hide the vodka bottle she planned to buy and hurried outside. When she passed the Hoot Owl a few blocks away and remembered how she used to go drinking every weekend when she'd first arrived in town, she nearly turned the baby carriage around and went home. She had wanted to change so badly, to be a good wife, a good mother. But the longing to forget her sorrow was just too great to resist.

She felt even worse when she reached the liquor store. What kind of an unfit mother was she to take a baby into a place like that? But she couldn't leave Joey outside. The ride hadn't soothed him at all, and he was still whining and acting fussy as she set the carriage brake and lifted him into her arms. The woman behind the counter smiled at Rosa as she walked inside, jiggling Joey to quiet him.

"Let me guess," the woman said. "He's teething, isn't he?"

"How did you know?"

"Why else would you bring a baby to a liquor store?" The woman took a pint bottle from the shelf behind her and set it on the counter. "Rubbing a little brandy on his gums works every time. Poor little guy."

Rosa didn't particularly like brandy, but it would get her just as drunk as vodka would. "Do you have a bigger bottle?" she asked as she pulled some money from her purse with one hand.

"Sure. But you don't need to get the little fellow drunk, you know."

Rosa tried to laugh. "I know. But this is only his first tooth and

I figure he'll be getting lots more of them, right? I want to save myself a trip." She felt bad for lying.

As soon as she was out of sight of the store, Rosa opened the bottle and took a long swig. Then another. And another. She felt pleasantly lightheaded by the time she reached home and parked the carriage on the back porch. But the question of where to hide the bottle quickly arose. She recalled the night of the Ladies' Missionary Society meeting and Tena's spiked punch, and for a moment the memory almost made her smile. Then little Joey cried for her, wanting to be picked up, and Rosa's eyes filled with tears. She didn't want to be like her own mother, drunk and unavailable most of the time. Rosa lifted her son into her arms and carried him into their bedroom.

"I'm sorry, baby," she murmured. "Mommy's so sorry. . . ."

Jean had told her she could talk to God whenever she needed to—like talking to someone on the telephone. Rosa closed her eyes to pray, swaying as she rocked Joey in her arms.

Hello, God? Are you there? Listen, I don't know any of those fancy words like the minister says in church. Besides, I just don't feel right saying Thou *and stuff like that. But, God? I need Dirk really badly. I'm not strong enough to go through what Jean and her family are going through.*

Rosa opened her eyes to shift Joey to her other arm and saw the brandy bottle sticking out of her purse. The attraction seemed stronger than ever.

I know what will happen to me if Dirk doesn't come home, God. And I don't want that to happen. Please bring him home. Please . . . please . . .

The baby kept Rosa awake half the night as she walked the floor with him, rocking him. She had drunk a good amount of brandy before he finally fell asleep. When Tena woke her up for church the next morning, Rosa had such a terrible headache that she nearly rolled over and went back to sleep. But in the end she forced herself to get up and get dressed, afraid that God would get mad at her if she skipped church. She made it through most of the service with her fears and her tears under control until the pastor announced to the congregation that Dirk Voorhees had been listed as missing in action. A collective gasp shuddered through the sanctuary, then everyone bowed to pray for him.

Rosa hated the word *missing*. That was how the men from the navy had described Dirk, and they'd made it sound as if he had vanished into thin air. He wasn't missing. He had to be somewhere. Even if he were dead he still lived in heaven, according to Jean's mom. He hadn't stopped existing. God knew where he was. Hadn't Mr. Voorhees always said that Dirk was in God's hands?

Jean's mother had also said that trusting in God didn't mean He would never let anything bad happen. It meant that no matter what happened, we could trust God's love. He would never stop loving us. Rosa bowed her head with everyone else and prayed.

God? If you really do love me, please let me find out where Dirk is. Even ... even if he's up there with you. Because not knowing for sure ... that's the hardest thing for me.

Later that afternoon at the dinner table, Rosa's father-in-law was unusually quiet. She knew him well enough by now to know that he had something on his mind. "We must talk, Rosa," he finally said. His eyes looked weary and sad, and he spoke in a voice that was so soft it didn't even sound like his. "Now that Dirk is missing, it is more important than ever that little Joseph becomes part of Christ's family. We need to have him baptized."

"Dirk *will* come home," she said in a trembling voice. "He promised me that he would come home."

"He shouldn't have promised such a thing," Wolter said. His tone was gentle, not demanding or bossy. "It wasn't Dirk's promise to make. Whether or not he comes home is up to God."

If Mr. Voorhees had spoken harshly to her, Rosa could have gotten angry in return and could have stood up for herself. Instead, she knew that he was gradually wearing her down. She could barely reply.

"But I want to wait for Dirk," she said, trying not to cry. "He should be here to hold his son when he's baptized."

Mr. Voorhees shook his head. "Rosa, you heard what the men from the navy said—"

"Leave her alone, Wolter." Mrs. Voorhees' voice wasn't loud, but her husband stopped abruptly. He stared at her as if she had smacked him in the face with a snowball.

"What did you say?"

Rosa didn't know who was more surprised that Tena had spoken up—Wolter or Rosa or Tena herself. In the year and a half that Rosa had lived here, Mrs. Voorhees had never once argued with her husband. She had probably never contradicted him in her life.

"I said, leave her alone," Tena repeated. "I understand how Rosa feels."

"Then maybe you don't understand what the Bible teaches. Baptism is a sign of our covenant with God. We are disobeying God when we fail to have Joseph baptized."

"He will be baptized when Dirk comes home. Dirk should present his own son. You need to stop hounding the poor girl about it."

His eyes widened in surprise, as if she had lobbed a second snowball smack into his face. "Tena! You know that I am the head of this household."

"Yes, I know. The Bible says I must honor you, and I always have. But that doesn't mean that I must always agree with you. And it doesn't mean that I can't tell you what I think. So I am telling you. If Rosa wants to wait, then we should respect her wishes and wait. And not nag her anymore."

"You are taking her side?"

"Yes, Wolter. I am."

He seemed too stunned to speak. He snatched up his knife and fork and sawed off a piece of meat, then chewed it in silence. He wouldn't look at either of them for the remainder of the meal.

Later, when Rosa stood to clear the table, she turned to Mrs. Voorhees. "Thank you for sticking up for me," she whispered, then hugged her mother-in-law.

"You are welcome, dear." Mrs. Voorhees' entire body was still trembling.

That afternoon while Joey napped, Rosa went to the hospital with Helen to visit Ginny. Harold Mitchell came out to the waiting room to talk to them, looking like a man who hadn't slept or eaten in days.

"There have been a few signs of improvement," he told them. "Ginny opened her eyes a few times, and she seemed to recognize me. She hasn't tried to talk yet. The doctor said she probably isn't comatose anymore, just sleeping very deeply. And her reflexes are good. They don't think there will be any paralysis. It's hard to tell because she fractured her leg and both arms when she fell. They've told me to keep talking to her. It might help her come around. That's what I've been doing."

From the way Ginny had described her husband, Rosa figured he'd probably talked to her more in the past few days than in their entire married life. No wonder he looked worn out.

"We'll sign up for shifts and talk to her around the clock," Rosa said.

Harold gave her a weary smile. "Thanks. I think it will help."

Rosa and Helen were still in the waiting room talking with Mr. Mitchell when Earl and Jean arrived. "I brought Ginny's purse and her clothes and things from her locker," Jean said.

Mr. Mitchell appeared shaken when he saw the items, as if reminded of the vibrant woman who had gone to work two days ago. He sank into a chair and opened the purse, sifting blindly through it.

"Her driver's license . . ." he mumbled. "I should have told her how proud I was of her. I should have given her a set of car keys. We should have celebrated. . . ." He pulled out the receipt from the flower shop and unfolded it. "What's this? The flowers? I looked everywhere for this! I was supposed to give it to our accountant so I'd get reimbursed."

"Who were the flowers for?" Rosa asked, not caring if it was a rude question.

"One of our secretaries. She had her appendix out. I ordered flowers from all of us at the firm."

"Ginny found it in your coat pocket, you know," Rosa said. "She worried herself sick that you'd bought them for some other woman and you were having an affair."

"What? Never!"

Rosa wanted to believe him, but she remembered how much grief he had caused her friend and couldn't control her temper. "Ginny worries all the time that you're cheating on her, Mr. Mitchell. I want you to know that if you ever do have an affair, or if you ever do *anything* to hurt Ginny, I'll hurt you in ways you'll never forget!"

"I would never have an affair! Why would I even look at another woman? Ginny is everything I've ever wanted."

"You need to tell her once in a while," Helen said quietly.

"Better yet, show her," Jean said.

Harold Mitchell looked truly baffled. "I show her all the time. I go to work to support her and our boys, I make sure she has a home, all of her needs are met. Doesn't that show her?"

"You should buy flowers for *her* once in a while," Rosa said.

"Take her out dancing," Jean added.

"Let her be herself, not what you want her to be," Helen said.

Harold sighed and ran his fingers through his hair. "I know I wasn't very supportive when she first started working at the shipyard. But I was so afraid that something like this would happen."

"This wasn't a random accident," Earl said. "This was an act of hatred, aimed at Ginny's friend Thelma. I offered to transfer your wife to another crew when the threats first started, but she wanted to stay and fight for her friend. Ginny showed a great deal of courage, Mr. Mitchell."

"And she was scared of her own shadow when she first started working there," Rosa added.

"I'm sure the police have told you that they've made two arrests," Earl said. "At least there will be some justice."

"I'm glad that Ginny stood up for Thelma," Harold said quietly. "I've met her and her grandmother, and they are good, good people. They've kept our home going since the day this happened. I'm very grateful to them. And to all of you."

The nurses gave permission for them to go into Ginny's room, one at a time, for a few minutes each. Rosa went first, and seeing Ginny lying there, all pale and bandaged up, was more than she could handle.

"You gotta get better, Ginny," she said, sniffling. "Joey's cutting teeth, and I sure could use your help. The lady at the liquor store said to rub brandy on his gums, but that don't sound right to me. It's bad enough that I got all the church ladies drunk that one time, but I really don't think I should get my own kid drunk—should I?"

Ginny opened her eyes and looked at Rosa for a few seconds before closing them again. Rosa could have sworn that she smiled.

The baby fussed again that night, keeping Rosa awake for hours. As she walked the floor with him, exhausted and alone, her worries grew into gigantic fears. She could tame them, maybe even forget them, if she finished off the bottle of brandy. She laid Joey on her bed and was digging beneath it for the bottle she'd hidden in her bedroom slipper when Mrs. Voorhees tapped on her bedroom door.

"Rosa?"

She scrambled to her feet and picked up the baby before opening the door. "I'm sorry he's keeping you awake, Mrs. Voorhees. I don't know what to do with him."

"It isn't that. I've come to take him for a while so you can rest." Rosa remembered Ginny's advice about letting Tena help. Maybe Mrs. Voorhees' arms felt empty without Dirk, too. The baby must remind her of him.

"He might be hungry again in a few hours," Rosa said.

"I'll bring him to you if he is." Rosa saw the loving look on Tena's face as she lifted Joseph from her arms. "Come on, little fellow. Let's see if Grandma can make you happy."

"Thank you," Rosa murmured.

She fell back into bed and was all the way beneath the covers before she remembered the brandy. Rosa began to cry and didn't know why. Within a few minutes, she had cried herself to sleep. She slept so soundly that the next thing she knew it was light outside.

She sat up. The baby wasn't in his bassinet.

Rosa jumped out of bed, wrapped her robe around her, and hurried into the living room. She froze in the doorway. It wasn't Tena who was walking the floor with Joseph, but Mr. Voorhees. He had his back to Rosa and didn't realize she was there. Rosa saw the top of Joey's head, with his dark, curly hair, resting on his grandfather's shoulder. The baby was asleep. Mr. Voorhees was saying something, murmuring softly, but Rosa couldn't hear what it was. Then the furnace shut off and the house grew quiet.

"Lord, Joseph needs his father to raise him," she heard Wolter say. "Please, Lord ... please bring our Dirk home so this child will have a father. ..."

Rosa turned and crept back into her room. She fished out the brandy bottle from beneath her bed, opened her bedroom window, and poured every last drop of it out onto the ground.

CHAPTER 38

★ *Virginia* ★

Voices. Why were there so many voices, men's and women's, talking to her endlessly? Ginny wanted to sleep, and they were keeping her awake. She opened her eyes and saw Harold sitting beside her bed. He sat hunched in a chair with his arms on his thighs, his hands dangling between his knees. He was talking and talking, on and on.

"... Minnie and Thelma are getting all the housework done and taking care of the boys, but it just isn't the same. We need you, Ginny. I ... I need you."

Harold's shirt was a wrinkled mess. It looked as though he'd slept in it or had dug it out of the ironing basket instead of the clothes closet. Why on earth would he go out in public looking like that? She tried to speak, to ask him why he was wearing such a wrinkled thing, but no sound came out. It was as if she had forgotten how to talk. Harold couldn't seem to stop talking.

"I've had a lot of time to think these past few days. Your friends from work said that I should tell you how I feel more often. Or better yet, show you. I know they're right, but I don't know why that's so hard for me to do...."

Her friends from work. Why wasn't she at work? Ginny looked around. She recognized this room. Every time she'd opened her eyes she had found herself in this strange room. It looked like a hospital.

But the only reason she could think of to be in a hospital was to have a baby—and no one had brought a baby to her. Rosa was the one who'd had a baby.

She tried to reach out to Harold and get his attention, but her arms wouldn't move. She looked down at her body, lying prone beneath the white sheets. Both of her arms were encased in white plaster casts.

". . . I know I act stern and demanding sometimes," Harold was saying. "I wish I could change. My father was the same way and I always hated the way he spoke to everybody—and now I'm doing the same thing. I think I come on strong to hide how weak I really feel. You told me once that the reason you fell in love with me was because I was so strong and decisive. Well . . . sometimes I don't feel that way at all, and I worry that you'll change your mind about me if you find out I'm a phony. Or if you discover that you're strong enough to make it without me. . . ."

Why was he talking this way, saying all these things? The man looked like Harold, spoke with Harold's voice, but Harold didn't talk this way in real life. She must be dreaming. Ginny closed her eyes again, but the Harold beside her bed kept on talking.

"My love for you and my need for you scare me sometimes. I need your tenderness and I don't know why I push you away. I guess I don't want to admit my own weakness. I know that you think I'm cold. I . . . I'm not cold, Ginny—I'm scared! Scared that you'll stop loving me. So I push you away, telling myself that I don't need you. But I do. Please come back to me. I love you so much."

She opened her eyes again. Harold was looking right at her. "I'm here," she wanted to say. "I love you, too." But she couldn't remember how to make the words travel from where they formed inside her head, out into the room. She must be ill. Something must have happened to her. Harold's eyes filled with tears.

"Say something, Ginny. Please be okay . . ."

She closed her eyes again, hoping that when she opened them this dream would be over and she would be in her own bed, in her own room, with Harold asleep beside her. But when she opened them,

the only thing that was different was Harold. He was no longer looking into her eyes but sat slumped in the chair again with his head
bowed.

"I loved you so much when we got married that I never wanted
you to change. And I was afraid that this job would change you . . .
that you would find out how strong and smart and capable you really
are, and then you wouldn't need me anymore. But you know what?
I've grown to love the stronger, more confident Ginny. I love the
woman you've become—a woman who can build ships and drive a
car . . . and who still loves her family more than herself. We need you,
Ginny. I need you. . . ."

Poor Harold. He looked so lost and alone as he sat in the cold
metal chair, pouring out his heart to her. She wanted to throw aside
the covers and climb out of bed and gather him into her arms. She
wanted to tell him that she loved him, too. Her mind and her heart
begged her to do it, but her body simply wouldn't obey.

Move! she screamed inside her head. *Move your arms! Your legs! Say
something!* Her vision blurred. Ginny felt tears of frustration roll down
her face.

Just then Harold lifted his head and looked at her again.
"Ginny?" he whispered. "Can you hear me?"

She blinked, and more tears rolled down her face. Harold scrambled to his feet and bent over her. He tenderly wiped her tears away.
"Ginny. . . ?"

"Hold me," she whispered. And this time the words exploded
from her head and out into the room.

Harold brushed aside all the wires and tubes that surrounded her
and lay down on the bed beside her. He was weeping as he gathered
her gently into his arms.

CHAPTER 39

June 1944

"D-day, the long-awaited Allied invasion of Europe,
began just after midnight on June 6. Military experts claim
it was the largest invasion force in history and included more
than 175,000 troops, 10,000 airplanes and 4,000 ships."

★ *Helen* ★

Helen rode her bicycle to Ginny Mitchell's house right after work, still dressed in her coveralls. She wished she had a bell or a horn she could toot as she coasted to a stop in her driveway. She pulled the large manila envelope from her carrier basket and hurried up the sidewalk to ring the doorbell. Ginny answered the door herself.

"Helen! Oh, it's so good to see you!" The casts were off Ginny's arms and she was able to give Helen a hug. It was so wonderful to hear Ginny's voice again, even if her speech was still a little slow and labored.

"I have something to show you." Helen held up the envelope.

"Well, come on in. Rosa is here with Joseph. Now, if only Jean were here, we'd all be together again." As she followed her into the living room, Helen noticed that Ginny had a slight limp and still walked with a cane. But when Helen remembered the terrible fall Ginny had taken and the tenuous hours she had spent between life and death, Helen thanked God that she had recovered at all.

"You look wonderful, Ginny."

"I'll look even better when I get rid of this cane. It's been frustrating at times, but I'm getting a little better every day."

Rosa jumped up to give Helen a hug, as well. Helen couldn't get over how much the baby had grown since the last time she'd seen him. When Rosa put him on the floor, he was able to sit up all by himself.

"I'm glad you're here, Rosa. You'll be interested in seeing these pictures, too." Helen slid the glossy black-and-white photos out of the envelope and passed them to the women. "Earl Seaborn had them posted on his bulletin board, but I coaxed him into letting me borrow them to show you. What do you think?"

"These are our ships!" Ginny said.

"That's right. The U.S. Army took these photos on D-day. Our landing craft were used in the invasion."

"Wow! I can't believe it," Rosa said. "Look at all our beautiful babies. Just think—we helped make them. We helped fight the war!"

"We have every right to be proud," Helen said.

"I wish I could come back to work," Ginny said. "I miss all of you so much. By the time I finish my therapy and get back to normal, the war will be over. But that's a good thing, right?"

"A very good thing," Helen agreed. She noticed that Rosa had tears in her eyes as she gazed at the pictures. "How are you doing, Rosa?" she asked.

"I'm okay. Joey keeps me pretty busy, as you can imagine. He has four teeth now." The baby had managed to maneuver onto his tummy and was inching across the floor, away from his mother. Helen wondered if there was news of Dirk, but she hesitated to ask.

"We still haven't heard any more about Dirk," Rosa said as she corralled the baby and sat him on the floor in front of her again. "It's hard, waiting and not knowing.... It's real hard. But Joey deserves to have a good mother, a happy mother, so I'm doing my best to be strong."

"How are Dirk's parents?" Ginny asked.

"They're holding up. And I'm getting along with them now. They've been good to me, and I know they'll take good care of Joey and me, even if . . . you know. I'm closer to Dirk's mom than I ever was to my own." Rosa scooped up the baby again as he crawled away, and he let out a howl. "The ladies at church help me, too. Almost everybody there has a loved one who is away in the service. We pray for each other."

"Rosa was just telling me that she works with the Ladies' Missionary Society now," Ginny said.

"Yeah, but I don't give them spiked punch anymore," Rosa said with a smile. Helen and Ginny laughed. "One of our projects is to take Bibles and things out to the POW camp and help them with church services. I got Mrs. Voorhees to help me bake some stuff for them, too. I keep thinking that if Dirk was in a POW camp somewhere, he would appreciate it if someone took him a Bible and some cookies, you know?"

"Say hello to Mr. Kesler for me if you see him—" Ginny began, then stopped. "Wait. I keep forgetting that you never worked with him, Rosa. I seem to forget a lot of things these days. My memory isn't quite the same, you know." Ginny's cheeks reddened, and Helen knew that she felt bad for mentioning Meinhard in front of her.

"Actually, I'd like to see Mr. Kesler again, too," Helen said. "Let me know the next time you're going out to the camp, Rosa. I'll give you a ride."

Helen didn't want to stay too long and make Ginny tired. As she retrieved her bicycle and headed home, she started thinking about how everything had changed in a few short months, how they were all going their separate ways. Only Helen and Jean still worked at the shipyard. And Thelma, of course. But Rosa and Ginny had entered new phases in their lives, new beginnings. And that made Helen think about her own life.

Production at the shipyard would be slowing down as the war neared an end. And when the soldiers returned home, they would come back to their old jobs. Perhaps it was time for Helen to make some changes, too.

She turned abruptly at the next intersection and pedaled over to Lincoln Elementary School. She certainly wasn't looking her best, wearing her work coveralls, and her hair disheveled from cycling, but she parked her bicycle in the rack and marched inside to see the principal.

"I know I turned down a perfectly good job last year," she told him without preamble. "And it's probably too much to hope that there will be another opening this year. But if there is, I'd like to be considered."

A slow smile spread across his face. "Well, you may be in luck, Miss Kimball. I know of at least one teacher whose circumstances have changed, and she may not be coming back this fall. But in addition, the town of Stockton has grown so quickly in the past few years that we may need to add additional classes to accommodate all the new students."

Helen couldn't help smiling, as well. "Please be sure to let me know," she said. As she walked back through the familiar hallways, it felt right to be here this time. She had learned a great deal at the shipyard, accomplished so much. But this was where she truly belonged.

She decided that she would tell Mr. Seaborn and Jean of her decision when she went to work the next day. But when Helen arrived, she realized there was one more loose end to tie up at the shipyard. Jean was still grieving. It would take a while to adjust to her brother's loss, Helen knew. But Jean needed to move on with her life, the way everyone else was doing.

"I saw Ginny and Rosa yesterday," Helen said as she and Jean worked side-by-side.

"How are they?"

"Good. Then I rode over to my old elementary school and asked to be considered for a position next fall."

Jean stopped working and stared at Helen for a long moment. "It will be lonely here without you."

"We're all moving on with our lives, Jean. And you need to move on, as well. The war is entering a new phase on all fronts. We're winning. And I think it's obvious that it won't last too much longer—another year at the most. Then everything is going to change again, just as it did after Pearl Harbor." Jean turned away to concentrate on her work again. But Helen knew by Jean's expression that she'd heard her words.

"I know this sounds harsh," Helen continued, "but I'm going to say it anyway. Your brother's life came to an end, but yours didn't. Suppose it were the other way around. Would you want him to continue grieving for you and to stop living?"

"No," Jean said quietly.

"When Jimmy wrote his last letter to me he said, 'Get married. Live the life you deserve. Be happy.' What do you suppose your brother's advice to you would be?"

"I know, I know," Jean said, frowning.

"And what do you suppose he would say to you about Earl Seaborn?" Helen waited for a reply, but Jean didn't respond. "Earl is afraid to intrude on your grief, but he cares for you very much. I hope you'll give him a chance." An awkward silence fell between them. Helen sighed. "Listen to me, meddling in your life. And to think, we used to give Rosa a hard time about meddling! But I have just one more thing to say, Jean, before I'm finished. One of those colleges I told you about is only twenty miles away from here. I think you and I should visit there this Saturday. We can have a look around, get an application form, maybe some information about classes. I've been able to save up plenty of ration stamps since I'm riding my bicycle again, so I can come by for you around nine o'clock—or is that too early?" Jean shot her a quick glance. Helen saw that she was smiling.

"Nine o'clock is okay."

Rosa telephoned Helen a few days later to say that she and the other church ladies were going out to the POW camp on Sunday afternoon to conduct a worship service. Helen hesitated, wondering if she was truly ready—not only to face Meinhard Kesler but to face God. But she had convinced Jean to move forward, and now Helen knew that she needed to follow her own advice.

The beautiful wooded area around the lake stirred up so many memories of Jimmy that it brought tears to her eyes. But Helen could look at those memories now and not feel quite as much pain. She missed Jimmy Bernard. She probably would never stop missing him. But Jimmy had loved her. He had truly loved her.

Helen sat beside Rosa in the mess hall, where she had once visited with the mayor, and listened to the Sunday service conducted in such a tangled mixture of English and German that it would have been humorous if it hadn't been so poignant. When Helen bowed her head to pray, she was aware that God understood all of their prayers, regardless of language, and all of their needs, spoken and unspoken. Afterward, as Rosa served the cake that she and Mrs. Voorhees had baked, Helen sought out Meinhard Kesler.

"I'm sorry for the way I treated you," she said. "You asked for my forgiveness, but I'm the one who needs to ask for yours. I was wrong to judge you without knowing you. Wrong to assume that because you were a German that you were also a Nazi. It's a terrible mistake to lump people into categories by nationality or race or gender, and I'm so very sorry, Mr. Kesler. The way I treated you was every bit as wrong as the racism that surfaced here in Stockton. Will you forgive me?"

He reached for both of her hands and took them in his. "Of course, Miss Kimball. Of course."

She felt awkward now that she had said her piece. She groped for something to say as her hands slid free again and she folded her arms across her chest. "It looks as though the war will be over before too much longer. Before another year ends, Lord willing. I'm sure you'll be glad to return home."

"I want to help my country heal," Meinhard said, "to rebuild it without the hatred this time. I have learned that the only way to do that is to do what we have done—to ask each other for forgiveness and to rebuild our lives one person at a time."

As Helen walked back through the gates to the parking lot with Rosa, she felt more peaceful than she had felt in a long time. "Here—catch," she said as she tossed the car keys to Rosa.

"What're these for?"

"You need to learn to drive a car, Rosa. Get behind the wheel. I'll teach you."

CHAPTER 40
August 25, 1944

*"After four years of Nazi occupation,
Allied forces liberated the city of Paris today."*

★ *Jean* ★

Jean knew that her last day at Stockton Shipyard had to come sooner
or later, but when it finally arrived, it still felt bittersweet. Rosa had
left the shipyard nine months ago, Ginny four months ago, and
Helen two weeks ago to prepare for her new class of second-grade
students. Now it was Jean's turn. Helen had been right; she needed
to move on. Jean had already registered for fall classes at the college
and was looking forward to her first day, but she still felt sad as she
stuck her time card into the slot and punched out for the last time.

"I hope you're going somewhere to celebrate."

Jean looked up and saw Earl Seaborn watching her, his shirtsleeves rolled up, his tie loosened, his withered hand safely stuffed
into his pocket.

"New beginnings should always be celebrated," he said. "Helen
told me that you're starting college soon. Congratulations."

"Thank you." Jean knew that Earl had deliberately remained in
the background these past few months, giving her time and space in
which to grieve. She appreciated his sensitivity—but she had missed
him.

"Actually, I don't have any plans—to celebrate, that is."

"How about if we went dancing?"

Jean hesitated as she wrestled with her heart. It felt disloyal to Johnny's memory to have fun once again. But she remembered Helen's advice, and before she had time to change her mind she said, "How about tomorrow night?"

"I'll pick you up at eight o'clock," Earl said with a grin.

They danced only to the slow songs. Jean still wasn't ready to kick up her heels on the peppier ones. But the music soothed her and brightened her spirits. "I'm glad we came," she told Earl. "Thank you."

"I'm just glad you decided to celebrate. It was an incredible thing that you and all the other women in America did—going to work in difficult, dangerous jobs. No one can ever say that women are the weaker sex or that a woman's place is only in the home. You showed the world, Jean. You have a right to be proud."

"Have you heard some of the latest radio advertisements?" she asked. "When the war first started we heard a whole load of government propaganda telling women it was our patriotic duty to work in the war industries. Now they're buttering us all up to return home. I heard one the other night that talked about all the great postwar jobs there were going to be for women as teachers and nurses and secretaries. It made me furious! They interviewed a woman who said she'd be glad to lay down her tools and live happily ever after as a housewife again. Another one said it was the right thing to do to give the men *their* jobs back." She saw Earl cover his mouth to hide a smile and stopped. "What's so funny?"

"Please don't take this the wrong way, but you sound like the Jean Erickson I remember from two years ago."

Jean punched his arm—then laughed at herself, too. "Thanks for getting me through a really hard time, Earl. I don't even remember if I thanked you for driving me to Indiana. But I appreciate your patience in putting up with me. I don't know what I would have done without you and all of my other friends. Helen finally took me aside and told me that enough was enough. She kicked me in the rear end and got me to sign up for college. My classes start in two weeks."

"Will you come back and visit during vacations?"

"Didn't I tell you? I've decided to commute. It's only twenty miles away, and I met two other girls I can drive there with. I'm going to live with Patty until Bill comes home."

"Even better." Earl smiled, and his heart was all over both of his sleeves.

Jean reached for his hand. "Come on, I feel like dancing to this song."

When Earl brought her home later that night, Jean noticed that the lights on the front porch were turned off. Her heart began to race in anticipation. Then she halted halfway up the steps as she suddenly remembered the last time Earl had brought her home—the night she'd learned that Johnny had died.

"Are you okay?" Earl asked. Jean knew that he must have remembered that night, too. And she knew with a certainty she couldn't explain that Johnny wouldn't want her to grieve for him forever.

"Yeah. I am," she said truthfully.

Earl drew her close, then slowly bent to kiss her. It was a gentle, tender kiss, nothing at all like the bruising, possessive kisses that Russ used to wrestle from her.

When they pulled apart again, Jean remembered the very first time Earl had come here and asked her to walk to the corner drugstore for an ice-cream cone. Ever since that evening two years ago, Earl Seaborn had used slow, steady persistence, moving step by step, to work his way into Jean's heart. It was the same kind of perseverance that it took to build a ship, day by day, from a million tiny pieces. She smiled at him.

"Penny for your thoughts?" he asked. She held out her hand, waiting for the penny. He fished in his pocket and laid one in her palm.

"I was just thinking how nice it would be if you kissed me again."

CHAPTER 41
October 20, 1944

*"Allied forces have begun the invasion and
re-occupation of the Philippine Islands."*

★ *Rosa* ★

Joey grinned mischievously as he knocked down the towering pile of blocks Rosa had built. She loved to sit and play with him on the living room floor in the evening, listening to the radio while Mrs. Voorhees' knitting needles clacked together and Mr. Voorhees read his newspaper. But Rosa could tell that Joey was growing bored with the game. He was strong and very active at ten months of age, rarely content to sit still for very long. He crawled away from the scattered blocks and headed toward the sofa, then pulled himself up to stand on his own two feet. When he reached for Tena's cat, sleeping peacefully on the cushions, Rosa snatched him away again. Joey howled in protest.

"Boy, he sure does want his own way all the time," she said. "Was Dirk this stubborn?"

"Not that I recall," Tena said. "Dirk was a very contented baby. And quite lazy. He would rather be carried than walk. And when he wanted something he would just point to it."

"I can't imagine where Joseph gets his strong will from," Mr. Voorhees said from behind his newspaper.

Rosa couldn't help laughing. "All right, I guess you've got a point." But in the next moment she remembered Dirk saying that he'd fallen in love with her because of her fiery Italian temperament, and she went from laughter to tears. She seemed to be doing that a lot these past few months. One minute she would be filled with hope as she listened to a good report about the war on the news, then she would remember that Dirk was still missing and her heart would plummet. Her joy would overflow at something cute that Joey did, then sorrow would overwhelm her as she wondered if Dirk would ever see his son. Up and down, day after day, like a never-ending seesaw ride. She sighed.

"Okay, you want to walk, big boy? Let's see you walk." She stood Joey on his feet and led him around the living room, gripping his hands. He crowed with delight, making Rosa laugh again. Then the doorbell rang.

Rosa froze. Tena's knitting needles stopped as she looked up. Mr. Voorhees lowered his newspaper. They looked at each other for a long moment, as if waiting for someone to say that they'd been expecting company. They'd never spoken about it, but Rosa knew they each feared the day when a telegram would finally come and the news would be final, the waiting over. Rosa was closest to the door.

"I'll get it," she said. She scooped up her son and held him close, bracing herself as she opened the door. This time only one naval officer stood on the step, holding his hat in his hand. It was the chaplain.

"Oh no," she said in a whimper.

"I've come with good news this time," he said quickly. He smiled as he gripped Rosa's arm to steady her. Her knees had gone weak at the sight of him, and she couldn't seem to move. "May I come in?" he asked. He brushed past her without waiting, as if he could see that she was frozen with fear and hope.

"It's good news, Mr. and Mrs. Voorhees," the chaplain repeated as he walked into the living room. The two of them had risen to their feet. "Your son Dirk has been found alive! He was discovered in a Japanese prisoner of war camp that was recently liberated. He and all of the others are very malnourished, some have been mistreated, most of them are suffering from malaria and dysentery—but they're alive!"

Rosa lowered Joey to the floor. Her limp arms could no longer hold him. Then she felt Mr. Voorhees' strong arms around her, embracing her.

"Thank God . . . Oh, thank God . . ." he murmured. Rosa hugged him tightly in return. Mrs. Voorhees' arms encircled them, as well. The three of them huddled together, weeping.

"We'll have more information at a later date about possible injuries," the chaplain continued, and Rosa suddenly remembered Dirk's fears that he might lose an arm or a leg. She knew that what she had assured him of a year and a half ago was still true: She didn't care how many arms and legs he had; she just wanted him back.

"I don't have any information at the moment about when the men will be well enough to be shipped home. But we wanted to notify all the next of kin immediately. It's such wonderful news."

"Yes. Thank you so much," Mr. Voorhees said. He wiped his eyes with his fist and turned to shake the chaplain's hand. "And we thank God for answering our prayers."

Joey gave a cry of delight, as if he understood the good news. But when Rosa looked around for him, he was standing beside the couch again, reaching for the cat.

"Come here, you!" she said, swooping him up. "Your daddy is coming home!"